A Tree Grows in Brooklyn

Betty Smith

A Tree Grows in Brooklyn

Pavanne

published by Pan Books

First published in Great Britain 1944 by William Heinemann Ltd
under the title *The Tree in the Yard*
Reprinted as *A Tree Grows in Brooklyn*
This Pavanne edition published 1985 by Pan Books Ltd,
Cavaye Place, London SW10 9PG
All rights reserved
ISBN 0 330 28548 3
Printed and bound in Great Britain by
Cox & Wyman Ltd, Reading

BOOK ONE

I

SERENE WAS a word you could put to Brooklyn, New York. Especially in the summer of 1912. Sombre, as a word, was better. But it did not apply to Williamsburg, Brooklyn. Prairie was lovely and Shenandoah had a beautiful sound, but you couldn't fit those words into Brooklyn. Serene was the only word for it, especially on a Saturday afternoon in summer.

Late in the afternoon the sun slanted down into the mossy yard belonging to Francie Nolan's house, and warmed the worn wooden fence. Looking at the shafted sun, Francie had that same fine feeling that came when she recalled the poem they recited in school.

> *This is the forest primeval. The murmuring*
> *pines and the hemlocks,*
> *Bearded with moss, and in garments green,*
> *indistinct in the twilight,*
> *Stand like Druids of eld.*

The one tree in Francie's yard was neither a pine nor a hemlock. It had pointed leaves which grew along green switches which radiated from the bough and made a tree which looked like a lot of opened green umbrellas. Some people called it the Tree of Heaven. No matter where its seed fell, it made a tree which struggled to reach the sky. It grew in boarded-up lots and out of neglected rubbish-heaps and it was the only tree that grew out of cement. It grew lushly, but only in the tenement districts.

You took a walk on a Sunday afternoon and came to a nice neighbourhood, very refined. You saw a small one of these trees through the iron gate leading to someone's yard and you knew that soon that section of Brooklyn would get to be a tenement district. The tree knew. It came there first. Afterwards, poor foreigners seeped in and the quiet old brownstone houses were hacked up into flats, feather beds were pushed out on the window-sills to air and the Tree of Heaven flourished.

That was the kind of tree it was. It liked poor people.

That was the kind of tree in Francie's yard. Its umbrellas curled over, around and under her third-floor fire-escape. An eleven-year-old girl sitting on this fire-escape could imagine that she was living in a tree. That's what Francie imagined every Saturday afternoon in summer.

Oh, what a wonderful day was Saturday in Brooklyn. Oh, how wonderful anywhere! People were paid on Saturday and it was a holiday without the rigidness of a Sunday. People had money to go out and buy things. They ate well for once, got drunk, had dates, made love and stayed up until all hours; singing, playing music, fighting and dancing because the morrow was their own free day. They could sleep late—until late mass, anyhow.

On Sunday, most people crowded into the eleven o'clock mass. Well, some people, a few, went to early six o'clock mass. They were given credit for this but they deserved none, for they were the ones who had stayed out so late that it was morning when they got home. So they went to this early mass, got it over with and went home and slept all day absolved from sin.

For Francie, Saturday started with the trip to the junkie. She and her brother, Neeley, like other Brooklyn kids, collected rags, paper, metal, rubber, and other junk and hoarded it in locked cellar bins or in boxes under the bed. All week Francie walked home slowly from school with her eyes in the gutter looking for tin foil from cigarette packets or chewing gum wrappers. This was melted in the lid of a jar. The junkie wouldn't take an unmelted ball of foil because too many kids put iron washers in the middle to make it weigh heavier. Sometimes Neeley found a seltzer bottle. Francie helped him break the top off and melt it down for lead. The junkie wouldn't buy a complete top because he'd get into trouble with the soda water people. A seltzer bottle top was fine. Melted, it was worth a nickel.

Francie and Neeley went down into the cellar each evening and emptied the dumb-waiter shelves of the day's accumulated trash. They owned this privilege because Francie's mother was the janitress. They looted the shelves of paper, rags and deposit bottles. Paper wasn't worth much. They got only a penny for ten pounds. Rags brought two cents a pound and iron, four. Copper was good—ten cents a pound. Sometimes Francie came across a bonanza: the bottom of a discarded wash boiler. She got it off with a can-opener, folded it, pounded it, folded it and pounded it again.

Soon after nine o'clock of a Saturday morning, kids began spraying out of all the side streets on to Manhattan Avenue, the main thoroughfare. They made their slow way up the Avenue to Scholes Street. Some carried their junk in their arms. Others had wagons made of a wooden soap-box with solid wooden wheels. A few pushed loaded baby buggies.

Francie and Neeley put all their junk into a burlap bag and each grabbed an end and dragged it along the street; up Manhattan Avenue, past Maujer, Ten Eyck, Stagg to Scholes Street. Beautiful names for ugly streets. From each side street hordes of little ragamuffins emerged to swell the main tide. On the way to Carney's, they met other kids coming back empty-handed. They had sold their junk and already squandered the pennies. Now, staggering back, they jeered at the other kids.

"Rag picker! Rag picker!"

Francie's face burned at the name. No comfort knowing that the taunters were rag pickers too. No matter that her brother would straggle back, empty-handed with his gang and taunt later comers the same way. Francie felt ashamed.

Carney plied his junk business in a tumble-down stable. Turning the corner, Francie saw that both doors were hooked back hospitably and she imagined that the large, bland dial of the swinging scale blinked a welcome. She saw Carney, with his rusty hair, rusty moustache and rusty eyes presiding at the scale. Carney liked girls better than boys. He would give a girl an extra penny if she did not shrink when he pinched her cheek.

Because of the possibility of this bonus, Neeley stepped aside and let Francie drag the bag into the stable. Carney jumped forward, dumped the contents of the bag on the floor and took a preliminary pinch out of her cheek. While he piled the stuff on to the scale, Francie blinked, adjusting her eyes to the darkness and was aware of the mossy air and the odour of wetted rags. Carney slewed his eyes at the dial and spoke two words: his offer. Francie knew that no dickering was permitted. She nodded yes, and Carney flipped the junk off and made her wait while he piled the paper in one corner, threw the rags in another and sorted out the metals. Only then did he reach down in his trousers pocket, haul up an old leather pouch tied with a wax string and count out old green pennies that looked like junk too. As she whispered, "Thank you," Carney fixed a rusty junked look on her and pinched her cheek hard. She stood her ground. He smiled and added an extra penny. Then his manner changed and he became loud and brisk.

"Come on," he hollered to the next one in line, a boy. "Get the lead out!" He timed the laugh. "And I don't mean junk." The children laughed dutifully. The laughter sounded like the bleating of lost little lambs, but Carney seemed satisfied.

Francie went outside to report to her brother. "He gave me sixteen cents and a pinching penny."

"That's your penny," he said, according to an old agreement.

She put the penny in her dress pocket and turned the rest of the money over to him. Neeley was ten, a year younger than Francie. But he was the boy; he handled the money. He divided the pennies carefully.

"Eight cents for the bank." That was the rule; half of any money they got from anywhere went into the tin-can bank that was nailed to the floor in the darkest corner of the closet. "And four cents for you and four cents for me."

Francie knotted the bank money in her handkerchief. She looked at her own five pennies, realizing happily that they could be changed into a whole nickel.

Neeley rolled up the burlap bag, tucked it under his arm and pushed his way in Cheap Charlie's with Francie right behind him. Cheap Charlie's was the penny candy store next to Carney's which catered to the junk trade. At the end of a Saturday, its cashbox was filled with greenish pennies. By an unwritten law, it was a boys' store. So Francie did not go all the way in. She stood by the doorway.

The boys, from eight to fourteen years of age, looked alike in straggling knickerbockers and broken-peaked caps. They stood around, hands in pockets and thin shoulders hunched forward tensely. They would grow up looking like that; standing the same way in other hang-outs. The only difference would be the cigarette seemingly permanently fastened between their lips, rising and falling in accent as they spoke.

Now the boys churned about nervously, their thin faces turning from Charlie to each other and back to Charlie again. Francie noticed that some already had their summer hair-cut: hair cropped so short that there were nicks in the scalp where the clippers had bitten too deeply. These fortunates had their caps crammed into their pockets or pushed back on the head. The unshorn ones, whose hair curled gently and still babyishly at the nape of the neck, were ashamed and wore their caps pulled so far down over their ears that there was something girlish about them in spite of their jerky profanity.

Cheap Charlie was not cheap and his name wasn't Charlie. He had taken that name and it said so on the store awning and Francie believed it. Charlie gave you a pick for your penny. A board with fifty numbered hooks and a prize hanging from each hook, hung behind the counter. There were a few fine prizes; roller-skates, a catcher's mitt, a doll with real hair, and so on. The other hooks held blotters, pencils and other penny articles. Francie watched as Neeley bought a pick. He removed the dirty card from the ragged envelope. Twenty-six! Hopefully Francie looked at the board. He had drawn a penny pen-wiper.

"Prize or candy?" Charlie asked him.

"Candy. What do you think?"

It was always the same. Francie had never heard of anyone winning above a penny prize. Indeed the skate wheels were rusted and the doll's hair was dust-filmed as though these things had waited there a long time like Little Boy Blue's toy dog and tin soldier. Some day, Francie resolved, when she had fifty cents, she would take all the picks and win everything on the board. She figured that would be a good business deal: skates, mitt, doll and all the other things for fifty cents. Why, the skates alone were worth four times that much! Neeley would have to come along that great day because girls seldom patronized Charlie's. True, there were a few girls there that Saturday . . . bold, brash ones, too developed for their age; girls who talked loud and horse-played around with the boys—girls whom the neighbours prophesied would come to no good.

Francie went across the street to Gimpy's candy store. Gimpy was lame. He was a gentle man, kind to little children . . . or so everyone thought until that sunny afternoon when he inveigled a little girl into his dismal back room.

Francie debated whether she should sacrifice one of her pennies for a Gimpy Special: the prize bag. Maudie Donavan, her once-in-a-while girl friend, was about to make a purchase. Francie pushed her way in until she was standing behind Maudie. She pretended that she was spending the penny. She held her breath as Maudie, after much speculation, pointed

9

dramatically at a bulging bag in the showcase. Francie would have picked a smaller bag. She looked over her friend's shoulder; saw her take out a few pieces of stale candy and examine her prize—a coarse cambric handkerchief. Once Francie had got a small bottle of strong scent. She debated again whether to spend a penny on a prize bag. It was nice to be surprised even if you couldn't eat the candy. But she reasoned she had been surprised by being with Maudie when she made her purchase, and that was almost as good.

Francie walked up Manhattan Avenue reading aloud the fine-sounding names of the streets she passed: Scholes, Meserole, Montrose and then Johnson Avenue. These last two Avenues were where the Italians had settled. The district called Jew Town started at Siegel Street, took in Moore and McKibbon and went past Broadway. Francie headed for Broadway.

And what was on Broadway in Williamsburg, Brooklyn? Nothing—only the finest nickel and dime store in all the world! It was big and glittering and had everything in the world in it ... or so it seemed to an eleven-year-old girl. Francie had a nickel. Francie had power. She could buy practically anything in that store! It was the only place in the world where that could be.

Arriving at the store, she walked up and down the aisles handling any object her fancy favoured. What a wonderful feeling to pick something up, hold it for a moment, feel its contour, run her hand over its surface and then replace it carefully. Her nickel gave her this privilege. If a floor-walker asked whether she intended buying anything, she could say yes, buy it and show him a thing or two. Money was a wonderful thing, she decided. After an orgy of touching things, she made her planned purchase—five cents' worth of pink-and-white peppermint wafers.

She walked back home from Graham Avenue, the Ghetto street. She was excited by the filled push-carts—each a little store in itself—the bargaining, emotional Jews and the peculiar smells of the neighbourhood; baked stuffed fish, sour rye bread fresh from the oven, and something that smelled like honey boiling. She stared at the bearded men in their alpaca skull-caps and silkolene coats and wondered what made their eyes so small and fierce. She looked into tiny hole-in-the-wall shops and smelled the dress fabrics arranged in disorder on the tables. She noticed the feather beds bellying out of windows, clothes of Oriental-bright colours drying on the fire-escapes and the half-naked children playing in the gutters. A woman, big with child, sat patiently at the kerb in a stiff wooden chair. She sat in the hot sunshine watching the life on the street and guarding within herself, her own mystery of life.

Francie remembered her surprise that time when mama told her that Jesus was a Jew. Francie had thought that He was a Catholic. But mama knew. Mama said that the Jews had never looked on Jesus as anything but a troublesome Yiddish boy who would not work at the carpentry trade, marry, settle down and raise a family. And the Jews believed that their Messiah was yet to come, mama said. Thinking of this, Francie stared at the pregnant Jewess.

"I guess that's why the Jews have so many babies," Francie thought. "And why they sit so quiet . . . waiting. And why they aren't ashamed the way they are fat. Each one thinks that she might be making the real little Jesus. That's why they walk so proud when they're that way. Now the Irish women always look so ashamed. They know that they can never make a Jesus. It will be just another Mick. When I grow up and know that I am going to have a baby, I will remember to walk proud and slow, even though I am not a Jew."

It was twelve when Francie got home. Mama came in soon after with her broom and pail which she banged into a corner with that final bang which meant that they wouldn't be touched again until Monday.

Mama was twenty-nine. She had black hair and brown eyes and was quick with her hands. She had a nice shape too. She worked as a janitress and kept three tenement houses clean. Who would ever believe that mama scrubbed floors to make a living for the four of them? She was so pretty and slight and vivid and always bubbling over with intensity and fun. Even though her hands were red and cracked from the sodaed water, they were beautifully shaped with lovely, curved, oval nails. Everyone said it was a pity that a slight pretty woman like Katie Nolan had to go out scrubbing floors. But what else could she do, considering the husband she had, they said. They admitted that, no matter which way you looked at it, Johnny Nolan was a handsome lovable fellow, far superior to any man on the block. But he was a drunk. That's what they said, and it was true.

*　　*　　*

11

Francie made mama watch while she put the eight cents in the tin-can bank. They had a pleasant five minutes conjecturing about how much was in the bank. Francie thought there must be nearly a hundred dollars. Mama said eight dollars would be nearer right.

Mama gave Francie instructions about going out to buy something for lunch. "Take eight cents from the cracked cup and get a quarter loaf of Jew rye bread and see that it's fresh. Then take a nickel, go to Sauerwein's and ask for the end-of-the-tongue for a nickel."

"But you have to have a pull with him to get it."

"Tell him that your mother *said*," insisted Katie firmly. She thought something over. "I wonder whether we ought to buy five cents' worth of sugar buns or put that money in the bank."

"Oh, Mama, it's *Saturday*. All week you said we could have dessert on Saturday."

"All right. Get the buns."

The little Jewish delicatessen was full of Christians buying Jew rye bread. She watched the man push her quarter loaf into a paper bag. With its wonderfully crisp yet tender crust and floury bottom, it was easily the most wonderful bread in the world, she thought, when it was fresh. She entered Sauerwein's store reluctantly. Sometimes he was agreeable about the tongue and sometimes he wasn't. Sliced tongue at seventy-five cents a pound was only for rich people. But when it was nearly all sold, you could get the square end for a nickel if you had a pull with Mr. Sauerwein. Of course there wasn't much tongue to the end. It was mostly soft, small bones and gristle with only the memory of meat.

It happened to be one of Sauerwein's agreeable days. "The tongue came to an end, yesterday," he told Francie. "But I saved it for you because I know your mama likes tongue and I like your mama. You tell her that. Hear?"

"Yes, sir," whispered Francie. She looked down on the floor as she felt her face getting warm. She hated Mr. Sauerwein and would *not* tell mama what he had said.

At the baker's, she picked out four buns, carefully choosing those with the most sugar. She met Neeley outside the store. He peeped into the bag and cut a caper of delight when he saw the buns. Although he had eaten four cents' worth of candy that morning, he was very hungry and made Francie run all the way home.

Papa did not come home for dinner. He was a free lance singing waiter, which meant that he didn't work very often. Usually he spent Saturday morning at Union Headquarters waiting for a job to come in for him.

Francie, Neeley, and mama had a very fine meal. Each had a thick slice of the "tongue," two pieces of sweet-smelling rye bread spread with unsalted butter, a sugar bun apiece and a mug of strong hot coffee with a teaspoon of sweetened condensed milk on the side.

There was a special Nolan idea about the coffee. It was their one great luxury. Mama made a big potful each morning and reheated it for dinner and supper and it got stronger as the day wore on. It was an awful lot of water and very little coffee, but mama put a lump of chicory in it which made it taste strong and bitter. Each one was allowed three cups a day *with milk*. Other times you could help yourself to a cup of black coffee any time you felt like it. Sometimes when you had nothing at all and it was raining and you were alone in the flat, it was wonderful to know that you could have *something*, even though it was only a cup of black and bitter coffee.

Neeley and Francie loved coffee but seldom drank it. Today, as usual, Neeley let his coffee stand black and ate his condensed milk spread on bread. He sipped a little of the black coffee for the sake of formality. Mama poured out Francie's coffee and put the milk in it even though she knew that the child wouldn't drink it.

Francie loved the smell of coffee and the way it was hot. As she ate her bread and meat, she kept one hand curved about the cup enjoying its warmth. From time to time, she'd smell the bitter sweetness of it. That was better than drinking it. At the end of the meal, it went down the sink.

Mama had two sisters, Sissy and Evy, who came to the flat often. Every time they saw the coffee thrown away, they gave mama a lecture about wasting things.

Mama explained: "Francie is entitled to one cup each meal like the rest. If it makes her feel better to throw it away rather than to drink it, all right. *I* think it's good that people like us can waste something once in a while and get the feeling of how it would be to have lots of money and not have to worry about scrounging."

This queer point of view satisfied mama and pleased Francie. It was one of the links between the ground-down poor and the wasteful rich. The girl felt that even if she had less than

13

anybody in Williamsburg, somehow she had more. She was richer because she had something to waste. She ate her sugar bun slowly, reluctant to have done with its sweet taste, while the coffee got ice-cold. Regally, she poured it down the sink feeling casually extravagant. After that, she was ready to go to Losher's for the family's semi-weekly supply of stale bread. Mama told her that she could take a nickel and buy a stale pie if she could get one that wasn't mashed too much.

Losher's bread factory supplied the neighbourhood stores. The bread was not wrapped in wax paper and grew stale quickly. Losher's redeemed the stale bread from the dealers and sold it at half price to the poor. The outlet store adjoined the bakery. Its long narrow counter filled one side and long narrow benches ran along the other two sides. A huge double door opened behind the counter. The bakery wagons backed up to it and unloaded the bread right on to the counter. They sold two loaves for a nickel, and when it was dumped out, a pushing crowd fought for the privilege of buying it. There was never enough bread and some waited until three or four wagons had reported before they could buy bread. At that price, the customers had to supply their own wrappings. Most of the purchasers were children. Some kids tucked the bread under their arms and walked home brazenly letting all the world know that they were poor. The proud ones wrapped up the bread, some in old newspapers, others in clean or dirty flour sacks. Francie brought along a large paper bag.

She didn't try to get her bread right away. She sat on a bench and watched. A dozen kids pushed and shouted at the counter. Four old men dozed on the opposite bench. The old men, pensioners on their families, were made to run errands and mind babies, the only work left for the old worn-out men in Williamsburg. They waited as long as they could before buying because Losher's smelled kindly of baking bread, and the sun coming in the windows felt good on their old backs. They sat and dozed while the hours passed and felt that they were filling up time. The waiting gave them a purpose in life for a little while and, almost, they felt necessary again.

Francie stared at the oldest man. She played her favourite game, figuring out about people. His thin tangled hair was the same dirty grey as the stubble standing on his sunken cheeks. Dried spittle caked the corners of his mouth. He yawned. He had no teeth. She watched, fascinated and revolted, as he closed his mouth, drew his lips inward until there was no

14

mouth, and made his chin come up to almost meet his nose. She studied his old coat with the padding hanging out of the torn sleeve seam. His legs were sprawled wide in helpless relaxation and one of the buttons was missing from his grease-caked trousers opening. She saw that his shoes were battered and broken open at the toes. One shoe was laced with a much-knotted shoe string, and the other with a bit of dirty twine. She saw two thick dirty toes with creased grey toenails. Her thoughts ran....

"He is old. He must be past seventy. He was born about the time Abraham Lincoln was living and getting himself ready to be president. Williamsburg must have been a little country place then and maybe Indians were still living in Flatbush. That was so long ago." She kept staring at his feet. "He was a baby once. He must have been sweet and clean and his mother kissed his little pink toes. Maybe when it thundered at night she came to his crib and fixed his blanket better and whispered that he mustn't be afraid, that mother was there. Then she picked him up and put her cheek on his head and said that he was her own sweet baby. He might have been a boy like my brother, running in and out of the house and slamming the door. And while his mother scolded him she was thinking that maybe he'll be president some day. Then he was a young man, strong and happy. When he walked down the street, the girls smiled and turned to watch him. He smiled back and maybe he winked at the prettiest one. I guess he must have married and had children and they thought he was the most wonderful papa in the world the way he worked hard and bought them toys for Christmas. Now his children are getting old too, like him, and *they* have children and nobody wants the old man any more and they are waiting for him to die. But he don't want to die. He wants to keep on living even though he's so old and there's nothing to be happy about any more."

The place was quiet. The summer sun streamed in and made dusty, down-slanting roads from the window to the floor. A big green fly buzzed in and out of the sunny dust. Excepting for herself and the dozing old men, the place was empty. The children who waited for bread had gone to play outside. Their high screaming voices seemed to come from far away.

Suddenly Francie jumped up. Her heart was beating fast. She was frightened. For no reason at all, she thought of an accordion pulled out full for a rich note. Then she had an idea that the accordion was closing ... closing ... closing.... A ter-

15

rible panic that had no name came over her as she realized that many of the sweet babies in the world were born to come to something like this old man some day. She had to get out of that place or it would happen to her. Suddenly she would be an old woman with toothless gums and feet that disgusted people.

At that moment, the double doors behind the counter were banged open as a bread truck backed up. A man came to stand behind the counter. The truck driver started throwing bread to him which he piled up on the counter. The kids in the street who had heard the doors thrown open piled in and milled around Francie, who had already reached the counter.

"I want bread!" Francie called out. A big girl gave her a strong shove and wanted to know who she thought she was. "Never mind! Never mind!" Francie told her. "I want six loaves and a pie not too crushed," she screamed out.

Impressed by her intensity, the counter man shoved six loaves and the least battered of the rejected pies at her and took her two dimes. She pushed her way out of the crowd dropping a loaf which she had trouble picking up as there was no room to stoop over in.

Outside, she sat on the kerb fitting the bread and the pie into the paper bag. A woman passed, wheeling a baby in a pram. The baby was waving his feet in the air. Francie looked and saw, not the baby's foot but a grotesque thing in a big, worn-out shoe. The panic came on her again and she ran all the way home.

The flat was empty. Mama had dressed and gone off with Aunt Sissy to see a matinee from a ten-cent gallery set. Francie put the bread and pie away and folded the bag neatly to be used the next time. She went into the tiny, windowless bedroom that she shared with Neeley and sat on her own cot in the dark waiting for the waves of panic to stop passing over her.

After a while Neeley came in, crawled under his cot and pulled out a ragged catcher's mitt.

"Where you going?" she asked.

"Play ball in the lots."

"Can I come along?"

"No."

She followed him down to the street. Three of his gang were waiting for him. One had a bat, another a baseball and the third had nothing, but wore a pair of baseball trousers. They

16

started out for an empty lot over towards Greenpoint. Neeley saw Francie following but said nothing. One of the boys nudged him and said:

"Hey! Your sister's followin' us."—

"Yeah," agreed Neeley. The boy turned around and yelled at Francie:

"Go chase yourself!"

"It's a free country," Francie stated.

"It's a free country," Neeley repeated to the boy. They took no notice of Francie after that. She continued to follow them. She had nothing to do until two o'clock, when the neighbourhood library opened up again.

It was a slow, horse-playing walk. The boys stopped to look for tin foil in the gutter and to pick up cigarette-butts which they would save and smoke in the cellar on the next rainy afternoon. They took time out to bedevil a little Jew boy on his way to the temple. They detained him while they debated what to do with him. The boy waited, smiling humbly. The Christians released him finally with detailed instructions as to his course of conduct for the coming week.

"Don't show your puss on Devoe Street," he was ordered.

"I won't," he promised. The boys were disappointed. They had expected more fight. One of them took out a bit of chalk from his pocket and drew a wavy line on the sidewalk. He commanded:

"Don't you even step over that line."

The little boy, knowing that he had offended them by giving in too easily, decided to play their game.

"Can't I even put one foot in the gutter, fellers?"

"You can't even *spit* in the gutter," he was told.

"All right." He sighed in pretended resignation.

One of the bigger boys had an inspiration. "And keep away from Christian girls. Get me?" They walked away leaving him staring after them.

"Gol-*lee!*" he whispered rolling his big brown Jewish eyes. The idea that those *Goyem* thought him man enough to be capable of thinking about *any* girl, Gentile or Jew, staggered him and he went his way saying gol-*lee* over and over.

The boys walked on slowly, looking slyly at the big boy who had made the remark about the girls, and wondering whether he would lead off into a dirty talk session. But before this could start, Francie heard her brother say:

"I know that kid. He's a white Jew." Neeley had heard papa

17

speak of a Jewish bar-tender that he liked.

"They ain't no such thing as a white Jew," said the big boy.

"Well, if there was such a thing as a white Jew," said Neeley, with that combination of agreeing with others and still sticking to his own opinions, which made him so amiable, "he would be it."

"There never could be a white Jew," said the big boy, "even in supposing."

"Our Lord was a Jew." Neeley was quoting mama.

"And other Jews turned right around and killed him," clinched the big boy.

Before they could go deeper in theology, they saw another little boy turn on to Ainslee Street from Humboldt Avenue carrying a basket on his arm. The basket was covered with a clean ragged cloth. A stick stuck up from one corner of the basket, and, on it, like a sluggish flag, stood six pretzels. The big boy of Neeley's gang gave a command and they made a tightly-packed run on the pretzel seller. He stood his ground, opened his mouth and bawled: "Mama!"

A second-storey window flew open and a woman clutching a crêpe-paperish kimono around her sprawling breasts, yelled out:

"Leave him alone and get off this block, you lousy bastards."

Francie's hands flew to cover her ears so that at confession she would not have to tell the priest that she had stood and listened to a bad word.

"We ain't doing nothing, Lady," said Neeley with that ingratiating smile which always won over his mother.

"You bet your life, you ain't. Not while I'm around." Then without changing her tone she called to her son, "And get upstairs here, you. I'll learn you to bother me when I'm taking a nap." The pretzel boy went upstairs and the gang ambled on.

"That lady's tough." The big boy jerked his head back at the window.

"Yeah," the others agreed.

"My old man's tough," offered a smaller boy.

"Who the hell cares?" inquired the big boy languidly.

"I was just saying," apologized the smaller boy.

"My old man ain't tough," said Neeley. The boys laughed.

They ambled along, stopping now and then to breathe deeply of the smell of Newtown Creek which flowed its narrow tormented way a few blocks up Grand Street.

"God, she stinks," commented the big boy.

"Yeah!" Neeley sounded deeply satisfied.

"I bet that's the worst stink in the world," bragged another boy.

"Yeah."

And Francie whispered yeah in agreement. She was proud of that smell. It let her know that nearby was a waterway which, dirty though it was, joined a river that flowed out to the sea. To her, the stupendous stench suggested far-sailing ships and adventure and she was pleased with the smell.

Just as the boys reached the lot in which there was a ragged diamond tramped out, a little yellow butterfly flew across the weeds. With man's instinct to capture anything running, flying, swimming or crawling, they gave chase, throwing their ragged caps at it in advance of their coming. Neeley caught it. The boys looked at it briefly, quickly lost interest in it and started up a four-man baseball game of their own devising.

They played furiously, cursing, sweating and punching each other. Every time a stumble bum passed and loitered for a moment, they clowned and showed off. There was a rumour that the Brooklyn Dodgers had a hundred scouts roaming the streets of a Saturday watching lot games and spotting promising players. And there wasn't a Brooklyn boy who wouldn't rather play on the Bums' team than be president of the United States.

After a while, Francie got tired of watching them. She knew that they would play and fight and show off until it was time to drift home for supper. It was two o'clock. The librarian should be back from lunch by now. With pleasant anticipation, Francie walked back towards the library.

II

THE LIBRARY was a little old shabby place. Francie thought it was beautiful. The feeling she had about it was as good as the feeling she had about church. She pushed open the door and went in. She liked the combined smell of worn leather bindings library paste and freshly-inked stamping pads better than she liked the smell of burning incense at high mass.

Francie thought that all the books in the world were in that library and she had a plan about reading all the books in the world. She was reading a book a day in alphabetical order and not skipping the dry ones. She remembered that the first author had been Abbott. She had been reading a book a day for a long time now and she was still in the B's. Already she had read about bees and buffaloes, Bermuda vacations and Byzantine architecture. For all of her enthusiasm she had to admit that some of the B's had been hard going. But Francie was a reader. She read everything she could find: trash, classics, time tables and the grocer's price list. Some of the reading had been wonderful; the Louisa Alcott books for example. She planned to read all the books over again when she had finished with the Z's.

Saturdays were different. She treated herself by reading a book not in the alphabetical sequence. On that day she asked the librarian to recommend a book.

After Francie had come in and closed the door quietly behind her—the way you were supposed to do in the library—she looked quickly at the little golden-brown pottery jug which stood at the end of the librarian's desk. It was a season indicator. In the autumn it held a few sprigs of bittersweet and at Christmas time it held holly. She knew spring was coming, even if there was snow on the ground, when she saw pussy willow in the bowl. And today, on this summer Saturday of 1912, what was the bowl holding? She moved her eyes slowly up the jug past the thin green stems and little round leaves and saw . . . nasturtiums! Red, yellow, gold and ivory-white. A head pain caught her between the eyes at the taking in of such a wonderful sight. It was something to be remembered all her life.

"When I get big," she thought, "I will have such a brown bowl and in hot August there will be nasturtiums in it."

She put her hand on the edge of the polished desk, liking the way it felt. She looked at the neat row of freshly-sharpened pencils, the clean green square of blotter, the fat white jar of creamy paste, the precise stack of cards and the returned books waiting to be put back on the shelves. The remarkable pencil with the date slug above its point was by itself near the blotter's edge.

"Yes, when I get big and have my own home, no plush chairs and lace curtains for me. And *no* rubber plants. I'll have a desk like this in my parlour and white walls and a clean green blotter every Saturday night and a row of shining yellow pencils always sharpened for writing and a golden-brown bowl with a flower or some leaves or berries always in it and books ... books ... books. ..."

She chose her book for Sunday; something by an author named Brown. Francie figured she had been reading on the Brown's for months. When she thought she was nearly finished, she noticed that the next shelf started up again with Browne. After that came Browning. She groaned, anxious to get into the C's, where there was a book by Marie Corelli that she had peeped into and found thrilling. Would she *ever* get to that? Maybe she ought to read two books a day. Maybe. . . .

She stood at the desk a long time before the librarian deigned to attend to her.

"Yes?" inquired that lady pettishly.

"This book. I want it." Francie pushed the book forward opened at the back with the little card pushed out of the envelope. The librarians had trained the children to present the books that way. It saved them the trouble of opening several hundred books a day and pulling several hundred cards from as many envelopes.

She took the card, stamped it, pushed it down a slot in the desk. She stamped Francie's card and pushed it at her. Francie picked it up but she did not go away.

"Yes?" The librarian did not bother to look up.

"Could you recommend a good book for a girl?"

"How old?"

"She is eleven."

Each week Francie made the same request and each week the librarian asked the same question. A name on a card meant nothing to her and since she never looked up into a child's face, she never did get to know the little girl who took a book out every day and two on Saturday. A smile would have meant a lot to Francie and a friendly comment would have made her so happy. She loved the library and was anxious to worship the lady in charge. But the librarian had other things on her mind. She hated children anyhow.

Francie trembled in anticipation as the woman reached under the desk. She saw the title as the book came up: *If I Were King,* by McCarthy. Wonderful! Last week it had been *Beverly of Graustark* and the same two weeks before that. She had had the McCarthy book only twice. The librarian recom-

21

mended these two books over and over again. Maybe they were the only ones she herself had read; maybe they were on a recommended list; maybe she had discovered that they were sure fire as far as eleven-year-old girls were concerned.

Francie held the books close and hurried home, resisting the temptation to sit on the first stoop she came to, to start reading.

Home at last and now it was the time she had been looking forward to all week: fire-escape-sitting time. She put a small rug on the fire-escape and got the pillow from her bed and propped it against the bars. Luckily there was ice in the icebox. She chipped off a small piece and put it in a glass of water. The pink-and-white peppermint wafers bought that morning were arranged in a little bowl, cracked, but of a pretty blue colour. She arranged glass, bowl and book on the window-sill and climbed out on the fire-escape. Once out there, she was living in a tree. No one upstairs, downstairs or across the way could see her. But she could look out through the leaves and see everything.

It was a sunny afternoon. A lazy warm wind carried a warm sea smell. The leaves of the tree made fugitive patterns on the white pillow-case. Nobody was in the yard and that was nice. Usually it was pre-empted by the boy whose father rented the store on the ground floor. The boy played an interminable game of graveyard. He dug miniature graves, put live captured caterpillars into little matchboxes, buried them with informal ceremony and erected little pebble headstones over the tiny earth mounds. The whole game was accompanied by fake sobbings and heavings of his chest. But today the dismal boy was away visiting an aunt in Bensonhurst. To know that he was away was almost as good as getting a birthday present.

Francie breathed the warm air, watched the dancing leaf shadows, ate the candy and took sips of the cooled water in-between reading the book.

If I were King, Love,
Ah, if I were King. . . .

The story of François Villon was more wonderful each time she read it. Sometimes she worried for fear the book would be lost in the library and she'd never be able to read it again. She had once started copying the book in a two-cent notebook. She wanted to own a book so badly and she had thought the copying would do it. But the pencilled sheets did not seem like

22

nor smell like the library book, so she had given it up, consoled herself with the vow that when she grew up she would work hard, save money and buy every single book that she liked.

As she read, at peace with the world and happy as only a little girl could be with a fine book and a little bowl of candy, and all alone in the house, the leaf shadows shifted and the afternoon passed. About four o'clock, the flats in the tenements across from Francie's yard came to life. Through the leaves, she looked into the open uncurtained windows and saw growlers being rushed out and returned overflowing with cool foaming beer. Kids ran in and out, going to and returning from the butcher's, the grocer's and the baker's. Women came in with bulky hock-shop bundles. The man's Sunday suit was home again. On Monday, it would go back to the pawnbroker's for another week. The hock-shop prospered on the weekly interest money and the suit benefited by being crushed and hung away in camphor where the moths couldn't get at it. In on Monday, out on Saturday. Ten cents' interest paid to Uncle Timmy. That was the cycle.

Francie saw young girls making preparations to go out with their fellers. Since none of the flats had bathrooms, the girls stood before the kitchen sinks in their camisoles and petticoats, and the line the arm made, curved over the head while they washed under the arm, was very beautiful. There were so many girls in so many windows washing this way that it seemed a kind of hushed and expectant ritual.

She stopped reading when Fraber's horse and wagon came into the yard next door because watching the beautiful horse was almost as good as reading. The next door yard was cobblestoned and had a good-looking stable at the end of it. A wrought-iron double gate separated the yard from the street. At the edge of the cobblestones was a bit of well-manured earth where a lovely rosebush grew and a row of bright red geraniums. The stable was finer than any house in the neighbourhood and the yard was the prettiest in Williamsburg.

Francie heard the gate click shut. The horse, a shining brown gelding with a black mane and tail, came into view first. He pulled a small maroon wagon that had *Dr. Fraber, Dentist,* and the address painted on the sides in golden letters. This trim wagon delivered nothing and carried nothing. It was driven slowly through the streets all day as an advertisement. It was a dreamily-moving billboard.

Frank, a nice young man with rosy cheeks—like the fabulous youth in the children's song—took the wagon out every morning and brought it back every afternoon. He had a fine life and all the girls flirted with him. All he had to do was to drive the wagon around slowly so that people could read the name and address on it. When it came to a set of plates or the pulling of a tooth, the people would remember the address on the wagon and come to Dr. Fraber.

Frank leisurely removed his coat and donned a leather apron while Bob, the horse, patiently shifted from one foot to the other. Frank then unharnessed him, wiped off the leather and hung the harness up in the stable. Next he washed the horse with a great wet yellow sponge. The horse enjoyed it. He stood there with the sunshine dappling him over and sometimes his hooves struck a spark from the stones as he pawed the ground. Frank squeezed water out on to the brown back and rubbed it down, talking to the big horse all the while.

"Steady now, Bob. That's a good boy. Back up there. Whoa now!"

Bob was not the only horse in Francie's life. Her Aunt Evy's husband, Uncle Willie Flittman, also drove a horse. His horse was named Drummer and pulled a milk wagon. Willie and Drummer were not friends the way Frank and his horse were friends. Willie and Drummer laid in wait for each other, figuring out injuries to do the other. Uncle Willie reviled Drummer by the hour. To hear him talk you would think that the horse never slept at night but stood awake in the milk company stable figuring out new torments for his driver.

Francie liked to play a game on which she imagined that people looked like their pets and vice versa. Little white poodles were favourite pets in Brooklyn. The woman who owned a poodle was usually small, plump, white, soiled and with rheumy eyes just like a poodle. Miss Tynmore, the tiny, bright chirping old maid who gave mama music lessons, was just like the canary whose cage hung in her kitchen. If Frank could turn into a horse, he'd look like Bob. Francie had never seen Uncle Willie's horse, but she knew what he looked like. Drummer, like Willie, would be small and thin and dark with nervous eyes which showed too much white. He'd be whimpery too, like Aunt Evy's husband. She let her thoughts go away from Uncle Flittman.

Out on the street, a dozen small boys clung to the iron gate watching the neighbourhood's only horse being washed. Francie couldn't see them but she heard them talking. They made up fearful stories about the gentle animal.

"Don't he look still and easy," a boy said. "But that's only a fake. He's layin' his chance for when Frank ain't lookin', then he'll bite him and kick him to death."

"Yeah," said another boy. "I seen him run over a little baby yesterday."

A third boy had an inspiration. "I seen him do number one on an old lady sittin' by the gutter sellin' apples. All over the apples, too," he added as an afterthought.

"They put them blinkers on him so's he can't see how little people is. If he could see how small they is, he would kill them all."

"Them blinkers make him think people is little?"

"Little like pee-wees."

"Gee!"

Each boy as he spoke knew that he was lying. Yet he believed what the other boys said about the horse. Eventually the boys tired of watching gentle Bob just stand there. One of them picked up a stone and threw it at the horse. Bob's skin rippled where it struck him and the boys shivered in anticipation of his going berserk. Frank looked up and spoke to them in a gentle Brooklyn voice.

"You don't want to go and do that now. The horse didn't do nothin' to you."

"Oh, no?" shouted a boy indignantly.

"No," answered Frank.

"Aw, go—yourself," came the inevitable *coup de grâce* from the smallest boy.

Still gently spoke Frank as he let a rill of water run over the horse's rump: "Do you want to go away from here or do I have to break a couple of your asses?"

"You and who else?"

"I'll show you who else!" Suddenly Frank swooped down and picked up a loose cobblestone and squared off as if to throw it. The boys backed away hollering out offended retorts.

"I guess this is a free country."

"Yeah. You don't own the streets."

"I'm gonna tell my uncle, the cop, on you."

"Beat it now," said Frank indifferently. He replaced the cobblestone carefully.

The big boys drifted away, tired of the game. But the little boys seeped back. They wanted to see Frank give Bob his oats.

25

Frank finished washing the horse and stood him under the tree where his head was in the shade. He hung a filled feed bag on his neck, then went to work washing the wagon, whistling: "Let Me Call You Sweetheart." As if this was a signal, Flossie Gaddis, who lived below the Nolans, stuck her head out of the window.

"Hello, there," she called vivaciously.

Frank knew who called. He waited a long time and then answered "Hello" without looking up. He walked around to the other side of the wagon where Floss couldn't see him, but her persistent voice followed.

"Done for the day?" she asked brightly.

"Soon. Yeah."

"I guess you're going out sporting beings it's a Saturday night tonight." No answer. "Don't tell me a good-looking feller like you ain't got no girl." No answer. "They're running a racket tonight at the Shamrock Club."

"Yeah?" He didn't sound interested.

"Yeah. I got a ticket admitting lady and gent."

"Sorry. I'm all tied up."

"Staying at home to keep your old lady company?"

"Maybe."

"Aw, go to hell!" She slammed the window down and Frank breathed a sigh of relief. *That* was over.

Francie felt sorry for Flossie. She never gave up hope no matter how many times she lost out with Frank. Flossie was always running after men and they were always running away from her. Francie's Aunt Sissy ran after men, too. But somehow they ran to meet her halfway.

The difference was that Flossie Gaddis was starved about men and Sissy was healthily hungry about them. And what a difference *that* made!

III

PAPA CAME home at five o'clock. By that time the horse and wagon had been locked up in Fraber's stable. Francie had finished her book and her candy and had noted how pale and thin the late afternoon sun was on the worn fence boards. She held the sun-warmed, wind-freshened pillow to her cheek a moment before she replaced it on her cot. Papa came in singing his favourite ballad, "Molly Malone." He always sang it coming up the stairs so that everyone would know he was home.

> *In Dublin's fair city,*
> *The girls are so pretty,*
> *'Twas there that I first met....*

Francie, smilingly happy, had the door open before he could sing the next line.

"Where's your mother?" he asked. He always asked that when he came in.

"She went to the show with Sissy."

"Oh!" He sounded disappointed. He was *always* disappointed if Katie wasn't there. "I work at Klommer's tonight. Big wedding party." He brushed his derby with his coat sleeve before he hung it up.

"Waiting or singing?" Francie asked.

"Both. Have I got a clean waiter's apron, Francie?"

"There's one clean but not ironed. I'll iron it for you."

She set up the ironing-board on two chairs and put the iron to heat. She got a square of thick wrinkled duck material with linen tape ties and sprinkled it. While she waited for the iron to get hot, she heated the coffee and poured him a cup. He drank it and ate the sugar bun that they had saved for him. He was very happy because he had a job that night and because it was a nice day.

"A day like this is like somebody giving you a present," he said.

"Yes, Papa."

"Isn't hot coffee a wonderful thing? How did people get along before it was invented?"

"I like the way it smells."

"Where did you buy these buns?"

"Winkler's. Why?"

"They make them better every day."

"There's some Jew bread left a piece."

"Fine!" He took the slice of bread and turned it over. The Union sticker was on that piece. "Good bread, well made by Union bakers." He pulled the sticker off. A thought struck him. "The Union label on my apron!"

"It's right here, sewn in the seam. I'll iron it out."

"That label is like an ornament," he explained, "like a rose

27

that you wear. Look at my Waiters' Union button." The pale green-and-white button was fastened in his lapel. He polished it with his sleeve. "Before I joined the Union the bosses paid me what they felt like. Sometimes they paid me nothing. The tips, they said, would take care of me. Some places even charged me for the privilege of working. The tips were so big, they said, that they could sell the waiting concession. Then I joined the Union. Your mother shouldn't begrudge the dues. The Union gets me jobs where the boss has to pay me certain wages, regardless of tips. All trades should be unionized."

"Yes, Papa." By now, Francie was ironing away. She loved to hear him talk.

Francie thought of the Union Headquarters. One time she had gone there to bring him an apron and car-fare to go to a job. She saw him sitting with some men. He wore his tuxedo all the time. It was the only suit he had. His black derby was cocked jauntily and he was smoking a cigar. He took his hat off and threw the cigar away when he saw Francie come in.

"My daughter," he said proudly. The waiters looked at the thin child in her ragged dress and then exchanged glances. They were different from Johnny Nolan. They had regular waiter jobs during the week and picked up extra money on Saturday night jobs. Johnny had no regular job. He worked at one-night places here and there.

"I want to tell you fellows," he said, "that I got a couple of fine children home and a pretty wife. And I want to tell you that I'm not good enough for them."

"Take it easy," said a friend, and patted him on the shoulder.

Francie overheard two men outside the group talking about her father. The short man said:

"I want you to hear this fellow talk about his wife and his kids. It's rich. He's a funny duck. He brings his wages home to his wife but keeps his tips for booze. He's got a funny arrangement at McGarrity's. He turns all his tips over to him and McGarrity supplies him with drinks. He don't know whether McGarrity owes him money or whether he owes McGarrity. The system must work out pretty good for him, though. He's always carrying a load." The men walked away.

There was a pain around Francie's heart, but when she saw how the men standing around her father liked him, how they smiled and laughed at what he said and how eagerly they listened to him, the pain lessened. Those two men were exceptions. She knew that everyone loved her father.

Yes, everyone loved Johnny Nolan. He was a sweet singer of sweet songs. Since the beginning of time, everyone, especially the Irish had loved and cared for the singer in their midst. His brother waiters really loved him. The men he worked for loved him. His wife and children loved him. He was still gay and young and handsome. His wife had not turned bitter against him and his children did not know that they were supposed to be ashamed of him.

Francie pulled her thoughts away from that day when she had visited the Union Headquarters. She listened to her father again. He was reminiscing.

"Take me. I'm nobody." Placidly, he lit up a nickel cigar. "My folks came over from Ireland the year the potatoes gave out. Fellow ran a steamship company said he'd take my father to America—had a job waiting for him. Said he'd take the boat fare from his wages. So my father and mother came over.

"My father was like me—never held the one job long." He smoked in silence for a while.

Francie ironed quietly. She knew that he was just thinking out loud. He did not expect her to understand. He just wanted someone to listen to him. He said practically the same things every Saturday. The rest of the week when he was drinking, he would come and go and say little. But today was Saturday. It was his day to talk.

"My folks never knew how to read or write. I only got to the sixth grade myself—had to leave school when the old man died. You kids are lucky. I'm going to see to it that you get through school."

"Yes, Papa."

"I was a boy of twelve then. I sang in saloons for the drunks and they threw pennies at me. Then I started working around saloons and restaurants . . . waiting on people. . . ." He was quiet a while with his thoughts.

"I always wanted to be a real singer, the kind that comes out on the stage all dressed up. But I didn't have no education and I didn't know the first way about how to start in being a stage singer. 'Mind your job,' my mother told me. 'You don't know how lucky you are to have work,' she said. So I drifted into the singing waiter business. It's not steady work. I'd be better off if I was just a plain waiter. That's why I drink," he finished up illogically.

She looked up at him as though she were going to ask a question. But she said nothing.

"I drink because I don't stand a chance and I know it. I couldn't drive a truck like other men and I couldn't get on the cops with my build. I got to sling beer and sing when I just want to sing. I drink because I got responsibilities that I can't handle." There was another long pause. Then he whispered: "I am not a happy man. I got a wife and children and I don't happen to be a hardworking man. I never wanted a family."

Again that hurt around Francie's heart. He didn't want her or Neeley?

"What does a man like me want a family for? But I fell in love with Katie Rommely. Oh, I'm not blaming your mother," he said quickly. "If it hadn't been her, it would have been Hildy O'Dair. You know, I think your mother is still jealous of her. But when I met Katie, I said to Hildy: 'You go your way and I'll go mine.' So I married your mother. We had children. Your mother is a good woman, Francie. Don't you ever forget that."

Francie knew that mama was a good woman. She *knew*. And papa said so. Then why did she like her father better than her mother? Why did she? Papa was no good. He said so himself. But she liked papa better.

"Yes, your mother works hard. I love my wife and I love my children." Francie was happy again. "But shouldn't a man have a better life? Maybe some day it will be that the Unions will arrange for a man to work and to have time for himself too. But that won't be in my time. Now, it's work hard all the time or be a bum ... no in-between. When I die, nobody will remember me for long. No one will say: 'He was a man who loved his family and believed in the Union.' All they will say is: 'Too bad. But he was nothing but a drunk no matter which way you look at it.' Yes, they'll say that."

The room was very quiet. Johnny Nolan threw his half-smoked cigar out of the unscreened window with a bitter gesture. He had a premonition that he was running his life out too fast. He looked at the little girl ironing away so quietly with her head bent over the board and he was stabbed by the soft sadness on the child's thin face.

"Listen!" He went to her and put an arm around her thin shoulders. "If I get a lot of tips tonight, I'll put the money on a good horse that I know is running Monday. I'll put a couple

30

of dollars on him and win ten. Then I'll put the ten on another horse I know and win a hundred. If I use my head and have any kind of luck at all, I'll run it up to five hundred."

Pipe dreams he thought to himself, even while he was telling her about his dream winnings. But oh, how wonderful, he thought, if everything you talked about could come true! He went on talking.

"Then do you know what I'm going to do, Prima Donna?" Francie smiled happily, pleased at his using the nickname he had given her when, as a baby, he swore that her crying was as varied and as tuneful as an opera singer's range.

"No. What are you going to do?"

"I'm going to take you on a trip. Just you and me, Prima Donna. We'll go way down south where the cotton blossoms blow." He was delighted with the sentence. He said it again. "Down where the cotton blossoms blow." Then he remembered that the sentence was a line in a song that he knew. He jammed his hands in his pockets, whistled, and started to do a waltz clog like Pat Rooney. Then he went into the song.

> ...a field of snowy white.
> Hear the darkies singing soft and low.
> I long there to be, for someone waits for me,
> Down where the cotton blossoms blow.

Francie kissed his cheek softly. "Oh, Papa, I love you so much," she whispered.

He held her tight. Again the stab-wound feeling. "Oh, God! Oh, God!" he repeated to himself in almost unendurable agony. "What a hell of a father I am." But when he spoke to her again, it was quietly enough.

"All this isn't getting my apron ironed, though."

"It's all done, Papa." She folded it into a careful square.

"Is there any money in the house, Baby?"

She looked into the cracked cup on the shelf. "A nickel and some pennies."

"Would you take seven cents and go out and get me a dicky and a paper collar?"

Francie went over to the dry-goods store to get her father's Saturday night linen. A dicky was a shirt-front made of stiffly starched muslin. It fastened around the neck with a collar button and the vest held it in place. It was used instead of a shirt. It was worn once and then thrown away. A paper collar was not exactly made out of paper. It was called that to

31

differentiate it from a celluloid collar, which was what poor men wore because it could be laundered simply by being wiped with a wet rag. A paper collar was made out of thin cambric stiffly starched. It could be used only once.

When Francie got back, papa had shaved, wetted his hair down, shined his shoes and put on a clean undershirt. It was unironed and had a big hole in the back, but it smelled nice and clean. He stood on a chair and took down a little box from the top cupboard shelf. It contained the pearl studs that Katie had given him for a wedding present. They had cost her a month's salary. Johnny was very proud of them. No matter how hard up the Nolans were, the studs were never pawned.

Francie helped him put the studs in the dicky. He fastened the wing collar on with a golden collar button, a present that Hildy O'Dair had given him before he became engaged to Katie. He wouldn't part with that either. His tie was a piece of heavy black silk and he tied an expert bow with it. Other waiters wore ready-made bows attached to elastics. But not Johnny Nolan. Other waiters wore soiled white shirts or clean shirts indifferently ironed and celluloid collars. But not Johnny. His linen was immaculate, if temporary.

He was dressed at last. His wavy blond hair gleamed and he smelled clean and fresh from washing and shaving. He put his coat on and buttoned it up jauntily. The satin lapels of the tuxedo were threadbare, but who would look at that when the suit fitted him so beautifully and the crease in his trousers was so perfect? Francie looked at his well-polished black shoes and noticed how the cuffless trousers came down in the back over the heel, and what a nice break they made across his instep. No other father's trousers hung just that way. Francie was proud of her father. She wrapped up his ironed apron carefully in a piece of clean paper saved for that purpose.

She walked with him to the trolley car. Women smiled at him until they noticed the little girl clinging to his hand. Johnny looked like a handsome, devil-may-care Irish boy instead of the husband of a scrub-woman and the father of two children who were always hungry.

They passed Gabriel's Hardware Store and stopped to look at the skates in the window. Mama never had time to do this. Papa talked as though he would buy Francie a pair some day. They walked to the corner. When a Graham Avenue trolley came along, he swung up on to the platform, suiting his rhythm to the car's slowing down. As the car started up again, he stood on the back platform holding on to the bar while he leaned way out to wave to Francie. No man had ever looked so gallant as her father, she thought.

IV

AFTER SHE had seen papa off, Francie went up to see what kind of costume Floss Gaddis had for the dance that night.

Flossie supported her mother and brother by working as a turner in a kid glove factory. The gloves were stitched on the wrong side and it was her job to turn them right side out. Often she brought work home to do at night. They needed every cent they could get on account of her brother not being able to work. He had consumption.

Francie had been told that Henry Gaddis was dying, but she didn't believe it. He didn't look it. In fact, he looked wonderful. He had clear skin with a beautiful pink colour in his cheeks. His eyes were large and dark and burned steadily like a lamp protected from the wind. But he knew. He was nineteen and avid for life and he couldn't understand why he was doomed. Mrs. Gaddis was glad to see Francie. Company took Henny's thoughts off himself.

"Henny, here's Francie," she called out cheerfully.

"Hello, Francie."

"Hello, Henny."

"Don't you think Henny's looking good, Francie? Tell him that he's looking good."

"You're looking good, Henny."

Henny addressed an unseen companion. "She tells a dying man that he's looking good."

"I mean it."

"No, you don't. You're just saying that."

"How you talk, Henny. Look at me—how skinny I am and I never think about dying."

"You won't die, Francie. You were born to lick this rotten life."

"Still and all, I wish I had nice red cheeks like you."

"No, you don't. Not if you know where they come from."

"Henny, you should sit on the roof more," said his mother.

"She tells a dying man he should sit on the roof," reported

33

Henny to his invisible companion.

"Fresh air is what you need, and sunshine."

"Leave me alone, Mama."

"For your own good."

"Mama, Mama, leave me alone! Leave me alone!"

Suddenly he put his head down on his arms and pulled tormented coughing sobs out of his body. Flossie and her mother looked at each other and silently agreed to let him alone. They left him coughing and sobbing in the kitchen and went into the front room to show Francie the costumes.

Flossie did three things each week. She worked on the gloves, she worked on her costumes, and she worked on Frank. She went to a masquerade ball every Saturday night, wearing a different costume each time. The costumes were especially designed to hide her disfigured right arm. As a child, she had fallen into a wash boiler of scalding hot water carelessly left standing on the kitchen floor. Her right arm had been horribly burned and she grew up with its skin withered and purple. She always wore long sleeves.

Since it was essential that a masquerade costume be *décolleté*, she had devised a backless costume, the front cut to display her over-full bust and with one long sleeve to cover that right arm. The judges thought that the one flowing sleeve symbolized something. Invariably, she won first prize.

Flossie got into the costume she was going to wear that night. It resembled the popular conception of what a Klondike dancehall girl wore. It was made of a purple satin sheath with layers of cerise tarleton underskirts. There was a black sequin butterfly stitched over the place where her left breast came to a blunt point. The one sleeve was made of pea-green chiffon. Francie admired the costume. Flossie's mother threw open the closet door and Francie looked at the row of brilliantly coloured garments.

Flossie had six sheaths of various colours and the same number of tarleton underskirts and at least twenty chiffon sleeves of every colour that a person could imagine. Each week, Flossie switched the combinations to make a new costume. Next week the cerise underskirt might froth out from beneath a sky-blue sheath with one black chiffon sleeve. And so on. There were two dozen tightly-rolled, never-used silk umbrellas in that closet; prizes she had won. Flossie collected them for display the way an athlete collects cups. Francie felt happy looking at all the umbrellas. Poor people have a great passion for huge quantities of things.

While Francie was admiring the costumes, she began to grow uneasy. While looking at the brilliant frothing colours, cerise, orange, bright blue, red and yellow, she had a feeling that something was stealthily concealed behind those costumes. It was something wrapped in a long sombre cloak with a grinning skull, and bones for hands. And it was hiding behind these brilliant colours waiting for Henny.

V

MAMA CAME home at six with Aunt Sissy. Francie was very glad to see Sissy. She was her favourite aunt. Francie loved her and was fascinated by her. So far, Sissy had led a very exciting life. She was thirty-five now, had been married three times, and had given birth to ten children, all of whom had died soon after being born. Sissy often said that Francie was all of her ten children.

Sissy worked in a rubber factory and was very wild as far as men were concerned. She had roving black eyes, black curling hair, and a high clear colour. She liked to wear a cherry-coloured bow in her hair. Mama was wearing her jade-green hat which made her skin look like cream off the top of the bottle. The roughness of her pretty hands was hidden by a pair of white cotton gloves. She and Sissy came in talking excitedly and laughing as they recalled to each other the jokes they had heard at the show.

Sissy brought Francie a present, a corn-cob pipe that you blew into and a rubber hen popped up and swelled over the pipe-bowl. The pipe came from Sissy's factory. The factory made a few rubber toys as a blind. It made its big profits from other rubber articles which were bought in whispers.

Francie hoped that Sissy would stay for supper. When Sissy was around, everything was gay and glamorous. Francie felt that Sissy understood how it was with little girls. Other people treated children like lovable but necessary evils. Sissy treated them like important human beings. But although mama urged her, Sissy wouldn't stay. She had to go home, she said, and see if her husband still loved her. This made mama laugh. Francie laughed too, although she didn't understand what Sissy meant.

Sissy left after promising that she would come back on the first of the month with the magazines. Sissy's current husband worked for a pulp magazine house. Each month he received copies of all their publications: love stories, wild west stories, detective stories, supernatural stories and what not. They had shiny colourful covers and he received them from the stockroom tied up in a length of new yellow twine. Sissy brought them over to Francie just as they came. Francie read them all avidly, then sold them at half price to the neighbourhood stationery store and put the money in mama's tin-can bank.

After Sissy left, Francie told mama about the old man at Losher's with the obscene feet.

"Nonsense," said mama. "Old age isn't such a tragedy. If he was the only old man in the world—yes. But he has other old men to keep him company. Old people are not unhappy. They don't long for the things we want. They just want to be warm and have soft food to eat and remember things with each other. Stop being so foolish. If there's one thing certain, it's that we all have to get old some day. So get used to the idea as quickly as you can."

Francie knew that mama was right. Still . . . she was glad when mama spoke of something else. She and mama planned what meals they'd make from the stale bread in the week to come.

The Nolans practically lived on that stale bread, and what amazing things Katie could make from it! She'd take a loaf of stale bread, pour boiling water over it, work it up into a paste, flavour it with salt, pepper, thyme, minced onion and an egg (if eggs were cheap), and bake it in the oven. When it was good and brown, she made a sauce from half a cup of ketchup, two cups of boiling water, seasoning, a dash of strong coffee, thickened it with flour and poured it over the baked stuff. It was good, hot, tasty and staying. What was left over was sliced thin the next day and fried in hot bacon fat.

Mama made a very fine bread pudding from slices of stale bread, sugar, cinnamon and a penny apple sliced thin. When this was baked brown, sugar was melted and poured over the top. Sometimes she made what she had named *Weckschnittens*, which, laboriously translated, meant something made with bread bits that usually would be thrown away. Bits of bread were dipped into a batter made from flour, water, salt and an egg and then fried in deep hot fat. While they were frying, Francie ran down to the candy store and bought a penny's worth of brown rock candy. This was crushed with a rolling-pin and sprinkled on top of the fried bits just before eating. The crystals didn't quite melt and that made it wonderful.

Saturday supper was a red-letter meal. The Nolans had fried meat! A loaf of stale bread was made into pulp with hot water and mixed with a dime's worth of chopped meat into which an onion had been cleavered. Salt and a penny's worth of minced parsley were added for flavour. This was made up into little balls, fried and served with hot ketchup. These meat balls had a name, *fricadellen,* which was a great joke with Francie and Neeley.

They lived mostly on these things made from stale bread, and condensed milk and coffee, onions, potatoes, and always the penny's worth of something bought at the last minute, added for fillip. Once in a while they had a banana. But Francie always longed for oranges and pineapple and especially tangerines, which she got only at Christmas.

Sometimes when she had a spare penny, she bought broken crackers. The groceryman would make a toot, which was a poke made of a bit of twisted paper, and fill it with bits of sweet crackers that had been broken in the box and could no longer be sold as whole crackers. Mama's rule was: don't buy candy or cake if you have a penny. Buy an apple. But what was an apple? Francie found that a raw potato tasted just as good, and this she could have for free.

There were times, though, especially towards the end of a long, cold, dark winter, when, no matter how hungry Francie was, nothing tasted good. That was big pickle time. She'd take a penny and go down to a store on Moore Street that had nothing in it but fat Jew pickles floating around in a heavy spiced brine. A patriarch with a long white beard, black skull-cap and toothless gums presided over the vats with a big forked wooden stick. Francie ordered the same as the other kids did.

"Gimme a penny sheeny pickle."

The Hebrew looked at the Irish child with his fierce red-rimmed eyes, small, tortured and fiery.

"*Goyem! Goyem!*" he spat at her, hating the word "sheeny."

Francie meant no harm. She didn't know what the word

37

meant really. It was a term applied to something alien, yet beloved. The Jew of course did not know this. Francie had been told that he had one vat from which he sold only to Gentiles. It was said that he spat or did worse in this vat once a day. That was his revenge. But this was never proven against the poor old Jew, and Francie for one did not believe it.

As he stirred with his stick, muttering curses into his stained white beard, he was thrown into a hysterical passion by Francie asking for a pickle from the bottom of the vat. This brought on eye rollings and clutchings of the beard. Eventually a fine fat pickle, greenish yellow and hard at the ends, was fished out and laid on a scrap of brown paper. Still cursing, the Jew received her penny in his vinegar-scarred palm and retired to the rear of his store, where his temper cooled as he sat nodding in his beard dreaming of old days in the old country.

The pickle lasted all day. Francie sucked and nibbled on it. She didn't exactly eat it. She just *had* it. When they had just bread and potatoes too many times at home, Francie's thoughts went to dripping sour pickles. She didn't know why, but after a day of the pickle, the bread and potatoes tasted good again. Yes, pickle day was something to look forward to.

VI

NEELEY CAME home and he and Francie were sent out for the week-end meat. This was an important ritual and called for detailed instructions by mama.

"Get a five-cent soup bone off of Hassler's. But don't get the chopped meat there. Go to Werner's for that. Get round steak chopped, ten cents' worth, and don't let him give it to you off the plate. Take an onion with you, too."

Francie and her brother stood at the counter a long time before the butcher noticed them.

"What's yours?" he asked finally.

Francie started the negotiations. "Ten cents' worth of round steak."

"Ground?"

"No."

"Lady was just in. Bought a quarter' worth of round steaks

ground. Only I ground too much and here's the rest on the plate. Just ten cents' worth. Honestly, I only just ground it."

This was the pitfall Francie had been told to watch against. Don't buy it off the plate, no matter what the butcher says.

"No. My mother said ten cents' worth of round steak."

Furiously the butcher hacked off a bit of meat and slammed it down on the paper after weighing it. He was just about to wrap it up when Francie said in a trembling voice:

"Oh, I forgot. My mother wants it ground."

"God-damn it to hell!" He hacked up the meat and shoved it into the chopper. Tricked again, he thought bitterly. The meat came out in fresh red spirals. He gathered it up in his hand and was just about to slam it down on the paper when . . .

"And mama said to chop up this onion in it." Timidly, she pushed the peeled onion that she had brought from home across the counter. Neeley stood by and said nothing. His function was to come along for moral support.

"Jesus!" the butcher said explosively. But he went to work with two cleavers chopping the onion up into the meat. Francie watched, loving the drum-beat rhythm of the cleavers. Again the butcher gathered up the meat, slammed it down on the paper and glared at Francie. She gulped. The last order would be hardest of all. The butcher had an idea of what was coming. He stood there trembling inwardly. Francie said all on one breath:

"And-a-piece-of-suet-to-fry-it-with."

"Son-of-a-bitchin' bastard," whispered the butcher bitterly. He slashed off a piece of white fat, let it fall to the floor in revenge, picked it up and slammed it on the mound of meat. He wrapped it furiously, snatched the dime, and as he turned it over to the boss for ringing up, he cursed the destiny that had made him a butcher.

After the chopped meat deal they went to Hassler's for the soup bone. Hassler was a fine butcher for bones but a bad butcher for chopped meat because he ground it behind closed doors, and God knows what you got. Neeley waited outside with the package because if Hassler noticed you had bought meat elsewhere, he'd proudly tell you to go get your bone where you got your other meat.

Francie ordered a nice bone with some meat on it for Sunday soup for five cents. Hassler made her wait while he told the stale joke: how a man had bought two cents' worth

39

of dog meat and how Hassler had asked, should he wrap it up or do you want to eat it here? Francie smiled shyly. The pleased butcher went into the ice-box and returned holding up a gleaming white bone with creamy marrow in it and shreds of red meat clinging to the ends. He made Francie admire it.

"After your mama cooks this," he said, "tell her to take the marrow out, spread it on a piece of bread· with pepper, salt, and make a nice samwish for you."

"I'll tell mama."

"You eat it and get some meat on your bones, ha, ha."

After the bone was wrapped and paid for, he sliced off a thick piece of liver *wurst* and gave it to her. Francie was sorry that she had deceived the kind man by buying the other meat elsewhere. Too bad mama didn't trust him about chopped meat.

It was still early in the evening and the street lights had not yet come on. But already, the horse-radish lady was sitting in front of Hassler's grinding away at her pungent roots. Francie held out the cup that she had brought from home. The old mother filled it half-way up for two cents. Happy that the meat business was over, Francie bought two cents' worth of soup greens from the greengrocer's. She got an emasculated carrot, a droopy leaf of celery, a soft tomato and a fresh sprig of parsley. These would be boiled with the bone to make a rich soup with shreds of meat floating in it. Fat, home-made noodles would be added. This, with the seasoned marrow spread on bread, would make a good Sunday dinner.

After a supper of fried *fricadellen,* potatoes, smashed pie, and coffee, Neeley went down on the street to play with his friends. Although there was no signal nor agreement, the boys always gathered on the corner after supper, where they stood the whole evening, hands in pockets, shoulders hunched forward, arguing, laughing, pushing each other around and jigging in time to whistled tunes.

Maudie Donavan came around to go to confession with Francie. Maudie was an orphan who lived with two maiden aunts who worked at home. They made ladies' shrouds for a living at so much per dozen for a casket company. They made satin tufted shrouds: white ones for dead virgins, pale lavender for the young married, purple for the middle-aged and black for the old. Maudie brought some pieces. She thought Francie might like to make something out of them. Francie pretended to be glad, but shuddered as she put the gleaming scraps away.

The church was smoky with incense and guttering candles. The nuns had put fresh flowers on the altars. The Blessed Mother's altar had the nicest flowers. She was more popular with the sisters than either Jesus or Joseph. People were lined up outside the confessionals. The girls and fellows wanted to get it over with before they went out on their dates. The line was longest at Father O'Flynn's cubicle. He was young, kind, tolerant and easy on the penances.

When her turn came, Francie pushed aside the heavy curtain and knelt in the confessional. The old, old mystery took hold as the priest slid open the tiny door that separated him from the sinner and made the sign of the cross before the grilled window. He started whispering rapidly and monotonously in Latin with his eyes closed. She caught the mingled odours of incense, candle wax, flowers, and the good black cloth and shaving lotion of the priest.

"Bless me, Father, for I have sinned...."

Quickly were her sins confessed and quickly absolved. She came out with her head bowed over her clapped hands. She genuflected before the altar, then knelt at the rail. She said her penance using her mother-of-pearl rosary to keep count of the prayers. Maudie, who lived a less complicated life, had had fewer sins to confess and had got out sooner. She was sitting outside on the steps waiting when Francie came out.

They walked up and down the block, arms about each other's waists, the way girl friends did in Brooklyn. Maudie had a penny. She bought an ice-cream sandwich and treated Francie to a bite. Soon Maudie had to go in. She wasn't allowed out on the street after eight at night. The girls parted after mutual promises were asked and given to go to confession together the following Saturday.

"Don't forget," called Maudie, walking backwards away from Francie, "I called for you this time and it's your turn to call for me next time."

"I won't forget," promised Francie.

There was company in the front room when Francie got home. Aunt Evy was there with her husband, Willie Flittman. Francie liked Aunt Evy. She looked a lot like mama. She was full of fun and said things to make you laugh like people did in a show, and she could mimic anybody in the world.

Uncle Flittman had brought his guitar along. He was playing it and all were singing. Flittman was a thin dark man with smooth black hair and a silky moustache. He played the guitar pretty well considering that the middle finger of his right hand wasn't there. When he came to where he was supposed to use that finger, he'd give the guitar a thumping whack to do for the time when the note should be played. This gave a queer rhythm to his songs. He had nearly reached the end of his repertoire when Francie came in. She was just in time to hear his last selection.

After the music, he went out and got a pitcher of beer. Aunt Evy treated to a loaf of pumpernickel bread and a dime's worth of limburger cheese and they had sandwiches and beer. Uncle Flittman got confidential after the beer.

"Look on me, Kate," he said to mama, "and you look on a man that's a failure." Aunt Evy rolled her eyes up and sighed, pulling in her lower lip. "My children don't respect me," he said. "My wife has no use for me and Drummer, my milk wagon horse, is got it in for me. Do you know what he did to me just the other day?"

He leaned forward and Francie saw his eyes brighten with unshed tears.

"I was washing him in the stable and I was washing under his belly and he went and wet on me."

Katie and Evy looked at each other. Their eyes were dancing with hidden laughter. Katie looked suddenly at Francie. The laughter was still in her eyes, but her mouth was stern. Francie looked down on the floor and frowned, although she was laughing inside.

"That's what he did. And all the men in the stable laughed at me. Everyone laughs at me." He drank another glass of beer.

"Don't talk like that, Will," said his wife.

"Evy doesn't love me," he said to mama.

"I love you, Will," Evy assured him in her soft tender voice that was a caress in itself.

"You loved me when you married me, but you don't love me now, do you?" He waited. Evy said nothing. "You see, she don't love me any more," he said to mama.

"It's time we went home," said Evy.

Before they went to bed, Francie and Neeley had to read a page of the Bible and a page from Shakespeare. That was a rule. Mama used to read the two pages to them each night until they were old enough to read for themselves. To save time, Neeley read the Bible page and Francie read from Shakespeare. They had been at this reading for six years and were half-way through the Bible and up to *Macbeth* in Shakespeare's *Complete Works*. They raced through the reading and by eleven all the Nolans, excepting Johnny, who was working, were in bed.

On Saturday nights Francie was allowed to sleep in the front room. She made a bed by pushing two chairs together in front of the window where she could watch the people on the street. Lying there, she was aware of the night-time noises in the house. People came in and went to their flats. Some were tired and dragged their feet. Others ran up the stairs lightly. One stumbled, cursing the torn linoleum in the hall. A baby cried half-heartedly and a drunken man in one of the downstairs flats synopsized the wicked life he claimed his wife had led.

At two in the morning, Francie heard papa singing softly as he came up the stairs.

> *...sweet Molly Malone.*
> *She drove her wheel-barrow,*
> *Through streets wide and narrow,*
> *Crying....*

Mama had the door open on "crying." It was a game papa had. If they got the door opened before he finished the verse, they won. If he was able to finish it out in the hall, he won.

Francie and Neeley got out of bed and they all sat around the table and ate after papa had put three dollars down on the table and given the children each a nickel, which mama made them put in the tin-can bank, explaining they had already received money that day from the junk. Papa had brought home a paper bagful of food not used at the wedding because some of the guests hadn't come. The bride had divided the unconsumed food among the waiters. There was half of a cold broiled lobster, five stone-cold fried oysters, an inch jar of caviar and a wedge of Roquefort cheese. The children didn't like the lobster and the cold oysters had ño taste and the caviar seemed too salty. But they were so hungry that they ate everything on the table and digested it too, during the night. They could have digested nails had they been able to chew them.

After she had eaten, Francie at last faced the fact that she had broken the fast which started at midnight and was to have lasted until after Mass next morning. Now she could not receive communion. Here was a real sin to confess to the priest next week.

Neeley went back to bed and resumed his sound sleep. Francie went into the dark front room and sat by the window. She didn't feel like sleeping. Mama and papa sat in the kitchen. They would sit there and talk until daybreak. Papa was telling about the night's work; the people he had seen, what they had looked like and how they spoke. The Nolans just couldn't get enough of life. They lived their own lives up to the hilt, but that wasn't enough. They had to fill in on the lives of all the people they made contact with.

So Johnny and Katie talked away the night, and the rise and fall of their voices was a safe and soothing sound in the dark. Now it was three in the morning and the street was very quiet. Francie saw a girl who lived in a flat across the street come home from a dance with her feller. They stood pressed close together in her vestibule. They stood embracing without talking until the girl leaned back and unknowingly pressed the bells. Then her father came down in his long under-drawers and, with quiet but intense profanity, told the fellow what he could go and do to himself. The girl ran upstairs giggling hysterically while the boy friend walked away down the street whistling: "When I Get You Alone, Tonight."

Mr Tomony, who owned the pawn-shop, came home in a hansom cab from his spendthrift evening in New York. He had never set foot inside his pawn-shop which he had inherited along with an efficient manager. No one knew why Mr. Tomony lived in the rooms above the shop—a man with his money. He lived the life of an aristocratic New Yorker in the squalor of Williamsburg. A plasterer who had been in his rooms reported them furnished with statues, oil-paintings, and white fur rugs. Mr. Tomony was a bachelor. No one saw him all week. No one saw him leave Saturday evenings. Only Francie and the cop on the beat saw him come home. Francie watched him, feeling like a spectator in a theatre box.

His high silk hat was tipped over an ear. The street light picked up the gleam of his silver-knobbed cane as he tucked it under his arm. He swung back his white satin-lined Inverness cape to get some money. The driver took the note, touched the butt of his whip to the rim of his plug hat and shook the horse's reins. Mr. Tomony watched him drive away as though the cab were the last link in a life that he had found good.

Then he went upstairs to his fabulous apartment.

He was supposed to frequent such legendary places as Riesenweber's and the Waldorf. Francie decided to see these places some day. Some day she would go across Williamsburg Bridge, which was only a few blocks away, and find her way up-town in New York to where these fine places were and take a good look at the outside. Then she'd be able to place Mr. Tomony more accurately.

A fresh breeze blew in over Brooklyn from the sea. From far away on the north side where the Italians lived and kept chickens in their yards, came the crowing of a rooster. It was answered by the distant barking of a dog and an inquiring whinny from the horse, Bob, comfortably bedded in his stable.

Francie was glad for Saturday and hated to end it by going to sleep. Already the dread of the week to come made her uneasy. She fixed the memory of this Saturday in her mind. It was without fault except for the old man waiting for bread.

Other nights in the week she would have to lie on her cot and from the air-shaft hear the indistinct voices of the child-like bride who lived in one of the other flats with her ape-like truck-driver husband. The bride's voice would be soft and pleading, his, rough and demanding. Then there would be a short silence. Then he would start snoring and the wife would cry piteously until nearly morning.

Recalling the sobs, Francie trembled and instinctively her hands flew to cover her ears. Then she remembered it was Saturday; she was in the front room, where she couldn't hear sounds from the air-shaft. Yes, it was still Saturday, and it was wonderful. Monday was a long time away. Peaceful Sunday would come in-between, when she could think long thoughts about the nasturtiums in the brown bowl and the way the horse had looked being washed while standing in sunshine and shadow. She was growing drowsy. She listened a moment to Katie and Johnny talking in the kitchen. They were reminiscing.

"I was seventeen when I first met you," Katie was saying, "and I was working in the Castle Braid Factory."

"I was nineteen then," recalled Johnny, "and keeping company with your best friend, Hildy O'Dair."

"Oh, *her*," sniffed Katie.

The sweet-smelling warm wind moved gently in Francie's hair. She folded her arms on the window-sill and laid her cheek on them. She could look up and see the stars high above the tenement roofs. After a while she went to sleep.

BOOK TWO

VII

IT WAS in another Brooklyn summer but twelve years earlier in nineteen hundred that Johnny Nolan first met Katie Rommely. He was nineteen and she was seventeen. Katie worked in the Castle Braid Factory. So did Hildy O'Dair, her best friend. They got along well, although Hildy was Irish and Katie came from parents who had been born in Austria. Katie was prettier, but Hildy was bolder. Hildy had brassy blonde hair, wore a garnet-coloured chiffon bow around her neck, chewed sensen, knew all the latest songs and was a good dancer.

Hildy had a feller, a beau who took her dancing Saturday nights. His name was Johnny Nolan. Sometimes he waited for Hildy outside the factory. He always brought some of the boys along to wait with him. They stood loafing on the corner, telling jokes and laughing.

One day, Hildy asked Johnny to bring someone for Katie, her girl friend, the next time they went dancing. Johnny obliged. The four of them rode out to Canarsie on the trolley. The boys wore straw katies with a cord attached to the brim and the other end to their coat lapel. The stiff ocean breeze blew the hats off and there was much laughter when the boys pulled the skimmers back by the cords.

Johnny danced with his girl, Hildy. Katie refused to dance with the feller provided for her, a vacuous, vulgar boy given to remarks like: "I thought you musta fallen in," when Katie returned from a trip to the ladies' room. However, she let him buy her a beer, and she sat at the table watching Johnny dancing with Hildy and thinking that in all the world there was nobody like Johnny.

Johnny's feet were long and slender and his shoes were shiny. He danced with his toes pointed in and rocked from heel to toe with beautiful rhythm. It was hot, dancing. Johnny hung his coat over the back of his chair. His trousers settled well on his hips and his white shirt bloused over his belt. He

46

wore a high stiff collar and a polka-dotted tie (which matched the band on his straw hat), baby-blue sleeve garters of satin ribbon shirred on to elastic which Katie jealously suspected Hildy had made for him. So jealous was she that for the rest of her life she hated that colour.

Katie couldn't stop looking at him. He was young, slender and shining with blond curly hair and deep blue eyes. His nose was straight and his shoulders broad and square. She heard the girls at the next table say that he was a nifty dresser. Their escorts said he was a nifty dancer, too. Although he did not belong to her, Katie was proud of him.

Johnny gave her a courtesy dance when the orchestra played "Sweet Rosie O'Grady." Feeling his arms around her and instinctively adjusting herself to his rhythm, Katie knew that he was the man she wanted. She'd ask nothing more than to look at him and to listen to him for the rest of her life. Then and there, she decided that those privileges were worth slaving for all her life.

Maybe that decision was her great mistake. She should have waited until some man came along who felt that way about *her*. Then her children would not have gone hungry; she would not have had to scrub floors for their living and her memory of him would have remained a tender shining thing. But she wanted Johnny Nolan and no one else and she set out to get him.

Her campaign started the following Monday. When the whistle blew dismissal, she ran out of the factory, reached the corner before Hildy did and sang out:

"Hello, Johnny Nolan."

"Hello, Katie dear," he answered.

After that, she'd managed to get a few words with him each day. Johnny found that he was waiting around on the corner for those few words.

One day Katie, falling back on a woman's always-respected excuse, told her forelady that it was the time of the month; she didn't feel so good. She got out fifteen minutes before closing time. Johnny was waiting on the corner with his friends. They were whistling "Annie Rooney" to pass the time away. Johnny cocked his skimmer over one eye, put his hands in his pockets and did a waltz clog there on the pavement. Passers-by stopped to admire. The cop, walking his beat, called out:

"You're losing time, Sport. You ought to be on the stage."

Johnny saw Katie coming along and stopped and grinned at

her. She looked mighty fetching in a tight-fitting grey suit, trimmed with black braid from the factory. Intricately whorled and squirled, the braid trimming was designed to call attention to her modest bust already helped out by two rows of ruffles pinned to her corset cover. With the grey suit, she wore a cherry-coloured tam pulled over one eye and vici-kid high-buttoned shoes with spool heels. Her black eyes sparkled and her cheeks glowed with excitement and shame as she thought how fresh she must look—running after a feller like that.

Johnny hailed her. The other boys drifted away. What Katie and Johnny said to each other on that special day they never remembered. Somehow during their aimless but oh-so-significant conversation with its delicious pauses and thrilling undercurrents of emotion, they came to know that they loved each other passionately.

The factory whistle blew and the girls streamed out of the Castle Braid. Hildy came along in a mud-coloured brown suit and a black sailor skewered on to her ratted brassy pompadour with an evil-looking hatpin. She smiled possessively when she saw Johnny. But the smile changed to a spasm of hurt, fear and then hate when she saw Katie with him. She rushed down on them, pulling her long hatpin from her sailor.

"He's my feller, Katie Rommely," she screamed, "and you can't steal him away."

"Hildy, Hildy," said Johnny in his soft unhurried voice.

"I guess this is a free country," said Katie, tossing her head.

"Not free for robbers," yelled Hildy as she lunged at Katie with her hatpin.

Johnny stepped between the girls and got the scratch down his cheek. By this time, a crowd of Castle Braid girls had gathered and were watching them with delighted cluckings. Johnny took each girl by the arm and steered them around the corner. He crowded them into a doorway and imprisoned them there with his arm while he talked to them.

"Hildy," he said, "I'm not much good. I shouldn't have led you on, because I see now that I can't marry you."

"It's all her fault," wept Hildy.

"Mine," acknowledged Johnny handsomely. "I never knew what true love was till I met Katie."

"But she's my best friend," said Hildy piteously, as though Johnny were committing a kind of incest.

"She's my best girl now and there's nothing more to say

about it."

Hildy wept and argued. Finally Johnny quieted her down and explained how it was with him and Katie. He ended by saying that Hildy was to go her way and he'd go his. He liked the sound of his words. He repeated them again, enjoying the drama of the moment.

"So you go your way and I'll go mine."

"You mean, I go my way and you go *her way*," said Hildy bitterly.

Finally Hildy went her way. She walked down the street with her shoulders sagging. Johnny ran after her, and there on the street put his arms about her and kissed her tenderly in farewell.

"I wish it could have been different with us," he said sadly.

"You wish no such thing," snapped Hildy. "If you did"— she started crying again—"you'd just give her the gate and start going out with me again."

Katie was crying too. After all, Hildy O'Dair had been her best friend. She, too, kissed Hildy. She looked away when she saw Hildy's tear-wetted eyes, so close to hers, grow small with hate.

So Hildy went her way and Johnny went Katie's way.

They kept company for a little while, became engaged and were married in Katie's church on New Year's Day, nineteen hundred and one. They had known each other not quite four months when they married.

Thomas Rommely never forgave his daughter. In fact he never forgave any of his daughters for marrying. His philosophy about children was simple and profitable: a man enjoyed himself begetting them, put in as little money and effort into their upbringing as was possible, and then put them to work earning money for the father as soon as they got into their teens. Katie, at seventeen, had only been working four years when she married. He figured that she owed him money.

Rommely hated everybody and everything. No one ever found out why. He was a massive handsome man with iron-grey curly hair covering a leonine head. He had run away from Austria with his bride to avoid being conscripted into the army. Although he hated the old country, he stubbornly refused to like the new country. He understood and could speak English if he wanted to. But he refused to answer when addressed in English and forbade the speaking of English in his home. His daughters understood very little German. (Their mother insisted that the girls speak only English in the home. She reasoned that the less they understood German, the less they would find out about the cruelty of their father.) Consequently, the four daughters grew up having little communion with their father. He never spoke to them except to curse them. His *Gott verdammte* came to be regarded as hello and good-bye. When very angry, he'd call the object of his temper *Du Russe*! This he considered his most obscene expletive. He hated Austria. He hated America. Most of all he hated Russia. He had never been to that country and had never laid eyes on a Russian. No one understood his hatred of that dimly-known country and its vaguely-known people. This was the man who was Francie's maternal grandfather. She hated him the way his daughters hated him.

Mary Rommely, his wife and Francie's grandmother, was a saint. She had no education; she could not read or write her own name, but she had in her memory over a thousand stories and legends. Some she had invented to entertain her children; others were old folk tales told to her by her own mother and her grandmother. She knew many old-country songs and understood all the wise sayings.

She was intensely religious and knew the life story of every Catholic saint. She believed in ghosts and fairies and all supernatural folk. She knew all about herbs and could brew you either a medicine or a charm—provided you intended no evil with the charm. Back in the old country she had been honoured for her wisdom and much sought out for advice. She was a blameless, sinless woman, yet she understood how it was with people who sinned. Inflexibly rigid in her own moral conduct, she condoned weaknesses in others. She revered God and loved Jesus, but she understood why people often turned away from these two.

She had been virgin when she married and had humbly submitted to her husband's brutal love. His brutality early killed all of her latent desires. Yet she could understand the fierce love hunger that made girls—as people put it—go wrong. She understood how a boy who had been driven from the neighbourhood for rape could still be a good boy at heart. She understood why people had to lie and steal and harm one another. She knew of all pitiful human weaknesses and of many cruel strengths.

Yet she could not read or write.

Her eyes were soft brown, limpid and innocent. She wore her shining brown hair parted in the middle and drawn down over her ears. Her skin was pale and translucent and her mouth was tender. She spoke in a low, soft, warmly melodious voice that soothed those who listened. All of her daughters and grand-daughters inherited this quality of voice from her.

Mary was convinced that because of some sin she had unwittingly committed in her life, she was mated with the devil himself. She really believed this because her husband told her so. "I am the devil himself," he told her frequently.

She often looked at him—the way two locks of his hair stood up on either side of his head, the way his cold grey eyes slanted upward at the outer corners, and she sighed and said to herself: "Yes, he is the devil."

He had a way of looking full into her saintly face and in a falsely caressing tone he would accuse Christ of unspeakable things. This always terrified her so much that she'd take her shawl from the nail behind the door, throw it over her head and rush forth into the street, where she would walk and walk until concern for her children drove her back into the house.

She went to the public school that the three youngest girls attended and in halting English told the teacher that the children must be encouraged to speak only English; they were not to use a German word or phrase ever. In that way she protected them against their father. She grieved when her children had to leave school after the sixth grade and go out working. She grieved when they married no-account men. She wept when they gave birth to daughters, knowing that to be born a woman meant a life of humble hardship.

Each time Francie began the prayer, *Hail, Mary, full of grace, the Lord is with thee,* her grandmother's face came before her.

Sissy was the oldest child of Thomas and Mary Rommely. She had been born three months after her parents landed in America. She had never gone to school. At the time when she should have started, Mary did not understand that free education was available for people like them. There were laws about sending children to school, but no one sought out these ignorant people in order to enforce the law. By the time the other girls reached school age, Mary had learned about free education. But Sissy was then too big to start with the six-year-olds. She stayed home and helped her mother.

At ten, Sissy was as fully developed as a woman of thirty and all the boys were after Sissy and Sissy was after all the boys. At twelve, she started keeping steady company with a lad of twenty. Her father nipped that romance by beating up the boy. At fourteen, she was going with a fireman of twenty-five. Because he licked her father, instead of the other way round, this romance ended in the fireman marrying Sissy.

They went to City Hall, where Sissy swore that she was eighteen, and were married by one of the clerks. The neighbours were shocked, but Mary knew that marriage was the best thing that could happen to her highly-sexed daughter.

Jim, the fireman, was a good man. He was considered educated, having graduated from grammar school. He made good money and wasn't home much. He was an ideal husband. They were very happy. Sissy demanded little from him except a lot of lovemaking, which made him very happy. Sometimes he was a little ashamed because his wife couldn't read or write. But she was so witty and clever and warm-hearted that she made of living a high, joyous thing, and in time he began to overlook her illiteracy. Sissy was very good to her mother and her younger sisters. Jim gave her a fair household allowance. She was very careful with it and usually had money left over to give her mother.

She became pregnant a month after marriage. She was still a hoyden girl of fourteen, in spite of her womanly status. The neighbours were horrified when they watched her skipping rope on the street with other children, heedless of the yet-to-be-born baby who was now an almost unwieldy bulge.

In the hours not devoted to cooking, cleaning, love-making, rope-skipping and trying to get into the baseball game with the boys, Sissy made plans for the coming baby. If it were a girl, she was going to call it Mary after her mother. If a boy, it would be named John. For some unknown reason, she had a great affection for the name John. She began calling Jim by the name of John. She said she wanted to name him after the baby. At first, it was an affectionate nickname, but soon everyone got to calling him John, and many people believed that that was his real name.

The baby was born. It was a girl and a very easy birth. The midwife down the block was called in. Everything went fine. Sissy was in labour only twenty-five minutes. It was a wonderful delivery. The only thing wrong with the whole business was that the baby was born dead. Coincidently, the baby was born and died on Sissy's fifteenth birthday.

She grieved a while and her grief changed her. She worked harder at keeping her house spotless and clean. She became even more thoughtful of her mother. She stopped being a tomboy. She was convinced that the rope-skipping had cost her the child. As she quieted down, she seemed younger and more child-like.

By the time she was twenty, she had had four children, all born dead. Finally she came to the conclusion that her husband was at fault. It wasn't her fault. Hadn't she stopped skipping rope after the first child? She told Jim that she didn't care for him any more, since nothing but death grew out of their love-making. She told him to leave her. He argued a little, but went finally. At first he sent her money from time to time. Sometimes when Sissy got lonesome for a man, she'd walk past the fire-house where Jim would be sitting outside with his chair tilted against the brick wall. She'd walk slow, smiling, and swaying her hips, and Jim would take unauthorized leave, run up to the flat and they'd be very happy together for a half-hour or so.

Eventually Sissy met another man who wanted to marry her. What his real name was nobody in her family knew, because she began calling him John right way. Her second marriage was arranged very simply. Divorce was complicated and expensive. Besides, she was a Catholic and didn't believe in divorce. She and Jim had been married by a clerk in City Hall. She reasoned that it hadn't been a church or real marriage, so why let it stand in her way? Using her marriage name and saying nothing about her previous marriage, she was married again in City Hall, but by a different clerk.

Mary, her mother, was distressed because Sissy hadn't married in the church. This second marriage provided Thomas with a new implement of torture for his wife. He often told her that he was going to tell a policeman and have Sissy arrested for bigamy. But before he could get around to it, Sissy and her second John had been married four years, she had given birth to four more children, all born dead, and she had decided that this second John wasn't her man either.

She dissolved the marriage very simply by telling her husband, a Protestant, that since the Catholic Church didn't recognize her marriage, she didn't recognize it either, and she now announced her freedom.

John Two took it in his stride. He liked Sissy and had been

fairly happy with her. But she was like quicksilver. In spite of her terrifying frankness and overwhelming naïveté, he really knew nothing about her and he was tired of living with an enigma. He didn't feel too bad about going away.

Sissy at twenty-four had borne eight children, none of whom had lived. She decided that God was against her marrying. She got a job in a rubber factory, where she told everyone she was an old maid (which no one believed), and went home to live with her mother. Between her second and third marriage, she had a succession of lovers, all of whom she called John.

After each futile birth, her love of children grew stronger. She had dark moods in which she thought she would go crazy if she didn't have a child to love. She poured out her frustrated maternity on the men she slept with, her two sisters, Evy and Katie, and on their children. Francie adored her. She had heard it whispered that Sissy was a bad girl, but she loved her fiercely just the same. Evy and Katie tried to be mad at their erring sister, but she was so good to them that they couldn't hold out against her.

Soon after Francie was eleven, Sissy married for the third time at City Hall. The third John was the one who worked in the magazine company and through him Francie had those fine, new magazines each month. She hoped the third marriage would endure because of the magazines.

Eliza, the second daughter of Mary and Thomas, lacked the prettiness and fire of her three sisters. She was plain and dull and indifferent to life. Mary, wanting to give one of her daughters to the Church, decided that Eliza was the one. Eliza entered a convent at sixteen. She chose a very rigid order of nuns. She was never permitted to leave the convent walls except on the occasion of her parents' death. She took the name of Ursula and as Sister Ursula she became an unreal legend to Francie.

Francie saw her once when she came out of the convent to attend Thomas Rommely's funeral. Francie was nine at the time. She had just made her First Communion and had given herself so wholeheartedly to the Church that she thought she might like to be a nun when she grew up.

She awaited Sister Ursula's coming with excitement. Just think of it! An aunt who was a nun! What an honour! But when Sister Ursula stooped to kiss her, Francie saw that she had a fine fringe of hair on her upper lip and chin. This frightened Francie into believing that hair grew on the faces of all nuns who entered the convent at a tender age. Francie decided against sisterhood.

Evy was the third Rommely girl. She, too, had married young. She married Willie Flittman, a handsome, black-haired man with a silky moustache and liquid eyes like an Italian. Francie thought that he had a very comical name and she laughed to herself every time she thought of it.

Flittman wasn't much good. He wasn't exactly a bum, he was just a weak man who whined all the time. *But* he played the guitar. Those Rommely women had a weakness for any kind of man who was by way of being a creator or a performer. Any kind of musical, artistic or story-telling talent was wonderful to them and they felt it their duty to nurture and guard these things.

Evy was the refined one of the family. She lived in a cheap basement flat on the fringes of a very refined neighbourhood and studied her betters.

She wanted to be somebody; wanted her children to have advantages she had never had. She had three children: a boy named after his father, a girl named Blossom and another boy called Paul Jones. Her first step towards refinement was to take her children out of the Catholic Sunday School and put them in the Episcopal Sunday School. She had got it into her head that the Protestants were more refined than the Catholics.

Evy, loving talent in music and lacking it herself, sought for it avidly in her children. She hoped that Blossom would like to sing and that Paul Jones would want to play the fiddle and Little Willie the piano. But there was no music in the children. Evy took the bull by the horns. They would have to love music whether they wanted to or not. If talent wasn't born in them, maybe it could be shoved in at so much per hour. She bought a second-hand fiddle for Paul Jones and negotiated lessons for him at fifty cents an hour from a man who called himself Professor Allegretto. He taught little Flittman fearsome scrapings and at the end of the year gave him the piece called "Humoresque." Evy thought it was wonderful when he got a piece to play. It was better than playing the scales all the time . . . well a little better. Then Evy got more ambitious.

"Beings," she said to her husband, "that we've got the fiddle for Paul Jones, little Blossom could take lessons too and both could practise on the same fiddle."

"At different times, I hope," replied her husband sourly.

"What do you think?" she answered indignantly.

So fifty cents more a week was scraped up and folded into Blossom's reluctant hand and she was sent off to take fiddle lessons, too.

It so happened that Professor Allegretto had a very slight peculiarity concerning his girl pupils. He made them take off their shoes and stockings and stand in their bare feet on his green carpet while they sawed away. Instead of beating time or correcting their fingering, he spent the hour in a reverie staring at their feet.

Evy was watching Blossom getting ready for a lesson one day. She noticed that the child removed her shoes and stockings and washed her feet carefully. Evy thought that commendable but a little strange.

"And why do you wash your feet now?"

"For my fiddle lesson."

"You play with your hands, not your feet."

"I feel ashamed standing in front of the professor with dirty feet."

"He can see through your shoes, maybe?"

"I don't think so because he always makes me take my shoes and stockings off."

This made Evy jump. She knew nothing of Freud and her scanty knowledge of sex did not include any of its deviations. But her common sense told her that Professor Allegretto should not charge fifty cents an hour and not attend to his work. Blossom's musical education was terminated then and there.

Upon being questioned, Paul Jones said that he had never been asked to take anything off but his hat when he went for a lesson. He was allowed to continue. In five years, he could play the fiddle almost as well as his father, who had never taken a lesson in his life, could play the guitar.

Apart from his music, Uncle Flittman was a dull man. At home, his only topic of conversation was the way Drummer the milk wagon horse, treated him. Flittman and the horse had been feuding for five years and Evy hoped that one of them would get the decision soon.

Evy really loved her husband although she could not resist mimicking him. She'd stand in the Nolan kitchen and pretend that she was the horse, Drummer, and she'd give a good imitation of Uncle Flittman trying to get the feedbag on the horse.

"The horse is standing at the kerb like this." Evy leaned over until her head was dangling at her knees. "Will comes along with the feedbag. He's just about to put it on when up goes the horse's head." Here Evy would jerk her head high and whinny like a horse. "Will waits. The horse's head goes down again. You'd think he never could get it up in the air. The horse makes out like he's got no bones." Evy's head lolled alarmingly. "Comes Will with the feedbag, up goes the head."

"*Then* what happens?" asked Francie.

"*I* go down and put the feedbag on the horse. That's what happens."

"Does he let you?"

"Does he let me!" Evy reported to Katie, then turned to Francie. "Why, he runs up on the sidewalk to meet me and sticks his head in the feedbag before I can lift it up, even. Does he let me!" she murmured indignantly. She turned again to Katie. "You know, Kate, sometimes I think my man is jealous the way the horse, Drummer likes me."

Katie stared at her a moment with her mouth open. Then she started to laugh. Evy laughed and Francie laughed. The two Rommely girls and Francie, who was half a Rommely, stood there laughing about a secret they shared concerning the weakness of a man.

Those were the Rommely women: Mary, the mother, Evy, Sissy, and Katie, her daughters, and Francie, who would grow up to be a Rommely woman even though her name was Nolan. They were all slender, frail creatures with wondering eyes and soft fluttery voices.

But they were made out of thin invisible steel.

VIII

THE ROMMELYS ran to women of strong personalities. The Nolans ran to weak and talented men. Johnny's family was dying out. The Nolan men grew handsomer, weaker and more beguiling with each generation. They had a way of falling in love but of ducking marriage. That was the main reason why they were dying out.

Ruthie Nolan had come from Ireland with her handsome young husband soon after their marriage. They had four sons born a year apart. Then Mickey Nolan died at thirty and Ruthie carried on. She managed to get Andy, George, Frankie, and Johnny through the sixth grade. As each boy reached the age of twelve, he had to leave school to go out to earn a few pennies.

The boys grew up, handsome, able to play music, to dance and to sing and with all the girls crazy for them. Though the Nolans lived in the shabbiest house in Irish Town, the boys were the dressiest in the neighbourhood. The ironing board was kept set up in the kitchen. One or the other was always pressing trousers, smoothing out a tie or ironing a shirt. They were the pride of Shantytown, the tall, blond, good-looking Nolan lads. They had quick feet in shoes that were kept highly polished. Their trousers hung just so and their hats set jauntily on their head. But they were all dead before they were thirty-five—all dead, and of the four, only Johnny left children.

Andy was the eldest and the handsomest. He had red-gold wavy hair and finely-moulded features. He had consumption, too. He was engaged to a girl named Francie Melaney. They kept putting off the marriage, waiting for him to get better, only he never did get better.

The Nolan boys were singing waiters. They had been the Nolan Quartette until Andy got too sick to work. They became the Nolan Trio then. They didn't earn much and spent more of that on liquor and horse-racing bets.

When Andy took to his bed for the last time, the boys bought him a genuine swansdown pillow that cost seven dollars. They wanted him to have a luxury before he died. Andy thought it was a wonderful pillow. Andy used it two days, then there was a last great rush of blood which stained the fine new pillow a rusty brown and Andy died. His mother keened over the body for three days. Francie Melaney made a vow that she would never marry. The three remaining Nolan boys swore that they would never leave their mother.

Six months later, Johnny married Katie. Ruthie hated Katie. She had hoped to keep all of her fine boys home with her until either she or they died. So far all had avoided marriage. But that girl—that girl, Katie Rommely! She did it! Ruthie was sure that Johnny had been tricked into marriage.

Georgie and Frankie liked Katie but thought it was a dirty trick for Johnny to skip out and leave them to take care of their mother. They made the best of it, however. They looked around for a wedding present and decided to give Katie the fine pillow they had bought for Andy and which he had used so briefly. The mother sewed a new ticking over it to hide the ugly stain that had been the last part of Andy's life. The pillow thus passed on to Johnny and Katie. It was considered too good for ordinary use and only brought out when one of them was sick. Francie called it "the sick pillow." Neither Katie nor Francie knew that it had been a death pillow.

About a year after Johnny's marriage, Frankie, whom many thought even handsomer than Andy, wavered home after a drinking party one night and stumbled over some taut wire that a bucolic Brooklynite had strung around a square foot of grass before his house stoop. The wire was held up by sharp little sticks. As Frankie stumbled, one of the sticks pierced his stomach. He got up somehow and went home. He died during the night. He died alone and without the priest's last absolution for all of his sins. For the rest of her days, his mother had a mass said once a month for the repose of his soul which she knew wandered about in Purgatory.

In little more than a year, Ruthie Nolan had lost three sons; two by death and one by marriage. She grieved for the three. Georgie, who never left her, died three years later when he was twenty-eight. Johnny, twenty-three, was the only Nolan boy left at the time.

These were the Nolan boys. All died young. All died sudden or violent deaths brought on by their own recklessness or their own bad way of living. Johnny was the only one who lived past his thirtieth birthday.

And the child, Francie Nolan, was of all of the Rommelys and all the Nolans. She had the violent weaknesses and passion for beauty of the shanty Nolans. She was a mosaic of her grandmother Rommely's mysticism, her tale-telling, her great belief in everything and her compassion for the weak ones. She had a lot of her grandfather Rommely's cruel will. She had some of her Aunt Evy's talent for mimicking, some of

Ruthie Nolan's possessiveness. She had Aunt Sissy's love for life and her love for children. She had Johnny's sentimentality without his good looks. She had all of Katie's soft ways and only half of the invisible steel of Katie. She was made up of all of these good and these bad things.

She was made up of more, too. She was the books she read in the library. She was of the flower in the brown bowl. Part of her life was made from the tree growing rankly in the yard. She was the bitter quarrels she had with her brother whom she loved dearly. She was Katie's secret, despairing weeping. She was the shame of her father staggering home drunk.

She was all of these things and of something more that did not come from the Rommelys or the Nolans, the reading, the observing, the living from day to day. It was something that had been born into her and her only—the something different from anyone else in the two families. It was what God or whatever is His equivalent puts into each soul that is given life—the one different thing such as that which makes no two finger-prints on the face of the earth alike.

IX

JOHNNY AND Katie were married and went to live on a quiet side street in Williamsburg called Bogart Street. Johnny chose the street because its name had a thrilling dark sound. They were very happy there the first year of their marriage.

Katie had married Johnny because she liked the way he sang and danced and dressed. Womanlike, she set about changing all those things in him after marriage. She persuaded him to give up the singing waiter business. He did so, since he was in love and anxious to please her. They got a job together taking care of a public school and they loved it. Their day started when the rest of the world went to bed. After supper, Katie put on her black coat with the big leg-o'-mutton sleeves, lavishly trimmed with braid—her last loot from the factory— and threw a cherry wool fascinator over her head (a "noobie" she called it), and she and Johnny set off for work.

The school was old and small and warm. They looked forward to spending the night there. They walked arm-in-arm; he in his patent leather dancing shoes and she in her high-laced boots. Sometimes when the night was frosty and full of stars, they ran a little, skipped a little and laughed a lot. They felt very important using their private key to get into the school. The school was their world for a night.

They played games while they worked. Johnny sat at one of the desks and Katie pretended she was a teacher. They wrote messages to each other on the blackboards. They pulled down the maps which rolled up like blinds and pointed out foreign countries with the rubber-tipped pointer. They were filled with wonder at the thought of strange lands and unknown languages. (He was nineteen and she was seventeen.)

They liked best to clean the assembly rooms. Johnny dusted the piano and, while doing so, ran his fingers over the keys. He picked out some chords. Katie sat in the front row and asked him to sing. He sang to her; sentimental songs of the time: "She May Have Seen Better Days," or "I'm Wearin' My Heart Away For You." People living near-by would be coaxed out of their midnight sleep by the singing. They'd lie in their warm beds, listening drowsily and murmur to each other:

"That feller, whoever he is, is losing time. He's losing time. He ought to be in a show."

Sometimes Johnny went into one of his dances on the little platform that he pretended was a stage. He was so graceful and handsome, so loving, so full of the grandness of just living, that Katie, watching him, thought she would die of being happy.

At two, they went into the teachers' lunch-room, where there was a gas plate. They made coffee. They kept a can of condensed milk in the cupboard. They enjoyed the boiling hot coffee which filled the room with a wonderful smell. Their rye bread and bologna sandwiches tasted good. Sometimes after supper, they'd go into the teachers' rest-room, where there was a chintz-covered couch, and lie there for a while with their arms about each other.

They emptied the wastebasket, last thing, and Katie salvaged the longer bits of discarded chalk and the pencils that were not too stubby. She took them home and saved them in a box. Later when Francie was growing up, she felt very rich having so much chalk and so many pencils to use.

At dawn, they left the school scrubbed, shiny, warm and ready for the daytime janitor. They walked home watching the stars fade from the sky. They passed the baker's, where the smell of freshly-baked rolls came up to them from the baking room in the basement. Johnny ran down and bought a nickel's worth of buns hot from the oven. Arriving home, they had a breakfast of hot coffee and warm sweet buns. Then Johnny ran out and got the morning *American* and read the news to her, with running comments, while she cleaned up their rooms. At noon, they had a hot dinner of pot roast and noodles or something good like that. After dinner they slept until it was time to get up for work.

They earned fifty dollars a month, which was good pay for people of their class in those days. They lived comfortably and it was a good life they had . . . happy and full of small adventures.

And they were so young and loved each other so much.

In a few months to their innocent amazement and consternation, Katie found out that she was pregnant. She told Johnny that she was "that way." Johnny was bewildered and confused at first. He didn't want her to work at the school. She told him she had been that way for quite a while without being sure and had been working and had not suffered. When she convinced him that it was good for her to work, he gave in. She continued working until she was too unwieldy to dust under the desks. Soon she could do little more than go along with him for company and lie on the gay couch no longer used for love-making. He did all the work now. At two in the morning he made clumsy sandwiches and over-boiled coffee for her. They were still very happy although Johnny was getting more and more worried as the time wore on.

Towards the end of a frosty December night, her pains started. She lay on the couch, holding them back, not wanting to tell Johnny until the work was finished. On the way home, there was a tearing pain that she couldn't keep back. She moaned and Johnny knew that the baby was on the way. He got her home and put her to bed without undressing her, and covered her warmly. He ran down the block to Mrs. Gindler, the midwife, and begged her to hurry. The good woman drove him crazy by taking her time.

She had to take dozens of curlers out of her hair. She couldn't find her teeth and refused to officiate without them. Johnny helped her search and they found them at last in a glass of water on the ledge outside the window. The water had frozen around the teeth and they had to be thawed before she could put them in. That done, she had to go about making a charm out of a piece of blessed palm taken from the altar on

Palm Sunday. To this, she added a medal of the Blessed Mother, a small bluebird feather, a broken blade from a penknife and a sprig of some herb. These things were tied together with a bit of dirty string from the corset of a woman who had given birth to twins after only ten minutes of labour. She sprinkled the whole business with holy water that was supposed to have come from a well in Jerusalem from which it was said that Jesus had once quenched His thirst. She explained to the frantic boy that this charm would cut the pains and assure him of a fine, well-born baby. Lastly she grabbed her crocodile satchel—familiar to everyone in the neighbourhood and believed by all the youngsters to be the satchel in which they had been delivered, kicking, to their mothers—and she was ready to go.

Katie was screaming in pain when they got to her. The flat was filled with neighbour women who stood around praying and reminiscing about their own child-bed experiences.

"When I had my Wincent," said one, "I . . ."

"I was even smaller than her," said another, "and when . . ."

"They didn't expect me to come through it," proudly declared a third, 'but . . ."

They welcomed the midwife and shooed Johnny out of the place. He sat on the stoop and trembled each time Katie cried out. He was confused, it had happened so suddenly. It was now seven in the morning. Her screams kept coming to him even though the windows were closed. Men passed on their way to work, looked at the window from behind which the screams were coming and then looked at Johnny huddled on the stoop and a sombre look came over their faces.

Katie was in labour all that day and there was nothing that Johnny could do—nothing that he could do. Towards night, he couldn't stand it any longer. He went to his mother's house for comforting. When he told her that Katie was having a baby, she nearly raised the roof with her lamentations.

"Now she's got you good," she wailed. "You'll never be able to come back to me." She would not be consoled.

Johnny hunted up his brother, Georgie, who was working a dance. He sat drinking, waiting for Georgie to finish, forgetting that he was supposed to be at the school. When Georgie was free for the night, they went to several all-night saloons, had a drink or two at each place and told everyone what Johnny was going through. The men listened sympathetically, treated Johnny to drinks and assured him that they had been through the same mill.

Towards dawn, the boys went to their mother's house where Johnny fell into a troubled sleep. At nine, he woke up with a feeling of coming trouble. He remembered Katie and, too late, he remembered the school. He washed and dressed and started for home. He passed a fruit stand which displayed avocados. He bought two for Katie.

He had no way of knowing that during the night, his wife in great pain, and after nearly twenty-four hours of labour, gave bloody birth to a fragile baby girl. The only notable thing about the birth was that the infant was born with a caul which was supposed to indicate that the child was set apart to do great things in the world. The midwife surreptitiously confiscated the caul and later sold it to a sailor from the Brooklyn Navy Yard for two dollars. Whoever wore a caul would never die by drowning, it was said. The sailor wore it in a flannel bag around his neck.

While he drank and slept the night away, Johnny did not know that the night had turned cold and the school fires which he was supposed to tend had gone out and the water pipes had burst and flooded the school basement and the first floor.

When he got home, he found Katie lying in the dark bedroom. The baby was beside her on Andy's pillow. The flat was scrupulously clean: the neighbour women had attended to that. There was a faint odour of acid mixed with Mennen's talcum powder. The midwife had gone after saying: "That will be five dollars and your husband knows where I live."

She left and Katie turned her face to the wall and tried not to cry. During the night, she had assured herself that Johnny was working at the school. She had hoped that he would run home for a moment during the two o'clock eating period. Now it was late morning and he should be home. Maybe he had gone to his mother's to snatch some sleep after the night's work. She made herself believe that no matter what Johnny was doing, it was all right and that his explanation would set her mind at ease.

Soon after the midwife left, Evy came over. A neighbour's boy had been sent for her. Evy brought along some sweet butter and a package of soda crackers and made tea. It tasted so good to Katie. Evy examined the baby and thought it didn't look like much, but she said nothing to Katie.

When Johnny got home, Evy started to lecture him. But when she saw how pale and frightened he looked and when she considered his age—just twenty years old—she choked up inside, kissed his cheek, told him not to worry and made fresh coffee for him.

Johnny hardly looked at the baby. Still clutching the avocados, he knelt by Katie's bed and sobbed out his fear and worry. Katie cried with him. During the night, she had wanted him with her. Now she wished she could have had that baby secretly and gone away somewhere and when it was over come back and tell him that everything was fine. She had had the pain; it had been like being boiled alive in scalding oil and not being able to die to get free of it. She had had the pain. Dear God! Wasn't that enough? Why did *he* have to suffer? *He* wasn't put together for suffering, but *she* was. She had borne a child but two hours ago. She was so weak that she couldn't lift her head an inch from the pillow, yet it was she who comforted him and told him not to worry, that she would take care of him.

Johnny began to feel better. He told her that after all it was nothing; that he had learned that a lot of husbands had been "through the mill."

"I've been through the mill, now, too," he said. "And now I'm a man."

He made a big fuss over the baby then. At his suggestion, Katie agreed to name her Francie, after the girl, Francie Melaney, who had never married his brother, Andy. They thought it would help to mend her broken heart if she were made godmother. The child would have the name *she* would have carried had Andy lived: Francie Nolan.

He fixed the avocados with sweet oil and pickle vinegar and brought the salad to Katie. She was disappointed at the flat taste. Johnny said you had to get used to it, like olives. For his sake and because she was touched by his thinking of her, Katie ate the salad. Evy was urged to try some. She did and said that she'd sooner have tomatoes.

While Johnny was in the kitchen drinking coffee, a boy came from the school with a note from the principal which said that Johnny was fired because of neglect. He was told to come around and get what money was due to him. The note ended by telling Johnny not to ask for a recommendation. Johnny's face got pale as he read it. He gave the kid a nickel for bringing the note and a message saying he would be around. He destroyed the note and said nothing about it to Katie.

65

Johnny saw the principal and tried to explain. The principal told Johnny that since he knew the baby was coming, he should have been more careful of his job. As a kindly afterthought, he told the boy that he wouldn't have to pay the damage caused by the burst pipes; the Board of Education would see to that. Johnny thanked him. The principal paid him from his own pocket after Johnny had signed a voucher turning over the coming pay cheque to the principal. All in all the principal did the best he could according to the way he saw things.

Johnny paid the midwife and gave the landlord the next month's rent. He got a little frightened when he realized that now there was a baby and that Katie wouldn't be strong enough to do much for quite some time, and that they were out of a job. He consoled himself with the thought that the rent was paid and that they were safe for thirty days. Surely something would turn up in that time.

In the afternoon, he walked over to tell Mary Rommely about the new baby. On the way there, he stopped at the rubber factory and asked for Sissy's foreman. He asked the man to tell her about the baby and would she stop over after work? The foreman said he would, winked, poked Johnny in the ribs and said: "Good for you, Mac." Johnny grinned and gave him ten cents with instructions.

"Buy a good cigar and smoke it on me."

"I'll do that, Mac," promised the foreman. He pumped Johnny's hand and again promised to tell Sissy.

Mary Rommely wept when she heard the news. "The poor child! The poor little one," she lamented. "Born into this world of sorrow; born for suffering and hardship. Ai, there'll be a little happiness, but more of hard work. Ai, ai."

Johnny was all for telling Thomas Rommely but Mary begged him not to just yet. Thomas hated Johnny Nolan because he was Irish. He hated the Germans, he hated Americans, he hated the Russians, but he just couldn't stand the Irish. He was fiercely racial in spite of his stupendous hatred of his race and he had a theory that marriage between two of alien races would result in mongrel children.

"What would I get if I mated a canary with a crow?" was his argument.

After Johnny had escorted his mother-in-law over to his house, he went out looking for work.

66

Katie was glad to see her mother. With her memory of her own birth pangs still lingering, she had knowledge now of what her mother had suffered when she, Katie, was born. She thought of her mother bearing seven children, bringing them up, watching three of them die, and knowing that those who lived were doomed to hunger and hardship. She had a vision that the same cycle was destined for her less than day-old child. She became frantic with worry.

"What do *I* know?" Katie asked her mother. "I can't teach her anything more than I, myself, know and I know so little. You are poor, Mother. Johnny and I are poor. The baby will grow up to be poor. We can't be any more than we are this day. Sometimes I think that the year past was the best we will ever know. As the years go by and Johnny and I get older, nothing will grow better. All we have now is that we are young and strong enough to work and that will go from us as time passes."

Then the real truth came to her. "I mean," she thought, "that *I* can work. I can't count on Johnny. I'll always have to look after him. Oh, God, don't send me any more children or I won't be able to look after Johnny and I've *got* to look after Johnny. He can't look after himself." Her mother interrupted her thoughts. Mary was saying:

"What did we have in the old country? Nothing. We were peasants. We starved. Well, then, we came over here. It wasn't so much better except that they didn't take your father for the military the way they would do in the old country. But otherwise, it's been harder. I miss the homeland, the trees and broad fields, the familiar way of living, the old friends."

"If you could expect nothing better, why did you come to America?"

"For the sake of my children whom I wished to be born in a free land."

"Your children haven't done so well, Mother." Katie smiled bitterly.

"There is here, what is not in the old country. In spite of hard unfamiliar things, there is hope—hope. In the old country, a man can be no more than his father, providing he works hard. If his father was a carpenter, he may be a carpenter. He may not be a teacher or a priest. He may rise—but only to his father's state. In the old country, a man is given to the past. Here he belongs to the future. In this land, he may be what he will, if he has the good heart and the way of working honestly

67

at the right things."

"That is not so. Your children have not done better than you."

Mary Rommely sighed. "That may be my fault. I knew not how to teach my daughters because I have nothing behind me excepting that for hundreds of years my family has worked on the land of some overlord. I did not send my first child to the school. I was ignorant and did not know at first that the children of folk like us were allowed the free education of this land. Thus, Sissy had no chance to do better than me. But the other three . . . you went to school."

"I finished the sixth grade, if that is what is called education."

"And your Yohnny" (she could not pronounce "j") "did too. Don't you see?" Excitement came into her voice. "Already, it is starting—the getting better." She picked up the baby and held it high in her arms. "This child was born of parents who can read and write," she said simply. "To me this is a great wonder."

"Mother, I am young. Mother, I am just eighteen. I am strong. I will work hard, Mother. But I do not want this child to grow up just to work hard. What must I do, Mother, what must I do to make a different world for her? How do I start?"

"The secret lies in the reading and the writing. You are able to read. Every day you must read one page from some good book to your child. Every day this must be until the child learns to read. Then *she* must read every day. I know this is the secret."

"I will read," promised Katie. "What is a good book?"

"There are two great books. Shakespeare is a great book. I have heard tell that all the wonder of life is in that book; all that man has learned of beauty, all that he may know of wisdom and living are on those pages. It is said that these stories are plays to be acted out on the stage. I have never spoken to anyone who has seen this great thing. But I heard the lord of our land back in Austria say that some of the pages sing themselves like songs."

"Is Shakespeare a book in the German?"

"It is of the English. I so heard our lord of the land tell his young son who was setting out for the great University of Heidelberg long ago."

"And what is the other great book?"

"It is the Bible that the Protestant people read."

68

"We have our own Bible, the Catholic one."

Mary looked around the room furtively. "It is not fitting for a good Catholic to say so, but I believe that the Protestant Bible contains more of the loveliness of the greatest story on this earth and beyond it. A much-loved Protestant friend once read some of her Bible to me and I found it as I have said.

"That is the book, then, and the book of Shakespeare. And every day you must read a page of each to your child—even though you yourself do not understand what is written down and cannot sound the words properly. You must do this that the child will grow up knowing of what is great—knowing that these tenements of Williamsburg are not the whole world."

"The Protestant Bible and Shakespeare."

"And you must tell the child the legends I told you—as my mother told them to me and her mother to her. You must tell the fairy tales of the old country. You must tell of those not of the earth who live for ever in the hearts of people—fairies, elves, dwarfs and such. You must tell of the great ghosts that haunted your father's people and of the evil eye which a *hex* put on your aunt. You must teach the child of the signs that come to the women of our family when there is trouble and death to be. And the child must believe in the Lord God and Jesus, His Only Son." She crossed herself.

"Oh, and you must not forget the *Kris Kringle*. The child must believe in him until she reaches the age of six."

"Mother, I know there are no ghosts or fairies. I would be teaching the child foolish lies."

Mary spoke sharply. "You do not *know* whether there are not ghosts on earth or angels in heaven."

"I *know* there is no Santa Claus."

"Yet you must teach the child that these things are so."

"Why? When I, myself, do not believe?"

"Because," explained Mary Rommely simply, "the child must have a valuable thing which is called imagination. The child must have a secret world in which live things that never were. It is necessary that she *believe*. She must start out by believing in things not of this world. That when the world becomes too ugly for living in, the child can reach back and live in her imagination. I, myself, even in this day and at my age, have great need of recalling the miraculous lives of the Saints and the great miracles that have come to pass on earth. Only by having these things in my mind can I live beyond what I *have* to live for."

"The child will grow up and find out things for herself. She will know that I lied. She will be disappointed."

"That is what is called learning the truth. It is a good thing to learn the truth one's self. To first believe with all your heart, and then not to believe, is good too. It fattens the emotions and makes them to stretch. When as a woman life and people disappoint her, she will have had practice in disappointment and it will not come so hard. In teaching your child, do not forget that suffering is good too. It makes a person rich in character."

"If that is so," commented Katie bitterly, "then we Rommelys are rich."

"We are poor, yes. We suffer. Our way is very hard. But we are better people because we know of the things I have told you. I could not read but I told you of all the things I learned from living. You must tell them to your child and add on to them such things as you will learn as you grow older."

"What more must I teach the child?"

"The child must be made to believe in heaven. A heaven, not filled with flying angels with God on a throne"—Mary articulated her thoughts painfully, half in German and half in English—"but a heaven which means a wondrous place that people may dream of—as of a place where desires come true. This is probably a different kind of a religion. I do not know."

"And then, what else?"

"Before you die, you must own a bit of land—maybe with a house on it that your child or children may inherit."

Katie laughed. "*Me* own *land*? A house? We're lucky if we can pay our rent."

"Even so." Mary spoke firmly. "Yet you must do that. For thousands of years, our people have been peasants working the land of others. This was in the old country. Here we do better working with our hands in the factory. There is a part of each day that does not belong to the master but which the worker owns himself. That is good. But to own a bit of land is better, a bit of land that we may hand down to our children . . . that will raise us up on the face of the earth."

"How can we ever get to own land? Johnny and I work and we earn so little. Sometimes after the rent is paid and the insurance there is hardly enough left for food. How could we save for land?"

"You must take an empty condensed milk can and wash it well."

70

"A can . . .?"

"Cut off the top neatly. Cut strips down into the can the length of your finger. Let each strip be so wide." She measured two inches with her fingers. "Bend the strips backward. The can will look like a clumsy star. Make a slit in the top. Then nail the can, a nail in each strip, in the darkest corner of your closet. Each day put five cents in it. In three years there will be a small fortune, fifty dollars. Take the money and buy a lot in the country. Get the papers that say it is yours. Thus you become a landowner. Once one has owned land, there is no going back to being a serf."

"Five cents a day. It seems a little. But where is it to come from? We haven't enough now and with another mouth to feed . . ."

"You must do it thus: You go to the greengrocer's and ask how much are carrots the bunch. The man will say three cents. Then look about until you see another bunch, not so fresh, not so large. You will say: May I have this damaged bunch for two cents? Speak strongly and it shall be yours for two cents. That is a saved penny that you put in the star bank. It is winter, say. You bought a bushel of coal for twenty-five cents. It is cold. You would start a fire in the stove. But wait! Wait one hour more. Suffer the cold for an hour. Put a shawl around you. Say I am cold because I am saving to buy land. That hour will save you three cents' worth of coal. That is three cents for the bank. When you are alone at night, do not light the lamp. Sit in the darkness and dream a while. Reckon out how much oil you saved and put its value in pennies in the bank. The money will grow. Some day there will be fifty dollars, and somewhere on this long island is a piece of land that you may buy for that money."

"Will it work, this saving?"

"I swear by the Holy Mother it will."

"Then why haven't you ever saved enough money to buy land?"

"I did. When we first landed, I had a star bank. It took me ten years to save that first fifty dollars. I took the money in my hand and went to a man in the neighbourhood of whom it was said that he dealt fairly with people who bought land. He showed me a beautiful piece of earth and told me in my own language: 'This is thine.' He took my money and gave me a paper. I could not read. Later, I saw men building the house of another on my land. I showed them my paper. They

71

laughed at me with pity in their eyes. It was that the land had not been the man's to sell. It was ... how do you say it in the English ... a schwindle."

"Swindle."

"Ai. People like us, known as greenhorns from the old country, were often robbed by men such as he because we could not read. But you have education. First you will read on the paper that the land is yours. Only then will you pay."

"And you never saved again, Mother?"

"I did. All over again. The second time it was harder because there were the many children. I saved, but when we moved your father found the bank and took the money. He would not buy land with it. He was always one for birds, so he bought a rooster and many hens with the money and put them in the back yard."

"I seem to remember those chickens," said Katie, "a long, long time ago."

"He said the eggs would bring much money in the neighbourhood. Ah, what dreams men have! The first night twenty starving cats came over the fence and killed and ate many chickens. The second night, the Italians climbed the fence and stole more. The third day the policeman came and said it was against the law to keep chickens in a yard in Brooklyn. We have to pay him five dollars not to take your father to the station house. Your father sold the few chickens that were left and bought canary birds which he could own without fear Thus I lost the second savings. But I am saving again. Maybe some time ..." She sat in silence for a while. Then she got up and put on her shawl.

"It grows dark. Your father will be coming home from his work. Holy Mary watch over thee and the child."

Sissy came over right from work. She didn't even take time to brush the grey rubber powder from her hair bow. She went into choking hysterics over the baby, pronouncing it the most beautiful baby in the world. Johnny looked sceptical. The baby looked blue and wizened to him and he felt that there must be something wrong with it. Sissy washed the baby. (It must have been bathed a dozen times the first day.) She rushed out to the delicatessen store and beguiled the man into letting her open a charge account until Saturday pay-day. She bought two dollars' worth of delicacies: sliced tongue, smoked salmon, creamy-white slices of smoked sturgeon and crisp rolls.

She bought a sack of charcoal and made the fire roar. She brought a tray of supper in to Katie, then she and Johnny sat in the kitchen and ate together. The house smelled of warmth, good food, sweet powder and the stronger candy-like smell that came from a hard chalkish disc that Sissy wore in an imitation-silver filigree heart on a chain around her neck.

Johnny studied Sissy as he smoked an after-supper cigar. He wondered what criterion people used when they applied the tags "good" and "bad" to their fellow-men. Take Sissy. She was bad. But she was good. She was bad where the men were concerned. But she was good because wherever she was, there was life, good, tender, overwhelming, fun-loving and strong-scented life. He hoped that his newly-born daughter would be a little like Sissy.

When Sissy announced that she was going to stay the night Katie looked worried and said there was but the one bed which she and Johnny shared. Sissy declared that she was willing to sleep with Johnny if he could guarantee her a fine baby like Francie. Katie frowned. She knew Sissy was joking, of course. Yet there was something true and direct about Sissy. She started to give her a lecture. Johnny cut the whole thing short by saying he had to get over to the school.

He couldn't bring himself to tell Katie that he had lost their job. He hunted up his brother, Georgie, who was working that night. Fortunately, they needed another man to wait tables and sing in between. Johnny got the job and was promised another for the following week. He drifted back into the singing waiter business and from that time on never worked at any other job.

Sissy got into bed with Katie and they talked most of the night away. Katie told of her worry about Johnny and her fears of the future. They talked about Mary Rommely; what a good mother she was to Evy and Sissy and Katie. They spoke of their father, Thomas Rommely. Sissy said he was an old rip and Katie said Sissy ought to show more respect. Sissy said: "Oh, fudge!" and Katie laughed.

Katie told Sissy of the talk she had had with their mother that day. The idea of the bank so fascinated Sissy, that she got up—even though it was the middle of the night—emptied out a can of milk into a bowl and made the bank then and there. She tried to crawl into the narrow crowded closet to nail it down, but her voluminous night-gown got her tangled up. She pulled it off and crawled naked into the closet. All of her couldn't fit into the closet. The large, luminous, naked back end of her stuck out as she crouched on her knees hammering the bank to the floor. Katie had such a fit of giggling that she was afraid she'd bring on a haemorrhage. The loud banging at three o'clock in the morning woke the other tenants. They pounded on the ceiling from below and on the floor above. Sissy threw Katie into another spasm of giggles by mumbling from the closet that the tenants had a nerve raising such a racket where there was a sick woman in the house. "How can anybody sleep?" she asked, giving the last nail a terrific bang.

The bank in place, she put on her nightgown again, started off the land account by putting a nickel in the bank and got back into bed. She listened excitedly while Katie told her about the two books. She promised that she would get the two books; they would be her christening present to the baby.

Francie spent her first night on earth sleeping snugly between her mother and Sissy.

The next day, Sissy set about getting the two books. She went to a public library and asked the librarian how she could get a Shakespeare and a Bible for keeps. The librarian couldn't help her out on the Bible, but said there was a worn-out copy of Shakespeare in the files, about to be discarded, which Sissy could have. She bought it. It was a tattered old volume containing all of the plays and sonnets. It had intricate footnotes and detailed explanations as to the playwright's meaning. There was a biography and picture of the author and steel-cut engravings illustrating scenes from each play. It was printed in small type, two columns to the page on thin paper. It cost Sissy twenty-five cents.

The Bible, while a little harder to come by, was cheaper in the long run. In fact, it cost Sissy nothing. It had a name, *Gideon*, on the front.

A few days after buying the volume of Shakespeare, Sissy woke up one morning and nudged her current lover, with whom she was spending the night in a quiet family hotel.

"John" (she called him John, although his name was Charlie), "what's that book on the dresser?"

"A Bible."

"A Protestant Bible?"

"That's right."

"I'm going to hook it."

"Go ahead. That's why they put it there."

"No!"

"Yeah!"

"No kidding!"

"People swipe it, read it, reform and repent. They bring it back and buy another one too, so that other people can swipe, read and reform. In that way, the firm that puts out the books loses nothing."

"Well, here's one they're not going to get back." She wrapped it up in a hotel towel that she was also swiping.

"Say!" A cold fear enveloped her John. "You might read it and reform and then I'd have to go back to my wife." He shuddered and put his arms around her. "Promise me that you won't reform."

"I won't."

"How do you know you won't?"

"I never listen to what people tell me and I can't read. The only way I know what is right and wrong is the way I feel about things. If I feel bad, it's wrong. If I feel good, it's right. And I feel good being here with you." She threw her arm across his chest and exploded a kiss in his ear.

"I sure wish we could get married, Sissy."

"So do I, John. I know we could hit it off. For a while, anyhow," she added honestly.

"But I'm married and that's the hell of the Catholic religion. No divorce."

"I don't believe in divorce, anyhow," said Sissy, who always remarried without the benefit of a divorce.

"You know what, Sissy?"

"What?"

"You got a heart of gold."

"No kidding?"

"No kidding." He watched her snap a red silk garter over the sheer lisle stocking she had just pulled up over her shapely leg. "Give us a kiss," he begged suddenly.

"Have we time?" she asked in a practical way. But she pulled the stocking off again.

That's how the library of Francie Nolan was started.

X

FRANCIE WASN'T much of a baby. She was skinny and had a blue look and didn't thrive. Katie nursed her doggedly, although the neighbour women told her that her milk was bad for the child.

Francie was put on the bottle soon enough because Katie's milk stopped suddenly when the child was three months old. Katie worried. She consulted her mother. Mary Rommely looked at her, sighed, but said nothing. Katie went to the midwife for advice. The woman asked her a foolish question.

"Where do you buy your fish of a Friday?"

"Paddy's market. Why?"

"You wouldn't be after seeing an old woman in there buying a cod-fish head for her cat, would you now?"

"Yes. I see her every week."

"She did it! She dried up your milk on you."

"Oh, no!"

"She put the eye on you."

"But why?"

"Jealous she is because you're too happy with that pretty Irish lad of yours."

"Jealous? An old woman like that?"

"A witch she is. I knew her back in the old country. Sure and didn't she come over on the same boat as meself. When she was young she was in love with a wild County Kerry boy. And didn't he go and get her that way and he wouldn't go to the priest with her when her old father went after him. He slipped away on a boat for America in the dead of the night. Her baby died when it was born. Then she sold her soul to the divil and he did give her the power of drying up the milk of cows and nanny-goats and of girls married to young boys."

"I remember she looked at me in a funny way."

"'Twas then she put the eye on you."

"How can I get my milk back?"

"I'll tell you what you must do. Wait until the moon is full. Then make a little image out of a lock of your curling hair, a cutting from your finger-nail and a bit of rag sprinkled with holy water. Christen it Nelly Grogan, and that's the witch's name, and stick three rusty pins in it. That will spoil her power over you and sure your milk will be flowing again like the River Shannon. That will be a quarter."

Katie paid her. When the moon was full, she made the little

doll and stabbed it and stabbed it. She remained dry. Francie sickened on the bottle. In desperation, Katie called Sissy in for advice. Sissy listened to the witch story.

"A witch my foot," she said scornfully. "It was Johnny who did it, and it wasn't with an eye."

In that way Katie knew that she was pregnant again. She told Johnny and he started to worry. He had been fairly happy back in the singing waiter business and he worked pretty often, was steady, didn't drink too much and brought home most of his money. The news that a second child was on the way made him feel trapped. He was only twenty and Katie was eighteen. He felt that they were both so young and so defeated already. He went out and got drunk after he heard the news.

The midwife came around later to see how the charm had worked. Katie told her that the charm had failed, since she was pregnant and the witch was not to blame. The midwife lifted her skirt and dug down into a capacious pocket made in her petticoat. She brought up a bottle of evil-looking dark brown stuff.

"Sure and there is nothing to worry about," she said. "A good dose of this night and morning for three days and you'll come around again." Katie shook her head negatively. "You're not afraid of what the priest would be saying to you if you did it?"

"No. It's just that I couldn't kill anything."

"It wouldn't be killing. It don't count until you've felt life. You're not after feeling it move, are you?"

"No."

"There!" she slammed her fist on the table triumphantly. "I'll only be charging you a dollar for the bottle."

"Thank you, I don't want it."

"Don't be foolish. You're just a bit of a girl and have trouble enough with the one you do be having already. And your man is pretty but not the steadiest boy in the world."

"The way my man is, is my own business, and my baby is no trouble."

"I'm only after trying to help you out."

"Thank you and good-bye."

The midwife returned the bottle to her petticoat pocket and got up to go. "When your time comes, you know where I live." At the door, she gave a last bit of optimistic advice. "If you keep running up and down the stairs, maybe you'll have a miscarriage."

That autumn, in the false warmth of a Brooklyn Indian summer, Katie sat on the stoop and held her sickly baby against the bigness which was another child soon to be born. Pitying neighbours stopped to commiserate over Francie.

"You'll never raise that one," they told her. "Her colour ain't good. If the good Lord takes her, it will be for the best. What good is a sickly baby in a poor family? There is too many children on this earth already and no room for the weak ones."

"Don't say that." Katie held her baby tightly. "It's not better to die. Who wants to die? Everything struggles to live. Look at that tree growing up there out of that grating. It gets no sun, and water only when it rains. It's growing out of sour earth. And it's strong because its hard struggle to live is making it strong. My children will be strong that way."

"Aw, somebody ought to cut that tree down, the homely thing."

"If there was only one tree like that in the world, you would think it was beautiful," said Katie. "But because there are so many, you just can't see how beautiful it really is. Look at those children." She pointed to a swarm of dirty children playing in the gutter. "You could take any one of them and wash him good and dress him up and sit him in a fine house and you would think he was beautiful."

"You've got fine ideas but a very sick baby, Katie," they told her.

"This baby will live," said Katie fiercely. "I'll *make* it live."

And Francie lived, choking and whimpering her way through that first year.

Francie's brother was born a week after her first birthday.

This time Katie was not working when the pains came. This time she bit her lip and did not scream out in her agony. Helpless in her pain, she was capable still of laying the foundation for bitterness and capability.

When the strong healthy boy, howling at the indignity of the birth process, was put to her breast, she felt a wild tenderness for him. The other baby, Francie, in the crib next her bed, began to whimper. Katie had a flash of contempt for the weak child she had borne a year ago, when she compared her to this new handsome son. She was quickly ashamed of her contempt. She knew it wasn't the little girl's fault. "I must watch myself carefully," she thought. "I am going to love this boy more than the girl, but I mustn't ever let her know. It is wrong to love one child more than the other, but this is something that I cannot help."

Sissy begged her to call the boy after Johnny, but Katie insisted that the boy had a right to a name all his own. Sissy got very angry and told Katie a thing or two. Finally Katie, more in anger than in truth, accused Sissy of being in love with Johnny. Sissy answered: "Maybe," and Katie shut up. She was a little afraid that if they quarrelled further, she would find out that it was so about Sissy loving Johnny.

Katie called the boy Cornelius after a noble character she had seen a handsome actor represent on the stage. As the boy grew up, the name was changed into Brooklynese, and he was known as Neeley.

Without devious reasoning or complicated emotional processes, the boy became Katie's whole world. Johnny took second place and Francie went to the back of her mother's heart. Katie loved the boy because he was more completely hers than either Johnny or Francie. Neeley looked exactly like Johnny. Katie would make him into the kind of man Johnny should have been. He would have everything that was good about Johnny; she would encourage that. She would stamp out all of the things that were bad about Johnny as they came up in the boy Neeley. He would grow up and she would be proud of him and he would take care of her all of her days. He was the one that she had to see through. Francie and Johnny would get by somehow, but she would take no chances with the boy. She'd see to it that he more than got by.

Gradually, as the children grew up, Katie lost all of her tenderness, although she gained in what people call character. She became capable, hard and far-seeing. She loved Johnny dearly, but all the old wild worship faded away. She loved her little girl because she felt sorry for her. It was pity and obligation towards her that she felt rather than love.

Johnny and Francie felt the growing change in Katie. As the boy grew stronger and handsomer, Johnny grew in weakness and went further and further down hill. Francie felt the way her mother thought about her. She grew an answering hardness against her mother, and this hardness, paradoxically enough, brought them a little closer together because it made them more alike.

By the time Neeley was a year old, Katie had stopped depending on Johnny. Johnny was drinking heavily. He worked when he was offered one-night jobs. He brought home his wages, but kept his tips for liquor. Life was going too swiftly for Johnny. He had a wife and two babies before he was old enough to vote. His life was finished before it had a chance to begin. He was doomed, and no one knew it better than Johnny Nolan.

Katie had the same hardships as Johnny and she was nineteen, two years younger. It might be said that she, too, was doomed. Her life, too, was over before it began. But there the similarity ended. Johnny knew he was doomed and accepted it. Katie *wouldn't* accept it. She started a new life where her old one left off.

She exchanged her tenderness for capability. She gave up her dreams and took over hard realities in their place.

Katie had a fierce desire for survival, which made her a fighter. Johnny had a hankering after immortality, which made him a useless dreamer. And that was the great difference between these two who loved each other so well.

XI

JOHNNY CELEBRATED his voting birthday by getting drunk for three days. When he was coming out of it, Katie locked him in the bedroom, where he couldn't get anything more to drink. Instead of sobering up, he started to get delirium tremens. He wept and begged by turns for a drink. He said he was suffering. She told him it was a good thing, that suffering would harden him, would teach him such a lesson that he'd stop drinking. But poor Johnny just wouldn't harden. He softened into a wailing, screaming banshee.

Neighbours banged on her door and told her to do something for the poor man. Katie's mouth set in a hard, cold line and she called out to them to mind their own business. But even as she defied the neighbours, she knew that they would have to move as soon as the month was up. They couldn't live in the neighbourhood after the way Johnny was disgracing them.

In the late afternoon, his tortured cries unnerved even Katie. Crowding the two babies in the buggy, she went over to the factory and had Sissy's long-suffering foreman get her away from her machine. She told Sissy about Johnny, and Sissy said she'd come over and fix him up as soon as she could get away.

Sissy consulted a gentleman friend about Johnny. The friend gave her instructions. Accordingly, she bought a half-pint of good whisky, concealed it between her full breasts and laced her corset cover and buttoned her dress over it.

She went over to Katie's and told her that if she could be left alone with Johnny she'd get him out of it. Katie locked Sissy in the bedroom with Johnny. She went back into the kitchen and spent the night with her head on her arms on the table, waiting.

When Johnny saw Sissy, his poor mixed-up brain unscrambled for a minute and he grabbed her arm. "You're my friend, Sissy. You're my sister. For God's sake give me a drink."

"Take it slow, Johnny," she said in her soft comforting voice. "I've got a drink right here for you."

She unbuttoned her waist, releasing a cascade of foaming white embroidered ruffles and dark pink ribbon. The room filled up with the sweet scent of the warm, strong sachet she used. Johnny stared as she undid an intricate bow and loosened her corset cover. The poor fellow remembered her reputation and misunderstood.

"No, no, Sissy. Please!" he moaned.

"Don't be a dockle, Johnny. There's a time and a place for everything and this isn't the time." She pulled out the bottle.

He grabbed it. It was warm from her. She let him take a long drink, then she dug the bottle out of his clutching fingers. He quieted down after the drink; got sleepy and begged her not to go away. She promised. Without bothering to tie up her ribbons or button her waist, she lay on the bed beside him. She put her arm under his shoulders and he rested his cheek on her bare, warm-scented breast. He slept and tears came from under his closed lids and they were warmer than the flesh they fell on.

She lay awake, holding him in her arms and staring into the darkness. She felt towards him as she would have felt towards her babies had they only lived to know her warm love. She stroked his curling hair and smoothed his cheek gently. When he moaned in his sleep, she soothed him with the kind of words she would have spoken to her babies. Her arm cramped and she tried to move it. He woke up for a moment, clutched her tightly and begged her not to leave him. When he spoke to her, he called her "mother."

Whenever he woke up and got afraid, she gave him a swallow of whisky. Towards morning he woke. His head was clearer, but he said it hurt. He jerked away from her and moaned.

"Come back to mama," she said in her soft fluttering voice.

She opened her arms wide and once more he crept into them and rested his cheek on her generous breast. He wept quietly. He sobbed out his fears and his worries and his bewilderment at the way things were in the world. She let him talk, she let him weep. She held him the way his mother should have held him as a child (which she never did). Sometimes Sissy wept with him. When he had talked himself out, she gave him what was left of the whisky, and at last he fell into a deep exhausted sleep.

She lay very still for a long time, not wanting him to feel her withdrawing from him. Towards dawn, his tight holding of her hand relaxed; peace came into his face and made it boyish again. Sissy put his head on the pillow, expertly undressed him and put him under the covers. She threw the empty whisky bottle down the air-shaft. She figured that what Katie didn't know couldn't possibly bother her. She tied her pink ribbons carelessly and adjusted her waist. She closed the door very softly when she went out.

Sissy had two great failings. She was a great lover and a great mother. She had so much of tenderness in her, so much of wanting to give of herself to whoever needed what she had, whether it was her money, her time, the clothes off her back, her pity, her understanding, her friendship or her companionship and love. She was mother to everything that came her way. She loved men, yes. She loved women too, and old people, and especially children. How she loved children! She loved the down-and-outers. She wanted to make everybody happy. She had tried to seduce the good priest who heard her infrequent confessions because she felt sorry for him. She thought he was missing the greatest joy on earth by being committed to a life of celibacy.

She loved all the scratching curs on the street and wept for the gaunt scavenging cats who slunk around Brooklyn corners with their sides swollen looking for a hole in which they might bring forth their young. She loved the sooty sparrows and thought that the very grass that grew in the lots was beautiful. She picked bouquets of white clover in the lots believing they were the most beautiful flowers God ever made. Once she saw a mouse in her room. The next night she set out a tiny box for him with cheese crumbs in it. Yes, she listened to everybody's troubles, but no one listened to hers. But that was right because Sissy was a giver and never a taker.

When Sissy came into the kitchen, Katie looked at Sissy's disordered clothing with swollen and suspicious eyes.

"I'm not forgetting," she said with pitiful dignity, "that you are my sister. And I hope you remembered that, too."

"Don't be such a *heimdiskischer* ass," said Sissy, knowing what Katie meant. But she smiled deeply into Katie's eyes. Katie was suddenly reassured.

"How's Johnny?"

"Johnny will be fine when he wakes up. But for Christ's sweet sake, don't nag him when he wakes up. Don't nag him, Katie."

"But he's got to be told...."

"If I hear that you nag him, I'll get him away from you. I swear it. Even though I am your sister."

Katie knew that she meant it, and was a little frightened. "I won't then," she mumbled. "Not this time."

"Now you're growing up into a woman," approved Sissy as she kissed Katie's cheek. She felt sorry for Katie as well as for Johnny.

Katie broke down then and cried. She made hard, ugly noises because she hated herself for crying, yet couldn't help it. Sissy had to listen, to go through again all she had gone through with Johnny, only this time from Katie's angle. Sissy handled Katie differently than she had handled Johnny. She had been gentle and maternal with Johnny because he needed that. Sissy acknowledged the steeliness that was in Katie. She hardened to that steeliness as Katie finished her story.

"And now you know it all, Sissy. Johnny's a drunk."

"Well, everybody's *something*. We all got a tag of some kind. Take me now: I never took a drink in my life. But do you know," she stated with honest and consummate ignorance, "that there are some people who talk about me and call *me* a bad woman? Can you imagine that? I admit that I smoke a Sweet Caporal once in a while. But bad...."

83

"Well, Sissy, the way you carry on with men makes people . . ."

"Katie! *Don't* nag! All of us are what we have to be and everyone lives the kind of life it's in him to live. You've got a good man, Katie."

"But he drinks."

"And he always will until he dies. There it is. He drinks. You must take that along with the rest."

"What rest? You mean the not working, the staying out all night, the bums he has for friends?"

"You married him. There was something about him that caught your heart. Hang on to that and forget the rest."

"Sometimes I don't know why I married him."

"You lie! You know why you married him. You married him because you wanted him to sleep with you, but you were too religious to take a chance without a church wedding."

"How you talk. The whole thing was that I wanted to get him away from someone else."

"It was the sleeping. It always is. If it is good, the marriage is good. If it is bad, the marriage is bad."

"No. There are other things."

"What other things? Well, maybe there are," conceded Sissy. "If there are other good things too, that's so much velvet."

"You're wrong. That might be important to you, but . . ."

"It's important to everybody, or should be. Then all marriages would be happy."

"Oh, I admit that I liked the way he danced, how he sang a song . . . the way he looked . . ."

"You're saying what I'm saying, but you're using your own words."

How can you win out with a person like Sissy, thought Katie. She's got everything figured out her way. Maybe her way is a good way to figure things out. I don't know. She is my own sister, but people talk about her. She is a bad girl and there is no getting around that. When she dies, her soul will wander through Purgatory through all eternity. I have often told her that, and she always answered that it wouldn't wander alone. If Sissy dies before I do, I must have Masses said for the repose of her soul. Maybe after a while she'll get out of Purgatory because even if they say she is bad, she is good to all the people in the world who are lucky enough to run across her. God will have to take that into consideration.

Suddenly Katie leaned over and kissed Sissy on the cheek. Sissy was astonished because she could not know Katie's thoughts.

"Maybe you're right, Sissy, maybe you're wrong. With me it comes down to this: Apart from his drinking, I love everything else about Johnny and I will try to be good to him. I will try to overlook ..." She said no more. In her heart, Katie knew that she was not the overlooking kind.

Francie lay awake in the wash-basket set up near the kitchen range. She lay sucking her thumb and listening to the conversation. But she learned nothing from it, being but two years old at the time.

XII

KATIE WAS ashamed to stay in the neighbourhood after Johnny's great spree. A good many of the neighbours' husbands were no better than Johnny, of course, but that was no standard for Katie. She wanted the Nolans to be *better* and not as good as anybody. Too, there was the question of money. Although it was no question, because they had very little, and now there were two children. Katie looked around for a place where she could work for their rent. At least, they'd have a roof over their heads.

She found a house where she would get rent free in return for keeping it clean. Johnny swore that he wouldn't have his wife a janitress. Katie told him in her new, crisp, hard way that it was janitor or no home, as it was harder and harder each month to get the rent money together. Johnny finally gave in after promising that he would do all of the janitor work until he got a steady job, when they would move again.

Katie packed their few belongings: a double bed, the babies' crib, a busted-down baby buggy, a green plush parlour suite, a carpet with pink roses, a pair of parlour lace curtains, a rubber plant and a rose geranium, a yellow canary in a gilt cage, a plush picture album, a kitchen table and some chairs, a box of dishes and pots and pans, a gilt crucifix with a music-box in its base that played "Ave Maria" when you wound it up, a plain wooden crucifix that her mother had given her, a wash-basket full of clothes, a roll of bedding, a pile of Johnny's sheet music and two books, the Bible and the *Complete Works of Wm. Shakespeare.*

There was such a little bit of stuff that the ice-man could load it all on his wagon and his one shaggy little horse could pull it. The four Nolans rode along on the ice wagon to their new home.

The last thing Katie did in their old home after it had been stripped bare and had that look of a near-sighted man with his glasses off, was to rip up the tin-can bank. It had three dollars and eighty cents in it. Out of that, she knew regretfully, she would have to give the ice-man a dollar for moving them.

The first thing she did in the new home, while Johnny was helping the ice-man carry in the furniture, was to nail down the bank in a closet. She put two dollars and eighty cents back in it. She added a dime from the few pennies in her own purse. That was the dime she wasn't going to give to the ice-man.

In Williamsburg, it was the custom to treat the movers to a pint of beer when they had completed their job. But Katie reasoned: "We'll never see *him* again. Besides, the dollar is enough. Think of all the ice he'd have to sell to make a dollar."

While Katie was putting up the lace curtains, Mary Rommely came over and sprinkled the rooms with holy water to drive out any devils that might be lurking in the corners. Who knows? Protestants might have been living there before. A Catholic might have died in the rooms without the last absolution of the Church. The holy water would purify the home again so that God might come in if He chose.

The baby Francie crowed with delight as her grandmother held up the cruet and the sun shone through it and made a small fat rainbow on the opposite wall. Mary smiled with the child and made the rainbow dance.

"Schöne! Schöne!" she said.

"Shame! Shame!" repeated Francie, and held out her two hands.

Mary let her hold the half-filled cruet while she went to help Katie. Francie was disappointed because the rainbow went away. She thought it must be hidden in the bottle. She poured the holy water out into her lap expecting a rainbow to come slithering from the bottle. Later Katie noticed that she was wet and paddled her softly, telling her that she was too big to wet her pants. Mary explained about the holy water.

"Ai, the child has but blessed herself and a spanking comes

from the blessing."

Katie laughed then. Francie laughed because her mama wasn't mad any more. Neeley exposed his three teeth in a baby laugh. Mary smiled at them all, and said it was good luck to start life in a new home with laughter.

They were settled by supper-time. Johnny stayed with the children while Katie went to the grocery store to establish credit. She told the grocer she had just moved into the neighbourhood and would he trust her with a few groceries until Saturday pay-day? The grocer obliged. He gave her a bag of groceries and a little book in which he jotted down her indebtedness. He told her she was to bring the book along each time she came to "trust." With that little ceremony Katie's family was assured of food until the next money came in.

After supper, Katie read the babies to sleep. She read a page of the introduction to Shakespeare and a page of begats from the Bible. That was as far as she had got to date. Neither the babies nor Katie understood what it was all about. The reading made Katie very drowsy, but doggedly she finished the two pages. She covered the babies carefully, then she and Johnny went to bed too. It was only eight o'clock, but they were tired out from moving.

The Nolans slept in their new home on Lorimer Street, which was still in Williamsburg, but almost near where Greenpoint began.

XIII

LORIMER STREET was more refined than Bogart Street. It was peopled by letter-carriers, firemen and those store owners who were affluent enough not to have to live in the rooms in the rear of the store.

The flat had a bathroom. The tub was an oblong wooden box lined with zinc. Francie couldn't get over the wonder of it when it was filled with water. It was the largest body of water she had seen up to that time. To her baby eyes, it seemed like an ocean.

They liked the new home. Katie and Johnny kept the cellar, halls, the roof, and the pavement before the house spotlessly clean in return for their rent. There was no air-shaft. There was a window in each bedroom and three each in the kitchen and front room. The first autumn there was pleasant. The sun came in all day long. They were warm that first winter, too. Johnny worked fairly steadily, did not drink much and there was money for coal.

When summer came, the children spent most of the day outdoors on the stoop. They were the only children in the house, so there was always room on the stoop. Francie, who was going on four, had to mind Neeley, who was going on three. She sat for long hours on the stoop with her thin arms hugging her thin legs and with her straight brown hair blowing in the slow breeze that came laden with the salt smell of the sea, the sea which was so near-by and which she had never seen. She kept an eye on Neeley as he scrambled up and down the steps. She sat, rocking to and fro, wondering about many things: what made the wind blow and what was grass and why Neeley was a boy instead of a girl like her.

Sometimes Francie and Neeley sat regarding each other with steady eyes. His eyes were the same as hers in shape and depth, but his were a bright clear blue and hers a dark clear grey. There was steady unbroken communications between the two children. Neeley spoke very little and Francie spoke a lot. Sometimes Francie talked and talked until the genial little boy fell asleep sitting upright on the steps with his head against the iron rail.

Francie did "stitching" that summer. Katie bought her a square of goods for a penny. It was the size of a lady's handkerchief and had a design outlined on it: a sitting New-foundland dog with his tongue lolling out. Another penny bought a small reel of red embroidery cotton and two cents went for a pair of small hoops. Francie's grandmother taught her how to work the running stitches. The child became adept at stitching. Women passing would stop and cluck in pitying admiration at the tiny girl, a deep line already showing at the inner edge of her right eyebrow, pushing the needle in and out of the taut material while Neeley hung over her to watch the bright sliver of steel disappear like magic and then come back up again through the cloth. Sissy gave her a fat little cloth strawberry for cleaning the needle. When Neely got restless, Francie let him push the needle through the strawberry for a while. You were supposed to stitch a hundred or so of these squares and then sew them together to make a bed-spread. Francie heard that some ladies had actually made a bed-spread that way, and that was Francie's great ambition. But though she worked intermittently on the square all summer, autumn found it only half done. The bed-spread had to be saved for the future.

The autumn came again, winter, spring and summer. Francie and Neeley kept getting bigger, Katie kept working harder and Johnny worked a little less and drank a little more with each season. The reading went on. Sometimes Katie skipped a page when she was tired at night, but most of the time she stuck with it. They were in "Julius Caesar" now and the stage direction "Alarum" confused Katie. She thought it had something to do with fire-engines, and whenever she came to that word, she shouted out: "Clang-clang." The children thought it was wonderful.

Pennies accumulated in the tin-can bank. Once it had to be ripped open and two dollars taken out to pay the doctor the time Francie ran a rusty nail into her knee. A dozen times one prong was unfastened and a nickel fished out with a knife to provide Johnny with car-fare to get to a job. But the rule was that he had to put ten cents back out of his tip money. So the bank profited.

On the warm days, Francie played alone on the streets or on the stoop. She yearned for playmates, but did not know how to make friends with the other little girls. The other youngsters avoided her because she talked funnily. Owing to Katie's nightly reading, Francie had a queer way of saying things. Once, when taunted by a youngster, she had retorted: "Aw, you don't know what you're saying. You're jus' full of soun' 'n furry siggaflying nothing."

Once, trying to make friends with a little girl, she said:

"Wait here and I'll go in and begat my rope and we'll play jumping."

"You mean you'll *git* your rope," the little girl corrected.

"No. I'll begat my rope. You don't git things. You begat things."

"What's that—begat?" asked the little girl who was just five years old.

"Begat. Like Eve begat Cain."

"You're buggy. Ladies don't git canes. Only men git canes when they can't walk good."

"Eve begat. She begat Abel too."

"She gits or she don't git. You know what?"

"What."

"You talk just like a Wop."

"I do not talk like no Wop," cried Francie. "I talk like . . . like . . . God talks."

"You'll be struck down dead saying a thing like that."

"I won't neither."

"Nobody home upstairs in your house." The little girl tapped her forehead.

"There is so."

"Why do you talk like that then?"

"My mother reads those things to me."

"Nobody home upstairs in your *mother's* house," corrected the little girl.

"Well, anyhow, my mother ain't a dirty slob like your mother." That was the only reply Francie could think of.

The little girl had heard this many times. She was shrewd enough not to debate it. "Well, I'd sooner have a dirty slob for a mother than a crazy woman. And I'd rather have no father than a drunken man for my father."

"Slob! Slob! Slob!" shouted Francie passionately.

"Crazy, crazy, crazy," chanted the little girl.

"Slob! Dirty slob," screamed Francie, sobbing in her impotence.

The little girl skipped away, her fat curls bouncing in the sun and sang in a clear high voice: "Sticks and stones will break my bones, but names will never hurt me. When I die, you will cry for all the names you called me."

And Francie did cry. Not for all the names called, but because she was lonesome and nobody wanted to play with her. The rougher children found Francie too quiet and the better-behaved ones seemed to shun her. Dimly, Francie felt that it wasn't all her fault. It had something to do with Aunt Sissy, who came to the house so often, the way Sissy looked and the way the men in the neighbourhood looked after Sissy when she passed. It had something to do with the way papa couldn't walk straight sometimes and walked sideways down the street when he came home. It had something to do with the way neighbour women asked her questions about papa and mama and Sissy. Their wheedling off-hand questions did not deceive Francie. Had not mama warned her: "Don't let the neighbours pick on you"?

So in the warm summer days the lonesome child sat on her stoop and pretended disdain for the group of children playing

90

on the pavement. Francie played with imaginary companions and made believe that they were better than real children. But all the while her heart beat in rhythm to the poignant sadness of the song the children sang while walking around in a ring with hands joined.

> *Walter, Walter Wildflower,*
> *Growing up so high,*
> *As we are all young ladies*
> *And very sure to die.*
> *Excepting Lizzie Wehner*
> *Who is the finest flower.*
> *Hide, hide, hide for shame.*
> *Turn your back and*
> *Tell your beau's name.*

They paused while the chosen girl, after much coaxing, finally whispered a boy's name. Francie wondered what name she'd give if they ever asked her to play. Would they laugh if she whispered Johnny Nolan?

The little girls whooped when Lizzie whispered a name. Again they joined hands and walked around in a circle genially advertising the boy.

> *Hermy Bachmeier*
> *Is a fine young man,*
> *He comes to the door*
> *With his hat in his hand*
> *Down comes she*
> *All dressed in silk.*
> *Tomorrow, tomorrow,*
> *The wedding shall begin.*

The girls stopped and clapped their hands joyously. Then without motivation, there was a change in mood. The girls went around the ring slower and with lowered heads.

> *Mother, Mother, I am sick.*
> *Send for the doctor,*
> *Quick, quick quick!*
> *Doctor, Doctor, shall I die?*
> *Yes, my darling,*
> *By and by.*
> *How many coaches shall I have?*
> *Enough for you and*
> *Your family, too.*

In other neighbourhoods there were different words to the song, but essentially it was the same game. No one knew where the words had come from. Little girls learned them from other little girls and it was the most frequently played game in Brooklyn.

There were other games. There were jacks that two little girls could play together sitting on the steps of a stoop. Francie played jacks by herself, first being Francie and then her opponent. She'd talk to the imaginary player. "I'm for threesies and you're for twosies," she'd say.

Potsy was a game that the boys started and the girls finished. A couple of boys would put a tin-can on the car-track and sit along the kerb and watch with a professional eye as the trolley wheels flattened the can. They'd fold it and put it on the track again. Again it was flattened, folded and flattened again. Soon there was a flat heavy square of metal. Numbered squares were marked off on the pavement and the game turned over to the girls, who hopped on one foot pushing the potsy from square to square. Whoever got through the squares with the least number of hops won the game.

Francie made a potsy. She put a can on the tracks. She watched with a professional frown as the car ran over it. She shuddered in delighted horror when she heard the scrunch. Would the motorman be mad, she wondered, if he knew that she was making his trolley-car work for her? She made the squares, but could only write one and seven. She hopped through a game ardently wishing someone were playing with her, as she was sure she won with less hops than any other little girl in the world.

Sometimes there was music in the streets. This was something that Francie could enjoy without companions. A three-piece band came around once a week. They wore ordinary suits but funny hats, like a motor-man's hat, only the top was squashed in. When Francie heard the children shouting: "Here comes the Bieble-boobers," she'd run out on the street, sometimes dragging Neeley with her.

The band consisted of a fiddle, drum and cornet. The men played old Viennese airs, and if they didn't play well they at least played loudly. Little girls waltzed with each other, round and round on the warm summer pavements. There were always two boys who did a grotesque dance together, mimicking the girls and bumping into them rudely. When the girls got angry, the boys would bow with great exaggeration (being sure their buttocks would bump another dancing couple), and apologize in flowery language.

Francie wished she could be one of the brave ones who took no part in the dancing but stood close to the horn-blower sucking noisily on big dripping pickles. This made saliva flow into the horn, which made the cornet-player very angry. If provoked enough, he'd let out a string of oaths in German, ending up with something that sounded like *Gott verdammte Ehrländiger Jude*. Most Brooklyn Germans had a habit of calling everyone who annoyed them a Jew.

Francie was fascinated by the money angle. After two songs, the fiddle and horn carried on alone while the drummer went around hat in hand ungraciously accepting the pennies doled out to him. After canvassing the street, he'd stand on the kerb's edge and look up at the house windows. Women wrapped two pennies in a bit of newspaper and tossed them down. The newspaper was essential. Any pennies thrown loose were considered fair game by the boys and they scrambled for them, picked them up and ran off down the street with an angry musician after them. For some reason, they wouldn't try to get the wrapped pennies. They'd pick them up sometimes and hand them to the musicians. It was some sort of code that made them agree as to whose pennies were whose.

If the musicians got enough, they'd play another song. If the take was meagre, they'd move on hoping for greener fields. Francie, usually dragging Neeley along, often followed the musicians from stop to stop, street to street, until it got dark and time for the musicians to disband. Francie was but one of a crowd, as many children followed the band Pied Piper fashion. Many of the little girls towed baby brothers and sisters along, some in home-made wagons, others in busted-down baby buggies. The music cast such a spell over them that they forgot about home and eating. And the little babies cried, wet their pants, slept, woke to cry again, wet their pants again and to sleep again. And "The Beautiful Blue Danube" played on and on.

Francie thought the musicians had a fine life. She made plans. When Neeley got bigger, he would play the hot-hot (his name for an accordion) and she would bang a tambourine on the street and people would throw them pennies, and they'd get rich, and mama wouldn't have to work any more.

Although she followed the band, Francie liked the organ-grinder better. Every once in a while a man came around lugging a small organ with a monkey perched atop it. The monkey wore a red jacket with gold braid and a red pill-box hat strapped under his chin. His red trousers had a convenient hole in them so that his tail could stick out. Francie loved that monkey. She'd give him her precious penny-for-candy just for the happiness of seeing him tip his hat to her. If mama were around, she'd come out with a penny that should have gone into the tin-can bank and give it to the man with sharp instruction not to mistreat his monkey, and if he did and she found out, she would report him. The Italian never understood a word she said and always made the same answer. He pulled off his hat, bowed humbly with a little crook of the leg and called eagerly: "*Sì, Sì.*"

The big organ was different. When that came around it was like a *fiesta*. The organ was pulled by a dark curly-haired man with very white teeth. He wore green velveteen trousers and a brown corduroy jacket from which hung a red bandana handkerchief. He wore one hoop ear-ring. The woman who helped him pull the organ wore a swirling red skirt and a yellow blouse and large hoop ear-rings.

The music tinkled out shrilly, a song from *Carmen* or *Il Trovatore*. The woman shook a dirty, be-ribboned tambourine and listlessly punched it with her elbow in time to the music. At the end of a song, she'd twirl suddenly, showing her stout legs in dirty white cotton stockings and a flash of multi-coloured petticoats.

Francie never noticed the dirt and the lassitude. She heard the music and saw the flashing colours and felt the glamour of a picturesque people. Katie warned her never to follow the big organ. Katie said that those organ-grinders who dressed up so were Sicilians. And all the world knew that the Sicilians belonged to the Black Hand, and that the Black Hand Society always kidnapped little children and held them for ransom. They took the child and left a note saying to leave a hundred dollars in the cemetery, and signed it with the black imprint of a hand. That's what mama said about those organ-grinders.

For days after the organ-grinder had been around, Francie played organ-grinder. She hummed what she recalled of Verdi and bumped her elbow on an old pie-tin, pretending it was a tambourine. She ended the game by drawing an outline of her hand on paper and filling it in with black crayon.

Sometimes Francie wavered. She didn't know whether it would be better to be a band when she grew up or an organ-grinder lady. It would be nice if she and Neeley could get a little organ and a cute monkey. All day they could have fun with him for nothing and go around playing and watching him tip his hat. And people would give them a lot of pennies and the monkey could eat with them and maybe sleep in her bed at night. This profession seemed so desirable that Francie announced her intentions to mama, but Katie threw cold water on the project, telling her not to be silly; that monkeys had fleas, and she wouldn't allow a monkey in one of her clean beds.

Francie toyed with the idea of being a tambourine lady. But then she'd have to be a Sicilian and kidnap little children, and she didn't want to do that, although drawing a black hand was fun.

There was always the music. There were songs and dancing on the Brooklyn streets in those long-ago summers, and the days should have been joyous. But there was something sad about those summers, something sad about the children, thin in body but with the baby curves still lingering in their faces, singing in sad monotony as they went through the figures of a ring game. It was sad the way they were still babies of four and five years of age, but so precocious about taking care of themselves. "The Blue Danube" that the band played was sad as well as bad. The monkey had sad eyes under his bright red cap. The organ-grinder's tune was sad under its lilting shrillness.

Even the minstrels who came in the back yards and sang:

> *If I had my way,*
> *You would never grow old,*

were sad, too. They were bums and they were hungry, and they didn't have talent for song-making. All they had in the world was the nerve to stand in a back yard with cap in hand and sing loudly. The sad thing was in the knowing that all their nerve would get them nowhere in the world, and that they were lost, as all people in Brooklyn seem lost when the day is nearly over, and even though the sun is still bright, it is thin and doesn't give you warmth when it shines on you.

LIFE WAS pleasant in Lorimer Street and the Nolans would have kept on living there if it hadn't been for Aunt Sissy and her big but mistaken heart. It was Sissy's business with the tricycle and the balloons that ruined and disgraced the Nolans.

One day Sissy was laid off from work and decided to go over and look after Francie and Neeley while Katie was working. A block before she got to their house, her eyes were dazzled by the sun glinting off the brass handle-bar of a handsome tricycle. It was a kind of vehicle that you don't see nowadays. It had a wide leather seat, big enough for two little children, with a back to it and an iron steering-bar leading to the small front wheel. There were two larger wheels in the back. There was a handle-bar of solid brass on top of the steering-rod. The pedals were in front of the seat and a child sat in it at ease, pedalled it while leaning back in the seat and steered it with the handle-bars which lay across the lap.

Sissy saw that tricycle standing there unattended in front of a stoop. She didn't hesitate. She took the tricycle, pulled it around to the Nolan house, got the children out and gave them a ride.

Francie thought it was wonderful! She and Neeley sat in the seat and Sissy pulled them around the block. The leather seat was warm from the sun and had a rich and expensive smell. The hot sun danced on the brass handle-bar and it looked like living fire. Francie thought that if she touched it, it would burn her hand surely. Then something happened.

A small crowd bore down on them headed by a hysterical woman and a bawling boy. The woman rushed at Sissy yelling: "Robber!" She grabbed the handle-bars and pulled. Sissy held on tightly. Francie almost got thrown out. The cop on the beat came rushing up.

"What's this? What's this?" Thus he took over.

"This lady is a robber," reported the woman. "She stole my little boy's tricycle."

"I didn't steal it, Sergeant," said Sissy in her soft appealing voice. "It was just standing there, I borrowed it to give the kids a ride. They never rode in such a fine tricycle. You know what a ride means to a kid. It's just heaven." The cop stared at the mute children in the seat. Francie grinned at him in trembling panic. "I was only going to ride them once around the block and then take it back. *Honest*, Sarge."

The cop let his eyes rest on Sissy's well-shaped bust which was not spoiled any by the tight waists that she liked to wear. He turned to the harassed mother.

"Why do you want to be so stingy for, Lady?" he said. "Let her give the kids a ride around the block. It ain't no skin off your teeth." (Only he didn't say "teeth," to the snickering delight of the youngsters clustered around.) "Let her give them a spin and I'll see that you get the bike back safe."

He was the law. What could the woman do? The cop gave the bawling kid a nickel and told him to shut up. He dispersed the crowd very simply by telling them he'd send for the pie wagon and take them all down to the station house if they didn't twenty-three skidoo.

The crowd scattered. The cop, swinging his club, gallantly escorted Sissy and her charges around the block. Sissy looked up at him and smiled into his eyes. Whereupon he stuck his club in his belt and insisted on pulling the bike for her. Sissy trotted along beside him on her tiny high-heeled shoes and cast a spell over him with her soft fluttering voice. They walked around the block three times, the cop pretending not to notice the hands that went up to hide smiles as the people saw a fully-uniformed officer of the law so engaged. He talked warmly to Sissy, mostly about his wife, who was a good woman, you understand, but, you know, a kind of invalid.

Sissy said she understood.

After the bike episode, people talked They talked enough about Johnny coming home drunk once in a while and about how the men looked at Sissy. Now they had this to add on. Katie thought of moving. It was getting like Bogart Street, where the neighbours knew too much about the Nolans. While Katie was thinking about looking for another place, something else happened and they had to move right away. The thing that finally drove them from Lorimer Street was stark raw sex. Only it was very innocent looked at in the right way.

One Saturday afternoon, Katie had an odd job at Gorling's, a large department store in Williamsburg. She fixed coffee and sandwiches for the Saturday night supper that the boss gave the girls in lieu of overtime money. Johnny was at Union Headquarters waiting for a job to find him. Sissy wasn't working that day. Knowing that the children would be left alone locked in the rooms, she decided to keep them company.

She knocked at the door, calling out that she was Aunt Sissy. Francie opened the door on the chain to make sure before she let her in. The children swarmed over Sissy, smothering her with hugs. They loved her. To them, she was a beautiful lady who always smelled sweet, wore beautiful clothes and brought them amazing presents.

Today she brought a sweet-smelling cedar cigar box, several sheets of tissue-paper, some red and some white, and a jar of paste. They sat around the kitchen table and went to work decorating the box. Sissy outlined circles on the paper with a quarter and Francie cut them out. Sissy showed her how to make them into little paper cups by moulding the circles around the end of a pencil. When they had a lot of cups made, Sissy drew a heart on the box cover. The bottom of each red cup was given a dab of paste and the cup was pasted on the pencilled heart. The heart was filled in with red cups. The rest of the lid was filled in with white. When the top was finished it looked like a bed of closely-packed white carnations with a heart of red ones. The sides were filled in with white cups and the inside lined with red tissue. You never could tell it had been a cigar box, it was that beautiful. The box took up most of the afternoon.

Sissy had a chop suey date at five and she got ready to leave. Francie clung to her and begged her not to go. Sissy hated to leave, yet she didn't want to miss her date. She searched in her purse for something to amuse them in her absence. They stood at her knee helping her look. Francie spied a cigarette box and pulled it out. On the cover was a picture of a man lying on a couch, knees crossed, one foot dangling in the air and smoking a cigarette which made a big smoke ring over his head. In the ring was a picture of a girl with her hair in her eyes and her bust popping out of her dress. The name on the box was *American Dreams*. It was out of the stock at Sissy's factory.

The children clamoured for the box. Sissy reluctantly let them have it after explaining that the box contained cigarettes and was only to hold and to look at and not under any circumstances to be opened. They must not touch the seals, she said.

After she left, the children amused themselves for a time by staring at the picture. They shook the box. A dull swishing mysterious sound resulted.

"They is snakes in there and not zingarettes," decided Neeley.

"No," corrected Francie. "Worms are in there. Live ones."

They argued, Francie saying the box was too small for snakes and Neeley insisting that they were rolled-up snakes like herring in a glass jar. Curiosity grew to such a pitch that Sissy's instructions were forgotten. The seals were so lightly pasted, it was a simple matter to pull them off. Francie opened the box. There was a sheet of soft dulled tin foil over the contents. Francie lifted the foil carefully. Neeley prepared to crawl under the table if the snakes became active. But there were neither snakes, worms nor cigarettes in the box and its contents were very uninteresting. After trying to devise some simple games, Francie and Neeley lost interest, clumsily tied the contents of the box to a string, trailed the string out of the window and finally secured the string by shutting the window on it. They took turns jumping on the denuded box and became so absorbed in breaking it into bits that they forgot all about the string hanging out of the window.

Consequently, there was a great surprise waiting for Johnny when he sauntered home to get a fresh dicky and collar for his evening job. He took one look and his face burned with shame. He told Katie when she came home.

Katie questioned Francie closely and found out everything. Sissy was condemned. That night after the children had been put to bed and Johnny was away working, Katie sat in her dark kitchen with blushes coming and going. Johnny went about his work with a dull feeling that the world had come to an end.

Evy came over later in the evening and she and Katie discussed Sissy.

"That's the end, Katie," said Evy, "the very end. What Sissy does is her own business until her own business makes a thing like this happen. I've got a growing girl, so have you, we mustn't let Sissy come into our homes again. She's bad and there's no getting around it."

"She's good in many ways," temporized Katie.

"You say that after what she did to you today?"

"Well ... I guess you're right. Only don't tell Mother. She doesn't know how Sissy lives and Sissy is her eye-apple."

When Johnny came home Katie told him that Sissy was never to come to their house again. Johnny sighed and said he guessed that was the only thing to do. Johnny and Katie talked away the night, and in the morning they had their plans all made for moving when the end of the month came.

Katie found a janitor place on Grand Street in Williamsburg. She took up the tin-can bank when they moved. There was a little over eight dollars in it. Two had to go to the movers, the rest was put back when the can was nailed down in the new home. Again Mary Rommely came and sprinkled the flat with holy water. Again there was the settling process and the establishing of trust or credit at the neighbourhood stores.

There was resigned regret that the new flat was not as nice as their Lorimer Street home. They lived on the top floor instead of the ground floor. There was no stoop, as a store occupied the street floor of the house. There was no bathroom and the toilet was in the hall and shared by two families.

The only bright spot was that the roof was theirs. By an unwritten agreement, the roof belonged to the people who lived on the top floor, as the yard belonged to the people who lived on the first floor. Another advantage was that there was no one living overhead to make vibrations on the ceiling and cause the Welsbach gas mantle to crumble into powder.

While Katie was arguing with the movers, Johnny took Francie up on the roof. She saw a whole new world. Not far away was the lovely span of the Williamsburg Bridge. Across the East River, like a fairy city made of silver cardboard, the skyscrapers loomed cleanly. There was the Brooklyn Bridge further away like an echo of the nearer bridge.

"It's pretty," said Francie. "It's pretty the same way pictures of in-the-country are pretty."

"I go over that bridge sometimes when I go to work," Johnny said.

Francie looked at him in wonder. He went over that magic bridge and still talked and looked like always? She couldn't get over it. She put out her hand and touched his arm. Surely the wonderful experience of going over that bridge would make him *feel* different? She was disappointed because his arm felt as it had always felt.

At the child's touch, Johnny put his arm around her and smiled down at her. "How old are you, Prima Donna?"

"Six going on seven."

"Why, you'll be going to school in September."

"No. Mama said I must wait until next year till Neeley's old enough so we can start together."

"Why?"

"So we can help each other against the older kids who might

lick us if there was only one."

"Your mother thinks of everything."

Francie turned around and looked at the other roofs. Nearby was one with a pigeon coop on it. The pigeons were safely locked up. But the pigeon owner, a youth of seventeen, stood on the edge of the roof with a long bamboo stick. It had a rag on the end and the boy stood waving the stick in circles. Another flock of pigeons was flying around in a circle. One of them left the group to follow the flying rag. The boy lowered the stick cautiously and the silly pigeon followed the rag. The boy grabbed him and stuck him in the coop. Francie was distressed.

"The boy stole a pigeon."

"And tomorrow someone will steal one of his," said Johnny.

"But the poor pigeon, taken away from his relations. Maybe he's got children." Tears came into her eyes.

"I wouldn't cry," said Johnny. "Maybe the pigeon wanted to get away from his relatives. If he doesn't like the new coop, he'll fly back to the old one when he gets out again." Francie was consoled.

They didn't say anything for a long time. They stood hand-in-hand on the roof's edge looking across the river to New York. Finally Johnny said, as if to himself: "Seven years."

"What, Papa?"

"Your mama and I have been married seven years already."

"Was I here when you got married?"

"No."

"I was here, though, when Neeley came."

"That's right." Johnny went back to thinking aloud. "Married seven years and we've had three homes. This will be my last home."

Francie didn't notice that he said my last home instead of our last home.

BOOK THREE

XV

FOUR ROOMS made up the new flat. They led one into the other and were called railroad rooms. The high narrow kitchen faced on the yard, which was a flagstone walk surrounding a square of cement-like sour earth out of which nothing could possibly grow.

Yet, there was this tree growing in the yard.

When Francie first saw it, it was only up to the second storey. She could look down on it from her window. It looked like a packed crowd of people of assorted sizes, standing umbrella-protected in the rain.

There was a lean clothes pole in the back of the yard from which six washlines on pulleys connected with six kitchen windows. The neighbourhood boys kept themselves in pocket money by climbing the poles to replace a washline when it slipped off a pulley. It was believed that the boys climbed the pole in the dead of night and sneaked the line off the pulley to guarantee the next day's dime.

On a sunny windy day, it was pretty to see the lines filled, the square white sheets taking the wind like the sails of a story-book boat and the red, green and yellow clothes straining at the wooden pins as though they had life.

The pole stood against a brick wall which was the window-less side of the neighbourhood school. Francie found that no two bricks were alike when she looked real close. It was a soothing rhythm the way they were put together with crumbly thin lines of white mortar. They glowed when the sun shone on them. They smelled warm and porous when Francie pressed her cheek against them. They were the first to receive the rain and they gave off a wet clay odour that was like the smell of life itself. In the winter, when the first snow was too delicate to last on the sidewalks, it clung to the rough surface of the brick and was like fairy lace.

Four feet of the school yard faced on Francie's yard and was segregated from it by an iron mesh fence. The few times

102

Francie got to play in the yard (it was pre-empted by the boy who lived on the ground floor, who would let no one in it while he was there), she managed to be there at recess time. She watched the horde of children playing in the yard. Recess consisted of getting several hundred children herded into this small, stone-paved enclosure and then getting them out again. Once in the yard, there was no room for games. The children milled about angrily and raised their voices in one steady monotonous shrieking which continued unabated for five minutes. It was cut off, as if with a sharp knife, when the end-of-recess bell clanged. For an instant after the bell there was dead silence and frozen motion. Then the milling changed to pushing. The children seemed as desperately anxious to get in as they had been to get out. The high shrieking changed to subdued wailing as they fought their way back.

Francie was in her yard one mid-afternoon when a little girl came out alone into the school yard and importantly clapped two blackboard erasers together to free them from chalk dust. To Francie, watching, her face close to the iron mesh, this seemed the most fascinating occupation ever devised. Mama had told her that this was a task reserved for teachers' pets. To Francie, pets meant cats, dogs and birds. She vowed that when she was old enough to go to school, she would meow, bark and chirp as best she could so that she would be a "pet" and get to clap the erasers together.

On this afternoon, she watched with a heart-full of admiration in her eyes. The clapper, aware of Francie's admiration, showed off. She clapped the erasers on the brick wall, on the stone walk and, as a finale, behind her back. She spoke to Francie.

"Want to see 'em real close?"

Francie nodded shyly. The girl brought an eraser close to the mesh. Francie poked a finger through to touch the vari-coloured felt layers blended together by a film of powdered chalk. As she was about to touch this soft beautifulness, the little girl snatched it away and spat full in Francie's face. Francie closed her eyes tightly to keep the hurt bitter tears from spilling out. The other girl stood there curiously, waiting for the tears. When none came, she taunted:

"Why don't you bust out crying, you dockle? Want I should spit in your face again?"

Francie turned and went down into the cellar and sat in the dark a long time waiting until the waves of hurt stopped breaking over her. It was the first of many disillusionments that were to come as her capacity to feel things grew. She never liked blackboard erasers after that.

The kitchen was living-room, dining-room, and cooking-room. There were two long narrow windows in one wall. An iron coal-range was recessed in another wall. Above the stove the recess was made of coral-coloured bricks and creamy white plaster. It had a stone mantelpiece and a slate hearth-stone on which Francie could draw pictures with chalk. Next to the stove was a water boiler which got hot when the fire was going. Often on a cold day, Francie came in chilled and put her arms around the boiler and pressed her frosty cheek gratefully against its warm silveriness.

Next to the boiler was a pair of soapstone washtubs with a hinged wooden cover. The partition could be removed and the two thrown into one for a bath tub. It didn't make a very good bath tub. Sometimes when Francie sat in it, the cover banged down on her head. The bottom was rubbly and she came out of what should have been a refreshing bath all sore from sitting on that wet roughness. Then there were four taps to contend with. No matter how the child tried to remember that they were inflexibly there and wouldn't give way, she would jump up suddenly out of the soapy water and get her back whacked good on a tap. Francie had a perpetual angry welt on her back.

Following the kitchen, there were two bedrooms, one leading into the other. An airshaft dimensioned like a coffin was built into the bedrooms. The windows were small and dingy grey. You could open an airshaft window, maybe, if you used a chisel and hammer. But when you did, you were rewarded with a blast of cold, dank air. The airshaft was topped by a miniature, slant-roofed skylight whose heavy opaque, wrinkled glass was protected from breakage by heavy, iron netting. The sides were corrugated iron slats. This arrangement supposedly supplied light and air to the bedrooms. But the heavy glass, iron fencing and dirt of many years refused to filter the light through. The openings in the sides were choked with dust, soot and cobwebs. No air could come in, but, stubbornly enough, rain and snow could get in. On stormy days, the wooden bottom of the airshaft was wet and smoky and gave out a tomby smell.

The airshaft was a horrible invention. Even with the windows tightly sealed, it served as a sounding box and you could hear everybody's business. Rats scurried around the bottom. There was always the danger of fire. A match absently tossed into the airshaft by a drunken teamster under the impression that he was throwing it into the yard or street would set the house afire in a moment. There were vile things cluttering up the bottom. Since this bottom couldn't be reached by man (the windows being too small to admit the passage of a body), it served as a fearful repository for things that people wanted to put out of their lives. Rusted razor blades and bloody cloths were the most innocent items. Once Francie looked down into the airshaft. She thought of what the priest said about Purgatory and figured it must be like the airshaft bottom, only on a larger scale. When Francie went into the parlour, she passed through the bedrooms shuddering and with her eyes shut.

The parlour or front room was The Room. Its two high narrow windows faced on the exciting street. The third floor was so high up that street noises were muted into a comforting sound. The room was a place of dignity. It had its own door leading into the hall. Company could be admitted without having to walk through the bedrooms from the kitchen. The high walls were covered with a sombre wall-paper, dark brown with golden stripes. The windows had inside shutters of slatted wood which telescoped into a narrow space on either side. Francie spent many happy hours pulling out these hinged shutters and watching them fold back again at a touch of her hand. It was a never-tiring miracle that that which could cover a whole window and blot out light and air could still meekly compress itself in its little closet and present an innocently panelled front to the eye.

A low parlour stove was built into a black marble fireplace. Only the front half of the stove was in view. It looked like a giant halved melon with the round side out. It was made of numerous isinglass windows with just enough thin carved iron to form a framework. At Christmas time, the only time Katie could afford to have a fire in the parlour, all of the little windows glowed and Francie felt a great joy sitting there, feeling the warmth and watching the windows change from rosy red to amber as the night wore on. And when Katie came in and lit the gas, chasing the shadows away and paling the light in the stove windows, it was like a great sin that she committed.

The most wonderful thing about the front room was the

piano. This was a miracle that you could pray for all your life and it would never come to pass. But there it stood in the Nolan parlour, a real true miracle that had come without a wish or a prayer. The piano had been left there by the previous tenants, who could not afford to pay to have it moved.

Piano-moving in those days was a project. No piano could be got down those narrow steep stairs. Pianos had to be bundled up, roped and hoisted out of the windows with an enormous pulley on the roof and with much shouting, arm-waving and brasshatting on the part of the boss mover. The street had to be roped off, the policeman had to keep the crowds back and children had to play hooky from school when there was a piano moving. There was always that great moment when the wrapped bulk swung clear of the windows and twisted dizzily in the air for a moment before it righted itself. Then began the slow perilous descent while the children cheered hoarsely.

It was a job that cost fifteen dollars, three times what it cost to move all the rest of the furniture. So the owner asked Katie could she leave it and would Katie mind it for her? Katie was glad to give her the promise. Wistfully the woman asked Katie not to let it get damp or cold, to leave the bedroom doors open in winter so a little heat would get through from the kitchen and prevent warping.

"Can you play it?" Katie asked her.

"No," said the woman sorrowfully. "No one in the family can play. I wish I could."

"Why did you ever buy it?"

"It was in a rich house. The people were selling it cheap. I wanted it so much. No, I couldn't play it. But it was so beautiful . . . It dresses up the whole room."

Katie promised to take good care of it until the woman could afford to send for it, but as things turned out, the woman never did send for it and the Nolans had this beautiful thing for always.

It was small and made of black polished wood that glowed darkly. The front of thin veneers was cut out to make a pretty pattern and there was old-rose silk behind this fretted wood design. Its lid did not fold back in sections like other uprights. It just turned back and rested against the designed wood like a lovely, dark, polished shell. There was a candle-holder on either side. You could put pure white candles in them and play by the candlelight which threw dreamy shadows over the creamy ivoried keys. And you could see the keys again in the dark cover.

When the Nolans walked into the front room on their first possessive tour of inspection, the piano was the only thing that Francie saw. She tried to get her arms around it, but it was too big. She had to be content to hug the faded-rose brocade stool.

Katie looked at the piano with dancing eyes. She had noticed a white card in the flat window below which said: "Piano Lessons." Katie had an idea.

Johnny sat on the magic stool, which turned around and went up or down according to your size, and played. He couldn't play, of course. He couldn't read notes in the first place, but he knew a few chords. He could sing a song and strike a chord now and then and really it sounded as though he were singing to music. He struck a minor chord, looked into the eyes of his oldest child and smiled a crooked smile. Francie smiled back, her heart waiting in anticipation. He struck the minor chord again; held it. To its soft echo, he sang in his clear true voice:

> Maxwelton's braes are bonny,
> Whe' early fae's the dew.
> (Chord—chord.)
> An' 'twas there that Annie Laurie,
> Gied me her promise true.
> (Chord—chord—chord—chord.)

Francie looked away, not wanting papa to see her tears. She was afraid he'd ask her why she was crying and she wouldn't be able to tell him. She loved him and she loved the piano. She could find no excuse for her easy tears.

Katie spoke. Her voice had some of the old soft tenderness in it which Johnny had been missing in the last year or so. "Is that an Irish song Johnny?"

"Scotch."

"I never heard you sing it before."

"No, I guess not. It's just a song I know. I never sing it because it's not the kind of song people want to hear at the rackets where I work. They'd sooner hear 'Call Me Up Some Rainy Afternoon.' Except when they're drunk. Then nothing but 'Sweet Adeline' will do."

They were quickly settled in the new place. The familiar

furniture looked strange. Francie sat on a chair and was surprised that it felt the same as it had in Lorimer Street. *She* felt different. Why didn't the chair feel different?

The front room looked pretty after papa and mama got it fixed up. There was a bright green carpet which had great pink roses. There were starched cream-coloured lace curtains for the windows, a table with a marble top for the centre of the room and a three-piece green plush parlour suite. A bamboo stand in the corner held a plush-covered album in which were pictures of the Rommely sisters as babies lying on their stomachs on a fur rug, and patient-looking great-aunts standing at the shoulders of seated, big-moustached husbands. Little souvenir cups stood on the small shelves. The cups were pink and blue and had gold-encrusted designs of blue forget-me-nots and red American beauty roses. There were phrases like *Remember Me* and *True Friendship* painted in gold. The tiny cups and saucers were memories of Katie's old girl friends and Francie was never permitted to play house with them.

On the bottom shelf stood a curly, bone-white conch shell with a delicate rosy interior. The children loved it dearly and had given it an affectionate name: Tootsy. When Francie held it to her ear, it sang of the great sea. Sometimes for the delight of his children Johnny listened to the shell, then held it dramatically at arm's length, looked at it meltingly and sang:

> *Upon the shore I found a shell.*
> *I held it to my ear.*
> *I listened gladly while it sang,*
> *A sea song sweet and clear.*

Later, Francie saw the sea for the first time when Johnny took them to Canarsie. The sea was remarkable only in that it sounded like the tiny sweet roar of Tootsy, the conch shell.

XVI

THE NEIGHBOURHOOD stores are an important part of a city child's life. They are his contact with the supplies that keep life going; they hold the beauty that his soul longs for; they hold the unattainable that he can only dream and wish for.

Francie liked the pawnshop almost the best—not for the

treasures prodigiously thrown into its barred windows; not for the shadowy adventure of shawled women slipping into the side entrance, but for the three golden balls that hung high above the shop and gleamed in the sun or swayed languorously like heavy golden apples when the wind blew.

There was a bakery store to one side of it which sold beautiful charlotte russes with red candied cherries on their whipped-cream tops for those who were rich enough to buy.

On the other side was Gollender's Paint Shop. There was a stand in front of it from which was suspended a plate with a dramatically mended crack across it and a hole bored into the bottom from which hung a heavy rock suspended on a chain. This proved how strong *Major's Cement* was. Some said the plate was made of iron and painted to resemble cracked china. But Francie preferred to believe it was a real plate that had been broken and then made whole again by the miracle of the cement.

The most interesting store was housed in a little shanty which had been there when the Indians prowled through Williamsburg. It looked queer among the tenements with its tiny small-paned windows, clap-boards and steep slanting roof. The store had a great small-panelled bay window behind which a dignified man sat at a table and made cigars—long thin dark-brown ones which sold four for a nickel. He chose the outside leaf very carefully from a hand of tobacco and filled it expertly with bits of tobacco of mixed browns and rolled it all very beautifully, so that it was tight and thin and the ends had squared corners. A craftsman of the old school, he scorned progress. He refused to have gaslight in his store. Sometimes when the days grew dark early and he still had a lot of cigars to finish, he worked by candlelight. He had a wooden Indian outside his store which stood in a threatening stance on a wooden block. He held a tomahawk in one hand and a hand of tobacco in the other. He wore Roman sandals with the lacings coming to his knees, a short skirt of feathers and a war bonnet, all of which were painted in bright reds, blues and yellows. The cigar-maker gave him a fresh coat of paint four times a year and carried him inside when it rained. The neighbourhood children called the Indian "Aunt Maimie."

One of Francie's favourite stores was the one which sold nothing but tea, coffee and spices. It was an exciting place of rows of lacquered bins and strange, romantic, exotic odours.

There were a dozen scarlet coffee bins with adventurous words written across the front in black China ink: Brazil! Argentine! Turkish! Java! Mixed Blend! The tea was in smaller bins: beautiful bins with sloping covers. They read: Oolong! Formosa! Orange Pekoe! Black China! Flowering Almond! Jasmine! Irish Tea! The spices were in miniature bins behind the counter. Their names marched in a row across the shelves: cinnamon—clover—ginger—all-spice—ball nutmeg—curry—peppercorns—sage—thyme—marjoram. All pepper, when purchased, was ground in a tiny pepper mill.

There was a large hand-turned coffee grinder. The beans were put into a shiny brass hopper, and the great wheel was turned with two hands. The fragrant grounds pattered down into a scarlet box that was shaped like a scoop at the back.

(The Nolans ground their coffee at home. Francie loved to see mama sitting debonairly in the kitchen with the coffee mill clutched between her knees, grinding away with a furious turn of her left wrist and looking up to talk sparklingly to papa while the room filled up with the rich satisfying odour of freshly-ground coffee.)

The tea man had a wonderful pair of scales: two gleaming brass plates which had been rubbed and polished daily for more than twenty-five years until now they were thin and delicate and looked like burnished gold. When Francie bought a pound of coffee or an ounce of pepper she watched while a polished silver block with the weight mark was placed in one scale and the fragrant purchase was conveyed gently by means of a silver-like scoop into the other. Francie, watching, held her breath while the scoop dropped in a few more grains or gently eased some out. It was a beautiful peaceful second when both golden plates were stilled and stood there in perfect balance. It was as if nothing wrong could happen in a world where things balanced so stilly.

The mystery of mysteries to Francie was the Chinaman's one-windowed store. The Chinaman wore his pigtail wound around his head. That was so he could go back to China if he wanted to, mama said. Once he cut it off, they would never let him return. He shuffled back and forth silently in his black felt slippers and listened patiently to instructions about shirts. When Francie spoke to him, he folded his hands in the wide sleeves of his Nankin shirt-coat and kept his eyes on the ground. She thought that he was wise and contemplative and listened with all his heart. But he understood nothing of what she said, having little English. All he knew was *tickee* and *shirtee*.

When Francie brought her father's soiled shirt there, he whisked it under the counter, took a square of mysteriously textured paper, dropped a thin brush into a pot of India ink, made a few strokes and gave her this magic document in exchange for a common dirty shirt. It seemed a wonderful barter.

The inside of the store had a clean warm but fragile scent, like odourless flowers in a hot room. He did the washing in some mysterious recess and it must have been in the dead of night because all day, from seven in the morning until ten at night, he stood in the store at his clean ironing-board pushing a heavy black iron back and forth. The iron must have had a tiny heating arrangement inside it to keep it hot. Francie did not know this. She thought it part of the mystery of his race that he could iron with an iron never heated on a stove. She had a vague theory that the heat came from something he used in place of starch in the shirts and collars.

When Francie brought a ticket and a dime back and pushed them across the counter, he gave her the wrapped shirt and two lichee nuts in exchange. Francie loved these lichee nuts. There was a crisp easily broken shell and the soft sweet meat inside. Inside the meat was a hard stone that no child had ever been able to break open. It was said that this stone contained a smaller stone and that the smaller stone contained a smaller stone which contained a yet smaller stone and so on. It was said that soon the stones got so small you could only see them with a magnifying glass and those smaller ones got still smaller until you couldn't see them with anything, but they were always there and would never stop coming. It was Francie's first experience with infinity.

The best times were when he had to make change. He brought out a small wooden frame strung with thin rods on which were blue, red, yellow and green balls. He slid the balls up the brass rods, pondered swiftly, clicked them all back into place and announced "dirty-nine cent." The tiny balls told him how much to charge and how much change to give.

Oh, to be a Chinaman, wished Francie, and have such a pretty toy to count on: oh, to eat all the lichee nuts she wanted and to know the mystery of the iron that was ever hot and yet never stood on a stove. Oh, to paint those symbols with a slight brush and a quick turn of the wrist and to make a

111

clear black mark as fragile as a piece of a butterfly wing! That was the mystery of the Orient in Brooklyn.

XVII

PIANO LESSONS: Magic words! As soon as the Nolans were settled, Katie called on the lady whose card announced piano lessons. There were two Miss Tynmores. Miss Lizzie taught the piano and Miss Maggie cultivated the voice. The charge was twenty-five cents per lesson. Katie proposed a bargain. She'd do one hour's cleaning for the Tynmores in exchange for a lesson each week. Miss Lizzie demurred, claiming her time had more value than Katie's time. Katie argued that time was time. Finally she got Miss Lizzie to agree that time was time and arrangements were made.

The history-making day of the first lesson arrived. Francie and Neeley were instructed to sit in the front room during the lesson and to keep their eyes and ears open. A chair was placed for the teacher. The children sat side by side on the other side of the piano, Katie nervously adjusted and read-justed the seat and the three sat waiting.

Miss Tynmore arrived on the dot of five. Although she only came from downstairs, she was formally attired in street clothes. A taut spotted veil was stretched over her face. Her hat was the breast and wing of a red bird tormentingly pierced by two hatpins. Francie stared at the cruel hat. Mama took her into the bedroom and whispered that the bird wasn't a bird at all, just some feathers glued together and that she mustn't stare. She believed mama, yet her eyes kept going back to the tormented effigy.

Miss Tynmore brought everything with her but the piano. She had a nickel alarm clock and a battered metronome. The clock said five o'clock. She set it for six and stood it on the piano. She took the privilege of using up part of the precious hour. She removed her pearl-grey, skin-tight kid gloves, blew into each finger, smoothed and folded them and placed them on the piano. She undid her veil and threw it back over her hat. She limbered up her fingers, glanced at the clock, was satisfied she had taken enough minutes, started the metronome, took her seat and the lesson began.

Francie was so fascinated by the metronome that she found it hard to listen to what Miss Tynmore said and to watch the way she placed mama's hands on the keys. She weaved dreams in time to the soothing monotonous clicking. As for Neeley, his round blue eyes rolled back and forth following the little swinging rod until he hypnotized himself into unconsciousness. His mouth relaxed and his blond head rolled over on his shoulder. A little bubble came and went as he breathed moistly. Katie dared not wake him lest Miss Tynmore catch on that she was teaching three for the price of one.

The metronome clicked on dreamily: the clock ticked querulously. Miss Tynmore, as if not trusting the metronome, counted, *one*, two, three; *one*, two, three. Katie's work-swollen fingers struggled doggedly with her first scale. Time passed and it grew dark in the room. Suddenly the alarm clock rang out shatteringly. Francie's heart jumped and Neeley fell off his chair. The first lesson was ended. Katie's words tumbled over each other in gratitude.

"Even if I never take another lesson, I could go on with what you taught me today. You are a good teacher."

Miss Tynmore, while pleased by the flattery, nevertheless told Katie what was what. "I won't charge extra for the children. I just want you to know you're not fooling me." Katie blushed and the children looked down on the floor, ashamed of being found out. "I will permit the children to stay in the room."

Katie thanked her. Miss Tynmore stood up and waited. Katie verified the time she was to do Miss Tynmore's housework. Still she waited. Katie felt that something was expected of her. Finally she inquired:

"Yes?"

Miss Tynmore flushed a shell pink and spoke proudly. "The ladies . . . where I give lessons . . . well . . . they offer me a cup of tea afterwards." She put her hand to her heart and explained vaguely: "Those stairs."

"Would you sooner take coffee?" Katie asked, "We have no tea."

"Gladly!" Miss Tynmore sat down in relief.

Katie rushed out to the kitchen and heated the coffee which was always standing on the stove. While it was warming, she put a sugar bun and a spoon on a round tin tray.

In the meantime, Neeley had fallen asleep on the sofa. Miss Tynmore and Francie sat exchanging stares. Finally Miss

113

Tynmore asked:

"What are you thinking about, little girl?"

"Just thinking," Francie said.

"Sometimes I see you sitting on the gutter kerb for hours. What do you think of then?"

"Nothing. I just tell myself stories."

Miss Tynmore pointed at her sternly. "Little girl, you'll be a story writer when you grow up." It was a command rather than a statement.

"Yes, ma'am," agreed Francie out of politeness.

Katie came in with the tray. "This may not be as refined as you're used to," she apologized, "but it's what we have in the house."

"It's very good," stated Miss Tynmore daintily. Then she concentrated on trying not to wolf it down.

To tell the truth, the Tynmores lived on the "tea" they got from their pupils. A few lessons a day at a quarter a lesson did not make for prosperity. After paying their rent, there was little left to eat on. Most of the ladies served them weak tea and soda crackers. The ladies knew what was polite and would come through with a cup of tea, but they had no intention of supplying a meal and paying a quarter, too. So Miss Tynmore came to look forward to the hour at the Nolans'. The coffee was heartening and there was always a bun or a bologna sandwich to sustain her.

After each lesson, Katie taught the children what she had been taught. She made them practise half an hour each day. In time, all three of them learned to play the piano.

When Johnny heard that Maggie Tynmore gave voice lessons, he figured that he could do no less than Katie. He offered to repair a broken sash cord in one of the Tynmore windows in exchange for two voice lessons for Francie. Johnny, who had never even seen a sash cord in all his life, got a hammer and screwdriver and took the whole window frame out of its case. He looked at the broken rope and that was as far as he could go. He experimented and got nowhere. His heart was willing but his skill was nil. In attempting to get the window back in to keep out the cold winter rain that was blowing into the room while he was figuring out about the sash cord, he broke a pane of glass. The deal fell through. The Tynmores had to get a regular window man in to fix it. Katie had to do two washings free for the girls to make up for it and Francie's voice lessons were abandoned for ever.

XVIII

SCHOOL DAYS were eagerly anticipated by Francie. She wanted all of the things that she thought came with school. She was a lonely child and she longed for the companionship of other children. She wanted to drink from the school water fountains in the yard. The taps were inverted and she thought that soda water came out instead of plain water. She had heard mama and papa speak of the school room. She wanted to see the map that pulled down like a blind. Most of all, she wanted "school supplies": a notebook and tablet and a pencil box with a sliding top filled with new pencils, an eraser, a little tin pencil sharpener made in the shape of a cannon, a pen wiper, and a six-inch, soft wood, yellow ruler.

Before school, there had to be vaccination. That was the law. How it was dreaded! When the health authorities tried to explain to the poor and illiterate that vaccination was a giving of the harmless form of smallpox to work up immunity against the deadly form, the parents didn't believe it. All they got out of the explanation was that germs would be put into a healthy child's body. Some foreign-born parents refused to permit their children to be vaccinated. They were not allowed to enter school. Then the law got after them for keeping the children out of school. A free country? they asked. You should live so long. What's free about it, they reasoned, when the law forces you to educate your children and then endangers their lives to get them into school? Weeping mothers brought bawling children to the Health Centre for inoculation. They carried on as though bringing their innocents to the slaughter. The children screamed hysterically at the first sight of the needle and their mothers, waiting in the ante-room, threw their shawls over their heads and keened loudly as if wailing for the dead.

Francie was seven and Neeley six. Katie had held Francie back, wishing both children to enter school together, so that they could protect each other against the older children. On a dreadful Saturday in August, she stopped in the bedroom to speak to them before she went off to work. She awakened them and gave instructions.

"Now when you get up, wash yourselves good and when it gets to be eleven o'clock, go around the corner to the public health place, tell them to vaccinate you because you're going to school in September."

Francie began to tremble. Neeley burst into tears.

"You coming with us, Mama?" Francie pleaded.

"I've got to go to work. Who's going to do my work if I don't?" asked Katie, covering up her conscience with indignation.

Francie said nothing more. Katie knew that she was letting them down. But she couldn't help it, she just couldn't help it. Yes, she should go with them to lend the comfort and authority of her presence, but she knew she couldn't stand the ordeal. Yet, they had to be vaccinated. Her being with them or somewhere else couldn't take that fact away. So why shouldn't one of the three be spared? Besides, she said to her conscience, it's a hard and bitter world. They've got to live in it. Let them get hardened young to take care of themselves.

"Papa's going with us then," said Francie hopefully.

"Papa's at Headquarters waiting for a job. He won't be home all day. You're big enough to go alone. Besides, it won't hurt."

Neeley wailed on a higher key. Katie could hardly stand that. She loved the boy so much. Part of her reason for not going with them was that she couldn't bear to see the boy hurt . . . not even by a pin-prick. Almost she decided to go with them. But no. If she went she'd lose half a day's work and she'd have to make it up on Sunday morning. Besides, she'd be sick afterwards. They'd manage somehow without her. She hurried off to her work.

Francie tried to console the terrified Neeley. Some older boys had told him that they cut your arm off when they got you in the Health Centre. To take his mind off the thing, Francie took him down into the yard and they made mud pies. They quite forgot to wash as mama had told them to.

They almost forgot about eleven o'clock, the mud-pie-making was so beguiling. Their hands and arms got very dirty playing in the mud. At ten to eleven, Mrs. Gaddis hung out the window and yelled down that their mother had told her to remind them when it was near eleven o'clock. Neeley finished off his last mud pie, watering it with his tears. Francie took his hand and with slow dragging steps the children walked around the corner.

They took their place on the bench. Next to them sat a Jewish mama who clutched a large six-year-old boy in her arms and wept and kissed his forehead passionately from time to time. Other mothers sat there with grim suffering furrowed on their faces. Behind the frosted-glass door where the terrifying business was going on, there was a steady bawling punctuated by a shrill scream, resumption of the bawling and then a pale child would come out with a strip of pure white gauze about his left arm. His mother would rush and grab him and with a foreign curse and a shaken fist at the frosted door, hurry him out of the torture chamber.

Francie went in trembling. She had never seen a doctor or a nurse in all of her small life. The whiteness of the uniforms, the shiny cruel instruments laid out in a napkin on a tray, the smell of antiseptics, and especially the cloudy sterilizer with its bloody red cross filled her with tongue-tied fright.

The nurse pulled up her sleeve and swabbed a spot clean on her left arm. Francie saw the white doctor coming towards her with the cruelly-poised needle. He loomed larger and larger until he seemed to blend into a great needle. She closed her eyes waiting to die. Nothing happened, she felt nothing. She opened her eyes slowly, hardly daring to hope that it was all over. She found, to her agony, that the doctor was still there, poised needle and all. He was staring at her arm in distaste. Francie looked too. She saw a small white area on a dirty dark brown arm. She heard the doctor talking to the nurse.

"Filth, filth, filth, from morning to night. I know they're poor but they could wash. Water is free and soap is cheap. Just look at that arm, nurse."

The nurse looked and clucked in horror. Francie stood there with the hot flamepoints of shame burning her face. The doctor was a Harvard man, interning at the neighbourhood hospital. Once a week, he was obliged to put in a few hours at one of the free clinics. He was going into a smart practice in Boston when his internship was over. Adopting the phraseology of the neighbourhood, he referred to his Brooklyn internship as going through Purgatory when he wrote to his socially prominent fiancée in Boston.

The nurse was a Williamsburg girl. You could tell that by her accent. The child of poor Polish immigrants, she had been ambitious, worked days in a sweatshop and gone to school at night. Somehow she had got her training. She hoped some day

117

to marry a doctor. She didn't want anyone to know she had come from the slums.

After the doctor's outburst, Francie stood hanging her head. She was a dirty girl. That's what the doctor meant. He was talking more quietly now, asking the nurse how that kind of people could survive; that it would be a better world if they were all sterilized and couldn't breed any more. Did that mean he wanted her to die? Would he do something to make her die because her hands and arms were dirty from the mud pies?

She looked at the nurse. To Francie, all women were mamas like her own mother and Aunt Sissy and Aunt Evy. She thought the nurse might say something like:

"Maybe this little girl's mother works and didn't have time to wash her good this morning," or: "You know how it is, Doctor, children *will* play in dirt." But what the nurse actually said was: "I know. Isn't it terrible? I sympathize with you, Doctor. There is no excuse for these people living in filth."

A person who pulls himself up from a low environment via the boot-strap route has two choices. Having risen above his environment, he can forget it; or, he can rise above it and never forget it and keep compassion and understanding in his heart for those he has left behind him in the cruel up-climb. The nurse had chosen the forgetting way. Yet, as she stood there, she knew that years later she would be haunted by the sorrow in the face of that starvelling child and that she would wish bitterly that she had said a comforting word then and done something towards the saving of her immortal soul. She had the knowledge that she was small, but she lacked the courage to be otherwise.

When the needle jabbed, Francie never felt it. The waves of hurt started by the doctor's words were racking her body and drove out all other feeling. While the nurse was expertly tying a strip of gauze around her arm and the doctor was putting his instrument in the sterilizer and taking out a fresh needle, Francie spoke up.

"My brother is next. His arm is just as dirty as mine, so don't be surprised. And you don't have to tell him. You told me." They stared at this bit of humanity who had become so strangely articulate. Francie's voice went ragged with a sob. "You don't have to tell him. Besides, it won't do no good. He's a boy and he don't care if he is dirty." She turned, stumbled a little and walked out of the room. As the door closed, she heard the doctor's surprised voice.

"I had no idea she'd understand what I was saying." She heard the nurse say: "Oh, well," on a sighing note.

Katie was home for lunch when the children got back. She looked at their bandaged arms with misery in her eyes. Francie spoke out passionately.

"Why, Mama, why? Why do they have to ... to ... say things and then stick a needle in your arm?"

"Vaccination," said mama firmly, now that it was all over, "is a very good thing. It makes you tell your left hand from your right. You had to write with your right hand when you go to school, and that sore will be there to say: "Uh-uh, not this hand. Use the other hand.' "

This explanation satisfied Francie because she had never been able to tell her left hand from her right. She ate, and drew pictures with her left hand. Katie was always correcting her and transferring the chalk or the needle from her left hand to her right. After mama explained about vaccination, Francie began to think that maybe it was a wonderful thing. It was a small price to pay if it simplified such a great problem and let you know which hand was which. Francie began using her right hand instead of the left after the vaccination and never had trouble afterwards.

Francie worked up a fever that night and the site of the injection itched painfully. She told mama, who became greatly alarmed. She gave intense instructions.

"You're not to scratch it, no matter how it bites you."

"Why can't I scratch it?"

"Because if you do, your whole arm will swell up and turn black and drop right off. So don't scratch it."

Katie did not mean to terrify the child. She, herself, was badly frightened. She believed that blood-poisoning would set in if the arm were touched. She wanted to frighten the child into not scratching it.

Francie had to concentrate on not scratching the painfully itching area. The next day, shots of pain were shooting up the arm. While preparing for bed, she peered under the bandage. To her horror, the place where the needle had entered was swollen, dark-green and festering yellowly. And Francie had not scratched it! *She knew she had not scratched it.* But wait! Maybe she had scratched it in her sleep the night before. Yes, she must have done it then. She was afraid to tell mama.

Mama would say: "I told you and I told you, and still you wouldn't listen. Now look."

It was Sunday night. Papa was out working. She couldn't sleep. She got up from her cot and went into the front room and sat at the window. She leaned her head on her arms and waited to die.

At three in the morning she heard a Graham Avenue trolley grind to a stop on the corner. That meant someone was getting off. She leaned out the window. Yes, it was papa. He sauntered down the street with his light dancer's step whistling "My Sweetheart's the Man in the Moon." The figure in its tuxedo and derby hat, with a rolled-up waiter's apron in a neat packet under his arm, seemed like life itself to Francie. She called to him when he got to the door. He looked up and tipped his hat gallantly. She opened the kitchen door for him.

"What are you doing up so late, Prima Donna?" he asked. "It's not Saturday night, you know."

"I was sitting at the window," she whispered, "waiting for my arm to drop off."

He choked back a laugh. She explained about the arm. He closed the door leading into the bedrooms and turned up the gas. He removed the bandage and his stomach turned over at sight of the swollen, festering arm. But he never let her know. He never let her know.

"Why, Baby, that's nothing at all. Just nothing at all. You should have seen my arm when I was vaccinated. It was twice as swollen and red, white and blue instead of green and yellow, and now look how hard and strong it is." He lied gallantly, for he had never been vaccinated.

He poured warm water into a basin and added a few drops of carbolic acid. He washed the ugly sore over and over again. She winced when it stung, but Johnny said that stinging meant curing. He sang a foolish sentimental song in a whisper as he washed it.

> He never cares to wander from his own fireside.
> He never cares to ramble or to roam ...

He looked around for a clean bit of cloth to serve as a bandage. Finding none, he took off his coat and shirt dicky, pulled his undershirt off over his head and dramatically ripped a strip of cloth from it.

"Your good undershirt," she protested.

"Aw, it was all full of holes, anyhow."

He bandaged the arm. The cloth smelled of Johnny, warm and cigarish. But it was a comforting thing to the child. It smelled of protection and love.

"There! You're all fixed up, Prima Donna. Whatever gave you the idea your arm was going to drop off?"

"Mama said it would if I scratched it. I didn't mean to scratch it, but I guess I did while I was sleeping."

"Maybe." He kissed her thin cheek. "Now go back to bed." She went and slept peacefully the rest of the night. In the morning, the throbbing had stopped and in a few days the arm was normal again.

After Francie had gone to bed, Johnny smoked another cigar. Then he undressed slowly and got into Katie's bed. She was sleepily aware of his presence, and in one of her rare impulses of affection, she threw her arm across his chest. He removed it gently and edged as far away from her as he could. He lay close to the wall. He folded his hands under his head and lay staring into the darkness all the rest of that night.

XIX

FRANCIE EXPECTED great things from school. Since vaccination taught her instantly the difference between left and right, she thought that school would bring forth even greater miracles. She thought she'd come home from school that first day knowing how to read and write. But all she came home with was a bloody nose gained by an older child slamming her head down on the stone rim of the water-trough when she had tried to drink from the taps that did not gush forth soda-water after all.

Francie was disappointed because she had to share a seat and desk (meant only for one) with another girl. She had wanted a desk to herself. She accepted with pride the pencil the monitor passed out to her in the morning and reluctantly surrendered it to another monitor at three o'clock.

She had been in school but half a day when she knew that she would never be a teacher's pet. That privilege was reserved for a small group of girls ... girls with freshly-curled hair, crisp clean pinafores and new silk hair-bows. They were the children of the prosperous storekeepers of the neighbourhood.

Francie noticed how Miss Briggs, the teacher, beamed on them and seated them in the choicest places in the front row. These darlings were not made to share seats. Miss Briggs' voice was gentle when she spoke to these fortune-favoured few, and snarling when she spoke to the great crowd of unwashed.

Francie, huddled with other children of her kind, learned more that first day than she realised. She learned of the class system of a great Democracy. She was puzzled and hurt by teacher's attitude. Obviously the teacher hated her and others like her for no other reason than that they were what they were. Teacher acted as though they had no right to be in the school, but that she was forced to accept them and was doing so with as little grace as possible. She begrudged them the few crumbs of learning she threw at them. Like the doctor at the Health Centre, she too acted as though they had no right to live.

It would seem as if all the unwanted children would stick together and be one against the things that were against them. But not so. They hated each other as much as the teacher hated them. They aped teacher's snarling manner when they spoke to each other.

There was always one unfortunate whom the teacher singled out and used for a scapegoat. This poor child was the nagged one, the tormented one, the one on whom she vented her spinsterly spleen. As soon as a child received this dubious recognition, the other children turned on him and duplicated the teacher's torments. Characteristically, they fawned on those close to teacher's heart. Maybe they figured they were nearer to the throne that way.

Three thousand children crowded into this ugly, brutalising school that had facilities for only one thousand. Dirty stories went the rounds of the children. One of them was that Miss Pfieffer, a bleached blonde teacher with a high giggle, went down to the basement to sleep with the assistant janitor those times when she put a monitor in charge and explained that she had to "step out to the office." Another, passed around by little boys who had been victims, was that the lady principal, a hard-bitten, heavy, cruel woman of middle years who wore sequin-decorated dresses and smelled always of raw gin, got recalcitrant boys into her offce and made them take down their trousers so that she could flay their naked buttocks with a rattan cane. (She whipped the little girls through their dresses.)

Of course, corporal punishment was forbidden in the schools. But who, outside, knew? Who would tell? Not the whipped children, certainly. It was a tradition in the neighbourhood that if a child reported that he had been whipped in school, he would receive a second home-whipping because he had not behaved in school. So the child took his punishment and kept quiet, leaving well enough alone.

The ugliest thing about these stories was that they were all sordidly true.

Brutalising is the only adjective for the public schools of that district around 1908 and '09. Child psychology had not been heard of in Williamsburg in those days. Teaching requirements were easy: graduation from high school and two years at Teachers' Training School. Few teachers had the true vocation for their work. They taught because it was one of the few jobs open to them; because it was better paying than factory work; because they had a long summer vacation; because they got a pension when they retired. They taught because no one wanted to marry them. Married women were not allowed to teach in those days, hence most of the teachers were women made neurotic by starved love instincts. These barren women spent their fury on other women's children in a twisted authoritative manner.

The cruellest teachers were those who had come from homes similar to those of the poor children. It seemed that in their bitterness towards those unfortunate little ones, they were somehow exorcising their own fearful background.

Of course, not all of the teachers were bad. Sometimes one who was sweet came along, one who suffered with the children and tried to help them. But these women did not last long as teachers. Either they married quickly and left the profession, or they were hounded out of their jobs by fellow-teachers.

The problem of what was delicately called "leaving the room" was a grim one. The children were instructed to "go" before they left home in the morning and then to wait until lunch-hour. There was supposed to be a time at recess, but few children were able to take advantage of that. Usually the press of the crowd prevented a child's getting near the wash-rooms. If he was lucky enough to get there (where there were but ten lavatories for five hundred children), he'd find the places pre-emptied by the ten most brutalised children in the school.

They'd stand in the doorways and prevent entrance to all comers. They were deaf to the piteous pleas of the tormented children who swarmed before them. A few exacted a fee of a penny which few children were able to pay. The overlords never relaxed their hold on the swinging doors until the bell clanged the end of recess. No one ever ascertained what pleasure they derived from this macabre game. They were never punished, since no teacher ever entered the children's wash-rooms. No child ever snitched. No matter how young he was, he knew that he mustn't squeal. If he tattled, he knew he would be tortured almost to death by the one he reported. So this evil game went on and on.

Technically, a child was permitted to leave the room if he asked permission. There was a system of coy evasion. One finger held aloft meant that a child wished to go out but a short time. Two fingers meant desire for a longer stay. But the harassed and unfeeling teachers assured each other that this was just a subterfuge for a child to get out of the classroom for a little while. They *knew* the child had ample opportunity at recess and at lunch-time. Thus they settled things among themselves.

Of course, Francie noted, the favoured children, the clean, the dainty, the cared-for in the front seats, were allowed to leave at any time. But that was different somehow.

As for the rest of the children, half of them learned to adjust their functions to the teachers' ideas of such things and the other half became chronic trouser-wetters.

It was Aunt Sissy who fixed up the leaving-the-room business for Francie. She had not seen the children since Katie and Johnny had told her she was not to visit the house again. She was lonesome for them. She knew they had started school and she just *had* to know how they were getting along.

It was in November. Work was slack and Sissy was laid off. She sauntered down the school street just as school was letting out. If the children reported meeting her, it would seem like an accident, she figured. She saw Neeley first in the crowd. A bigger boy snatched his cap off, trampled on it and ran away. Neeley turned to a smaller boy and did the same to *his* cap. Sissy grabbed Neeley's arm, but with a raucous cry he twisted loose and ran down the street. With poignancy, Sissy realised that he was growing up.

Francie saw Sissy and put her arms around her right there

on the street and kissed her. Sissy took her into a little candy store and treated her to a penny chocolate soda. Then she made Francie sit down on a stoop and tell her all about school. Francie showed her the primer and her homework book with block letters in it. Sissy was impressed. She looked long into the child's thin face and noticed that she was shivering. She saw that she was inadequately dressed against the raw November day in a threadbare cotton dress, ragged little sweater and thin cotton stockings. She put her arm around her and held her close to her own life warmth.

"Francie, baby, you're trembling like a leaf."

Francie had never heard that expression and it made her thoughtful. She looked at the little tree growing out of the concrete at the side of the house. There were still a few dried leaves clinging to it. One of them rustled dryly in the wind. "Trembling like a leaf." She stored the phrase away in her mind. Trembling . . .

"What's the matter?" Sissy asked. "You're ice-cold."

Francie wouldn't tell at first. But after being coaxed, she buried her shame-hot face in Sissy's neck and whispered something to her.

"Oh, my," said Sissy. "No wonder you're cold. Why didn't you ask to . . ."

"Teacher never looks at us when we raise our hands."

"Oh, well. Don't worry about it. It could happen to anyone. It happened to the Queen of England when she was a little girl."

But had the Queen been so shamed and sensitive about it? Francie wept quietly and rackingly, tears of shame and fear. She was afraid to go home, afraid that mama would make scornful shame of her.

"Your mama won't scold you . . . such an accident could happen to any little girl. Don't say I told you, but your mama wet her pants when she was little and your grandma did too. It's nothing new in the world, and you're not the first one it happened to."

"But I'm too big. Only babies do that. Mama'll make shame on me in front of Neeley."

"Tell her right out before she finds out for herself and promise never to do it again. She won't shame you then."

"I can't promise because it might happen again because teacher don't let us go."

"From now on, your teacher will let you leave the room any

125

time you have to. You believe Aunt Sissy, don't you?"

"Y-e-e-es. But how do you know?"

"I'll burn a candle in church about it."

Francie was consoled with the promise. When Francie went home, Katie did a little routine scolding, but Francie was armoured against it in the light of what Sissy had told her about the cycle of wetting.

The next morning, ten minutes before school started, Sissy was in that classroom confronting the teacher.

"There's a little girl named Francie Nolan in your room," she started out.

"*Frances* Nolan," corrected Miss Briggs.

"Is she smart?"

"Y-e-e-es."

"Is she good?"

"She had better be."

Sissy brought her face closer to Miss Briggs. Her voice went a tone slower and was gentler than before, but for some reason Miss Briggs backed away. "I just asked you is she a good girl?"

"Yes, she is," said Teacher hurriedly.

"I happen to be her mother," lied Sissy.

"No!"

"Yes!"

"Anything you want to know about the child's work, Mrs. Nolan . . ."

"Did it ever occur to you," lied Sissy, "that Francie's got kidney trouble?"

"Kidney what?"

"The doctor said that if she wants to go and some people don't let her go, she's liable to drop right down dead from overloaded kidneys."

"Surely you're exaggerating."

"How would you like her to drop dead in this room?"

"Naturally, I wouldn't, but . . ."

"And how would you like to get a ride to the station house in the pie wagon and stand up in front of this here doctor and the judge and say you wouldn't let her leave the room?"

Was Sissy lying? Miss Briggs couldn't tell. It was the most fantastic thing. Yet the woman spoke these sensational things in the calmest, softest voice she had ever heard. At this moment, Sissy happened to look out of the window and saw a burly cop sauntering by. She pointed.

"See that cop?" Miss Briggs nodded. "That's my husband."

"Frances's father?"

"Who else?" Sissy threw open the window and yelled: "Yoo, hoo, Johnny."

The astonished cop looked up. She blew him a great kiss. For a split second he thought it was some love-starved old-maid teacher gone crazy. Then his native masculine conceit assured him that it was one of the younger teachers who had long had a crush on him and had finally screwed up enough courage to make a passionate overture. He responded to the occasion, blew her a return kiss with a hammy fist, tipped his hat gallantly and sauntered off down his beat whistling "At the Devil's Ball." "Sure I'm a divil amongst the ladies," he thought. "I am that. And me with six kids at home."

Miss Briggs's eyes bugged out in astonishment. He had been a handsome cop and *strong*. Just then one of the little golden girls came in with a be-ribboned box of candy for Teacher. Miss Briggs gurgled with pleasure and kissed the child's satin pink cheek. Sissy had a mind like a freshly-honed razor. In a flash she saw which way the wind blew, she saw it blew against children like Francie.

"Look," she said. "I guess you don't think we got lots of money."

"I'm sure I never ..."

"We're not people that put on. Now Christmas is coming," she bribed.

"Maybe," conceded Miss Briggs, "I haven't always seen Frances when she raised her hand."

"Where does she sit that you don't see her so good?" Teacher indicated a dark back seat. "Maybe if she sat up front more, you could see her better."

"The seating arrangements are all set."

"Christmas is coming," warned Sissy coyly.

"I'll see what I can do."

"See, then. And see that you see good." Sissy walked to the door, then turned. "Because not only is Christmas coming but my husband, who is a cop, will come up here and beat hell out of you if you don't treat her right."

Francie had no more trouble after that parent-teacher conference. No matter how timorously her hand went up, Miss Briggs happened to see it. She even let her sit in the first row, first seat for a while. But when Christmas came and no expensive Christmas present came with it, Francie was again relegated to the dark back of the room.

Neither Francie nor Katie ever learned of Sissy's school visit. But Francie was never shamed again in that way, and if Miss Briggs did not treat her with kindness, at least she didn't nag at her. Of course, Miss Briggs knew that what that woman had told her was ridiculous. Yet, what was the use of taking chances? She didn't like children, but she was no fiend. She wouldn't want to see a child drop dead before her eyes.

A few weeks later, Sissy had one of the girls in her shop write a post-card message for her to Katie. She asked her sister to let bygones be bygones and permit her to come to the house at least to see the children once in a while. Katie ignored the card.

Mary Rommely came over to intercede for Sissy. "What is there that is bitter between you and your sister?" she asked Katie.

"I cannot tell you," replied Katie.

"Forgiveness," said Mary Rommely, "is a gift of high value. Yet its cost is nothing."

"I have my own ways," said Katie.

"Ai," agreed her mother. She sighed deeply and said no more.

Katie wouldn't admit it, but she missed Sissy. She missed her reckless good sense and her clear way of straightening out troubles. Evy never mentioned Sissy when she came to see Katie, and after that one attempt at reconciliation, Mary Rommely never mentioned Sissy's name again.

Katie got news of her sister through the official accredited family reporter, the insurance agent. All of the Rommelys were insured by the same company and the same agent collected the nickels and dimes from each of the sisters weekly. He brought news, carried gossip, and was the round-robin messenger of the family. One day he brought news that Sissy had given birth to another child which she had been unable to insure since it had lived but two hours. Katie felt ashamed of herself at last for being so bitter against poor Sissy.

"Next time you see my sister," she told the collector, "tell her not to be such a stranger." The collector relayed the message of forgiveness and Sissy came back into the Nolan family again.

XX

KATIE'S CAMPAIGN against vermin and disease started the day her children entered school. The battle was fierce, brief, and successful.

Packed closely together, the children innocently bred vermin and became lousy from each other. Through no fault of their own, they were subjected to the most humiliating procedure that a child could go through.

Once a week, the school nurse came and stationed herself with her back to the window. The little girls lined up, and when they came to her, turned round, lifted their heavy braids and bent over. Nurse probed about the hair with a long thin stick. If lice or nits were in evidence, the little one was told to stand aside. At the end of the examination, the pariahs were made to stand before the class while Nurse gave a lecture about how filthy those little girls were and how they had to be shunned. The untouchables were then dismissed for the day with instructions to get "blue ointment" from Knipe's Drug Store and have their mothers treat their heads. When they returned to school, they were tormented by their peers. Each offender would have an escort of children following her home, chanting:

"Lousy, ye'r lousy! Teacher said ye'r lousy. Hadda go home, hadda go home, hadda go home because ye'r lousy."

It might be that the infected child would be given a clean bill next examination. In that case, she, in turn, would torment those found guilty, forgetting her own hurt at being tormented. They learned no compassion from their own anguish. Thus their suffering was wasted.

There was no room in Katie's crowded life for additional trouble and worry. She shouldn't accept it. The first day that Francie came home from school and reported that she sat next to a girl who had bugs walking up and down the lanes of her hair, Katie went into action. She scrubbed Francie's head with a cake of her coarse, strong, yellow scrub-woman's soap until her scalp tingled with rawness. The next morning, she dipped the hairbrush into a bowl of kerosene oil, brushed Francie's hair vigorously, braided it into braids so tightly that the veins on Francie's temples stuck out, instructed her to keep away from lighted gas-jets and sent her off to school.

Francie smelled up the whole classroom. Her seat sharer edged as far away from her as possible. Teacher sent a note home forbidding Katie to use kerosene on Francie's head. Katie remarked that it was a free country and ignored the note. Once a week she scrubbed Francie's head with the yellow soap. Every day she anointed it with the kerosene.

When an epidemic of mumps broke out in the school, Katie went into action against communicable diseases. She made two flannel bags, sewed a bud of garlic in each one, attached a clean corset string and made the children wear them around their necks under their shirts.

Francie attended school stinking of garlic and kerosene oil. Everyone avoided her. In the crowded yard, there was always a cleared space around her. In crowded trolley-cars people huddled away from those Nolan children.

And it worked! Now whether there was a witch's charm in the garlic, whether the strong fumes killed the germs or whether Francie escaped contracting anything because infected children gave her a wide berth, or whether she and Neeley had naturally strong constitutions, is not known. However, it was a fact that not once in all the years of school were Katie's children ever sick. They never so much as came down with a cold. And they never had lice.

Francie, of course, became an outsider shunned by all because of her stench. But she had become accustomed to being lonely. She was used to walking alone and to being considered "different." She did not suffer too much.

XXI

FRANCIE LIKED school in spite of all the meanness, cruelty, and unhappiness. The regimented routine of many children, all doing the same thing at once, gave her a feeling of safety. She felt that she was a definite part of something, part of a community gathered under a leader for the one purpose. The Nolans were individualists. They conformed to nothing except what was essential to their being able to live in their world. They followed their own standards of living. They were part of no set social group. This was fine for the making of individualists, but sometimes bewildering to a small child. So Francie felt a certain safety and security in school. Although it was a cruel and ugly routine, it had a purpose and a progression.

School was not all unrelieved grimness. There was a great golden glory lasting a half-hour each week when Mr. Morton came to Francie's room to teach music. He was a specialised teacher who went around to all of the schools in that area. It was holiday-time when he appeared. He wore a swallow-tailed coat and a puffed-up tie. He was so vibrant, gay and jolly—so intoxicated with living—that he was like a god come from the clouds. He was homely in a gallant vital way. He understood and loved children and they worshipped him. The teachers adored him. There was a carnival spirit in the room on the day of his visit. Teacher wore her best dress and wasn't quite so mean. Sometimes she curled her hair and wore perfume. That's what Mr. Morton did to those ladies.

He arrived like a tornado. The door burst open and he flew in with his coat-tails streaming behind him. He leaped to the platform and looked around smiling and saying: "Well-well," in a happy voice. The children sat there and laughed and laughed out of happiness and Teacher smiled and smiled.

He drew notes on the blackboard; he drew little legs on them to make them look as though they were running out of the scale. He'd make a flat note look like humpty-dumpty. A sharp note would rate a thin beak-like nose zooming off it. All the while he'd burst into singing just as spontaneously as a bird. Sometimes his happiness was so overflowing that he couldn't hold it and he'd cut a dance caper to spill some of it out.

He taught them good music without letting them know it was good. He set his own words to the great classics and gave them simple names like "Lullaby" and "Serenade" and "Street Song" and "Song for a Sunshiny Day." Their baby voices shrilled out in Handel's "Largo," and they knew it merely by the title of "Hymn." Little boys whistled part of Dvorak's *New World Symphony* as they played marbles. When asked the name of the song, they'd reply: "Oh, 'Going Home.'" They played potsy, humming "The Soldiers' Chorus" from *Faust*, which they called "Glory."

Not so well loved as Mr. Morton, but as much admired, was Miss Bernstone, the special drawing teacher, who also came once a week. Ah, she was from another world, a world of beautiful dresses of muted greens and garnets. Her face was sweet and tender, and, like Mr. Morton, she loved the vast hordes of unwashed and unwanted children more than she loved the cared-for ones. The teachers did not like *her*. Yes, they fawned on her when she spoke to them and glowered at her when her back was turned. They were jealous of her charm, her sweetness and her lovely appeal to men. She was warm and glowing and richly feminine. They knew that she didn't sleep alone nights as they were forced to do.

She spoke softly in a clear singing voice. Her hands were beautiful and quick with a bit of chalk or a stick of charcoal. There was magic in the way her wrist turned when she held a crayon. One wrist twist and there was an apple. Two more twists and there was a child's sweet hand holding the apple. On a rainy day, she wouldn't give a lesson. She'd take a block of paper and a stick of charcoal and sketch the poorest, meanest kid in the room. And when the picture was finished, you didn't see the dirt or the meanness; you saw the glory of innocence and the poignancy of a baby growing up too soon. Oh, Miss Bernstone was grand.

The two visiting teachers were the gold and silver sun-splash in the great muddy river of school days, days made up of dreary hours in which Teacher made her pupils sit rigid with their hands folded behind their back while she read a novel hidden in her lap. If all the teachers had been like Miss Bernstone and Mr. Morton, Francie would have known plain what heaven was. But it was just as well. There had to be the dark and muddy waters so that the sun could have something to background its flashing glory.

XXII

OH, MAGIC hour when a child first knows it can read printed words!

For quite a while, Francie had been spelling out letters, sounding them and then putting the sounds together to mean a word. But one day she looked at a page and the word "mouse" had instantaneous meaning. She looked at the word and the picture of a grey mouse scampered through her mind. She looked further and when she saw "horse" she heard him pawing the ground and saw the sun glint on his glossy coat. The word "running" hit her suddenly and she breathed hard as though running herself. The barrier between the individual sound of each letter and the whole meaning of the word was removed and the printed word meant a thing at one quick glance. She read a few pages rapidly and almost became ill with excitement. She wanted to shout it out. She could read! She could read!

From that time on, the world was hers for the reading. She would never be lonely again, never miss the lack of intimate friends. Books became her friends, and there was one for every mood. There was poetry for quiet companionship. There was adventure when she tired of quiet hours. There would be love-stories when she came into adolescence and when she wanted to feel a closeness to someone she could read a biography. On that day when she first knew she could read, she made a vow to read one book a day as long as she lived.

She liked numbers and sums. She devised a game in which each number was a family member and the "answer" made a family grouping with a story to it. Naught was a babe in arms. He gave no trouble. Whenever he appeared you just "carried" him. The figure 1 was a pretty baby girl just learning to walk, and easy to handle; 2 was a baby boy who could walk and talk a little. He went into family life (into sums, etc.) with very little trouble. And 3 was an older boy in kindergarten, who had to be watched a little. Then there was 4, a girl of Francie's age. She was almost as easy to "mind" as 2. The mother was 5, gentle and kind. In large sums, she came along and made everything easy the way a mother should. The father, 6, was harder than the others but very just. But 7 was mean. He was a crotchety old grandfather and not at all accountable for how he came out. The grandmother, 8, was hard too, but easier to understand than 7. Hardest of all was 9. He was company, and what a hard time fitting *him* into family life!

When Francie added a sum, she would fix a little story to go with the result. If the answer was 924, it meant that the little boy and girl were being minded by company while the rest of the family went out. When a number such as 1024 appeared, it meant that all the little children were playing together in the yard. The number 62 meant that papa was taking the little boy for a walk; 50 meant that mama had the baby out in the buggy for an airing, and 78 meant grandfather and grandmother sitting home by the fire of a winter's evening. Each single combination of numbers was a new set-up for the family, and no two stories were ever the same.

Francie took the game with her up into algebra. X was the

boy's sweetheart, who came into the family life and complicated it. Y was the boy friend who caused trouble. So arithmetic was a warm and human thing to Francie and occupied many lonely hours of her time.

XXIII

SCHOOL DAYS went along. Some were made up of meanness, brutality and heart-break; others were bright and beautiful because of Miss Bernstone and Mr. Morton. And always there was the magic of learning things.

Francie was out walking one Saturday in October and she chanced on an unfamiliar neighbourhood. Here were no tenements or raucous shabby stores. There were old houses that had been standing there when Washington manoeuvred his troops across Long Island. They were old and decrepit, but there were picket fences around them with gates on which Francie longed to swing. There were bright autumn flowers in the front yard and maple trees with crimson and yellow leaves on the kerb. The neighbourhood stood old, quiet, and serene in the Saturday sunshine. There was a brooding quality about the neighbourhood, a quiet, deep, timeless, shabby peace. Francie was as happy as though, like Alice, she had stepped through a magic mirror. She was in an enchanted land.

She walked on further and came to a little old school. Its old bricks glowed garnet in the late afternoon sun. There was no fence around the school yard and the school grounds were grass and not cement. Across from the school, it was practically open country—a meadow with golden-rod, wild asters and clover growing in it.

Francie's heart turned over. This was it! This was the school she wanted to go to. But how could she get to go there? There was a strict law about attending the school in your own district. Her parents would have to move to that neighbourhood if she wanted to go to that school. Francie knew that mama wouldn't move just because *she* felt like going to another school. She walked home slowly thinking about it.

She sat up that night waiting for papa to come home from work. After Johnny had come home whistling his "Molly Malone" as he ran up the steps, after all had eaten of the lobster, caviar, and liverwurst that he brought home, mama and Neeley went to bed. Francie kept papa company while he smoked his last cigar. Francie whispered all about the school in papa's ear. He looked at her, nodded, and said: "We'll see tomorrow."

"You mean we can move near that school?"

"No, but there has to be another way. I'll go there with you tomorrow and we'll see what we can see."

Francie was so excited she couldn't sleep the rest of the night. She was up at seven, but Johnny was still sleeping soundly. She waited in a perspiration of impatience. Each time he sighed in his sleep, she ran in to see if he was waking up.

He woke about noon and the Nolans sat down to dinner. Francie couldn't eat. She kept looking at papa, but he made her no sign. Had he forgotten? Had he forgotten? No, because while Katie was pouring the coffee he said carelessly:

"I guess me and the Prima Donna will take a little walk later on."

Francie's heart jumped. He had not forgotten. He had not forgotten. She waited. Mama had to answer. Mama might object. Mama might ask why. Mama might say she guessed she'd go along too. But all mama said was: "All right."

Francie did the dishes. Then she had to go down to the candy store to get the Sunday paper; then to the cigar store to get papa a nickel Corona. Johnny had to read the paper. He had to read every column of it, including the society section, in which he couldn't possibly be interested. Worse than that, he had to make comments to mama on every item he read. Each time he'd put the paper aside, turn to mama and say: "Funny things in the papers nowadays. Take this case." Francie would almost cry.

Four o'clock came. The cigar had long since been smoked, the paper lay gutted on the floor, Katie had tired of having the news analysed and had taken Neeley and gone over to visit Mary Rommely.

Francie and papa set out hand in hand. He was wearing his only suit, the tuxedo and his derby hat, and he looked very grand. It was a splendid October day. There was a warm sun and a refreshing wind working together to bring the tang of the ocean around each corner. They walked a few blocks, turned a corner and were in this other neighbourhood. Only in a great sprawling place like Brooklyn could there be such a sharp division. It was a neighbourhood peopled with fifth and sixth generation Americans, whereas in the Nolan neighbour-hood, if you could prove you had been born in America, it was equivalent to a *Mayflower* standing.

Indeed, Francie was the only one in her classroom whose parents were American-born. At the beginning of the term, Teacher called the roll and asked each child her lineage. The answers were typical.

"I'm Polish-American. My father was born in Warsaw."

"Irish-American. Me fayther and mither were born in County Cork."

When Nolan was called, Francie answered proudly: "I'm an American."

"I *know* you're American," said the easily exasperated teacher. "But what's your nationality?"

"American!" insisted Francie even more proudly.

"Will you tell me what your parents are or do I have to send you to the principal?"

"My parents are American. They were born in Brooklyn."

All the children turned around to look at a little girl whose parents had *not* come from the old country. And when Teacher said: "Brooklyn? Hm. I guess that makes you American, all right," Francie was proud and happy. How wonderful was Brooklyn, she thought, when just being born there automatically made you an American!

Papa had told her about this strange neighbourhood: how its families had been Americans for more than a hundred years back; how they were mostly Scotch, English and Welsh extraction. The men worked as cabinet-makers and fine carpenters. They worked with metals: gold, silver and copper.

He promised to take Francie to the Spanish section of Brooklyn some day. There the men worked as cigar-makers, and each chipped in a few pennies a day to hire a man to read to them while they worked. And the man read fine literature.

They walked along the quiet Sunday street. Francie saw a leaf flutter from a tree and she skipped ahead to get it. It was a clear scarlet with an edging of gold. She stared at it, wondering if she'd ever see anything as beautiful again. A woman came from around the corner. She was rouged heavily and wore a feather boa. She smiled at Johnny and said:

"Lonesome, Mister?"

Johnny looked at her a moment before he answered gently:

"No, Sister."

"Sure?" she inquired archly.

"Sure," he answered quietly.

She went her way. Francie skipped back and took papa's hand.

"Was that a bad lady, Papa?" she asked eagerly.

"No."

"But she *looked* bad."

"There are very few bad people. There are just a lot of people that are unlucky."

"But she was all painted and . . ."

"She was one who had seen better days." He liked the phrase. "Yes, she may have seen better days." He fell into a thoughtful mood. Francie kept skipping ahead and collecting leaves.

They came upon the school and Francie proudly showed it to papa. The late afternoon sun warmed its softly-coloured bricks and the small-paned windows seemed to dance in the sunshine. Johnny looked at it a long time, then he said:

"Yes, this is the school. This is it."

Then, as whenever he was moved or stirred, he had to put it into a song. He held his worn derby over his heart, stood up

> School days, school days,
> Dear old golden rule days,
> Readin' 'n writin' 'n 'rithmetic . . .

straight looking up at the school house and sang:

To a passing stranger it might have looked silly—Johnny standing there in his greenish tuxedo and fresh linen holding the hand of a thin, ragged child and singing the banal song so un-self-consciously on the street. But to Francie it seemed right and beautiful.

They crossed the street and wandered in the meadow that folks called "lots." Francie picked a bunch of golden-rod and wild asters to take home. Johnny explained that the place had once been an Indian burying-ground, and how, as a boy, he had often come there to hunt arrow-heads. Francie suggested they hunt for some. They searched for half an hour and found none. Johnny recalled that as a boy he hadn't found any either. This struck Francie as funny and she laughed. Papa confessed that maybe it hadn't been an Indian cemetery after all; maybe someone had made up that story. Johnny was more than right, because he had made up the whole story himself.

Soon it was time to go home, and tears came into Francie's eyes because papa hadn't said anything about getting her into the new school. He saw the tears and figured out a scheme immediately.

"Tell you what we'll do, Baby. We'll walk around and pick out a nice house and take down the number. I'll write a letter to your principal saying you're moving there and want to be transferred to this school."

They found a house—a one-storey white one with a slanting roof and late chrysanthemums growing in the yard. He copied the address carefully.

"You know that what we are going to do is wrong?"

"Is it, Papa?"

"But it's a wrong to gain a bigger good."

"Like a white lie?"

"Like a lie that helps someone out. So you must make up for the wrong by being twice as good. You must never be bad or absent or late. You must never do anything to make them send a letter home through the mails."

"I'll always be good, Papa, if I can go to that school."

"Yes. Now I'll show you a way to go to school through a little park. I know right where it is. Yes, sir, I know right where it is."

He showed her the park and how she could walk through it diagonally to go to school.

"That should make you happy. You can see the seasons change as you come and go. What do you say to that?"

Francie, recalling something her mother had once read to her, answered: "My cup runneth over." And she meant it.

When Katie heard of the plan, she said: "Suit yourself. But I'll have nothing to do with it. If the police come and arrest you for giving a false address, I'll say honestly that I had nothing to do with it. One school's as good or as bad as another. I don't know why she wants to change. There's homework, no matter what school you go to."

"It's settled then," Johnny said. "Francie, here's a penny. Run down to the candy store and get a sheet of writing-paper and an envelope."

Francie ran down and ran back. Johnny wrote a note saying Francie was going to live with relatives at such and such an address and wanted a transfer. He added that Neeley would continue living at home and wouldn't require a transfer. He signed his name and underlined it authoritatively.

Tremblingly, Francie handed the note to her principal next morning. That lady read it, grunted, made out the transfer, handed her her report card and told her to go; that the school was too crowded, anyhow.

Francie presented herself and documents to the principal of the new school. He shook hands with her and said he hoped she'd be happy in the new school. A monitor took her to the classroom. The teacher stopped the work and introduced Francie to the class. Francie looked out over the rows of little girls. All were shabby but most were clean. She was given a seat to herself and happily fell into the routine of the new school.

The teachers and children here were not as brutalized as in the old school. Yes, some of the children were mean, but it seemed a natural child-meanness and not a campaign. Often the teachers were impatient and cross, but never naggingly cruel. There was no corporal punishment either. The parents were too American, too aware of the rights granted them by their Constitution to accept injustices meekly. They could not be bulldozed and exploited as could the immigrants and the second generation Americans.

Francie found that the different feeling in this school came mostly from the janitor. He was a ruddy white-haired man whom even the principal addressed as *Mister* Jenson. He had many children and grandchildren of his own, all of whom he loved dearly. He was father to all children. On rainy days when children came to school soaked, he insisted that they be sent down to the furnace-room to dry out. He made them take off their wet shoes and hung their wet stockings on a line to dry. The little shabby shoes stood in a row before the furnace.

It was pleasant down in the furnace-room. The walls were whitewashed and the big red-painted furnace was a comforting thing. The windows were high up in the walls. Francie liked to sit there and enjoy the warmth and watch the orange-and-blue flames dancing an inch above the bed of small black coals. (He left the furnace door open when the children were drying out.) On rainy days she left earlier and walked to school slower so that she would be soaking wet and rate the privilege of drying in the furnace-room.

It was unorthodox for Mr. Jenson to keep the children out of class to dry but everyone liked and respected him too much to protest. Francie heard stories around the school concerning

Mr. Jenson. She heard that he had been to college and knew more than the principal did. They said he had married, but when the children came, had decided that there was more money in being a school engineer than in being a school-teacher. Whatever it was, he was liked and respected. Once Francie saw him in the principal's office. He was in his clean striped overalls sitting there with his knees crossed and talking politics. Francie heard that the principal often came down to Mr. Jenson's furnace-room to sit and talk for a few moments while he smoked a pipeful of tobacco.

When a boy was bad, he wasn't sent to the principal's office for a licking; he was sent down to Mr. Jenson's room for a talking to.

Mr. Jenson never scolded a bad boy. He talked to him about his own youngest son who was a pitcher on the Dodgers' team. He talked about democracy and good citizen-ship and about a good world where everyone did the best he could for the common good of all. After a talk with Mr. Jenson, the boy could be counted upon not to cause any more trouble.

At graduation, the children asked the principal to sign the first page of their autograph-book out of respect to his posi-tion, but they valued Mr. Jenson's autograph more and he always got the second page to sign. The principal signed quickly in a great sprawling hand. But not Mr. Jenson. He made a ceremony out of it. He took the book over to his big roll-top desk and lit the light over it. He sat down, carefully polished his spectacles and chose a pen. He dipped it in ink, squinted at it, wiped it off and re-dipped it. Then he signed his name in a fine steel-engraving script and blotted it carefully. His signature was always the finest in the book. If you had the nerve to ask him, he'd take the book home and ask his son, who was with the Dodgers, to sign it too. This was a wonder-ful thing for the boys. The girls didn't care.

Mr. Jenson's handwriting was so wonderful that he wrote out all the diplomas by request.

Mr. Morton and Miss Bernstone came to that school, too. When they were teaching, Mr. Jenson would often come in and squeeze himself into one of the back seats and enjoy the lesson too. On a cold day, he'd have Mr. Morton or Miss Bernstone come down to his furnace-room for a hot cup of coffee before they went on to the next school. He had a gas plate and coffee-making equipment on a little table. He served strong, hot, black coffee in thick cups, and these visiting teachers blessed his good soul.

Francie was happy in this school. She was very careful about being a good girl. Each day, as she passed the house whose number she claimed, she looked at it with gratitude and affection. On windy days, when papers blew before it, she went about picking up the debris and depositing it in the gutter before the house. Mornings after the rubbish-man had emptied the burlap bag and had carelessly tossed the empty bag on the walk instead of in the yard, Francie picked it up and hung it on a fence paling. The people who lived in the house came to look on her as a quiet child who had a queer complex about tidiness.

Francie loved that school. It meant that she had to walk forty-eight blocks each day, but she loved the walk, too. She had to leave earlier in the morning than Neeley and she got home much later. She didn't mind, except that it was a little hard at lunchtime. There were twelve blocks to come home and twelve to go back—all in the hour. It left little time for eating. Mama wouldn't let her carry a lunch. Her reason was:

"She'll be weaned away from her home and family soon enough the way she's growing up. But while she's still a child she has to act like a child and come home and eat the way children should. Is it my fault that she has to go so far to school? Didn't she pick it out herself?"

"But, Katie," argued papa, "it's such a good school."

"Then let her take the bad along with this good."

The lunch question was settled. Francie had about five minutes for lunch—just time enough to report home for a sandwich which she ate walking back to school. She never considered herself put upon. She was so happy in the new school that she was anxious to pay in some way for this joy.

It was a good thing that she got herself into this other school. It showed her that there were other worlds beside the world she had been born into, and that these other worlds were not unattainable.

XXIV

FRANCIE COUNTED the year's passing not by the days or the month but by the holidays that came along. Her year started with the Fourth of July because it was the first holiday that came along after school closed. A week before the day she began accumulating firecrackers. Every available penny went for packets of small crackers. She hoarded them in a box under the bed. At least ten times a day she'd take the box out, re-arrange the fireworks and look long at the pale red tissue and white corded stem and wonder about how they were made. She smelled the thick bit of punk which was given gratis with each purchase and which, when lit, smouldered for hours and was used to set off the firecrackers.

When the great day came, she was reluctant to set them off. It was better to have them than to use them. One year when times were harder than usual and pennies could not be had, Francie and Neeley hoarded paper bags, and on the day filled them with water, twisted the tops shut and dropped them from the roof on to the street below. They made a nice plop which was almost like a firecracker. Passers-by were irritated and looked up angrily when a bag just missed them, but they did nothing about it, accepting the fact that poor children had a custom of celebrating the Fourth that way.

The next holiday was Hallowe'en. Neeley blackened his face with soot, wore his cap backwards and his coat inside out. He filled one of his mother's long black stockings with ashes and roamed the streets with his gang swinging his homely black-jack and crying out raucously from time to time.

Francie, in company with other little girls, roamed the streets carrying a bit of white chalk. She went about drawing a large quick cross on the back of each coated figure that came by. The children performed the ritual without meaning. The symbol was remembered but the reason forgotten. It may have been something that had survived from the Middle Ages, when houses and probably individuals were so marked to indicate where plague had struck. Probably the ruffians of that time so marked innocent people as a cruel joke and the practice had persisted down through the centuries to be distorted into a meaningless Hallowe'en prank.

Election Day seemed the greatest holiday of all to Francie. It, more than any other time, belonged to the whole neigh-bourhood. Maybe people voted in other parts of the country too, but it couldn't be the way it was in Brooklyn, thought Francie.

Johnny showed Francie an Oyster House on Scholes Street. It was housed in a building that had been standing there more than a hundred years before, when Big Chief Tammany himself skulked around with his braves. Its oyster fries were known throughout the State. But there was something else that made this place famous. It was the secret meeting-place of the great City Hall politicans. The party sachems met here in secret pow-wow in a private dining-room and over succulent oysters they decided who'd be elected and who mowed down.

Francie often passed by the store, looked at it and was thrilled. It had no name over its door and its window was empty save for a potted fern and a half curtain of brown linen run on brass rods along the back of it. Once Francie saw the door open to admit someone. She had a glimpse of a low room dimly lit with dulled red-shaded lamps and thick with the smoke of cigars.

Francie, along with the other neighbourhood children, went through some of the Election rites without knowing their meaning or reason. On Election night, she got in line, her hands on the shoulders of the child in front, and snake-danced through the streets singing:

> Tammany, Tammany,
> Big Chief sits in his teepee,
> Cheering braves to victory,
> Tamma-nee, Tamma-nee.

She was an interested listener at the debates between mama and papa on the merits and faults of the party. Papa was an ardent Democrat but mama just didn't care. Mama criticized the party and told Johnny he was throwing his vote away.

"Don't say that, Katie," he protested. "By and large the party does a lot of good for the people."

"I can just imagine it," sniffed mama.

"All they want is a vote from the man of the family, and look what they give in exchange."

"Name one thing *they* give."

"Well, you need advice on a legal matter. You don't need a lawyer. Just ask your Assembly-man."

"The blind leading the blind."

"Don't you believe it. They may be dumb in many ways, but they know the City's statutes backward and forward."

"Sue the City for something and see how far Tammany will help you."

"Take Civil Service," said Johnny, starting on another angle. "They know when the examinations for cops, firemen or lettercarriers are coming up. They'll always put a voter wise if he's interested."

"Mrs. Lavey's husband took the examination for letter-carrier three years ago. He's still working on a truck."

"Ah! That's because he's a Republican. If he was a Democrat, they'd take his name and put it on the top of the list. I heard about a teacher who wanted to be transferred to another school. Tammany fixed it up."

"Why? Unless she was pretty."

"That's not the point. It was a shrewd move. Teachers are educating future voters. This teacher, for instance, will always say a good word for Tammany to her pupils whenever she can. Every boy has to grow up to vote, you know."

"Why?"

"Because it's a privilege."

"Privilege! Humpf!" sneered Katie.

"Now, for instance, if you had a poodle and it died, what would you do?"

"What would I do with a poodle in the first place?"

"Can't you make out like you have a dead poodle just for the sake of conversation?"

"All right. My poodle's dead. Now what?"

"You go around to Headquarters and the boys will take it away for you. Suppose Francie wanted to get working papers but was too young."

"They'd get them, I suppose."

"Certainly."

"Do you think that's right to fix it so little children can work in factories?"

"Well, supposing you had a bad boy who played hooky from school and was getting to be a loafer hanging around street corners but the law wouldn't let him work. Wouldn't it be better if he got faked working papers?"

"In that case, yes," conceded Katie.

"Look at all the jobs they get for voters."

"You know how they get them, don't you? They inspect a factory and overlook the fact that they're violating the factory laws. Naturally, the boss pays back by letting them know when they need men and Tammany gets all the credit for

144

finding jobs."

"Here's another case. A man has relatives in the old country but he can't get them over here on account of the quotas. Well, Tammany can fix that up."

"Sure, they get them foreigners over here and see to it that they start on their citizenship papers and then tell them they must vote the Democratic ticket or go back where they came from."

"No matter what you say, Tammany's good to the poor people. Say a man's been sick and can't pay his rent. Do you think the organization would let the landlord dispossess him? No, sir. Not if he's a Democrat."

"I suppose the landlords are all Republicans, then," Katie said.

"No. The system works both ways. Suppose the landlord has a bum for a tenant who gives him a punch in the nose instead of the rent. What happens? The Organization dispossesses him for the landlord."

"For what Tammany gives to the people, it takes from them double. You wait until us women vote." Johnny's laugh interrupted her. "You don't believe we will? That day will come. Mark my words. We'll put all those crooked politicians where they belong—behind iron bars."

"If that day ever comes when women vote, you'll go along to the polls with me—arm in arm—and vote the way I do." He put his arm around her and gave her a quick hug.

Katie smiled up at him. Francie couldn't help noticing that mama was smiling sidewise, the way the lady did in the picture in the school auditorium, the one they called *Mona Lisa*.

Tammany owed much of its power to the fact that it got the children young and educated them in the party ways. The dumbest ward heeler was smart enough to know that time, no matter what else it did, passed, and that the schoolboy of today was the voter of tomorrow. They got the boys on their side and the girls, too. A woman couldn't vote in those days, but the politicians knew that the women of Brooklyn had a great influence on their men. Bring a little girl up in the party way and when she married she'd see to it that her man voted the straight Democratic ticket. To woo the children, the Mattie Mahony Association ran an excursion for them and their parents each summer. Although Katie had nothing but contempt for the Organization, she saw no reason why they shouldn't take advantage of the good time. When Francie heard that they were going, she was as excited as only a ten-year-old, who had never been on a boat before, could be.

Johnny refused to go and couldn't see why Katie wanted to go.

"I'm going because I like life," was her strange reason.

"If that racket's life, I wouldn't take it with coupons," he said.

But he went anyhow. He figured the boat trip might be educational and he wanted to be on hand to educate the children. It was a hot sweltering day. The decks teemed with kids, wild with excitement, racing up and down and trying to fall into the Hudson River. Francie stared and stared at the moving water until she worked up the first headache of her life. Johnny told his children how Hendrick Hudson had sailed up that same river so long ago. Francie wondered whether Mr. Hudson got sick to his stomach like she did. Mama sat on deck looking very pretty in her jade-green straw hat and a yellow dotted-swiss dress that she had borrowed from Aunt Evy. People around her were laughing. Mama was a vivid conversationalist and people liked to hear her talk.

Soon after noon, the boat docked at a wooded glen upstate and the Democrats got off the boat and took over. The kids ran around spending their tickets. The week before, each child had been given a strip of ten tickets labelled "hot dog," "soda water," "merry-go-round" and so on. Francie and Neeley had each been given a strip but Francie had been tempted by some shrewd boys into gambling her tickets in a marble game. They had told her how she might possibly win fifty strips and have a grand day on the excursion. Francie was a poor marble player and quickly lost her tickets. Neeley, on the other hand, had three strips. He had been lucky. Francie asked mama could she have one of Neeley's tickets. Mama seized the opportunity to give her a lecture on gambling.

"You had tickets but you thought you could be smart and get something you weren't entitled to. When people gamble, they think only of winning. They never think of losing. Remember this: Someone has to lose and it's just as apt to be you as the other fellow. If you learn this lesson by giving up a strip of tickets, you're paying cheap for the education."

Mama was right. Francie *knew* she was right. But it didn't make her happy at all. She wanted to go on the merry-go-round like the other kids. She wanted a drink of soda. She was standing disconsolately near the hot-dog stand watching other children stuff themselves when a man paused to speak to her. He wore a policeman's uniform, only with more gold on it.

"No tickets, little girl?" he asked.

"I forgot them," lied Francie.

"Sure and I was no good at marbles meself as a boy." He pulled three strips from his pocket. "We count on making up a certain number of losses each year. But it's seldom the girls are the losin' ones. They hang on to what they have, be it ever so little." Francie took the tickets, thanked him and was backing off when he asked: "Would that be your mother sittin' over there in the green hat?"

"Yes." She waited. He said nothing. Finally she asked "Why?"

"Do you be sayin' your prayers to the Little Flower each night askin' that you grow up half as pretty as your mother. Do that now."

"And that's my papa next to my mama." Francie waited to hear him say that papa was good-looking, too. He stared at Johnny and said nothing. Francie ran off.

Francie was instructed to report back to her mother at half-hour intervals during the day. At the next interval when Francie came back, Johnny was over at the free beer keg. Mamma teased her.

"You're like Aunt Sissy—always talking to men in uniform."

"He gave me extra tickets."

"I saw." Katie's next words were casual enough. "What did he ask you?"

"He asked was you my mama." Francie did not tell her what he said about mama being pretty.

"Yes, I thought he was asking that." Katie stared at her hands. They were rough and red and cut into with cleansing fluids. She took a pair of mended cotton gloves from her purse. Although it was a hot day, she pulled them on. She sighed. "I work so hard, sometimes I forgot that I'm a woman."

Francie was startled. It was the nearest thing to a complaint she had ever heard from mama. She wondered why mama was ashamed of her hands all of a sudden. As she skipped away, she heard mama ask the lady next to her:

"Who's that man over there—the one in the uniform looking this way?"

"That would be Sergeant Michael McShane. It's funny you don't know who he is seein' that it's from your own precinct he is."

The day of joy went on. There was a keg of beer set up at the end of each long table and it was free to all good Democrats. Francie was caught up in the excitement and tore around, screamed and fought like the other children. Beer flowed like a Brooklyn gutter after a rain-storm. A brass band played doggedly. It played "The Kerry Dancers" and "When Irish Eyes are Smiling" and "Harrigan, That's Me." It played "The River Shannon" and New York's own folk song. "The Sidewalks of New York."

The conductor announced each selection: "Mattie Mahony's Band will now play. . . ." Each song ended with the band members shouting in unison, "Hurray for Mattie Mahony." With each glass of beer drawn, the attendants said, "Compliments of Mattie Mahony." Each event was labelled, "The Mattie Mahony Foot Race," "The Mattie Mahony Peanut Race," and so on. Before the day was over, Francie was convinced that Mattie Mahony was a very great man indeed.

Late in the afternoon, Francie got the idea that she ought to find Mr. Mahony and thank him personally for a very nice time. She searched and searched, and asked and asked and a strange thing happened. No one knew Mattie Mahony; no one had ever seen him. Certainly he was not at the picnic. His presence was felt everywhere but the man was invisible. Some man told her that maybe there was no Mattie Mahony; it was just the name they gave to whatever man was head of the Organization.

"I been votin' the straight ticket for forty years," he said. "Seems like the candidate was always the same man, Mattie Mahony; or else it was a different man but with the same name. I don't know who he is, Girlie. All I know is that I vote the straight Democratic ticket."

The trip home down the moonlit Hudson was notable only for the many fights that broke out among the men. Most of the children were sick and sunburnt and fretful. Neeley fell asleep on mama's lap. Francie sat on deck and listened to mama and papa talking.

"Do you happen to know Sergeant McShane?" Katie asked.

"I know who he is. They call him the Honest Cop. The

party has its eye on him. It wouldn't surprise me if he was put up for Assembly-man."

A man sitting near-by leaned forward and touched Johnny's arm. "Police Commissioner is more like it, Mac," he said.

"What about his life?" Katie asked.

"It's like one of those Alger stories. He came from Ireland twenty-five years ago with nothing but a trunk small enough to be carried on his back. He worked as a dock walloper, studied nights and got on the force. He kept on studying and taking examinations and finally got to be Sergeant," said Johnny.

"I suppose he's married to an educated woman who helped him?"

"Matter of fact, no. When he first came over, an Irish family took him in and kept him till he got on his feet. The daughter of the family married a bum who ran out on her after the honeymoon and got himself killed in a brawl. Well, the girl was going to have a baby and you couldn't make the neighbours believe she had ever been married. Seems like the family would be disgraced, but McShane married her and gave the child his name to kind of repay the family. It wasn't a love marriage, exactly, but he's been very good to her, I hear."

"Did they have children together?"

"Fourteen, I heard."

"Fourteen!"

"But he only raised four. Seemed like they all died before they grew up. They were all born with consumption, you know, inherited it from their mother, who had it from a girl."

"He's had more than his share of trouble," mused Johnny. "And he's a good man."

"She's still alive, I suppose."

"But very sick. They say she hasn't long to live."

"Oh, those kind hang on."

"Katie!" Johnny was startled by his wife's remark.

"I don't care! I don't blame her for marrying a bum and having a child by him. That's her privilege. But I do blame her for not taking her medicine when the time came due. Why did she put her troubles off on a good man?"

"That's no way to talk."

"I hope she dies and dies soon."

"Hush, Katie."

"Yes, I do. So that he can marry again—marry a cheerful healthy woman, who'll give him children that can live. That's

149

every good man's right."

Johnny said nothing. A nameless fear had grown within Francie while she listened to her mother talking. Now she got up and went over to papa, took his hand and pressed it hard. In the moonlight, Johnny's eyes flew open in startled surprise.. He pulled the child to him and held her tightly. But all he said was:

"Look how the moon walks on the water."

Soon after the picnic, the Organization began to prepare for Election Day. They distributed shiny white buttons with Mattie's mug on them to the neighbourhood kids. Francie got some and stared long at the face. Mattie had grown so mysterious to her that he took the place of someone like the Holy Ghost—he was never seen but his presence was felt. The picture was of a bland-faced man with roached hair and handlebar moustaches. It looked like the face of any small-time politician. Francie wished she could see him—just once in the flesh.

There was a lot of excitement about these buttons. The children used them for trading purposes, for games and coins of the realm. Neeley sold his top to a boy for ten buttons. Gimpy, the candy-store man, redeemed fifteen of Francie's buttons for a penny's worth of candy. (He had an arrangement with the Organization whereby he got the money back for the buttons.) Francie went around looking for Mattie and found him all over. She found boys playing pitch games with his face. She found him flattened out on a car track to make a miniature potsy. He was in the debris of Neeley's pocket. She peered down the sewer and saw him floating face upward. She found him in the sour soil at the bottoms of gratings. She saw Punky Perkins, next to her in church, drop two buttons in the plate in lieu of the two pennies his mother had given him. She saw him go into the candy store and buy four Sweet Caporal cigarettes with the two cents after mass. She saw Mattie's face everywhere but she never saw Mattie.

The week before Election she went around with Neeley and the boys gathering "lection," which was what they called the lumber for the big bonfires which would be lighted Election night. She helped store the lection in the cellar.

She was up early on Election day and saw the man who came and knocked on the door. When Johnny answered, the

150

man said:

"Nolan?"

"Yes," admitted Johnny.

"At the polls, eleven o'clock." He checked Johnny's name on his list. He handed Johnny a cigar. "Compliments of Mattie Mahony." He went on to the next Democrat.

"Wouldn't you go anyhow without being told?" Francie asked.

"Yes, but they give us each a time so that the voting is staggered . . . you know, not everyone coming in a bunch."

"Why?" persisted Francie.

" 'Cause," Johnny evaded.

"I'll tell you why," broke in mama. "They want to keep tabs on who's voting and how. They know when each man's due at the polls and God help him if he doesn't show up to vote for Mattie."

"Women don't know anything about politics," said Johnny lighting up Mattie's cigar.

Francie helped Neeley drag their wood out on Election night. They contributed it to the biggest bonfire on the block. Francie got in line with the other children and danced around the fire Indian fashion, singing "Tammany." When the fire had burned down to embers, the boys raided the pushcarts of the Jewish merchants and stole potatoes which they roasted in the ashes. So cooked, they were called "mickies." There weren't enough to go around and Francie didn't get any.

She stood on the street watching the returns come in on a bed sheet stretched from window to window of a house on the corner. A magic lantern across the street threw the figures on the sheet. Each time new returns came in, Francie shouted with the other kids:

"Another county heard from!"

Mattie's picture appeared on the screen from time to time and the crowd cheered itself hoarse. A Democratic president was elected that year and the Democratic governor of the State was re-elected, but all that Francie knew was that Mattie Mahony got in again.

After Election, the politicians forgot their promises and enjoyed an earned rest until New Year, when they started work on the next Election. January second was Ladies' Day at Democratic Headquarters. On that day, and no other, ladies were received into this strictly masculine precinct and treated

151

to sherry wine and little seeded cakes. All day, the ladies kept calling and were received gallantly by Mattie's henchmen. Mattie himself never showed up. As the ladies went out, they left their little decorated cards with their names written on them in the cut-glass dish on the hall table.

Katie's contempt for the politicians did not interfere with her making her yearly call. She put on her brushed and pressed grey suit with all the braid on it and tilted her jade-green velvet hat over her right eye. She even gave the penman, who set up temporary shop outside Headquarters, a dime to make a card for her. He wrote *Mrs. John Nolan* with flowers and angels crawling out of the capitals. It was a dime that should have gone into the bank, but Katie figured she could be extravagant once a year.

The family awaited her homecoming. They wanted to hear all about the call.

"How was it this year?" asked Johnny.

"The same as always. The same old push was there. A lot of women had new clothes which I bet they bought on time. Of course, the prostitutes were the best dressed," said Katie in her forthright way, "and, like always, they outnumbered the decent women two to one."

XXV

JOHNNY WAS one for taking notions. He'd take a notion that life was too much for him and start drinking heavier to forget it. Francie got to know when he was drinking more than usual. He walked straighter coming home. He walked carefully and slightly sidewise. When he was drunk, he was a quiet man. He didn't brawl, he didn't sing, he didn't grow sentimental. He grew thoughtful. People who didn't know him thought that he was drunk when he was sober, because sober he was full of song and excitement. When he was drunk, strangers looked on him as a quiet, thoughtful man who minded his own business.

Francie dreaded the drinking periods—not on moral grounds but because papa wasn't a man she knew then. He wouldn't talk to her or anybody. He looked at her with the eyes of a stranger. When mama spoke to him, he turned his head away from her.

When he got over a drinking time, he'd take a notion that he had to be a better father to his children. He felt that he had to teach them things. He'd stop drinking for a while, take a notion to work hard and devote all his spare time to Francie and Neeley. He had the same idea that Katie's mother, Mary Rommely, had about education. He wanted to teach his children all he knew so that at fourteen or fifteen they would know as much as he knew at thirty. He figured they could go on from there picking up their own knowledge and according to his calculations, when they reached thirty they would be twice as smart as he had been at thirty.

He felt that they needed lessons in—for what passed in his mind—geography, civics and sociology. So he took them over to Bushwick Avenue.

Bushwick Avenue was the high-toned boulevard of old Brooklyn. It was a wide, tree-shaded avenue and the houses were rich and impressively built of large granite blocks with long stone stoops. Here lived the big-time politicians, the moneyed brewery families, the well-to-do immigrants who had been able to come over first-class instead of steerage. They had taken their money, their statuary and their gloomy oil paintings and had come to America and settled in Brooklyn.

Automobiles were coming into use but most of these families still clung to their handsome horses and magnificent carriages. Papa pointed out and described the various equipages to Francie. She watched in awe as they rolled by.

There were small lacquered dainty ones lined with tufted white satin, with a large fringed umbrella that was used by fine and delicate ladies. There were adorable wicker ones with a bench along each side on which lucky children sat while they were pulled along by a Shetland pony. She stared at the capable-looking governesses who accompanied these children—women from another world, in capes and starch-stringed bonnets, who sat sideways to the seat to drive the pony.

Francie saw practical black two-seaters drawn by a single high-stepping horse controlled by dandified young men in kid gloves with edges turned back to look like inverted cuffs.

She saw staid family vehicles drawn by dependable-looking teams. These coaches did not impress Francie very much because every undertaker in Williamsburg had a string of them.

Francie liked the hansom cabs best. How magic they were

with only two wheels and that funny door that closed by itself when a passenger sat back in the seat! (Francie thought in her innocence that the doors were meant to protect the passenger from flying horse manure.) If I were a man, thought Francie, that's the job I'd like to have, driving one of them. Oh, to sit high up in the back with a great-coat with large buttons and a velvet collar and a squashed-down high hat with a ribbon cockade in the band! Oh, to have such an expensive-looking blanket folded over her knees! Francie imitated the driver's cry under her breath.

"Kerridge, sir? Kerridge?"

"Anybody," said Johnny, carried away by his personal dream of Democracy, "can ride in one of those hansom cabs, provided," he qualified, "they got the money. So you can see what a free country we got here."

"What's free about it if you have to *pay*?" asked Francie.

"It's free in this way: If you have the money you're allowed to ride in them no matter who you are. In the old countries, certain people aren't free to ride in them, even if they have the money."

"Wouldn't it be more of a free country," persisted Francie, "if we could ride in them free?"

"No."

"Why?"

"Because that would be Socialism," concluded Johnny triumphantly, "and we don't want that over here."

"Why?"

"Because we're not Russians and don't ever want to be," clinched Johnny.

New York City had a Mayor from Brooklyn who lived on Bushwick Avenue. "Look up and down this block, Francie, and show me where our Mayor lives," said Johnny.

Francie looked, then had to hang her head and say: "I don't know, Papa."

"There!" announced Johnny as though he were blowing a trumpet fanfare. "That's it! The house with the two lamp posts at the bottom of the stoop. No matter where you roam in this great city," he orated, "and you come across a house with two lamp-posts like that, you'll know that the Mayor of the greatest city in the world lives there."

"Why does he need two lamp-posts for?" Francie wanted to know.

"Because this is America and in a country where such things are," concluded Johnny vaguely but very patriotically, "you know that the government is by the people, for the people, of the people and shall not perish from the face of the earth the way it does in the old country." He began to sing under his breath. Soon he was carried away by his feeling and started to sing louder. Francie joined in. Johnny sang:

> You're a grand old flag,
> You're a high-flying flag,
> And for ever in peace may you wave ...

People stared at Johnny curiously and one kind lady threw him a penny.

Francie had another memory about Bushwick Avenue. It was tied up with the scent of roses. There were roses ... roses ... Bushwick Avenue. Streets emptied of traffic. Crowds on the sidewalk, the police holding them back. Always the scent of roses. Then came the cavalcade: mounted policemen and a large open motor-car in which was seated a genial, kindly-looking man with a wreath of roses around his neck. Some people were weeping with joy as they looked at him. Francie clung to papa's hand. She heard people around her talking:

"Just think! He was a Brooklyn boy, too."

"*Was?* You dope, he *still* lives in Brooklyn."

"Yeah?"

"Yeah. And he lives right here on Bushwick Avenue."

"Look at him! Look at him!" a woman cried out. "He did such a great thing and he's still an ordinary man like my husband only better-looking."

"It musta been cold up there," said a man. "It wonders me he didn't freeze his whatzis off," said a bawdy boy.

A cadaverous-looking man tapped Johnny on the shoulder. "Mac," he inquired, "do you actually believe there's a pole up there sticking out on top of the world?"

"Sure," answered Johnny. "Didn't he go up there and turn around and hang the American flag on it?"

Just then a small boy hollered out: "Here he comes!"

"Aw-w-w-w-w!"

Francie was thrilled by the sound of admiration that swayed the crowd when the car came past where they were standing.

155

Carried away by the excitement, she yelled out shrilly:
"Hurray for Captain Cook! Hurray for Brooklyn!"

XXVI

MOST CHILDREN brought up in Brooklyn before the first World War remember Thanksgiving Day there with a peculiar tenderness. It was the day children went around "ragamuffin" or "slamming gates," wearing costumes topped off by a penny mask.

Francie chose her mask with great care She bought a yellow Chinaman one with sleazy rope mandarin moustaches. Neeley bought a chalk-white death's-head with grinning black teeth. Papa came through at the last minute with a penny tin horn for each, red for Francie, green for Neeley.

What a time Francie had getting Neeley into his costume! He wore one of mama's discarded dresses hacked off anklelength in the front to enable him to walk. The uncut back made a dirty dragging train. He stuffed wadded newspapers in the front to make an enormous bust. His broken-out, brasstipped shoes stuck out in front of the dress. Lest he freeze, he wore a ragged sweater over the *ensemble*. With this costume, he wore the death mask and one of papa's discarded derbies cocked on his head. Only it was too big and wouldn't cock and rested on his ears.

Francie wore one of mama's yellow bodices, a bright blue skirt and a red sash. She held the Chinaman mask on by a red bandanna over her head and tied under her chin. Mama made her wear her zitful cap (Katie's own name for a wool stocking cap) over her headgear because it was a cold day. Francie put two walnuts for decoy in her last year's Easter basket and the children set out.

The street was jammed with masked and costumed children making a deafening din with their penny tin horns. Some kids were too poor to buy a penny mask. They had blackened their faces with burnt cork. Other children with more prosperous parents had store costumes: sleazy Indian suits, cowboy suits and cheesecloth Dutch maiden dresses. A few indifferent ones simply draped a dirty sheet over themselves and called it a costume.

Francie got pushed in with a compact group of children and went the rounds with them. Some shopkeepers locked their doors against them, but most of them had something for the children. The candy-store man had hoarded all broken bits of candy for weeks and now passed it out in little bags for all who came begging. He had to do this because he lived on the pennies of the youngsters and he didn't want to be boycotted. The bakery stores obliged by baking up batches of soft doughy cookies which they gave away. Children were the marketers of the neighbourhood and they would only patronize those stores that treated them well. The bakery people were aware of this. The greengrocer obliged with decaying bananas and half-rotted apples. Some stores which had nothing to gain from the children neither locked them out nor gave them anything save a profane lecture on the evils of begging. These people were rewarded by terrific and repeated bangings of the front door by the children. Hence the term "slamming gates."

By noon it was all over. Francie was tired of her unwieldy costume. Her mask had crumpled. (It was made of cheap gauze, heavily starched and dried in shape over a mould.) A boy had taken her tin horn and broken it in two across his knee. She met Neeley coming along with a bloody nose. He had been in a fight with another boy who wanted to take his basket. Neeley wouldn't say who won, but he had the other boy's basket besides his own. They went home to a good Thanksgiving dinner of pot roast and home-made noodles and spent the afternoon listening to papa reminisce how he had gone around Thanksgiving Day as a boy.

It was at a Thanksgiving time that Francie told her first organized lie, was found out and determined to become a writer.

The day before Thanksgiving, there were exercises in Francie's room. Each of four chosen girls recited a Thanksgiving poem and held in her hand a symbol of the day. One held an ear of dried-up corn, another a turkey's foot, meant to stand for a whole turkey. A third girl held a basket of apples and the fourth held a five-cent pumpkin pie which was the size of a small saucer.

After the exercises, the turkey foot and corn were thrown into the wastebasket. Teacher set aside the apples to take home. She asked if anyone wanted the little pumpkin pie. Thirty mouths watered; thirty hands itched to go up into the air but no one moved. Some were poor, many were hungry and all were too proud to accept charitable food. When no one responded, Teacher ordered the pie to be thrown away.

Francie couldn't stand it; that beautiful pie thrown away and she had never tasted pumpkin pie. To her it was the food of covered-wagon people, of Indian fighters. She was dying to taste it. In a flash she invented a lie and up went her hand.

"I'm glad someone wants it," said Teacher.

"I don't want it for myself," lied Francie proudly. "I know a very poor family I'd like to give it to."

"Good," said Teacher. "That's the real Thanksgiving spirit."

Francie ate the pie while walking home that afternoon. Whether it was her conscience or the unfamiliar flavour, she didn't enjoy the pie. It tasted like soap. The Monday following, teacher saw her in the hall before class and asked her how the poor family had enjoyed the pie.

"They liked it a whole lot," Francie told her. Then when she saw Teacher there looking so interested, she embellished the story. "This family has two little girls with golden curls and big blue eyes."

"And?" prompted Teacher.

"And...and...they're twins."

"How interesting."

Francie was inspired. "One of them has the name Pamela and the other Camilla." (These were names that Francie had once chosen for her non-existent dolls.)

"And they are very, very poor," suggested Teacher.

"Oh, very poor. They didn't have anything to eat for three days and just would have died, the doctor said, if I didn't bring them that pie."

"That was such a tiny pie," commented Teacher gently, "to save two lives."

Francie knew then that she had gone too far. She hated whatever that thing was inside her that made her invent such whoppers. Teacher bent down and put her arms around Francie. Francie saw that there were tears in her eyes. Francie went to pieces and remorse rose in her like bitter flood waters.

"That's all a big lie," she confessed. "I ate the pie myself."

"I know you did."

"Don't send a letter home," begged Francie, thinking of the address she didn't own. "I'll stay after school every day for ..."

"I'll not punish you for having an imagination."

Gently, Teacher explained the difference between a lie and a story. A lie was something you told because you were mean or a coward. A story was something you made up out of something that might have happened. Only you didn't tell it like it was: you told it like you thought it should have been.

As Teacher talked, a great trouble left Francie. Lately, she had been given to exaggerating things. She did not report happenings truthfully, but gave them colour, excitement and dramatic twists. Katie was annoyed at this tendency and kept warning Francie to tell the plain truth and to stop romancing. But Francie just couldn't tell the plain undecorated truth. She had to put something to it.

Although Katie had this same flair for colouring an incident and Johnny himself lived in a half-dream world, yet they tried to squelch these things in their child. Maybe they had a good reason. Maybe they knew their own gift of imagination coloured too rosily the poverty and brutality of their lives and made them able to endure it. Perhaps Katie thought that if they did not have this faculty, they would be clearer-minded; see things as they really were, and seeing them loathe them and somehow find a way to make them better.

Francie always remembered what that kind teacher told her. "You know, Francie, a lot of people would think that these stories that you're making up all the time were terrible lies because they are not the truth as people see the truth. In the future, when something comes up, you *tell* exactly what happened but *write down for yourself the way you think it should have happened. Tell* the truth and *write* the story. Then you won't get mixed up."

It was the best advice Francie ever got. Truth and fancy were so mixed up in her mind—as they are in the mind of every lonely child—that she didn't know which was which. But Teacher made these two things clear to her. From that time on, she wrote little stories about things she saw and felt and did. In time, she got so that she was able to speak the truth with but a slight and instinctive colouring of the facts.

Francie was ten years old when she first found an outlet in writing. What she wrote was of little consequence. What was important was that the attempt to write stories kept her straight on the dividing line between truth and fiction.

If she had not found this outlet in writing, she might have grown up to be a tremendous liar.

XXVII

CHRISTMAS WAS a charmed time in Brooklyn. It was in the air,
long before it came. The first hint of it was Mr. Morton going
around the schools teaching Christmas carols, but the first sure
sign was the store windows.

You have to be a child to know how wonderful is a store
window filled with dolls and sleds and other toys. And this
wonder came free to Francie. It was nearly as good as actually
having the toys to be permitted to look at them through the
glass window.

Oh, what a thrill there was for Francie when she turned a
street corner and saw another store all fixed up for Christmas!
Ah, the clean shining window with cotton batting sprinkled
with star dust for a carpet! There were flaxen-haired dolls and
others which Francie liked better who had hair the colour of
good coffee with lots of cream in it. Their faces were perfectly
tinted and they wore clothes the like of which Francie had
never seen on earth. The dolls stood upright in flimsy cardboard boxes. They stood with the help of a bit of tape passed
around the neck and ankles and through holes at the back of
the box. Oh, the deep blue eyes framed by thick lashes that
stared straight into a little girl's heart and the perfect miniature hands extended, appealingly asking: "Please, won't you
be my mama?" And Francie had never had a doll except a
two-inch one that cost a nickel.

And the sleds! (Or, as the Williamsburg children called
them, the sleighs.) There was a child's dream of heaven come
true! A new sled with a flower someone had dreamed up
painted on it—a deep blue flower with bright green leaves—
the ebony-black painted runners, the smooth steering bar
made of hard wood and gleaming varnish over all! And the
names painted on them! "Rosebud!" "Magnolia!" "Snow
King" "The Flyer!" Thought Francie, "If I could only have
one of those, I'd never ask God for another thing as long as I
live."

There were roller skates made of shining nickel straps of
good brown leather and silvered nervous wheels, tensed for
rolling, needing but a breath to start them turning, as they lay
crossed one over the other, sprinkled with mica snow on a bed
of cloud-like cotton.

There were other marvellous things. Francie couldn't take
them all in. Her head spun and she was dizzy with the impact

of all the seeing and all the making up of stories about the toys in the shop windows.

The spruce trees began coming into the neighbourhood the week before Christmas. Their branches were corded to hold back the glory of their spreading and probably to make shipping easier. Vendors rented space on the kerb before a store and stretched a rope from pole to pole and leaned the trees against it. All day they walked up and down this one-sided avenue of aromatic leaning trees, blowing on stiff ungloved fingers and looking with bleak hope at those people who paused. A few ordered a tree set aside for the day; others stopped to price, inspect and conjecture. But most came just to touch the boughs and surreptitiously pinch a fingerful of spruce needles together to release the fragrance. And the air was cold and still, and full of the pine smell and the smell of tangerines, which appeared in the stores only at Christmas-time and the mean street was truly wonderful for a little while.

There was a cruel custom in the neighbourhood. It was about the trees still unsold when midnight of Christmas Eve approached. There was a saying that if you waited until then, you wouldn't have to buy a tree; that "they'd chuck 'em at you." This was literally true.

At midnight on the Eve of our dear Saviour's birth, the kids gathered where there were unsold trees. The man threw each tree in turn, starting with the biggest. Kids volunteered to stand up against the throwing. If a boy didn't fall down under the impact, the tree was his. If he fell, he forfeited his chance at winning a tree. Only the roughest boys and some of the young men elected to be hit by the big trees. The others waited shrewdly until a tree came up that they could stand against. The littlest kids waited for the tiny, foot-high trees and shrieked in delight when they won one.

On the Christmas Eve when Francie was ten and Neeley nine, mama consented to let them go down and have their first try for a tree. Francie had picked out her tree earlier in the day. She had stood near it all afternoon and evening praying that no one would buy it. To her joy, it was still there at midnight. It was the biggest tree in the neighbourhood and its price was so high that no one could afford to buy it. It was ten feet high. Its branches were wound with new white rope and it came to a sure point at the top.

The man took this tree out first. Before Francie could speak up, a neighbourhood bully, a boy of eighteen known as Punky Perkins, stepped forward and ordered the man to chuck the tree at him. The man hated the way Punky was so confident. He looked around and asked:

"Anybody else wanna take a chance on it?"

Francie stepped forward. "Me, Mister."

A spurt of derisive laughter came from the tree man. The kids snickered. A few adults, who had gathered to watch the fun, guffawed.

"Aw g'wan. You're too little," the tree man objected.

"Me and my brother—we're not too little together."

She pulled Neeley forward. The man looked at them—a thin girl of ten with starveling hollows in her cheeks but with the chin still baby-round. He looked at the little boy with his fair hair and round blue eyes—Neeley Nolan, all innocence and trust.

"Two ain't fair," yelped Punky.

"Shut your lousy trap," advised the man who held all power in that hour. "Those here kids is got nerve. Stand back, the rest of youse. These kids is goin' to have a show at this tree."

The others made a wavering lane. Francie and Neeley stood at one end of it and the big man with the big tree at the other. It was a human funnel with Francie and her brother making the small end of it. The man flexed his great arms to throw the great tree. He noticed how tiny the children looked at the end of the short lane. For a split part of a moment, the tree-thrower went through a kind of gethsemane.

"Oh, Jesus Christ," his soul agonized, "why don't I just give 'em the tree, say 'Merry Christmas' and let 'em go? What's the tree to me? I can't sell it no more this year and it won't keep till next year." The kids watched him solemnly as he stood there in his moment of thought. "But then," he rationalized, "if I did that, all the others would expect to get 'em handed to 'em. And next year, nobody a-tall would buy a tree off of me. They'd all wait to get 'em handed to 'em on a silver plate. I ain't a big enough man to give this tree away for nothin'. No, I ain't big enough. I ain't big enough to do a thing like that. I gotta think of myself and my own kids." He finally came to his conclusion. "Oh, what the hell! Them kids is gotta live in this world. They *got* to get used to it. They got to learn to give and to take punishment. And by Jesus, it ain't *give* but *take, take, take* all the time in this God-damned world." As he threw the tree with all his strength, his heart wailed out: "It's a God-damned, rotten, lousy world."

Francie saw the tree leave his hands. There was a split bit of being when time and space had no meaning. The whole world stood still as something dark and monstrous came through the air. The tree came towards her, blotting out all memory of her ever having lived. There was nothing—nothing but pungent darkness and something that grew as it rushed at her. She staggered as the tree hit them. Neeley went to his knees, but she pulled him up fiercely before he could go down. There was a mighty swishing sound as the tree settled. Everything was dark, green and prickly. Then she felt a sharp pain at the side of her head where the trunk of the tree had hit her. She felt Neeley trembling.

When some of the older boys pulled the tree away, they found Francie and her brother standing upright, hand in hand. Blood was coming from scratches on Neeley's face. He looked more like a baby than ever with his bewildered blue eyes and the fairness of his skin made more noticeable because of the clear red blood. But they were smiling. Had they not won the biggest tree in the neighbourhood? Some of the boys hollered "Hooray!" A few adults clapped. The tree man eulogized them by screaming.

"And now get the hell out of here with your tree, you lousy bastards."

Francie had heard swearing since she had heard words. Obscenity and profanity had no meaning as such among those people. They were emotional expressions of inarticulate people with small vocabularies; they made a kind of dialect. The phrases could mean many things according to the expression and tone used in saying them. So now, when Francie heard themselves called lousy bastards, she smiled tremulously at the kind man. She knew that he was really saying: "Goodbye—God bless you."

It wasn't easy dragging that tree home. They had to pull it inch by inch. They were handicapped by a boy who ran alongside yelping: "Free ride! All aboard!" who'd jump on and make them drag him along. But he got sick of the game eventually and went away.

In a way, it was good that it took them so long to get the tree home. It made their triumph more drawn out. Francie glowed when she heard a lady say: "I never saw such a big

163

tree!" A man called after them: "You kids musta robbed a bank to buy such a big tree." The cop on their corner stopped them, examined the tree and solemnly offered to buy it for ten cents—fifteen cents if they'd deliver it to his home. Francie nearly burst with pride, although she knew he was joking. She said she wouldn't sell it for a dollar, even. He shook his head and said she was foolish not to grab the offer. He went up to a quarter, but Francie kept smiling and shaking her head, "No."

It was like acting in a Christmas play where the setting was a street corner and the time, a frosty Christmas Eve and the characters, a kind cop, her brother and herself. Francie knew all the dialogue. The cop gave his lines and Francie picked up her cues happily and the stage directions were the smiles between the spoken lines.

They had to call up to papa to help them get the tree up the narrow stairs. Papa came running down. To Francie's relief, he ran down straight and not sidewise, which proved that he was still sober.

Papa's amazement at the size of the tree was flattering. He pretended to believe that it wasn't theirs. Francie had a lot of fun convincing him, although she knew all the while that the whole thing was make-believe. Papa pulled in front and Francie and Neeley pushed in back and they began forcing the big tree up the three narrow flights of stairs. Johnny was so excited that he started singing, not caring that it was rather late at night. He sang "Holy Night." The narrow walls took up his clear sweet voice, held it for a breath and gave it back with doubled sweetness. Doors creaked open and families gathered on the landings, pleased and amazed at the something unexpected being added to that moment of their lives.

Francie saw the Tynmore girls standing together in their doorway, their grey hair in crimpers, and ruffled, starched nightgowns showing under their voluminous wrappers. They added their thin poignant voices to Johnny's. Floss Gaddis, her mother and her brother, Henny, who was dying of consumption, stood in their doorway. Henny was crying and when Johnny saw him he let the song trail off; he thought maybe it made Henny too sad.

Flossie was in costume waiting for an escort to take her to a masquerade ball which started soon after midnight. She stood there in her Klondike-dance-hall-girl costume with sheer black silk stockings, spool-heeled slippers, one red garter fastened under a knee and swinging a black mask in her hand. She smiled into Johnny's eyes. She put her hand on her hip and leaned seductively—or so she thought—against the door jamb. More to make Henny smile than anything else, Johnny said:

"Floss, we got no angel for the top of this Christmas tree. How about you obliging?"

Floss was all ready to make a dirty reply about the wind blowing her drawers off if she was up that high. But she changed her mind. There was something about the big proud tree, now so humble in its being dragged; something about the beaming children; something about the rare good will of the neighbours and the way the lights looked turned low in the halls, that made her ashamed of her unspoken reply. All she said was:

"Gee, ain't you the kidder, Johnny Nolan."

Katie stood alone on the top of the last flight of steps with her hands clasped before her. She listened to the singing. She looked down and watched their slow progress up the stairs. She was thinking deeply.

"They think this is so good," she thought. "They think it's good—the tree they got for nothing and their father playing up to them and the singing and the way the neighbours are happy. They think they're mighty lucky that they're living and that it's Christmas again. They can't see that we live on a dirty street in a dirty house among people who aren't much good. Johnny and the children can't see how pitiful it is that our neighbours have to make happiness out of this filth and dirt. My children must get out of this. They must come to more than Johnny or me or all these people around us. But how is this to come about? Reading a page from those books every day and saving pennies in the tincan bank isn't enough. Money! Would that make it better for them? Yes, it would make it easy. But no, the money wouldn't be enough. McGarrity owns the saloon standing on the corner and he has a lot of money. His wife wears diamond ear-rings. But her children are not as good and smart as my children. They are mean and greedy towards others because they have the things to taunt poor children with. I have seen the McGarrity girl eating from a bag of candy on the street while a ring of hungry children watched her. I saw those children looking at her and crying in their hearts. And when she couldn't eat any more, she threw the rest down the sewer rather than give it to them. Ah, no, it

165

isn't the money alone. The McGarrity girl wears a different hair-bow each day and they cost fifty cents apiece and that would feed the four of us here for one day. But her hair is thin and pale red. My Neeley has a big hole in his zitful cap and it's stretched out of shape, but he has thick, deep golden hair that curls. My Francie wears no hair-bow but her hair is long and shining. Can money buy things like that? No. That means there must be something bigger than money. Miss Jackson teaches at the Settlement House and she has no money. She works for charity. She lives in a little room there on the top floor. She only has the one dress but she keeps it clean and pressed. Her eyes look straight into yours when you talk with her. When you listen to her, it's like you used to be sick but hearing her voice, it's making you well again. She knows about things—Miss Jackson. She understands about things. She can live in the middle of a dirty neighbourhood and be fine and clean and like an actress in a play; someone you can look at but who is too fine to touch. That is the difference between her and Mrs. McGarrity, who has so much money but is too fat and acts in a dirty way with the truck-drivers who deliver her husband's beer. So what is this difference between her and this Miss Jackson who has no money?"

An answer came to Katie. It was so simple that a flash of astonishment that felt like a pain shot through her head. Education! That was it! It was education that made the difference! Education would pull them out of the grime and dirt. Proof? Miss Jackson was educated, the McGarrity wasn't. Ah! That's what Mary Rommely, her mother, had been telling her all those years. Only her mother did not have the one clear word: education!

Watching the children struggling up the stairs with their tree, listening to their voices, still so baby-like, she got these ideas about education.

"Francie is smart," she thought. "She must go to High School and maybe beyond that. She's a learner and she'll be somebody some day. But when she gets educated, she will grow away from me. Why, she's growing away from me now. She does not love me the way the boy loves me. I feel her turn away from me. She does not understand me. All she understands is that I don't understand her. Maybe when she gets education she will be ashamed of me—the way I talk. But she will have too much character to show it. Instead she will try to make me different. She will come to see me and try to make

166

me live in a better way and I will be mean to her because I'll know she's above me. She will figure out too much about things as she grows older; she'll get to know too much for her own happiness. She'll find out that I don't love her as much as I love the boy. I cannot help it that this is so. But she won't understand that. Sometimes I think she knows that now. Already she is growing away from me; she will fight to get away soon. Changing over to that far-away school was the first step in her getting away from me. But Neeley will never leave me, that is why I love him best. He will cling to me and understand me. I want him to be a doctor. He *must* be a doctor. Maybe he will play the fiddle, too. There is music in him. He got that from his father. He has gone further on the piano than Francie or me. Yes, his father has the music in him, but it does him no good. It is ruining him. If he couldn't sing, those men who treat him to drinks wouldn't want him around. What good is the fine way he can sing when it doesn't make him or us any better? With the boy, it will be different. He'll be educated. I must think out ways. We'll not have Johnny with us long. Dear God, I loved him so much once— and sometimes I still do. But he's worthless . . . worthless. And God forgive me for ever finding it out."

Thus Katie figured out everything in the moment it took them to climb the stairs. People looked up at her—at her smooth pretty vivacious face—had no way of knowing about the painfully articulated resolves formulating in her mind.

They set the tree up in the front room after spreading a sheet to protect the carpet of pink roses from falling pine needles. The tree stood in a big tin bucket with broken bricks to hold it upright. When the rope was cut away, the branches spread out to fill the whole room. They draped over the piano and it was so that some of the chairs stood among the branches. There was no money to buy tree decorations or lights. But the great tree standing there was enough. The room was cold. It was a poor year, that one—too poor for them to buy the extra coal for the front-room stove. The room smelled cold and clean and aromatic. Every day, during the week the tree stood there, Francie put on her sweater and zitful cap and went in and sat under the tree. She sat there and enjoyed the smell and the dark greenness of it.

Oh, the mystery of a great tree, a prisoner in a tin wash bucket in a tenement front room!

Poor as they were that year, it was a very nice Christmas and the children did not lack for gifts. Mama gave each of them a pair of long woollen drawers, drop seat style, and a woollen shirt with long sleeves and itchy insides. Aunt Evy gave them a joint present: a box of dominoes. Papa showed them how to play. Neeley didn't like the game, so papa and Francie played together and he pretended to be disgusted when he lost.

Grandma Mary Rommely brought over something very nice that she had made herself. She brought each a scapular. To make it, she cut two small ovals of bright red wool. On the one she embroidered a cross of bright blue yarn and on the other a golden heart crowned with brown thorns. A black dagger went through the heart and two drops of deep red blood dripped from the dagger point. The cross and heart were very tiny and made with microscopic stitches. The two ovals were stitched together and attached to a piece of corset string. Mary Rommely had taken the scapulars to be blessed by the priest before she brought them over. As she slipped the scapular over Francie's head, she said, "*Heiliges Weibnachten.*" Then she added, "May you walk with the angels always."

Aunt Sissy gave Francie a tiny package. She opened it and found a tiny matchbox. It was very fragile and covered with crinkly paper and a miniature spray of purple wisteria painted on the top. Francie pushed the box open. It held ten discs individually wrapped in pink tissue. The discs turned out to be bright golden pennies. Sissy explained that she had bought a bit of gold paint powder, mixed it with a few drops of banana oil and had gilded each penny. Francie loved Sissy's present the best of all. A dozen times within the hour of receiving it, she slid open the box slowly, gaining great pleasure from holding the box and looking at it and watching the cobalt-blue paper and the clean wafer-thin wood of the inside of the box appear. The golden pennies wrapped in the dream-like tissue were a never-tiring miracle. Everyone agreed that the pennies were too beautiful to be spent. During the day, Francie lost two of her pennies somewhere. Mama suggested they'd be safest in the tin-can bank. She promised that Francie could have them back when the bank was opened. Francie was sure that Mama was right about the pennies being safest in the bank, yet it was a wrench to let those golden pennies drop down into the darkness.

*   *   *

Papa had a special present for Francie. It was a postcard with a church on it. Powdered isinglass was pasted on the roof and it glistened more brightly than real snow. The church window-panes were made of tiny squares of shiny orange paper. The magic in this card was that when Francie held it up, light streamed through the paper panes and threw golden shadows on the glistening snow. It was a beautiful thing. Mama said that since it wasn't written on, Francie could save it for next year and mail it to someone.

"Oh, no," said Francie. She put both hands over the card and held it to her chest.

Mama laughed. "You must learn to take a joke, Francie, otherwise life will be pretty hard on you."

"Christmas is no day for lessons," said papa.

"But it is a day for getting drunk, isn't it?" she flared up.

"Two drinks is all I had, Katie," Johnny pleaded. "I was treated for Christmas."

Francie went into the bedroom and shut the door. She couldn't bear to hear mama scolding papa.

Just before supper, Francie distributed the gifts she had for them. She had a hat-pin holder for mama. She had made it with a penny test tube brought at Knipe's drug store. She had covered it with a sheath of blue satin ribbon ruffled at the sides. A length of baby ribbon was sewn to the top. It was meant to hang on the side of the dresser and hold hat-pins.

She had a watch-fob for papa. She had made it on a spool which had four nails driven into the top. It took two shoe-laces. These were worked over and around the nails and a thick braided fob kept growing out of the bottom of the spool as she worked it. Johnny had no watch but he took an iron tap-washer, attached the fob to it and wore it in his vest pocket all day pretending it was a watch. Francie had a very fine present for Neeley: a five-cent shooter which looked like an over-size opal rather than a marble. Neeley had a boxful of "miggies," small brown marbles made of clay which cost a penny for twenty. But he had no good shooter and couldn't get into any important games. Francie watched him as he crooked his forefinger and cradled the marble in it with his thumb behind it. It looked nice and natural that way and she was glad she had got it for him rather than the nickel pop-gun she had first thought of buying.

Neeley shoved the marble in his pocket and announced that

he had presents, too. He ran into the bedroom, crawled under his cot and came out with a ticky bag. He thrust it at mama, saying: "You share them out." He stood in a corner. Mama opened the bag. There was a striped candy cane for each one. Mama went into ecstasies. She said it was the prettiest present she had ever had. She kissed Neeley three times. Francie tried very hard not to be jealous because mama made more fuss over Neeley's present than hers.

It was in that same week that Francie told another great lie. Aunt Evy brought over two tickets. Some Protestant organization was giving a celebration for the poor of all faiths. There would be a decorated Christmas tree on the stage, a Christmas play, carol singing and a gift for each child. Katie couldn't see it—Catholic children at a Protestant party! Evy urged tolerance. Mama finally gave in and Francie and Neeley went to the party.

It was in a large auditorium. The boys sat on one side and the girls on the other. The celebration was fine except that the play was religious and dull. After the play, church ladies went down the aisle and gave each child a gift. All the girls got checker boards and all the boys got lotto games. After a little more singing, a lady came out on the stage and announced a special surprise.

The surprise was a lovely little girl, exquisitely dressed, who came from the wings carrying a beautiful doll. The doll was a foot high, had real yellow hair and blue eyes that opened and shut with real eyelashes. The lady led the child forward and made a speech.

"This little girl is named Mary." Little Mary smiled and bowed. The little girls in the audience smiled up at her and some of the boys who were approaching adolescence whistled shrilly. "Mary's mother bought this doll and had clothes made for it just like the clothes little Mary is wearing."

Little Mary stepped forward and held the doll high in the air. Then she let the lady hold it while she spread her skirt and made a curtsey. It was true, saw Francie. The doll's lace-trimmed blue silk dress, pink hair bow, black patent leather slippers and white silk socks duplicated exactly the clothes of the beautiful Mary.

"Now," said the lady, "this doll is named Mary after the kind little girl who is giving her away." Again the little girl smiled graciously. "Mary wants to give the doll to some poor little girl in the audience who is named Mary." Like wind on growing corn a rippling murmur came from all the little girls in the audience. "Is there any poor little girl in the audience named Mary?"

There was a great hush. There were at least a hundred Marys in that audience. It was that adjective "poor" that struck them dumb. No Mary would stand up, no matter how much she wanted the doll, and be a symbol of all the poor little girls in the audience. They began whispering to each other that they weren't poor and had better dolls at home and better clothes than that girl, too, only they didn't feel like wearing them. Francie sat numb, longing for that doll with all her soul.

"What?" said the lady. "No Marys?" She waited and made her announcement again. No response. She spoke regretfully. "Too bad there are no Marys. Little Mary will have to take the doll home again." The little girl smiled and bowed and turned to leave the stage with the doll.

Francie couldn't stand it, she couldn't stand it. It was like when the teacher was going to throw the pumpkin pie in the wastebasket. She stood up and held her hand high in the air. The lady saw it and stopped the little girl from leaving the stage.

"Ah! We do have a Mary, a very bashful Mary, but a Mary just the same. Come right up on the stage, Mary."

Feverish with embarrassment, Francie walked up the long aisle and on to the stage. She stumbled on the steps and all the girls snickered and boys guffawed.

"What is your name?" asked the lady.

"Mary Frances Nolan," whispered Francie.

"Louder. And look at the audience."

Miserably, Francie faced the audience and said loudly: "Mary Frances Nolan." All the faces looked like bloated balloons on thick strings. She thought that if she kept on looking, the faces would float away up to the ceiling.

The beautiful girl came forward and put the doll in Francie's arms. Francie's arms took a natural curve around it. It was as if her arms had waited and grown so just for that doll. The beautiful Mary extended her hand for Francie to shake. In spite of embarrassment and confusion, Francie noticed the delicate white hand with the tracery of pale blue veins and the oval nails that glowed like delicate pink sea-shells.

The lady talked as Francie walked back awkwardly to her seat. She said: "You have all seen an example of the true

Christmas spirit. Little Mary is a very rich little girl and received many beautiful dolls for Christmas. But she was not selfish. She wanted to make some poor little Mary, who is not as fortunate as herself, happy. So she gave the doll to that poor little girl who is named Mary, too."

Francie's eyes smarted with hot tears. "Why can't they," she thought bitterly, "just give the doll away without saying I am poor and she is rich? Why couldn't they just give it away without all the talking about it?"

That was not all of Francie's shame. As she walked down the aisle, the girls leaned towards her and whispered hissingly: "Beggar! beggar! beggar!"

It was beggar, beggar, beggar, all the way down the aisle. Those girls felt richer than Francie. They were as poor as she, but they had something she lacked—pride. And Francie knew it. She had no compunctions about the lie and getting the doll under false pretences. She was paying for the lie and for the doll by giving up her pride.

She remembered the teacher who had told her to write her lies instead of speaking them. Maybe she shouldn't have gone up for the doll but should have written a story about it instead. But no! No! *Having* the doll was better than any story about having a doll. When they stood to sing the "Star-Spangled Banner" in closing, Francie put her face down close to the doll's face. There was the cool delicate smell of painted china, the wonderful unforgettable smell of a doll's hair, the heavenly feel of new-gauze doll's clothes. The doll's red eyelashes touched her cheek and she trembled in ecstasy. The children were singing:

> *O'er the land of the free,*
> *And the home of the brave.*

Francie held one of the doll's tiny hands tightly. A nerve in her thumb throbbed and she thought the doll's hand twitched She almost believed the doll was real.

She told mama the doll had been given her as a prize. She dared not tell the truth. Mama hated anything that smacked of charity and if she knew she'd throw the doll away. Neeley didn't snitch on her. Francie now owned the doll but had yet another lie on her soul. That afternoon she wrote a story about a little girl who wanted a dolly so much that she was willing to give over her immortal soul to Purgatory for eternity if she could have the doll. It was a strong story but when Francie read it over, she thought, "that's all right for the girl in the story but it doesn't make me feel any better."

She thought of the confession she would have to make the next Saturday. She resolved that no matter what penancy Father gave her, she would triple it voluntarily. Still she felt no better.

Then she remembered something! Maybe she could make the lie a truth! She knew that when Catholic children received Confirmation, they were expected to take some saint's name for a middle name. What a simple solution! She would take the name of Mary when she was confirmed.

That night, after the page from the Bible and the page from Shakespeare had been read, Francie consulted mama.

"Mama, when I make my Confirmation, can I take Mary for a middle name?"

"No."

Francie's heart sank. "Why?"

"Because when you were christened you were named Francie after Andy's girl."

"I know."

"But you were also named Mary after my mother. Your real name is Mary Frances Nolan."

Francie took the doll to bed with her. She lay very still so as not to disturb it. She woke up from time to time in the night and whispered "Mary" and touched the doll's infinitesimal slipper with a light finger. She trembled at feeling the thin soft bit of smooth leather.

It was to be her first and her last doll.

XXVIII

THE FUTURE was a near thing to Katie. She had a way of saying, "Christmas will be here before you know it." Or, at the beginning of vacation, "School will be starting up before you know it." In the spring when Francie discarded her long drawers and joyously flung them away, mama made her pick them up again saying, "You'll need them soon enough again. Winter will be here before you know it." What was mama talking about? Spring had just started. The winter would never come again.

A small child has little idea of the future. Next week is as far ahead as his future stretches and the year between Christmas and Christmas again is an eternity. So time was with Francie up until her eleventh year.

Between her eleventh and twelfth birthdays, things changed. The future came along quicker; the days seemed shorter and the weeks seemed to have less days in them. Henny Gaddis died and this had something to do with it. She had always heard that Henny was going to die. She heard about it so much that she finally got to believe he would die. But that would be a long, long time away. Now the long time away had come. The something which had been a future was now a present and would become a past. Francie wondered whether someone had to die to make that clear to a child. But no, Grandfather Rommely had died when she was nine, a week after she made her first Communion and as she remembered, Christmas still ha'd seemed far away at that time.

Things were changing so fast for Francie now that she got mixed up. Neeley, who was a year younger than she, grew suddenly and got to be a head taller. Maudie Donavan moved away. When she returned on a visit three months later, Francie found her different. Maudie had developed in a womanly way during those three months.

Francie, who *knew* mama was always right, found out that she was wrong once in a while. She discovered that some of the things she loved so much in her father were considered very comical to other people. The scales at the tea store did not shine so brightly any more and she found the bins were chipped and shabby-looking.

She stopped watching for Mr. Tomony to come home on Saturday nights from his New York jaunts. All of a sudden she thought it was silly that he lived so and went to New York and came home longing for where he had been. He had money. Why didn't he just go over to New York and live there if he liked it so much?

Everything was changing. Francie was in a panic. Her world was slipping away from her and what would take its place? *Still, what was different anyhow?* She read a page from the Bible and Shakespeare every night the same as always. She practised the piano every day for an hour. She put pennies in the tin-can bank. The junk shop was still there; the stores were all the same. Nothing was changing. *She was the one who was changing.*

She told papa about it. He made her stick out her tongue and he felt her wrist. He shook his head sadly and said:

"You have a bad case, a very bad case."

"Of what?"

"Growing-up."

Growing up spoiled a lot of things. It spoiled the nice game they had when there was nothing to eat in the house. When money gave out and food ran low, Katie and the children pretended they were explorers discovering the North Pole and had been trapped by a blizzard in a cave with just a little food. They had to make it last till help came. Mama divided up what food there was in the cupboard and called it rations and when the children were still hungry after a meal, she'd say: "Courage, my men, help will come soon." When some money came in and mama bought a lot of groceries, she bought a little cake as celebration, and she'd stick a penny flag in it and say: "We made it, men. We got to the North Pole."

One day after one of those "rescues" Francie asked mama:

"When explorers get hungry and suffer like this, it's for a *reason*. Something big comes out of it. They discover the North Pole. But what big thing comes out of us being hungry like that?"

Katie looked tired all of a sudden. She said something Francie didn't understand at the time. She said: "You found the catch in it."

Growing up spoiled the theatre for Francie—well, not the theatre exactly, but the plays. She found she was becoming dissatisfied with the way things just happened in the nick of time.

Francie loved the theatre dearly. She had once wanted to be a hand-organ lady, then a school teacher. After her first Communion, she wanted to be a nun. At eleven, she wanted to be an actress.

If the Williamsburg kids knew nothing else, they knew their theatre. In those days, there were many good stock companies in the neighbourhood: Blaney's, Corse Payton's and Phillip's Lyceum. The Lyceum was just around the corner. Local residents called it first "The Lyce," and then changed that into "The Louse." Francie went there every Saturday afternoon (except when it was closed for the summer) when she could

175

scrape up a dime. She sat in the gallery and often waited in line an hour before the show opened in order to get a seat in the first row.

She was in love with Harold Clarence, the leading man. She waited at the stage door after the Saturday matinee and followed him to the shabby brown-stone house where he lived untheatrically in a modest furnished room. Even on the street he had the stiff-legged walk of the old-time actor and his face was baby pink as though he still had juvenile 2 grease-paint on it. He walked stiff-leggedly and leisurely, looking neither to right nor left and smoking an important-looking cigar which he threw away before he entered the house, as his landlady did not permit the great man to smoke in her rooms. Francie stood at the kerb, looking down reverently at the discarded butt. She took the paper ring off it and wore it for a week, pretending it was his engagement ring to her.

One Saturday, Harold and his company put on *The Minister's Sweetheart*, in which the handsome village minister was in love with Gerry Morehouse, the leading lady. Somehow, the heroine had to seek work in a grocery store. There was a villainess, also in love with the handsome young minister, and out to get the heroine. She swaggered into the store in her un-village-like furs and diamonds and regally ordered a pound of coffee. There was a dreadful moment when she uttered the fatal words: "Grind it!" The audience groaned. It had been planted that the delicate beautiful heroine wasn't strong enough to turn the great wheel. It had also been planted that her job was contingent on her being able to grind coffee. She struggled like anything but couldn't get the wheel to go round even once. She pleaded with the villainess; told her how much she needed the job. The villainess repeated, "Grind it!" When all seemed lost, Handsome Harold entered with his pink face and his clerical garb. Taking in the situation, he threw his wide minister's hat clear across the stage in a dramatic but unseemly gesture, stepped stiff-leggedly to the machine and ground the coffee and thus saved the heroine. There was an awed silence as the odour of freshly-ground coffee permeated the theatre. Then bedlam broke loose. Real coffee! Realism in the theatre! Everyone had seen coffee ground a thousand times, but on the stage it was a revolutionary thing. The villainess gnashed her teeth, and said: "Foiled again!" Harold embraced Gerry, making her face up-stage, and the curtain came down.

During intermission, Francie did not join the other kids in the interim pastime of spitting down on the plutocrats in the thirty-cent orchestra seats. Instead, she pondered over the situation at curtain. All very well and good that the hero came in the nick of time to grind the coffee. If he hadn't dropped in, what then? The heroine would have been discharged. All right and so what? After she got hungry enough she'd go out and find another job. She'd go out scrubbing floors like mama or graft chop suey off of her men friends like Floss Gaddis did. The grocery store job was important only because it said so in the play.

She wasn't satisfied with the play she saw the following Saturday, either. All right. The long-lost lover came home just in time to pay the mortgage. What if he had been held up and couldn't make it? The landlord would have to give them thirty days to get out—at least that's how it was in Brooklyn. In that month something might turn up. If it didn't and they had to get out, well, they'd have to make the best of it. The pretty heroine would have to get on piecework in the factory, her sensitive brother would have to go out peddling papers. The mother would have to do cleaning by the day. But they'd live. You betcha they'd live, thought Francie grimly. It takes a lot of doing to die.

Francie couldn't understand why the heroine didn't marry the villain. It would solve the rent problem and surely a man who loved her so much that he was willing to go through all kinds of fuss because she wouldn't have him, wasn't a man to ignore. At least, he was around while the hero was off on a wild-goose chase.

She wrote her own third act to that play—what would happen *if*. She wrote it out in conversation and found it a remarkably easy way of writing. In a story you had to explain why people were the way they were, but when you wrote in conversation you didn't have to do that because the things the people said explained what they were. Francie had no trouble selling herself on dialogue. Once more she changed her mind about what profession she'd follow. She decided she wouldn't be an actress after all. She'd be a writer of plays.

XXIX

IN THE summer of that same year, Johnny got the notion that the children were growing up ignorant of the great ocean that washed the shores of Brooklyn. Johnny felt that they ought to go out to sea in a ship. So he decided to take them for a rowboat ride at Canarsie and do a little deep-sea fishing on the side. He had never gone fishing and he'd never been in a rowboat. But that's the idea he got.

Weirdly tied up with this idea, and by a reasoning process known only to Johnny, was the idea of taking Little Tilly along on the trip. Little Tilly was the four-year-old child of neighbours whom he had never met. In fact, he had never seen Little Tilly, but he got this idea that he had to make something up to her on account of her brother Gussie. It all tied up with the notion of going to Canarsie.

Gussie, a boy of six, was a murky legend in the neighbourhood. A tough little hellion, with an over-developed underlip, he had been born like other babies and nursed at his mother's great breasts. But there, all resemblance to any child, living or dead, ceased. His mother tried to wean him when he was nine months old, but Gussie wouldn't stand for it. Denied the breast, he refused a bottle, food or water. He lay in his crib and whimpered. His mother, fearful that he would starve, resumed nursing him. He sucked contentedly, refusing all other food, and lived off his mother's milk until he was nearly two years old. The milk stopped then because his mother was with child again. Gussie sulked and bided his time for nine long months. He refused cow's milk in any form or container and took to drinking black coffee.

Little Tilly was born and the mother flowed with milk again. Gussie went into hysterics the first time he saw the baby nursing. He lay on the floor, screaming and banging his head. He wouldn't eat for four days and he refused to go to the toilet. He got haggard and his mother got frightened. She thought it wouldn't do any harm to give him the breast just once. That was her big mistake. He was like a dope fiend getting the stuff after a long period of deprivation. He wouldn't let go.

He took all of his mother's milk from that time on and Little Tilly, a sickly baby, had to go on the bottle.

Gussie was three years old at this time and big for his age.

Like other boys, he wore knee pants and heavy shoes with brass toe-tips. As soon as he saw his mother unbutton her dress, he ran to her. He stood up while nursing, an elbow on his mother's knee, his feet crossed jauntily and his eyes roving around the room. Standing to nurse was not such a remarkable feat, as his mother's breasts were mountainous and practically rested in her lap when released. Gussie was indeed a fearful sight nursing that way and he looked not unlike a man with his foot on a bar rail, smoking a fat pale cigar.

The neighbours found out about Gussie and discussed his pathological state in hushed whispers. Gussie's father got so that he wouldn't sleep with his wife; he said that she bred monsters. The poor woman figured and figured on a way to wean Gussie. He was too big to nurse, she decided. He was going on for four. She was afraid his second teeth wouldn't come in straight.

One day she took a can of stove blackening and the brush and closed herself in the bedroom, where she copiously blackened her left breast with the stove polish. With a lipstick she drew a wide ugly mouth with frightening teeth in the vicinity of the nipple. She buttoned her dress and went into the kitchen and sat in her nursing rocker near the window. When Gussie saw her, he threw the dice, with which he had been playing, under the wash-tubs and trotted over for feeding. He crossed his feet, planted his elbows on her knee and waited.

"Gussie want tiddy?" asked his mother wheedlingly.

"Yup!"

"All right. Gussie's gonna get nice tiddy."

Suddenly she ripped open her dress and thrust the horribly made-up breast into his face. Gussie was paralysed with fright for a moment, then he ran away screaming and hid under the bed, where he stayed for twenty-four hours. He came out at last, trembling. He went back to drinking black coffee and shuddered every time his eyes went to his mother's bosom. Gussie was weaned.

The mother reported her success all over the neighbourhood. It started a new fashion in weaning called: "Giving the baby the Gussie."

Johnny heard the story and contemptuously dismissed Gussie from his mind. He was concerned about Little Tilly. He thought she had been cheated out of something very important and might grow up thwarted. He got a notion that a boat ride off the Canarsie shore might wipe out some of the wrong her unnatural brother had done her. He sent Francie around to ask could Little Tilly go with them. The harassed mother consented happily.

The next Sunday, Johnny and the three children set out for Canarsie. Francie was eleven years old, Neeley ten and Little Tilly well past three. Johnny wore his tuxedo and derby and a fresh collar and dicky. Francie and Neeley wore their everyday clothes. Little Tilly's mother, in honour of the day, had dressed her up in a cheap but fancy lace dress trimmed with dark pink ribbon.

On the trolley ride out, they sat in the front seat and Johnny made friends with the motor-man and they talked politics. They got off at the last stop, which was Canarsie, and found their way to a little wharf on which was a tiny shack; a couple of waterlogged rowboats bobbed up and down on the frayed ropes which held them to the wharf. A sign over the shack read:

"Fishing tackle and boats for rent."

Underneath was a bigger sign which said:

FRESH FISH TO TAKE HOME FOR SALE HERE.

Johnny negotiated with the man and, as was his way, made a friend of him. The man invited him into the shack for an eyeopener, saying that he himself only used the stuff for a nightcap.

While Johnny was inside getting his eyes opened, Neeley and Francie pondered how a nightcap could also be an eyeopener. Little Tilly stood there in her lace dress and said nothing.

Johnny came out with a fishing pole and a rusty tin can filled with worms in mud. The friendly man untied the rope from the least sorry of the rowboats, put the rope in Johnny's hand, wished him luck and went back to his shack.

Johnny put the fishing stuff in the bottom of the boat and helped the children in. Then he crouched on the wharf, the bit of rope in his hand, and gave instructions about boats.

"There is always a wrong and a right way to get on a boat," said Johnny, who had never been on any boat except an excursion boat once. "The right way is to give the boat a shove and then jump for it before it drifts out to sea. Like this."

He straightened up, pushed the boat from him, leaped ... and fell into the water. The petrified children stared at him. A second before, papa had been standing on the dock above them. Now he was below them in the water. The water came to his neck and his small waxed moustache and derby hat were in the clear. His derby was still straight on his forehead. Johnny, as surprised as the children, stared at them a moment before he said:

"Don't any of you damned kids dare to laugh!"

He climbed into the boat, almost upsetting it. They didn't dare laugh aloud, but Francie laughed so hard inside that her ribs hurt. Neeley was afraid to look at his sister. He knew that if their eyes met he'd burst out laughing. Little Tilly said nothing. Johnny's collar and dicky were a sodden paperish mess. He stripped them off and threw them overboard. He rowed out to sea waveringly, but with silent dignity. When he came to what he thought was a likely spot, he announced that he was going to "drop anchor." The children were disappointed when they discovered that the romantic phrase simply meant that you threw a lump of iron attached to a rope overboard.

Horrified, they watched papa squeamishly impale a muddy worm on the hook. The fishing started. It consisted in baiting the hook, casting it dramatically, waiting a while, pulling it up minus the worm and fish and starting the whole thing over again.

The sun grew bright and hot. Johnny's tuxedo dried to a stiff wrinkled greenish outfit. The children started to get a whopping case of sunburn. After what seemed hours papa announced, to their intense relief and happiness, that it was time to eat. He wound up the tackle, put it away, pulled up the anchor and made for the wharf. The boat seemed to go in a circle which made the wharf get further away. Finally they made shore a few hundred yards further down. Johnny tied up the boat, told the children to wait in it and went ashore. He said he was going to treat them to a nice lunch.

He came back after a while walking sideways, carrying hot dogs, huckleberry pie and strawberry pop. They sat in the rocking boat tied to the rotting wharf, looked down into the slimy green water that smelled of decaying fish, and ate. Johnny had had a few drinks ashore, which made him sorry that he had hollered at the kids. He told them they could laugh at his falling into the water if they wanted to. But somehow, they couldn't bring up a laugh. The time was past for that. Papa was very cheerful, Francie thought.

"This is the life," he said. "Away from the maddening crowd. Ah, there's nothing like going down to the sea in a ship. We're getting away from it all," he ended up cryptically.

After their amazing lunch, Johnny rowed them out to sea again. Perspiration poured down from under his derby and the wax in the points of his moustache melted, causing his neat adornment to change into disorganized hair on his upper lip. He felt fine. He sang lustily as he rowed:

Sailing, sailing, over the bounding main.

He rowed and rowed and kept going around in a circle and never did get out to sea. Eventually his hands got so blistered that he didn't feel like rowing any more. Dramatically he announced that he was going to pull for the shore. He pulled and pulled and finally made it by rowing in smaller and smaller circles and making the circles come nearer the wharf. He never noticed that the three children were pea-green in the spots where they were not beet-red from the sunburn. If he had only known it, the hot dogs, huckleberry pie, strawberry pop and worms squirming on the hook weren't doing them much good.

At the wharf, he leaped to the dock and the children followed his example. All made it excepting Tilly, who fell into the water. Johnny threw himself flat on the dock, reached in and fished her out. Little Tilly stood there, her lace dress wet and ruined, but she said nothing. Although it was a broiling hot day, Johnny peeled off his tuxedo jacket, kneeled down and wrapped it around the child. The arms dragged in the sand. Then Johnny took her up in his arms and strode up and down the dock patting her back soothingly and singing her a lullaby. Little Tilly didn't understand a thing of all that had happened that day. She didn't understand why she had been put into a boat, why she had fallen into the water or why the man was making such a fuss over her. She said nothing.

When Johnny felt that she was comforted, he set her down and went into the shack, where he had either an eye-opener or a nightcap. He bought three flounders from the man for a quarter. He came out with the wet fish wrapped in a newspaper. He told his children that he had promised to bring home some fresh-caught fish to mama.

"The principal thing," said papa, "is that I am bringing home fish that were caught at Canarsie. It makes no difference who caught them. The point is that we went fishing and we're bringing home fish."

His children knew that he wanted mama to think he caught

the fish. Papa didn't ask them to lie. He just asked them not to be too fussy about the truth. The children understood.

They boarded one of those trolley cars that had two long benches facing each other. They made a queer row. First there was Johnny in green wrinkled salt-stiff trousers, an undershirt full of big holes, a derby hat and a disorderly moustache. Next came Little Tilly swallowed up in his coat and salt water dripping from under it and forming a brackish pool on the floor. Francie and Neeley came next. Their faces were brick-red and they sat very rigid, trying not to be sick.

People got on the car, sat across from them and stared curiously. Johnny sat upright, the fish in his lap, trying not to think of the holes in his exposed undershirt. He looked over the heads of the passengers, pretending to study an Ex-Lax advertisement.

More people got on, the car got crowded, but no one would sit next to them. Finally one of the fish worked its way out of the sodden newspaper and fell on the floor, where it lay slimily in the dust. It was too much for Little Tilly. She looked into the fish's glazed eye, said nothing but vomited silently and thoroughly all over Johnny's tuxedo jacket. Francie and Neeley, as if waiting for that cue, also threw up. Johnny sat there with two exposed fish in his lap, one at his feet and kept staring at the ad. He didn't know what else to do.

When the grisly trip was ended, Johnny took Tilly home, feeling that his was the responsibility of explaining. The mother never gave him a chance to explain. She screamed when she saw her dripping, befouled child. She snatched the coat off, threw it into Johnny's face and called him a Jack-the-Ripper. Johnny tried and tried to explain, but she wouldn't listen. Little Tilly said nothing. Finally Johnny got a word in edgewise.

"Lady, I think your little girl has lost her speech."

Whereupon the mother went into hysterics. "You did it, you did it," she screamed at Johnny.

"Can't you make her say something?"

The mother grabbed the child and shook her and shook her. "Speak!" She screamed. "Say something." Finally, Little Tilly opened her mouth, smiled happily and said:

"T'anks."

Katie gave Johnny a tongue-lashing and said that he wasn't fit to have children. The children in question were alternating between the chills and hot flashes of a bad case of sunburn. Katie nearly cried when she saw the ruin of Johnny's only suit. It would cost a dollar to get it cleaned, steamed and pressed and she knew it would never be the same again. As for the fish, they were found to be in an advanced state of decay and had to be thrown into the garbage can.

The children went to bed. Between chills and fever and bouts of nausea, they buried their heads under the covers and laughed silently and bed-shakingly at the remembrance of papa standing in the water.

Johnny sat at the kitchen window until far into the night trying to figure out why everything had been so wrong. He had sung many a song about ships and going down to the sea in them with a heave-ho and a heave-to. He wondered why it hadn't turned out the way it said in songs. The children should have returned exhilarated and with a deep and abiding love for the sea and he should have returned with a fine mess of fish. Why, oh why hadn't it turned out the way it did in a song? Why did there have to be his blistered hands and his spoiled suit and sunburn and rotting fish and nausea? Why didn't Little Tilly's mother understand the intention and overlook the result? He couldn't figure it out—he couldn't figure it out.

The songs of the sea had betrayed him.

XXX

"TODAY, I *am* a woman," wrote Francie in her diary in the summer when she was thirteen. She looked at the sentence and absently scratched a mosquito bite on her bare leg. She looked down on her long thin and as yet formless legs. She crossed out the sentence and started over. "Soon, I shall become a woman." She looked down on her chest, which was as flat as a washboard, and ripped the page out of the book. She started afresh on a new page.

"Intolerance," she wrote, pressing down hard on the pencil, "is a thing that causes war, pogroms, crucifixions, lynchings, and makes people cruel to little children and to each other. It is responsible for most of the viciousness, violence, terror and heart- and soul-breaking of the world."

She read the words over aloud. They sounded like words that came in a can; the freshness was cooked out of them. She closed the book and put it away.

That summer Saturday was a day that should have gone down in her diary as one of the happiest days of her life. She saw her name in print for the first time. The school got out a magazine at the end of the year in which the best story written in composition class from each grade was published. Francie's composition called "Winter Time" had been chosen as the best of the seventh-grade work. The magazine cost a dime and Francie had had to wait until Saturday to get it. School closed for the summer the day before and Francie worried that she wouldn't get the magazine. But Mr. Jenson said he'd be working around on Saturday and if she brought the dime over he'd give her a copy.

Now in the early afternoon, she stood in front of her door with the magazine opened to the page of her story. She hoped someone would come along to whom she could show it.

She had shown it to mama at lunch-time but mama had to get back to work and didn't have time to read it. At least five times during lunch, Francie mentioned that she had a story published. At last mama said:

"Yes, yes. I know. I saw it all coming. There'll be more stories printed and you'll get used to it. Now don't let it go to your head. There are dishes to be washed."

Papa was at Union Headquarters. He wouldn't see the story till Sunday, but Francie knew he'd be pleased. So she stood on the street with her glory tucked under her arm. She couldn't let the magazine out of her hands even for a moment. From time to time she'd glance at her name in print and the excitement about it never grew less.

She saw a girl named Joanna come out of her house a few doors away. Joanna was taking her baby out for an airing in its carriage. A gasp came up from some housewives who had stopped to gossip on the sidewalk while going to and fro about their shopping. You see, Joanna was not married. She was a girl who had got into trouble. Her baby was illegitimate— bastard was the word they used in the neighbourhood—and these good women felt that Joanna had no right to act like a proud mother and bring her baby out into the light of day. They felt that she should have kept it hidden in some dark place.

Francie was curious about Joanna and the baby. She had heard mama and papa talking about them. She stared at the baby when the carriage came by. It was a beautiful little thing sitting up happily in its carriage. Maybe Joanna *was* a bad girl but certainly she kept her baby sweeter and daintier than these good women kept theirs. The baby wore a pretty frilled bonnet and a clean white dress and bib. The carriage cover was spotless and showed much loving handiwork in its embroidery.

Joanna worked in a factory while her mother took care of the baby. The mother was too ashamed to take it out, so the baby got an airing only on week-ends, when Joanna wasn't working.

Yes, Francie decided, it was a beautiful baby. It looked just like Joanna. Francie remembered how papa had described her that day he and mama were talking about her.

"She has skin like a magnolia petal." (Johnny had never seen a magnolia.) "Her hair is as black as a raven's wing." (He had never seen such a bird.) "And her eyes are deep and dark like forest pools." (He had never been in a forest and the only pool he knew was where each man put in a dime and guessed what the Dodgers' score would be, and whoever guessed right got all the dimes.) But he had described Joanna accurately. She was a beautiful girl.

"That may be," answered Katie. "But what good is her looks? They're a curse to the girl. I heard that her mother was never married but had two children just the same. And now the mother's son is in Sing Sing and her daughter has this baby. There must be bad blood all along the line, and no use getting sentimental about it. Of course," she added with a detachment of which she was astonishingly capable at times, "it's none of my business. I don't need to do anything about it one way or the other. I don't need to go out and spit on the girl because she did wrong. Neither do I have to take her in my house and adopt her because she did wrong. She suffered as much pain bringing that child into the world as though she *was* married. If she's a good girl at heart, she'll learn from the pain and the shame and she won't do it again. If she's naturally bad it won't bother her the way people treat her. So, if I was you, Johnny, I wouldn't feel too sorry for her."

Suddenly she turned to Francie and said: "Let Joanna be a lesson to you."

On this Saturday afternoon, Francie watched Joanna walk up and down and wondered in what way she was a lesson. Joanna acted proud about her baby. Was the lesson there? Joanna was only seventeen and friendly and she wanted everybody to be friendly with her. She smiled at the grim good women, but the smile went away when she saw that they answered her with frowns. She smiled at the little children playing on the street. Some smiled back. She smiled at Francie. Francie wanted to smile back but didn't. Was the lesson that she mustn't be friendly with girls like Joanna?

The good housewives, their arms filled with bags of vegetables and brown-paper parcels of meat, seemed to have little to do that afternoon. They kept gathering into little knots and whispered to each other. The whispering stopped when Joanna came by and started up when she had passed.

Each time Joanna passed, her cheeks got pinker, her head went higher and her skirt flipped behind her more defiantly. She seemed to grow prettier and prouder as she walked. She stopped oftener than needed to adjust the baby's coverlet. She maddened the women by touching the baby's cheek and smiling tenderly at it. How dare she! How dare she, they thought, act as though she had a right to all that?

Many of these good women had children which they brought up by scream and cuff. Many of them hated the husbands who lay by their sides at night. There was no longer high joy for them in the act of love. They endured the love-making rigidly praying all the while that another child would not result. This bitter submissiveness made the man ugly and brutal. To most of them the love act had become a brutality on both sides; the sooner over with, the better. They resented the girl because they felt this had not been so with her and the father of her child.

Joanna recognized their hate, but wouldn't cringe before it. She would not give in and take the baby indoors. Something *had* to give. The women broke first. They couldn't endure it any longer. They had to do something about it. The next time Joanna passed, a stringy woman called out:

"Ain't you ashamed of yourself?"

"What for?" Joanna wanted to know.

This infuriated the woman. "'What for?' she asks," she

reported to the other women. "I'll tell you what for. Because you're a disgrace and a bum. You got no right to parade the streets with your bastard where innocent children can see you."

"I guess this is a free country," said Joanna.

"Not free for the likes of you. Get off the street, get off the street."

"Try and make me!"

"Get off the street, you whore," ordered the stringy woman.

The girl's voice trembled when she answered: "Be careful what you're saying."

"We don't have to be careful what we say to no street-walker," chipped in another woman.

A man passing by stopped a moment to take it in. He touched Joanna's arm. "Look, Sister, why don't you go home till these battle-axes cool off? You can't win with them."

Joanna jerked her arm away. "You mind your own business!"

"I meant it in the right way, Sister. Sorry." He walked on.

"Why don't you go with him?" taunted the stringy woman. "He might be good for a quarter." The others laughed.

"You're all jealous," said Joanna evenly.

"She says we're jealous," reported the interlocutor. "Jealous of what. You?" (She said "you" as though it were the girl's name.)

"Jealous that men like me. That's what. Lucky you're married already," she told the stringy one. "You'd never get a man otherwise. I bet your husband spits on you—afterwards. I bet that's just what he does."

"Bitch! You bitch!" screamed the stringy one hysterically. Then, acting on an instinct which was strong even in Christ's day, she picked a stone out of the gutter and threw it at Joanna.

It was the signal for the other women to start throwing stones. One, droller than the rest, threw a ball of horse manure. Some of the stones hit Joanna, but a sharp-pointed one missed and struck the baby's forehead. Immediately, a thin clear trickle of blood ran down the baby's face and spotted its clean bib. The baby whimpered and held out its arms for its mother to pick it up.

A few women, poised to throw the next stones, dropped them quietly back into the gutter. The baiting was all over. Suddenly the women were ashamed. They had not wanted to hurt the baby. They only wanted to drive Joanna off the street. They dispersed and went home quietly. Some children who had been standing around listening, resumed their play.

Joanna, crying now, lifted the baby from the carriage. The baby continued to whimper quietly as though it had no right to cry out loud. Joanna pressed her cheek to her baby's face and her tears mixed with its blood. The women won. Joanna carried her baby into the house not caring that the carriage stood in the middle of the pavement.

And Francie had seen it all; had seen it all. She had heard every word. She remembered how Joanna had smiled at her and how she had turned her head away without smiling back. Why hadn't she smiled back? Why hadn't she smiled back? Now she would suffer—she would suffer all the rest of her life every time that she remembered that she had not smiled back.

Some small boys started to play tag around the empty carriage, holding on to its sides and pulling it away over while being chased. Francie scattered them and wheeled the carriage over to Joanna's door and put the brake on. There was an unwritten law that nothing was to be molested that stood outside the door where it belonged.

She was still holding the magazine with her story in. She stood next to the braked carriage and looked at her name once more.

" 'Winter Time,' by Frances Nolan." She wanted to do something, sacrifice something to pay for not having smiled at Joanna. She thought of her story, she was so proud of it; so eager to show papa and Aunt Evy and Sissy. She wanted to keep it always to look at and to get that nice warm feeling when she looked at it. If she gave it away, there was no means by which she could get another copy. She slipped the magazine under the baby's pillow. She left it open at the page of her story.

She saw some tiny drops of blood on the baby's snowy pillow. Again she saw the baby; the thin trickle of blood on its face; the way it held out its arms to be taken up. A wave of hurt broke over Francie and left her weak when it passed. Another wave came, broke and receded. She found her way down to the cellar of her house and sat in the darkest corner in a heap of burlap sacks and waited while the hurt waves swept over her. As each wave spent itself and a new one gathered, she trembled. Tensely she sat there waiting for them to stop. If they didn't stop, she'd have to die—she'd have to die.

After a while they came fainter and there was a longer time between each one. She began to think. She was now getting her lesson from Joanna, but it was not the kind of lesson her mother meant.

She remembered Joanna. Often at night, on her way home from the library, she had passed Joanna's house and seen her and the boy standing close together in the narrow vestibule. She had seen the boy stroke Joanna's pretty hair tenderly; had seen Joanna put up her hand to touch his cheek. And Joanna's face looked peaceful and dreamy in the light from the street lamp. Out of that beginning, then, had come the shame and the baby. Why? Why? The beginning had seemed so tender and so right. Why?

She knew that one of the women stone-throwers had had a baby only three months after her marriage. Francie had been one of the children standing at the kerb watching the party leave for the church. She saw the bulge of pregnancy under the virginal veil of the bride as she stepped into the hired carriage. She saw the hand of the father closed tight on the bridegroom's arm. The groom had black shadows under his eyes and looked very sad.

Joanna had no father, no men kin. There was no one to hold her boy's arm tight on the way to the altar. That was Joanna's crime, decided Francie—not that she had been bad but that she had not been smart enough to get the boy to the church.

Francie had no way of knowing the whole story. As a matter of fact, the boy loved Joanna and was willing to marry her after—as the saying goes—he had got her into trouble. The boy had a family—a mother and three sisters. He told them he wanted to marry Joanna and they talked him out of it.

Don't be a fool, they told him. She's no good. Her whole family's no good. Besides, how do you know you're the one? If she had you she had others. Oh, women are tricky. We know. We are women. You are good and tender-hearted. You take her word for it that you are the man. She lies. Don't be tricked, my son, don't be tricked, our brother. If you must marry, marry a good girl, one who won't sleep with you without the priest saying the words that make it right. If you marry this girl, you are no longer my son; you are no longer our brother. You'll never be sure whether the child is yours. You will worry while you are at your work. You'll wonder who slips into your bed beside her after you have left in the morning. Oh yes, my son, our brother, that is how women do. *We* know. *We* are women. *We* know how they do.

The boy had let himself be persuaded. His women-folk gave him money and he got a room and a new job over in Jersey. They wouldn't tell Joanna where he was. He never saw her again. Joanna wasn't married. Joanna had the baby.

The waves had almost stopped passing over Francie when she discovered, to her fright, that something was wrong with her. She pressed her hand over her heart trying to feel a jagged edge under the flesh. She had heard papa sing so many songs about the heart; the heart that was breaking—was aching— was dancing—was heavy laden—that leaped for joy—that was heavy in sorrow—that turned over—that stood still. She really believed that the heart actually did those things. She was terrified thinking her heart had broken inside her over Joanna's baby and that blood was now leaving her heart and flowing from her body.

She went upstairs to the flat and looked into the mirror. Her eyes had dark shadows beneath them and her head was aching. She lay on the old leather couch in the kitchen and waited for mama to come home.

She told mama what had happened to her in the cellar. She said nothing about Joanna. Katie sighed and said: "So soon? You're just thirteen. I didn't think it would come for another year yet. I was fifteen."

"Then . . . then . . . this is all right what's happening?"

"It's a natural thing that comes to all women."

"I'm not a woman."

"It means you're changing from a girl into a woman."

"Do you think it will go away?"

"In a few days. But it will come back again in a month."

"For how long?"

"For a long time. Until you are forty or even fifty." She mused a while. "My mother was fifty when I was born."

"Oh, it has something to do with having babies."

"Yes. Remember always to be a good girl because you can have a baby now." Joanna and her baby flashed through Francie's mind. "You mustn't let the boys kiss you," said mama.

"Is that how you get a baby?"

"No. But what makes you get a baby often starts with a kiss."

She added: "Remember Joanna."

Now Katie didn't know about the street scene. Joanna happened to pop into her mind. But Francie thought she had wonderful powers of insight. She looked at mama with new respect.

Remember Joanna. Remember Joanna. Francie could never forget her. From that time on, remembering the stoning women, she hated women. She feared them for their devious ways, she mistrusted their instincts. She began to hate them for this disloyalty and their cruelty to each other. Of all the stone-throwers, not one had dared to speak a word for the girl for fear that she would be tarred with Joanna's brush. The passing man had been the only one who spoke with kindness in his voice.

Most women had the one thing in common; they had great pain when they gave birth to their children. This should make a bond that held them all together; it should make them love and protect each other against the man-world. But it was not so. It seemed like their great birth pains shrank their hearts and their souls. They stuck together for only one thing: to trample on some other woman . . . whether it was by throwing stones or by mean gossip. It was the only kind of loyalty they seemed to have.

Men were different. They might hate each other, but they stuck together against the world and against any woman who would ensnare one of them.

Francie opened the copy-book which she used for a diary. She skipped a line under the paragraph that she had written about intolerance and wrote:

"As long as I live, I will never have a woman for a friend. I will never trust any woman again, except maybe mama and sometimes Aunt Evy and Aunt Sissy."

XXXI

Two VERY important things happened in the year that Francie was thirteen. War broke out in Europe and a horse fell in love with Aunt Evy.

Evy's husband and his horse, Drummer, had been bitter enemies for eight years. He was mean to the horse; he kicked him and punched him and cursed at him and pulled too hard on the bit. The horse was mean to Uncle Willie Flittman. The horse knew the route and stopped automatically at each delivery. It had been his habit to start up again as soon as Flittman mounted the wagon. Lately, he had taken to starting up the instant Flittman got off to deliver milk. He'd break into a trot and often Flittman had to run more than half a block to catch up with him.

Flittman was through delivering at noon. He'd go home to eat dinner, then bring the horse and wagon back to the stable where he was supposed to wash Drummer and the wagon. The horse had a mean trick. Often when Flittman was washing under his belly, he'd wet on him. The other fellows would stand around waiting for this to happen so that they could have a good laugh. Flittman couldn't stand it, so he got in the habit of washing the horse in front of his house. That was all right in the summer, but it was a little hard on the horse in the winter. Often, on a bitterly cold day, Evy would go down and tell Willie that it was a mean thing to wash Drummer in the cold and with cold water, too. The horse seemed to know that Evy was taking his part. As she argued with her husband, Drummer would whinny pitifully and lay his head on her shoulder.

One cold day, Drummer took matters into his own hands— or as aunt Evy said it, into his own feet. Francie listened enchanted while Aunt Evy told the story to the Nolans. No one could tell a story like Evy. She acted out all the parts— even the horse and, in a funny way, she'd put in what she thought each one was secretly thinking at the time. It happened like this, according to Evy:

Willie was down on the street washing the shivering horse with cold water and hard yellow soap. Evy was standing at the window watching. He leaned under to wash the horse's belly and the horse tensed. Flittman thought Drummer was going to wet on him again, and it was more than the harassed and futile little man could stand. He hauled off and punched the horse in the belly. The horse lifted a leg and kicked him decisively in the head. Flittman rolled under the horse and lay unconscious.

Evy ran down. The horse whinnied happily when he saw her, but she paid no attention to him. When he looked over his shoulder and saw that Evy was trying to drag Flittman out from under, he started to walk. Maybe he wanted to help Evy by pulling the wagon clear of the unconscious man or maybe he wanted to finish the job by rolling the wagon over him. Evy hollered out: "Whoa there, boy," and Drummer stopped just in time.

A little boy had gone for a policeman who had gone for the ambulance. The ambulance doctor couldn't make out whether Flittman had a fracture or a concussion. He took him to a Greenpoint hospital.

Well, there was the horse and a wagon full of empty milk bottles to be got back to the stables. Evy had never driven a horse, but that was no reason why she couldn't. She put on one of her husband's old overcoats, wrapped a shawl around her head, climbed up into the seat, picked up the reins and called out: "Git for home, Drummer." The horse swung his head back to give her a loving look, then set off at a cheerful trot.

It was lucky he knew the way. Evy hadn't the slightest idea where the stables were. He was a smart horse. He stopped at each intersection and waited while Evy looked up and down the cross-street. If all was clear she'd say: "Giddy-yap, boy." If another vehicle was coming she'd say: "Just a minute, boy." In this way they reached the stables without mishap and the horse cantered in proudly to his usual place in the row. Other drivers, washing their wagons, were surprised to see a lady driver. They made such a commotion that the stable boss came running, and Evy told him what had happened.

"I saw it coming," the boss said. "Flittman never did like that horse and the horse never liked him. Well, we'll have to take on another man."

Evy, fearful lest her husband lose his job, asked whether she couldn't take his route while he was in the hospital. She argued that the milk was delivered in the dark and no one would ever know. The boss laughed at her. She told him how much they needed that twenty-two-fifty a week. She pleaded so hard, and looked so little and pretty and spunky, that he gave in at last. He gave her the list of customers and told her the boys would load the wagon for her. The horse knew the route, he said, and it wouldn't be too hard. One of the drivers suggested that she take the stable dog along for company and protection against milk thieves. The boss agreed to that. He told her to report to the stables at 2 a.m. Evy was the first milk-woman on the route.

She got along fine. The fellows at the stable liked her and said that she was a better worker than Flittman. In spite of her practicalness, she was soft and feminine and the men loved the low and breathless way she had of talking. And the horse was very happy and co-operated as much as he could. He stopped automatically before each house where milk was to be left and never started up again until she was safely in the seat.

Like Flittman, she brought him to her house while she ate her dinner. Because the weather was so cold, she took an old quilt from her bed and threw it over him so he wouldn't catch cold while he waited for her. She took his oats upstairs and heated them for a few minutes in the oven before she fed him. She didn't think ice-cold oats were appetizing. The horse enjoyed the warmed oats. After he finished munching, she treated him to half an apple or a lump of sugar.

She thought it was too cold to wash him on the street. She took him back to the stable for that. She thought the yellow soap was too biting, so she brought along a cake of Sweetheart soap and a big old bath-towel to dry him with. The men at the stable offered to wash the horse and wagon for her, but she insisted on washing the horse herself. Two men got into a fight over who should wash the wagon. Evy settled it by saying one would wash it one day and the other the next day.

She heated Drummer's wash water on a gas plate in the boss's office. She'd never think of washing him in cold water. She washed him with the warm water and the sweet-scented soap and dried him carefully bit by bit with the towel. He never committed an indignity on her while she washed him. He snorted and whinnied happily throughout the washing. His skin rippled in voluptuous delight when Evy rubbed him dry. When she worked around his chest, he rested his tremendous head on her small shoulders. There was no doubt about it. The horse was madly in love with Evy.

When Flittman recovered and reported back for work, the horse refused to leave the stable with him on the wagon seat. They had to give Flittman another route and another horse. But Drummer wouldn't go out with any other driver either.

195

The boss had just about made up his mind to have him sold, when he got an idea. Among the drivers, there was an effeminate young man who talked with a lisp. They put him on Flittman's wagon. Drummer seemed satisfied and consented to go out with the lady-like driver on the seat.

So Drummer took up his regular duties again. But every day at noon he turned into the street where Evy lived and stood in front of her door. He wouldn't go back to the stables until Evy had come down, given him a bit of apple or some sugar, stroked his nose and called him a good boy.

"He was a funny horse," said Francie after she heard the story.

"He may have been funny," said Aunt Evy, "but he sure knew what he wanted."

XXXII

FRANCIE HAD started a diary on her thirteenth birthday with the entry:

Dec. 15. Today I enter my teens. What will the year bring forth? I wonder.

The year brought forth little, according to the entries which became sparser as the year wore on. She had been prompted to start a diary because fictional heroines kept them and filled them with lush sighing thoughts. Francie thought her diary would be like that, but excepting for some romantic observations on Harold Clarence, actor, the entries were prosaic. Towards the end of the year she riffled through the pages reading an item here and there.

Jan. 8. Granma Mary Rommely has a pretty carved box that her great-grandfather made in Austria over a hundred years ago. She has a black dress and white petticoat and shoes and stockings in it. They are her burying clothes she doesn't want to be buried in a shroud. Uncle Will Flittman said he wants to be cremated and his ashes scattered from the Statue of Liberty. He thinks he'll be a bird the next life and he wants a good start. Aunt Evy said he's a bird already, a cuckoo. Mama scolded me for laughing.

cremation better than burying? I wonder.

Jan. 10. Papa sick today.

March 21. Neeley stole pussy willows from McCarren's Park and gave them to Gretchen Hahn. Mama said he's too young to be thinking about girls. There's time enough, she said.

April 2. Papa hasn't worked for three weeks. There's something wrong with his hands. They shake so much he can't hold anything.

April 20. Aunt Sissy says she's going to have a baby. I don't believe it because she's flat in front. I heard her tell mama she's carrying it in the back. I wonder.

May 8. Papa sick today.

May 9. Papa went to work tonight but had to come home. Said the people didn't need him.

May 10. Papa sick. Had bad nightmares in the day-time and screamed. I had to get Aunt Sissy.

May 12. Papa hasn't worked for over a month. Neeley wants to get his working papers and leave school. Mama said no.

May 15. Papa worked tonight. He said he's going to take charge of things from now on. He scolded Neeley about the working papers.

May 17. Papa came home sick. Some kids were following him on the street and making fun of him. I hate kids.

May 20. Neeley has a paper route now. He won't let me help sell papers.

May 28. Carney did not pinch my cheek today. He pinched something else. I guess I'm getting too big to sell junk.

May 30. Miss Garnder said they are going to publish my winter time compositions in the magazine.

June 2. Papa came home sick today. Neeley and I had to help mama get him upstairs. Papa cried.

June 4. I got A on my composition today. We had to write on My Ambition. I only made one mistake. I wrote play-writer and Miss Garnder said the right word was play-wright.

June 7. Two men brought papa home today. He was sick. Mama was away. I put papa to bed and gave him black coffee. When mama came home she said that was the right thing to do.

June 12. Miss Tynmore gave me Schubert's Serenade today. Mama's ahead of me. She got Tannhauser's Evening

197

Star. Neeley says he's ahead of both of us. He can play Alexander's Ragtime Band without notes.

June 20. Went to show. Saw The Girl of the Golden West. It was the best show I ever saw, the way the blood dripped through the ceiling.

June 21. Papa was away for two nights. We didn't know where he was. He came home sick.

June 22. Mama turned my mattress today and found my diary and read it. Everywhere I had the word drunk, she made me cross it out and write sick. It's lucky I didn't have anything against mama written down. If ever I have children I will not read their diaries, as I believe that even a child is entitled to some privacy. If mama finds this again and reads it, I hope she will take the hint.

June 23. Neeley says he has a girl. Mama says he's too young. I wonder.

June 25. Uncle Willie, Aunt Evy, Sissy and her John over tonight. Uncle Willie drank a lot of beer and cried. He said the new horse he's got, Bessie, did worse than wet on him. Mama scolded me for laughing.

June 27. We finished the Bible today. Now we got to start all over. We've gone through Shakespeare four times already.

July 1. Intolerance....

Francie put her hand over the entry to hide the words. For a moment, she thought the waves would pass over her again. But the feeling went away. She turned the page and read another entry.

July 4. Sergeant McShane brought papa home today. Papa wasn't arrested as we thought at first. He was sick. Mr. McShane gave Neeley and me a quarter. Mama made us give it back.

July 5. Papa still sick. Will he ever work again? I wonder.

July 6. We started playing the North Pole game today.

July 7. North Pole.

July 8. North Pole.

July 9. North Pole. Expected rescue did not come.

July 10. We opened the tin-can bank today. There was eight dollars and twenty cents in it. My golden pennies had turned black.

July 20. All the money from the tin-can bank is gone. Mama took some washing to do for Mrs. McGarrity.

helped iron, but burnt a hole on Mrs. McGarrity's drawers. Mama won't let me iron any more.

July 23. I got a job at Hendler's Restaurant just for the summer. I wash dishes during the dinner and supper rush. I use gobs of soft soap out of a barrel. On Monday a man comes and collects three barrels of scraps of fat and brings back one barrel of soft soap on Wednesday. Nothing is wasted in this world. I get two dollars a week and my meals. It isn't hard work, but I don't like that soap.

July 24. Mama said I'd be a woman before I knew it. I wonder.

July 28. Floss Gaddis and Frank are going to get married as soon as he gets a raise. Frank says that the way President Wilson is running things we'll be in the war before you know it. He says he's marrying because he wants a wife and kids so that when war comes he doesn't have to fight. Flossie says that's not true; it's a case of true love. I wonder. I remember how Flossie used to chase him years ago when he was washing the horse.

July 29. Papa wasn't sick today. He's going to get a job. He said mama has to stop washing for Mrs. McGarrity and I have to give up my job. He says we'll be rich and all go to live in the country. I wonder.

Aug. 10. Sissy says she's going to have a baby soon. I wonder. She's as flat as a pancake.

Aug. 17. Papa has been working for three weeks now. We have wonderful suppers.

Aug. 18. Papa's sick.

Aug. 19. Papa's sick because he lost his job. Mr. Hendler won't take me back in the restaurant. He says I'm not reliable.

Sept. 1. Aunt Evy, Uncle Willie over tonight. Willie sang Frankie and Johnny and put dirty words in it. Aunt Evy stood on a chair and punched him on the nose. Mama scolded me for laughing.

Sept. 10. I started my last year of school. Miss Garnder said if I keep on getting A's on my compositions, she might let me write a play for graduation. I have a very beautiful idea. There will be a girl in a white dress and her hair hanging down her back and she will be Fate. Other girls will come out on the stage and tell what they *want* from Life, and Fate will tell them what they'll *get*. At the end a girl in a blue dress will spread out her arms and say: "Is life worth living then?" And there will be a chorus that says "Yes." Only it will all be in rhyme. I told papa about it, but he was too sick to understand. Poor papa.

Sept. 18. I asked mama could I get a Castle Clip, and she said no, that hair was a woman's crowning beauty. Does that mean she expects me to be a woman soon? I hope so because I want to be my own boss and get my hair cut off if I feel like it.

Sept. 24. Tonight, when I took a bath, I discovered that I was changing into a woman. It's about time.

Oct. 25. I will be glad when this book is filled up as I am getting tired of keeping a diary. Nothing important ever happens.

Francie came to the last entry. Only one more blank page left. Well, the sooner she got it filled, the sooner the diary-keeping would be over and she wouldn't have to bother with it any more. She wet her pencil.

Nov. 2. Sex is something that invariably comes into everyone's life. People write pieces against it. The priests preach against it. They even make laws against it. But it keeps going on just the same. All the girls in school have but the one topic of conversation: sex and boys. They are very curious about it. Am I curious about sex?

She studied the last sentence. The line on the inner edge of her right eyebrow deepened. She crossed out the sentence and re-wrote it to read: "I am curious about sex."

XXXIII

YES, THERE was a great curiosity about sex among the adolescent children of Williamsburg. There was a lot of talk about it.

Among the younger children there was some exhibitionism (you show me and I'll show you). A few hypocrites devised such evasive games as "playing house" or "doctor." A few uninhibited ones did what they called "play dirty."

There was a great hush-hush about sex in that neighbourhood. When children asked questions, the parents didn't know

200

how to answer them, for the reason that these people did not know the correct words to use. Each married couple had its own secret words for things which were whispered in bed in the quiet of night. But there were few mothers brave enough to bring these words out into the daylight and present them to the child. When the children grew up, they in turn invented words which they couldn't tell *their* children.

Katie Nolan was neither a mental nor a physical coward. She tackled every problem masterfully. She didn't volunteer sex information, but when Francie asked questions she answered as best she knew how. Once when Francie and Neeley were young children, they had agreed to ask their mother certain questions. They stood before her one day. Francie was the spokesman.

"Mama, where did we come from?"

"God gave you to me."

The Catholic children were willing to accept that, but the next question was a sticker. "How did God get us to you?"

"I can't explain that because I'd have to use a lot of big words that you wouldn't understand."

"Say the big words and see if we understand them."

"If you understand them, I wouldn't have to tell you."

"Say it in some kind of words. Tell us how babies get here."

"No, you're too little yet. If I told you, you'd go around telling all the other children what you know and their mothers would come up here and say I was a dirty lady and there would be fights."

"Well, tell us why girls are different from boys."

Mama thought a while. "The main difference is that a little girl sits down when she goes to the bathroom and a little boy stands up."

"But, Mama," said Francie. "I stand up when I'm afraid in that dark toilet."

"And I," confessed little Neeley, "sit down when . . ."

Mama interrupted. "Well, there's a little bit of a man in every woman and a little of woman in every man."

That ended the discussion, because it was so puzzling to the children that they decided to go no further with it.

When Francie, as she wrote in her diary, started to change into a woman, she went to mama about her sex curiosity. And Katie told her simply and plainly all that she herself knew.

201

There were times in the telling when Katie had to use words which were considered dirty, but she used them bravely and unflinchingly because she knew no other words. No one had ever told her about the things she told her daughter. And in those days there were no books available for people like Katie from which they could learn about sex in the right way. In spite of the blunt words and homely phrasing, there was nothing revolting in Katie's explanations.

Francie was luckier than most children of the neighbourhood. She found out all she needed to know at the time she had to know about it. She never needed to slink into dark hallways with other girls and exchange guilty confidences. She never had to learn things in a distorted way.

If normal sex was a great mystery in the neighbourhood, criminal sex was an open book. In all poor and congested city areas, the prowling sex fiend is a nightmarish horror that haunts parents. There seems to be one in every neighbourhood. There was one in Williamsburg in that year when Francie turned fourteen. For a long time he had been molesting little girls, and although the police were on a continual look-out for him, he was never caught. One of the reasons was that when a little girl was attacked, the parents kept it secret so that no one would know and discriminate against the child and look on her as a thing apart and make it impossible for her to resume a normal childhood with her playmates.

One day, a little girl on Francie's block was killed and it had to come out in the open. She had been a quiet little thing of seven, well behaved and obedient. When she didn't come home from school, her mother didn't worry; she thought the child had stopped somewhere to play. After supper, they went looking for her; they questioned her playmates. No one had seen the child since school let out.

A fear wave swept over the neighbourhood. Children were called in off the streets and kept behind locked doors. McShane came over with half a dozen policemen and they began combing the roofs and cellars.

The child was found at last by her loutish seventeen-year-old brother. Her little body was lying across a busted-down doll carriage in the cellar of a near-by house. Her torn dress and undergarments, her shoes and her little red socks were thrown on an ash-heap. The brother was questioned. He was excited and stuttered when he answered. They arrested him on suspicion. McShane wasn't stupid. The arrest was a blind to put the killer off guard. McShane knew the killer would feel safe and strike again; and this time the police would be waiting for him.

Parents went into action. The children were told (and to hell with finding the right words) about the fiend and the horrible things he did. Little girls were warned not to take candy from strangers, not to speak to strange men. Mothers took to waiting in the doorways for their children when school let out. The streets were deserted. It was as if the Pied Piper had led all the children off to some mountain fastness. The whole neighbourhood was terrorized. Johnny got so worried about Francie that he got a gun.

Johnny had a friend named Burt, who was night watchman at the corner bank. Burt was forty years old and married to a girl half his age, of whom he was insanely jealous. He suspected that she took a lover in nights when he was at the bank. He brooded over this so much that he came to the conclusion that it would be a relief if he knew for sure that this was so. He was willing to exchange soul-destroying suspicion for heart-breaking reality. Accordingly, he slipped home at odd hours during the night while his friend, Johnny Nolan, watched the bank for him. They had signals. When, in the night, poor Burt got so tormented that he had to go home, he asked the cop on the beat to ring the Nolan bell three times. If Johnny was home when the signal came, he jumped out of bed like a fireman, dressed hurriedly and ran to the bank as though his life depended on it.

After the watchman slipped out, Johnny lay on Burt's narrow cot and felt the hard revolver through the thin pillow. He hoped someone would attempt to rob the bank so he could save the money and be a hero. But all the hours of his night watching were without event. There wasn't even the excitement of the watchman catching his wife in adultery. The girl always was sleeping soundly and alone when her husband sneaked into their flat.

When Johnny heard of the rape and murder, he went over to the bank to see his friend Burt. He asked the watchman whether he had another gun.

"Sure. Why?"

"I'd like the lend of it, Burt."

"Why, Johnny?"

"There's this fellow loose that killed the little girl on our block."

"I hope they ketch him, Johnny. I sure hope they ketch the son-of-a-bitch."

"I have a daughter of my own."

"Yeah, yeah, I know, Johnny."

"So I'd like you to loan me a gun."

"It's against the Sullivan Law."

"It's against some other law for you to go away from the bank and leave me here. How do you know? I may be a robber."

"Aw, no, Johnny."

"I figure if we break one law we might as well break another."

"All right. All right. I'll lend it." He opened a desk drawer and took out a revolver. "Now I'll show you. When you want to kill somebody, you point it at 'em like this," he pointed it at Johnny, "and pull this thing."

"I see. Let me try it." In his turn, Johnny aimed it at Burt.

" 'Course," said Burt. "I ain't never shot off the God-damned thing myself."

"This is the first time I ever held a gun in my hands," explained Johnny.

"Watch out then," said the watchman quietly. "It's loaded!"

Johnny shivered and put the gun down carefully. "Say, Burt, I didn't know. We might have killed each other."

"Jesus, you're right." The watchman shuddered.

"One jerk of a finger and a man is dead," mused Johnny.

"Johnny, you ain't thinking of killing yourself?"

"No, I'm letting the booze do that." Johnny started to laugh, but stopped abruptly. As he left with the gun Burt said:

"Let me know if you catch the bastard."

"I'll do that," promised Johnny.

"Yeah. So long."

"So long, Burt."

Johnny gathered his family around him and explained about the gun. He warned Francie and Neeley not to touch it. "This little cylinder holds death for five people in it," he explained dramatically.

Francie thought the revolver looked like a grotesque beckoning finger, a finger that beckoned to death and made it come running. She was glad when papa put it out of sight under his pillow.

The gun lay under Johnny's pillow for a month and was never touched. There were no further outrages in the neighbourhood. It seemed that the fiend had moved on. Mothers began to relax. A few, however, like Katie, continued to watch in door or hallway when they knew the children were due home from school. It was the killer's habit to lurk in dark hallways for his victims. Katie felt that it cost nothing to be careful.

When most of the people were lulled into a feeling of security, the pervert struck again.

One afternoon, Katie was cleaning in the halls of the second house away from her own. She heard children in the street and knew that school was out. She wondered whether it was necessary to go back and wait in their hallway for Francie as she had been doing since the murder. Francie was nearly fourteen and old enough to take care of herself. Besides, the killer usually attacked little girls of six or seven. Maybe he had been caught in some other neighbourhood and was safe in jail. Still. . . . She hesitated, then decided to go home. She'd be needing a fresh bar of soap within the hour, and could kill two birds with one stone if she got it now.

She looked up and down the street and grew uneasy when she didn't see Francie among the children. Then she remembered that Francie went farther to school and came home a bit later. Once in the flat, Katie decided to heat the coffee and have a cupful. By that time Francie should be home, and her mind would be at peace. She went into the bedroom to see if the gun was still under the pillow. Of course it was, and she felt foolish for looking. She drank the coffee, took her bag of yellow soap and started back for work.

Francie got home at her usual time. She opened the hall door, stared up and down the long narrow hall, saw nothing, and closed the solid wood door behind her. Now the hall was darkened. She walked the short length of hall towards the stairs. As she put her foot on the first step, she saw a man.

He stepped out from a small recess under the stairs that had an entrance to the cellar. He walked softly but with lunging steps. He was thin and under-sized. His thick bushy hair grew down on his forehead almost to his eyebrows. He had a beaked nose and his mouth was a thin crooked line. Even in the semi-darkness Francie was aware of his wet-looking eyes. She took another step, then, as she got a better look at him, her legs turned into cement. She couldn't lift them to take the next step! Her hands clutched two banister spokes and she clung to them. What hypnotized her into being unable to move was the fact that the man was coming towards her with his lower garments opened. Francie stared at the exposed part of his body in paralyzed horror. It was wormy white contrasted with the ugly dark sallowness of his face and hands. She felt the same kind of nausea she had once felt when she saw a swarm of fat white maggots crawling over the putrid carcass of a rat. She tried to scream "mama," but her throat closed over and only air came out. It was like a horrible dream where you tried to scream but no sound came. She couldn't move! She couldn't move! Her hands hurt from gripping the banister spokes. Irrelevantly, she wondered why they didn't snap off in her tight grasp. And now he was coming towards her and she couldn't run! She couldn't run! Please God, she prayed, let some tenant come along.

At this moment Katie was walking down the stairs quietly with the bar of yellow soap in her hand. When she came to the top of the flight she looked down and saw the man coming at Francie, and saw that Francie was frozen to the banister spokes. Katie made no sound. Neither one saw her. She turned quietly and ran up the two flights to her flat. Her hand was steady as she took the key from under the mat and opened the door. She took precious time, not aware of what she was doing, to set the cake of yellow soap on the washtub cover. She got the gun from under the pillow, aimed it, and keeping it aimed, put it under her apron. Now her hand was trembling. She put her other hand under her apron and steadied the gun with her two hands. Holding the gun in this way, she ran down the stairs.

The murderer reached the foot of the stairs, rounded it, leaped up the two steps, and, quick as a cat, threw one arm about Francie's neck and pressed his palm to her mouth to prevent her screaming. He put his other arm around her waist and started to pull her away. He slipped and the exposed part of his body touched her bare leg. The leg jerked as though a live flame had been put to it. Her legs came out of the paralysis then and she kicked and struggled. At that the pervert pressed his body close to hers, pinning her against the banister. He began undoing her clenched fingers, one by one. He got one hand free, forced it behind her back and leaned hard against it while he started to work on her other hand.

There was a sound. Francie looked up and saw her mother running down that last flight of stairs. Katie was running awkwardly, not balancing well on account of having both hands clutched under her apron. The man saw her. He couldn't see that she had a gun. Reluctantly, he loosed his hold and backed down the two steps, keeping his wet eyes on Katie. Francie stood there, one hand still gripping the banister spoke. She couldn't get her hand opened. The man got off the steps, pressed his back to the wall and started sliding against it to the cellar door. Katie stopped, knelt on a step, pushed her apron bulge between two banister spokes, stared at the exposed part of his body and pulled the trigger.

There was a loud explosion and the smell of burnt cloth as the hole in Katie's apron smouldered. The pervert's lips curled back to show broken dirty teeth. He put both hands on his stomach and fell. His hands came away as he hit the floor and blood was all over that part of him that had been worm-white. The narrow hall was full of smoke.

Women screamed. Doors banged open. There was the sound of running feet in the halls. People in the street started pouring into the hall. In a second, the doorway was jammed and no one could get in or out.

Katie grabbed Francie's hand and tried to pull her up the stairs, but the child's hand was frozen to the spoke. She couldn't open her fingers. In desperation, Katie hit Francie's wrist with the gunbutt and the numb fingers relaxed at last. Katie pulled her up the steps and through the halls. She kept meeting women coming out of their flats.

"What's the matter? What's the matter?" they screamed.

"It's all right now. It's all right now," Katie told them.

Francie kept stumbling and going to her knees. Katie had to drag her on her knees the length of the last hall. She got her into the flat and on to the couch in the kitchen. Then she put the chain bolt on the door. As she put the gun down carefully next to the bar of yellow soap, her hand accidentally touched the muzzle. She was frightened when she found it warm. Katie knew nothing about guns; she had never shot one before. Now she thought the heat might make the gun go off by itself. She opened the washtub cover and threw the gun into the water in which some soiled clothes were soaking. Because the bar of yellow soap was mixed up with the whole thing, she threw that in after the gun. She went to Francie.

"Did he hurt you, Francie?"

"No, mama," she moaned. "Only he ... his ... I mean it ... touched my leg."

"Where?"

Francie pointed to a spot above her blue sock. The skin was white and unharmed. Francie looked at it in surprise. She had an idea that the skin would be eaten away there.

"There's nothing the matter with it," mama said.

"But I can still feel where it touched." She moaned and cried out insanely: "I want my leg cut off."

People pounded on the door demanding to know what had happened. Katie ignored them and kept the door bolted. She made Francie swallow a cup of scalding hot black coffee. Then she walked up and down the room. She was trembling now. She didn't know what to do next.

Neeley had been loitering on the street when the shot sounded. When he saw people crowding into the hallway, he, too, worked his way in. He got up on the stairs and looked over the banisters. The pervert was huddled where he had fallen. The crowd of women had torn the trousers from his body and all who could get near were grinding their heels into his flesh. Others were kicking at him and spitting on him. All were shrieking obscenities at him. Neeley heard his sister's name.

"Francie Nolan?"

"Yeah, Francie Nolan."

"You sure? Francie Nolan?"

"I tell you I seen."

"Her mother went and ..."

"Francie Nolan!"

He heard the ambulance gong. He thought Francie had been killed. He raced up the stairs sobbing. He pounded on the door, screaming: "Let me in, Mama! Let me in!"

Katie let him in. When he saw Francie lying on the couch, he bawled louder. Now Francie started to bawl. "Stop it! Stop it!" Katie screamed. She shook Neeley until he didn't have a sob left in him.

"Run and get your father. Look all over until you find him."

Neeley found papa in McGarrity's saloon. Johnny was just about to settle down to a long afternoon of slow drinking. When he heard Neeley's story, he dropped his glass and ran out with him. They couldn't get back into the house. The ambulance was at the door and four policemen were fighting a

208

way through the crowd trying to get the ambulance doctor in.

Johnny and Neeley went through the next-door cellar into the yard, helped each other over the board fence into their own yard and climbed up on the fire-escape. When Katie saw Johnny's derby looming up outside the window she screamed and ran around frantically looking for the gun. Fortunately for Johnny, she had forgotten where she had thrown it.

Johnny ran to Francie, and, big as she was, he picked her up in his arms as though she were a baby. He rocked her and told her to go to sleep. Francie kept insisting that she wanted her leg cut off.

"Did he get her?" asked Johnny.

"No, but I got him," Katie said grimly.

"Did you shoot him with the pistol?"

"With what else?" She showed him the hole in her apron.

"Did you shoot him good?"

"As good as I could. But she keeps talking about her leg. His . . ." her eyes slid towards Neeley, ". . . well, you know, touched her leg." She pointed to the spot. Johnny looked, but he saw nothing. "That's too bad it had to happen to her," Katie said. "She's such a one for remembering. She might never get married, remembering."

"We'll fix that leg," promised papa.

He put Francie back on the couch, got the carbolic acid and swabbed the spot with the strong raw stuff. Francie welcomed the burning pain of the acid. She felt that the evil of the man's touch was being seared away.

Someone pounded at the door. They remained quiet and unanswering. They wanted no outsiders in their home at this time. A strong Irish voice called:

"Open up the door. 'Tis the law, now."

Katie opened the door. A policeman walked in followed by an ambulance intern carrying a bag. The cop pointed to Francie.

"This the kid he tried to get?"

"Yes."

"Doc, here, has to make an examination."

"I won't allow it," protested Katie.

"It's the law," he answered quietly.

So Katie and the intern took Francie into the bedroom and the terrified child had to submit to the indignity of an examination. The jaunty intern made a quick and careful examination. He straightened up and started to put his instru-

209

ments back into the bag. He said:

"She's okay. He never got near her." He took her swollen wrist in his hand. "How did this happen?"

"I had to hit her with the gun to make her let go of the banister," Katie explained. He noticed her bruised knee.

"What's this?"

"That's where I had to drag her along the hall." Then he got to the ᴜngry burn just above her ankle. "And what in the name of God is this?"

"That's where her father washed her leg with carbolic acid where that man touched her."

"My God!" exploded the intern. "You trying to give her third-degree burns?" He opened the bag again, put cooling salve on the burn and bandaged it neatly. "My God!" he said again, "between the two of you, you did more damage than the criminal!" He smoothed down Francie's dress, patted her cheek and said: "You'll be all right, girlie. I'm going to give you something to put you to sleep. When you wake up, just remember that you had a bad dream. That's all it was; a bad dream. Hear?"

"Yes, sir," said Francie gratefully. Again she saw a poised needle. She remembered something from a long time ago. She worried. Was her arm clean? Would he say . . .

"That's a brave girl," he said as the needle jabbed.

"Why he's on my side," thought Francie hazily. She went to sleep immediately after the hypodermic.

Katie and the doctor came out into the kitchen. Johnny and the cop were sitting at the table. The cop had a bit of pencil clutched in his big paw and he was painfully making small notes in a small notebook.

"Kid all right?" asked the cop.

"Fine," the intern told him, "just suffering from shock and parentitus." He winked at the cop. "When she wakes up," he said to Katie, "remember to keep telling her that she had a bad dream. Don't talk about it otherwise."

"What do I owe you, Doc?" asked Johnny.

"Nothing, Mac. This is on the city."

"Thank you," whispered Johnny.

The intern noticed Johnny's trembling hands. He pulled a pint flask from his hip pocket and thrust it at Johnny. "Here!" Johnny looked up at him. "Go ahead, Mac," insisted the intern. Gratefully, Johnny took a long swallow. The intern passed the flask to Katie. "You too, Lady. You look as if you need it." Katie took a big drink. The cop spoke up.

"What do you take me for? A orphan?"

When the intern got the flask back from the cop, there was only an inch left in it. He sighed and emptied the bottle. The cop sighed, too, and turned to Johnny.

"Now. Where do you keep the gun?"

"Under my pillow."

"Get it. I got to take it over to the station house."

Katie, forgetting how she had disposed of the gun, went into the bedroom to look under the pillow. She came back, looking worried.

"Why, it's not there!"

The cop laughed. "Naturally. You took it out to shoot the louse."

It took Katie a long time to remember that she had thrown it into the washtub. She fished it out. The cop wiped it off and took out the bullets. He asked Johnny a question.

"You got a permit for this, Mac?"

"No."

"That's tough."

"It's not my gun."

"Who gave it to you?"

"No—— Nobody." Johnny did not want to get the watchman into trouble.

"How'd you get it then?"

"I found it. Yes, I found it in the gutter."

"All oiled and loaded?"

"Honest."

"And that's your story?"

"That's my story."

"It's okay by me, Mac. See that you stick to it."

The ambulance driver hollered from the hall that he was back from taking the man to the hospital and was Doc ready to leave.

"Hospital?" Katie asked. "Then I didn't kill him."

"Not quite," said the intern. "We'll get him on his feet so's he can walk to the electric chair by himself."

"I'm sorry," said Katie. "I meant to kill him."

"I got a statement from him before he passed out," said the cop. "That little kid down the block: he killed her. He was responsible for two other jobs, too. I got his statement, signed and witnessed." He patted his pocket. "I wouldn't be surprised

211

if I got a promotion out of this when the Commissioner hears."

"I hope so," said Katie bleakly. "I hope somebody gets some good out of it."

When Francie woke the next morning, papa was there to tell her that it was all a dream. And as time passed it did seem like a dream to Francie. If left no ugliness in her memories. Her physical terror had blunted her emotional perceptions. The terror on the stairs had been brief—a bare three minutes in time—and terror had served as an anaesthetic. The events that followed were hazy in her mind on account of the unaccustomed hypodermic. Even the hearing in court where she had to tell her story seemed like a part in an unreal play in which her lines were brief.

There was a hearing, but Katie was told beforehand that it was a technicality. Francie remembered little of it except that she told her story and Katie told hers. Few words were needed.

"I was coming home from school," testified Francie, "and when I got in the hall, this man came out and grabbed me before I could scream. While he was trying to drag me off the stairs, my mother came down."

Katie said: "I came down the stairs and saw him there pulling my daughter. I ran up and got the gun (it didn't take long) and I ran down and shot him while he was trying to sneak down the cellar."

Francie wondered whether mama would be arrested for shooting a man. But no, it ended up with the judge shaking mama's hand and hers too.

A lucky thing happened about the newspapers. A soused reporter, going through his nightly routine of calling up the station houses for police blotter news, got the facts of the story, but confused the Nolan name with the name of the policeman on the case. There was a half-column item in a Brooklyn paper which said that Mrs. O'Leary, of Williamsburg, had shot a prowler in the hallway of her home. The next day, two of the New York newspapers gave it two inches, in which they stated that Mrs. O'Leary, of Williamsburg, had been shot by a prowler in the hallway of her home.

* * *

Eventually, the whole affair faded away into the background. Katie was a neighbourhood heroine for a while, but as time passed, the neighbourhood forgot the murdering pervert. They remembered only that Katie Nolan had shot a man. And in speaking of her, they said that she's not one to get into a fight with. Why, she'd shoot a person just as soon as look at him.

The scar from the carbolic acid never left Francie's leg, but it dwindled down to the size of a dime. Francie got used to it in time, and as she grew older, she seldom noticed it any more.

As for Johnny, they fined him five dollars for violating the Sullivan Law—having a gun without a permit. And, oh, yes! The watchman's young wife eventually ran away with an Italian a little nearer her own age.

Some days later Sergeant McShane came over looking for Katie. He saw her lugging a can of ashes out to the kerb and his heart turned over with pity. He gave her a hand with the ash can. Katie thanked him and looked up at him. She had seen him once since the Mattie Mahony outing, the day he had asked Francie was she her mother. The other time was when he had brought Johnny home, the time when Johnny couldn't get himself home. Katie had heard that Mrs. McShane was now in a sanatorium for incurable tuberculosis patients. She was not expected to live long. "Would he marry again—afterwards?" Katie wondered. "Of course he will," she answered her own question. "He is a fine-looking, upstanding man with a good job and some woman will snap him up." He took off his hat while he spoke to her.

"Mrs. Nolan, the boys down at the station house and myself do be thankin' you for helpin' us out in the catchin' of the murtherer."

"You're welcome," said Katie conventionally.

"And to show their appreciation, what did the boys do but pass the hat for you!" He extended an envelope.

"Money?" she asked.

"It is that."

"Keep it!"

"Sure you'll be needin' it with your man not workin' steady and the childthern needin' this and that."

"That's none of your business, Sergeant McShane. You can see that I work hard and we don't need anything from nobody."

"Just as you say."

He put the envelope back into his pocket, looking at her steadily all the while. "Here's a woman," he thought, "with a trim figure on her and a pretty white-faced skin and black curling hair. And she's got courage enough and pride for six like her. I'm a middle-aged man of forty-five," his thoughts went on, "and she's but a slip of a girl." (Katie was thirty-one, but looked much younger.) "We've both had hard luck when it came to marryin'. That we did." McShane knew all about Johnny and knew that he wouldn't last long the way he was going on. He had nothing but pity for Johnny; he had nothing but pity for Molly, his wife. He wouldn't have harmed either of them. He had never once considered being physically unfaithful to his sickly wife. "But is hoping in my heart harming either one of them?" he asked himself. "Of course, there'll be the waitin'. How many years? Two? Five? Ah, well, I've waited a long time without hope of happiness. Sure and I can wait a bit longer, now."

He thanked her again and said good-bye formally. As he held her hand in the handclasp, he thought: "She'll be my wife, some day, God and she willin'."

Kate could not know what he was thinking. (Or could she?) Maybe. Because something prompted her to call after him:

"I hope that some day you'll be as happy as you deserve to be, Sergeant McShane."

XXXIV

WHEN FRANCIE heard Aunt Sissy tell mama that she was going to *get* a baby, she wondered why Sissy didn't say *have* a baby like other women said. She found out there was a reason why Sissy said *get* instead of *have*.

Sissy had had three husbands. There were ten tiny head stones on a small plot in St. John's Cemetery in Cypress Hills belonging to Sissy. And on each stone the date of death was the same as the date of birth. Sissy was thirty-five, now, and desperate about not having children. Katie and Johnny often talked it over and Katie was afraid that Sissy would kidnap a child some day.

Sissy wanted to adopt a child, but her John wouldn't hear of it.

"I'll not support another man's bastard, see?" was his way of putting it.

"Don't you like children, Lover?" she asked wheedlingly.

"Sure I like children. But they got to be my own and not some other bum's," he answered, unintentionally insulting himself.

In most things her John was like soft dough in Sissy's hands. But in this one thing he refused to allow himself to be kneaded her way. If there was to be a child, he kept insisting, it would have to be his and no other man's. Sissy knew he meant it. She even had a kind of respect for his attitude. But she *had* to have a living baby.

By chance, Sissy found out that a beautiful sixteen-year-old girl out in Maspeth had got into trouble with a married man and was going to have a baby. Her parents, Sicilians lately come over from the other side, had shut up the girl in a dark room so that the neighbours could not see her shame increase. Her father kept her on a diet of bread and water. He had a theory that this would weaken her so, that she and her child would die in childbirth. Lest the kind-hearted mother feed Lucia during his absence, the father left no money in the house when he went to work in the mornings. He brought a bagful of groceries each night when he returned home and watched that no food was sneaked out and set aside for the girl. After the family had eaten, he gave the girl her daily ration of half a loaf of bread and a jug of water.

Sissy was shocked when she heard of this story of starvation and cruelty. She thought out a plan. Feeling as they did, she thought the family would be glad to give away the baby when it was born. She decided to have a look at the people. If they seemed normal and healthy, she'd offer to take the baby.

The mother wouldn't let her into the house when she called. Sissy came back the next day with a badge pinned to her coat. She knocked on the door. When it was opened a crack, she pointed to the badge and sternly demanded admittance. The frightened mother, thinking Sissy was from the immigration department, let her in. The mother could not read, else she would have seen that the badge said "Chicken Inspector."

Sissy took charge. The mother-to-be was frightened and defiant and also very thin from the starvation diet. Sissy threatened the girl's mother with arrest if she didn't treat the girl better. With many tears and in badly broken English, the mother told of the disgrace and of the father's plan to starve

215

the girl and the unborn child to death. Sissy had a day-long talk with the mother and Lucia, the daughter. It was mostly in pantomime. At last Sissy made it understood that she was willing to take the child off their hands as soon as it was born. When the mother understood finally, she covered Sissy's hands with grateful kisses. From that day, Sissy became the adored and trusted friend of the family.

After her John left for work in the morning, Sissy cleaned up her flat, cooked a potful of food for Lucia and took it over to the Italian home. She fed Lucia well on a combination Irish-German diet. She had a theory that if the child absorbed such food before birth, it wouldn't be so much of an Italian.

Sissy took good care oi Lucia. On nice days she took her out to the park and made her sit in the sun. During the time of their unusual relationship, Sissy was a devoted friend and a gay companion to the girl. Lucia adored Sissy, who was the only one in this new world who had treated her kindly. The whole family (except the father, who didn't know of her existence) loved Sissy. The mother and other children gladly entered into a conspiracy to keep the father in ignorance. They locked Lucia up in her dark room again when they heard the father's step on the stairs.

The family couldn't speak much English and Sissy knew no Italian, but as the months passed, they learned some English from her and she learned Italian from them and they were able to talk together. Sissy never told her name, so they called her "Statch' Lib'ty," after the lady with the torch, which had been the first thing they saw of America.

Sissy took over Lucia, her unborn child and the family. When everything was settled and agreed upon, Sissy announced to her friends and family that she was starting another baby. No one paid any attention. Sissy was always starting babies.

She found an obscure midwife and paid her in advance for the delivery. She gave her a paper on which she had asked Katie to write her name, her John's name and Sissy's maiden name. She told the midwife that the paper was to be turned over to the Board of Health immediately after the birth. The ignorant woman, who could not speak Italian (Sissy had made sure of that when she hired her), assumed that the names handed her were the names of the mother and father. Sissy wanted the birth certificate to be in order.

Sissy was so realistic about her pregnancy by proxy that she simulated morning sickness in the beginning weeks. When Lucia announced that she felt life, Sissy told her husband that *she* felt life.

On the afternoon that Lucia's labour pains started, Sissy went home and got into bed. When her John came home from work, she told him the baby was starting to come. He looked at her. She was as trim as a balletdancer. He argued, but she was so insistent that he went and got her mother. Mary Rommely looked at Sissy and said she couldn't possibly be having a baby. For answer, Sissy let out a blood curdling yell and said that her pains were killing her. Mary looked at her thoughtfully. She didn't know what Sissy had in mind, but she did know it was useless to argue with her. If Sissy said she was going to have a baby, she was going to have a baby, and that's all there was to it. Her John protested.

"But look how skinny she is. There's no baby in that belly, see?"

"Maybe it will come from her head. That's big enough as one may see," said Mary Rommely.

"Aw, there don't give such things," said the John.

"Who are you to say?" demanded Sissy. "Didn't the Virgin Mary herself get a baby without a man? If she could do it, I'm sure I could do it easier, being's I'm married and have a man."

"Who knows?" asked Mary. She turned to the harassed husband and spoke gently. "There are a lot of things that men don't understand about." She urged the confused man to forget the whole thing, eat a nice supper which she would cook for him, and then go to bed and get a good night's sleep.

The puzzled man lay beside his wife throughout the night. He couldn't get a good night's sleep. From time to time, he'd rise on his elbows and stare at her. From time to time he'd run his hand over her flat stomach. Sissy slept soundly through the night.

When he left for work the next morning, Sissy announced that he'd be a father before he returned that night.

"I give up," shouted the tormented man and went off to his work in the pulp magazine house.

Sissy rushed over to Lucia's house. The baby had been born just an hour after the father had left. It was a beautiful healthy girl. Sissy was so happy. She said Lucia would have to nurse the baby for ten days to give it a start, then she'd take it home. She went out and bought a roasting chicken and a bakery store pie. The mother cooked the chicken Italian style. Sissy trusted a bottle of Chianti wine from the Italian grocer on the block and they all had a fine dinner. It was like a *fiesta* in the house. Everybody was happy. Lucia's stomach was almost flat again. There was no longer any monument to her disgrace. Now all was as it had been before ... or would be when Sissy took the baby away.

Sissy washed the baby every hour. She changed its shirt and band three times during the day. The diapers were changed every five minutes, whether they needed to be or not. She washed Lucia and made her clean and sweet. She brushed and brushed her hair until it glowed like satin. She couldn't do enough for Lucia and the baby. She had to tear herself away when it came time for the father's returning.

The father came home and went into the dark room to give Lucia her daily food pittance. He turned up the gas and found a radiant Lucia and a fat healthy baby sleeping contentedly at her side. He was amazed. All this on bread and water! Then fright grew on him. It was a miracle! Surely the Virgin Mary had intervened for the young mother. She had been known to work such miracles in Italy. Maybe he would be punished for treating his flesh and blood so inhumanly. Contrite, he brought her a plate heaped with spaghetti. Lucia declined it, saying she had grown used to bread and water. The mother sided with Lucia and explained that the bread and water had formed the perfect baby. More and more the father believed a miracle had come about. Frantically, he tried to be nice to Lucia, but the family were punishing him. They wouldn't permit him to show any kindness to his daughter.

Sissy was lying peacefully in bed when her John came home that evening. Jokingly, he asked:

"Did you have that baby today?"

"Yes," she said in a weak voice.

"Aw, go on!"

"It was born an hour after you left this morning."

"It was not!"

"I swear!"

He looked around the room. "Where is it, then?"

"In the incubator at Coney Island."

"In the *where?*"

"It was a seven month's baby, you know. Only weighed three pounds. That's why I didn't show."

"You lie, see?"

"As soon as I get my strength back, I'll take you to Coney Island, right to the glass case where it is."

"What are you trying to do? Drive me crazy?"

"I'm going to bring it home in ten days. Just as soon as it grows finger-nails." She put that in on the spur of the moment.

"*What's* got into you, Sissy? You know God-damned well you didn't have a baby this morning."

"I had a baby. It weighed three pounds. They took it to the incubator so that it wouldn't die and I'm going to get it back in ten days."

"I give up! I give up," he shouted and went out and got drunk.

Sissy brought the baby home ten days later. It was a big baby and weighed almost eleven pounds. Her John asserted himself for the last time.

"It seems mighty big for a ten-day-old baby."

"You're a mighty big man yourself, Lover," she whispered. She saw a pleased look come into his face. She put her arms around him. "I'm all right now," she said in his ear, "if you want to sleep with me."

"You know," he said afterwards, "it does look a little like me."

"Especially around the ears," murmured Sissy drowsily.

The Italian family went back to Italy a few months later. They were glad to go, because the new world had brought them nothing but sorrow, poverty and shame. Sissy never heard of them again.

Everybody knew that it wasn't Sissy's baby—that it *couldn't* be her baby. But she stuck to her story and since there was no other explanation, people had to accept it. After all, strange things did happen in the world. She christened the child Sarah, but in time everyone called it Little Sissy.

Katie was the only one to whom Sissy told the truth about the origin of the baby. She confided in her when she asked her to write out the names for the birth certificate. Ah, but Francie knew too. Often in the night she had been awakened by the sound of voices and heard mama and Aunt Sissy talking in the kitchen about the baby. Francie vowed always to keep Sissy's secret.

Johnny was the only other person (outside of the Italian family) who knew. Katie told him. Francie heard them talking about it when they thought she was sound asleep. Papa took the part of Sissy's husband.

"That's a dirty trick to play on a man, any man. Somebody ought to tell him. I'll tell him."

"No!" said mama sharply. "He's a happy man. Let him be that way."

"Happy? With another man's child palmed off on him? I don't see it."

"He's crazy for Sissy; he's always afraid she's going to leave him and he'd die if she left him. And you know Sissy. She went from one man to another, one husband to another—always trying to get a child. She was on the verge of leaving this one when the baby happened along. Sissy will be a different woman from now on. Mark my words. She'll settle down at last and make him a much better wife than he deserves to have. Who *is* this John, anyhow?" she interrupted herself. "She'll be a good mother. The child will be her whole world and she won't need to be going after the men any more. So don't monkey around with it, Johnny."

"You Rommely women are too deep for us men," decided Johnny. A thought struck him. "Say! You didn't do that to me, did you?"

In answer, Katie got the children out of bed. She had them stand before him in their long white nightgowns. "Look at them," she commanded. Johnny looked at his son. It was as if he were looking in a trick mirror where he saw himself perfectly, but on a smaller scale. He looked at Francie. There was Katie's face all over again (only more solemn) except for the eyes. They were Johnny's eyes. On an impulse, Francie picked up a plate and held it over her heart the way Johnny held his hat when he sang. She sang one of his songs:

They called her frivolous Sal.
A peculiar sort of a gal...

She had Johnny's expressions and Johnny's gestures.

"I know, I know," papa whispered. He kissed his children, gave them each a pat on the backside and told them to go back to bed. After they had gone, Katie pulled Johnny's head down and whispered something to him.

"No!" he said in a surprised voice.

"Yes, Johnny," she said quietly. He put his hat on. "Where

are you going, Johnny?"

"Out."

"Johnny, please don't come home . . ." she looked towards the bedroom door.

"I won't, Katie," he promised. He kissed her gently and went out.

Francie woke in the middle of the night wondering what had taken her out of her sleep. Ah! Papa hadn't come home yet. That was it. She never slept soundly until she knew he had come home. Once awake, she started thinking. She thought of Sissy's baby. She thought of birth. Her thoughts went to birth's corollary: death. She didn't want to think of death; how everybody was born but to die. While she was fighting off thoughts of death, she heard papa coming up the stairs singing softly. She shivered when she heard that he was singing the last verse of "Molly Malone." He never sang that verse. *Never!* Why . . .?

> *She died of a fever,*
> *And no one could save her,*
> *And that's how I lo-ost*
> *Sweet Molly Malone . . .*

Francie didn't stir. It was a rule that when papa came home late, mama was to open the door. She didn't want the children to lose their sleep. The song was coming to an end. Mama didn't hear—she wasn't getting up. Francie jumped out of bed. The song was ended before she reached the door. When she opened it, papa was standing there quietly, his hat in his hand. He was looking straight before him, over her head.

"You won Papa," she said.

"Did I?" he asked. He walked into the room, not looking at her.

"You finished the song."

"Yes, I finished the song, I guess." He sat in the chair by the window.

"Papa . . ."

"Turn out the light and go back to bed." (The light was kept burning low against his return.) She turned out the light.

"Papa, are . . . are you sick?"

"No. I'm not drunk," he said clearly from the dark. And Francie knew that he spoke the truth.

221

She went to bed and buried her face in the pillow. She did not know why, but she wept.

XXXV

ONCE MORE it was in the week before Christmas. Francie had just had her fourteenth birthday. Neeley, as he put it, was waiting to turn thirteen any moment. It looked as though it wouldn't be a good Christmas. There was something wrong with Johnny. Johnny wasn't drinking. There had been other times, of course, when Johnny stopped drinking, but that was when he was working. Now he wasn't drinking at all and he wasn't working, and the wrong thing about Johnny was that he wasn't drinking, but he was acting like he was drinking.

He hadn't spoken to his family in more than two weeks. Francie remembered the last time papa had said anything to her was that night when he came home sober singing the last verse of "Molly Malone." Come to think of it, he hadn't sung since that night either. He came and went without speaking. He stayed out late nights and came home sober and nobody knew where he spent that time. His hands were trembling badly. He could hardly hold the fork when he ate. And suddenly he looked very old.

Yesterday he had come in while they were eating supper. He looked at them as though he were going to say something. Instead of speaking, he closed his eyes for a second and then went into the bedroom. He had no regular hours for anything. He came and went at odd hours of the day and night. When he was home, he spent the time lying on his bed fully clothed with his eyes shut.

Katie went about white and quiet. There was a foreboding about her as though she were carrying tragedy within herself. Her face was thin and there were hollows under her cheeks.

She had taken on an extra job in this week before Christmas. She got up earlier and worked faster at her flat cleaning and was finished in early afternoon. She rushed down to Gorling's, the department store at the Polish end of the Grand Street, where she worked from four to seven, serving coffee and sandwiches to the shop girls, who were not allowed to take the time to go out for supper on account of the Christmas rush. Her family desperately needed that seventy-five cents that she earned each day.

It was nearly seven o'clock. Neeley had come home from his paper route and Francie was back from the library. There was no fire in the flat. They had to wait until mama came home with some money with which to buy a bundle of wood. The children wore their coats and zitful caps as it was very cold in the flat. Francie saw that mama had washing on the line and she pulled it in. The garments had frozen into grotesque shapes and didn't want to come in through the window.

"Here, let me at 'em," said Neeley, referring to a frozen suit of underwear. The legs of the long drawers had frozen in a spread-out position and Neeley's struggles did no good.

"I'll break the damn thing's legs," said Francie. She whacked it fiercely and it crackled and collapsed. She pulled it in viciously. She looked like Katie at that moment.

"Francie?"

"Huh?"

"You . . . you *cursed*."

"I know it."

"God heard you."

"Oh, shoot!"

"Yes, He did. He sees and hears everything."

"Neeley, do you believe that He looks right in this little old room?"

"You betcha He does."

"Don't you believe it, Neeley. He's too busy watching all the little sparrows fall and worrying about whether the little buds will burst into flowers to have time to investigate us."

"Don't talk like that, Francie."

"I will so. If He went around looking into people's windows like you say, He'd see how things were here; He'd see that it was cold and that there was no food in the house; He'd see that mama isn't strong enough to work so hard. And He'd see how papa was and He'd do something about papa. Yes, He would!"

"Francie . . ." the boy looked around the room uneasily. Francie saw that he was uneasy.

"I'm getting too big to tease him," she thought. Aloud she said: "All right, Neeley." They talked about other things until

Katie came home.

Katie came in with a rush. She had a bundle of wood blocks which she had bought for two cents, a can of condensed milk and three bananas in a bag. She stuffed paper and the wood into the range and had a fire going in no time.

"Well, children, I guess we'll have to have oatmeal for supper tonight."

"Again?" groaned Francie.

"It won't be so bad," said mama. "We have condensed milk and I bought bananas to slice on top."

"Mama," ordered Neeley, "don't mix my condensed milk with the oatmeal. Let it stay on top."

"Slice the bananas and cook them with the oatmeal," suggested Francie.

"I want to eat my banana whole," protested Neeley.

Mama settled the argument. "I'll give you each a banana and you eat it the way you want."

When the oatmeal was cooked, Katie filled two soup plates full, set them on the table, punched two holes in the can of milk and set a banana by each plate.

"Aren't you going to eat, Mama?" asked Neeley.

"I'll eat after. I'm not hungry now," Katie sighed.

Francie said: "Mama, if you don't feel like eating, why don't you play the piano so it's like a restaurant while we're eating."

"It's cold in the front room."

"Light the oil stove," chorused the children.

"All right." Katie took a portable oil stove from the cupboard. "Only you know I don't play so good."

"You play grand, Mama," said Francie sincerely.

Katie was pleased. She knelt to light the oil stove. "What do you want me to play?"

"'Come Little Leaves,'" called Francie.

"'Welcome, Sweet Springtime,'" shouted Neeley.

"I'll play 'Little Leaves' first," decided mama, "because I didn't give Francie a birthday present." She went into the cold front room.

"I think I'll slice my banana on top of my oatmeal. I'll slice it very thin so that there's a whole lot of it," said Francie.

"I'm going to eat mine whole," decided Neeley, "and slow, so that it lasts a long time."

Mama was playing Francie's song, now. It was one that Mr. Morton had taught the children. She sang to the music:

Come, little leaves, said the wind one day.
Come o'er the meadows with me and play.
Put on your dresses of red and gold . . .

"Aw, that's a baby song," interrupted Neeley. Francie stopped singing. When Katie finished Francie's song, she started to play Rubinstein's "Melody in F." Mr. Morton had taught them that song too, calling it "Welcome, Sweet Springtime." Neeley started to sing:

Welcome, sweet springtime, we greet thee in song.

His voice changed suddenly from tenor to bass on the high note in "song." Francie giggled and soon Neeley was giggling so much that he couldn't sing.

"You know what mama would say if she was sitting here now?" asked Francie.

"What?"

"She'd say, 'Spring will be here before you know it.' " They laughed.

"Christmas is coming soon," commented Neeley.

"Remember when we were children," said Francie, who had just finished being thirteen, "how we used to smell if Christmas was coming?"

"Let's see if we can still smell it," Neeley said impulsively. He opened the window a crack and put his nose to it. "Yup."

"What does it smell like?"

"I smell snow. Remember how, when we were kids we used to look up at the sky and holler, 'Feather boy, feather boy, shake down some feathers from the sky.' "

"And when it snowed we thought there was a feather boy up there. Let me smell," she asked suddenly. She put her nose to the crack. "Yes, I can smell it. It smells like orange peel and Christmas trees put together." They closed the window.

"I never snitched on you that time you got the doll when you said your name was Mary."

"No," said Francie gratefully. "And I didn't tell on you either, the time you made a cigarette out of coffee grounds and when you smoked it the paper caught fire and fell on her blouse and burned a big hole in it. I helped you hide it."

"You know," mused Neeley, "mama found that blouse and sewed a patch over the hole and she never asked me about it."

"Mama is funny," said Francie. They pondered a while over their mother's inscrutable ways. The fire was dying down now, but the kitchen was still warm. Neeley sat on top of the far end of the stove, where it wasn't so hot. Mama had warned him that he'd get piles from sitting on a hot stove. But Neeley didn't care. He liked his backside to be warm.

The children were almost happy. The kitchen was warm and they were fed and mama's playing made them safe and comfortable. They reminisced about past Christmases, or, as Francie put it, they talked about olden times.

While they were talking, someone pounded on the door. "It's papa," said Francie.

"No. Papa always sings coming up the stairs, so we know it's him."

"Neeley, papa hasn't sung coming home since that night...."

"Let me in!" shouted Johnny's voice and he beat on the door as though he would break it down. Mama came running out from the front room. Her eyes looked very dark in her white face. She opened the door. Johnny lunged in. They stared at him. They had never seen papa looking like that. He was always so neat and now his tuxedo jacket was dirty, as though he had been lying in the gutter and his derby hat was bashed in. He didn't own an overcoat or gloves. His cold red hands were trembling. He lunged to the table.

"No, I'm not drunk," he said.

"Nobody said . . ." began Katie.

"At last I'm through with it. I hate it, I hate it, I hate it!" He pounded the table. They knew he was speaking the truth. "I haven't touched a drop since that night . . ." he broke off suddenly. "But no one would believe me any more. No one...."

"There, Johnny," said mama soothingly.

"What's the matter, Papa?" asked Francie.

"Sh! Don't bother your father," said mama. She spoke to Johnny. "There's coffee left from this morning, Johnny. It's nice and hot and we've got milk tonight. I was waiting until you came home, so that we could eat together." She poured coffee.

"We ate already," said Neeley.

"Hush!" mama told him. She put milk into the coffee and sat opposite Johnny. "Drink it, Johnny, while it's hot."

Johnny stared at the cup. Suddenly, he pushed it from him and Katie drew a sharp breath as it clattered to the floor. Johnny buried his head in his arms and sobbed shudderingly.

226

Katie went to him.

"What's the matter, Johnny, what's the matter?" she asked soothingly. Finally he sobbed out:

"They threw me out of the Waiters' Union today. They said I was a bum and a drunk. They said they'd never give me another job as long as I live." He controlled his sobs for a moment and his voice was frightened as he said: "as long as I live!" He wept bitterly. "They wanted me to turn in my Union button." He put his hand over the tiny green-and-white button he wore in his lapel. Francie's throat got tight as she remembered how he often said he wore it like an ornament, a rose. He was so proud to be a Union man. "But I wouldn't give it up," he sobbed.

"That's nothing, Johnny. You just get a good rest and get on your feet again and they'll be glad to take you in. You're a good waiter and the best singer they've got."

"I'm no good any more. I can't sing any more. Katie, they laugh at me now when I sing. The last few jobs I had, they hired me to give the people a laugh. It's come to that, now. I'm finished." He sobbed wildly; he sobbed as though he never could stop.

Francie wanted to run into the bedroom and hide her head under the pillow. She edged towards the door. Mama saw her.

"Stay here!" she said sharply. She spoke to papa again. "Come, Johnny. Rest a while and you'll feel better. The oil stove is lit and I'll put it in the bedroom and it will be nice and warm. I'll sit with you until you fall asleep." She put her arms around him. Gently, he put her arms away and went into the bedroom alone, sobbing more quietly. Katie spoke to the children. "I'm going to stay with papa for a while. Keep on talking or doing whatever you were doing." The children stared at her numbly. "What are you looking at me like that for?" her voice broke. "Nothing's the matter." They looked away. She went into the front room to get the oil stove.

Francie and Neeley did not look at each other for a long time. Finally he said: "Do you want to talk about olden times?"

"No," said Francie.

XXXVI

JOHNNY DIED three days later.

He had gone to bed that night and Katie had sat by him
until he went to sleep. Later she slept with Francie so as not to
disturb him. Some time during the night he got up, dressed
quietly and went out. He did not return the next night. The
second day they began looking for him. They looked all over,
but Johnny hadn't been in any of his accustomed haunts for a
week.

The second night, McShane came over to take Katie to a
nearby Catholic Hospital. On the way over he told her, as
gently as he could, about Johnny. Johnny had been found
early that morning huddled in a doorway. He was unconscious
when a cop found him. His tuxedo jacket was buttoned up
over his undershirt and the cop saw the St. Anthony's medal
around his neck and called up the Catholic Hospital ambulance. There were no marks of identification on him. Later the
cop made his report to the station house and gave a description of the unconscious man. In the routine of checking the
reports, McShane came across the description. His sixth sense
told him who the man was. He went to the hospital and saw
that it was Johnny Nolan.

Johnny was still living when Katie got there. He had pneumonia, the doctor told her, and there wasn't a chance. It was
merely a question of hours. Already he was in the coma that
came before death. They took Katie to him. His bed was in a
long corridor-like ward. There were fifty other beds in the
ward. Katie thanked McShane and said good-bye. He went
away knowing that she wanted to be alone with Johnny.

There was a screen, connoting dying, around Johnny's bed.
They brought a chair for Katie and she sat there all day
watching him. He was breathing harshly and there were dried
tears on his face. Katie stayed there until he died. He had
never opened his eyes. He had not spoken a word to his wife.

It was night when she came home. She decided not to tell the
children until the morning. "Let them have a night's sleep
behind them," she thought, "one more night of griefless sleep."
She told them only that their father was in the hospital and
very sick. She said no more. There was something about
the way she looked that discouraged the children from asking
questions.

Just as dawn came, Francie woke. She looked across the

narrow bedroom and saw mama sitting next to Neeley's bed and looking down into his face. Her eyes were dark underneath and she looked as though she had been sitting there all night. When she saw that Francie was awake, she told her to get up and get dressed right away. She shook Neeley gently to awaken him and told him the same thing. She went out into the kitchen.

The bedroom was grey and cold and Francie shivered as she got into her clothes. She waited for Neeley, not wanting to go out to mama alone. Katie was sitting by the window. They came before her and stood waiting.

"Your father is dead," she told them.

Francie stood numb. There was no feeling of surprise or grief. There was no feeling of anything. What mama just said had no meaning.

"You're not to cry for him," ordered mama. Her next words had no sense either. "He's out of it now and maybe he's luckier than we are."

An orderly at the hospital was in the pay of an undertaker whom he notified as soon as a death occurred. This wide-awake undertaker gained an advantage over his competitors in that he went after the business, while the others waited for the business to come after them. This enterprising fellow called on Katie early in the morning.

"Mrs. Nolan," he said, surreptitiously referring to the slip of paper on which the orderly had written her name and address, "I sympathize with you in your great grief. I give you a thought: What has come to you has to come to all of us."

"What do you want?" asked Katie bluntly.

"To be your friend." He hurried on before she could misunderstand. "There are details connected with . . . ah . . . the remains, I mean . . ." again a quick look at the slip, "I mean Mr. Nolan. I ask you to look on me as a friend who brings comfort at a time when . . . who will . . . well, I want you to leave everything in my hands."

Katie understood. "How much would you charge for a simple funeral?"

"Now don't you worry about costs," he hedged. "I'll give him a fine funeral. There's no man I respected more than Mr. Nolan." (He had never known Mr. Nolan.) "I'll make it my personal business to see that he gets the best there is. Don't worry about the money."

"I won't. Because there's none to worry about."

He wet his lips. "Aside from the insurance money of course." It was a question, not a statement.

"There's insurance. A little."

"Ah!" He rubbed his hands together happily. "There's where I can be of service. There's red tape connected with collecting insurance. Take a long time before you get the money. Now supposing you (and understand I'm not charging you for this) let me take care of it. You just sign this," he whisked a paper out of his pocket, "turning your policy over to me. I'll advance the money and collect on the policy."

All undertakers gave this "service." It was a trick to ascertain how much insurance there was. Once they knew the amount, the funeral cost eighty per cent of it. They *had* to leave a little money for mourning clothes to keep the people satisfied.

Katie got the policy. As she put it on the table, his practised eye picked out the amount: two hundred dollars. He appeared not to have looked at the policy. After Katie had signed the paper, he talked of other things for a while. Finally, as if coming to a decision, he said:

"Tell you what I'll do, Mrs. Nolan. I'll give the departed a first-class four-coach funeral with a nickel handle coffin for one hundred and seventy-five dollars. That's my regular two-hundred-and-fifty-dollar job and I'm not making a penny on it."

"Why are you doing it then for?" asked Katie.

He wasn't at all put out. "I'm doing it because I liked Mr. Nolan. A splendid man and a hard-working man." He noticed the surprised look Katie gave him.

"I don't know," she hesitated. "A hundred and seventy-five . . ."

"That includes the Mass, too," he put in hastily.

"All right," said Katie dully. She was tired of talking about it.

The undertaker picked up the policy and pretended to see the amount for the first time. "Say! This is for two hundred," he said in stagey surprise. "That means you got twenty-five dollars coming to you after the funeral is paid." He dug into his pocket, stretching his leg out straight before him to do so. "Well, I always say that a little cash comes in handy at a time like this . . . at any time, if you ask me." He chuckled understandingly. "So I'll just advance you the balance out of my own pocket." He put twenty-five dollars in new notes on the table.

Katie thanked him. He wasn't fooling her, but she made no protest. She knew that was the way things were done. He was only working at his trade. He asked her to get the death certificate from the officiating doctor.

"And please inform them that I'll call for the re ... I mean for the depart ... well, I'll come and get Mr. Nolan."

When Katie went to the hospital again, she was taken to the doctor's office. The priest of the parish was there. He was trying to supply information for the making out of the death certificate. When he saw Katie he made the sign of the cross in blessing and then shook her hand.

"Mrs. Nolan can tell you more than I can," said the priest.

The doctor asked necessary questions; the full name and place of birth and date of birth and so on. Finally Katie asked *him* a question.

"What are you writing down there—what he died from, I mean?"

"Acute alcoholism and pneumonia."

"They said he died of pneumonia."

"That was the direct cause of death. But this acute alcoholism was a definite contributing factor; probably the main cause of death, if you wish the truth."

"I don't want you to write down," said Katie slowly and steadily, "that he died from drinking too much. Write that he died of pneumonia alone."

"Madam, I have to state the entire truth."

"He's dead. What can it mean to you what he died of?"

"The law requires ..."

"Look," said Katie. "I got two nice children. They're going to grow up to amount to something. It isn't their fault that their father ... that he died from what you said. It would mean a lot to me if I could tell them that their father died of pneumonia alone."

The priest took a hand in it. "You can do it, Doctor," he said, "without hurt to yourself and with benefit to others. Don't be kicking around of a poor lad that's dead and gone. Write down pneumonia, which is no lie, and this lady will be remembering you in her prayers for a long time to come. Besides," he added practically, "it's no skin off your teeth."

All of a sudden the doctor recalled two things; he remembered that the priest was a member of the hospital board and he remembered that he liked being head doctor at that particular hospital.

"All right," he conceded. "I'll do it. But don't let it get around. It's a personal favour to you, Father." He wrote down "pneumonia" in the blank after "Cause of death."

And it was nowhere on record that John Nolan had died a drunkard.

Katie used the twenty-five dollars to buy mourning clothes. She bought Neeley a new black suit with long trousers. It was his first long-trousers suit, and pride, pleasure and grief fought in Neeley's heart. For herself, Katie got a new black hat and a three foot widow's veil, according to the custom of Brooklyn. Francie got new shoes, which she had been needing for a long time anyhow. It was decided not to buy Francie a black coat as she was growing fast and it wouldn't fit her next winter. Mama said her old green coat would do with a black band around the arm. Francie was glad because she hated black and had worried lest her mother put her in deep mourning. The little money left over after the shopping was finished was put in the tin-can bank.

The undertaker came again to report that Johnny was at his funeral parlour and was being fixed up fine and would be brought home that evening. Katie told him, rather sharply, not to give them the details.

Then the blow fell.

"Mrs. Nolan, I have to have the deed to your lot."

"What lot?"

"The cemetery plot. I need the deed to get the grave opened."

"I thought that was all in the hundred and seventy-five dollars."

"No, no, no! I'm giving you a bargain. The coffin alone cost me ..."

"I don't like you," said Katie in her blunt way. "I don't like the business you're in. But then," she added with her amazing detachment, "suppose someone has to bury the dead. How much is a plot?"

"Twenty dollars."

"Where in the world would I get ..." She stopped short. "Francie, get the screwdriver."

They prised up the tin-can bank. There was eighteen dollars and sixty-two cents in it.

"It's not enough," said the undertaker, "but I'll lay out the rest." He held out his hand for the money.

"I'll get all the money together," Katie told him. "But I'll not turn over the money until I have the deed in my hand."

He fussed and argued and finally went away saying he'd bring back the deed. Mama sent Francie over to Sissy's house to borrow two dollars. When the undertaker came back with the deed, Katie, remembering something her mother had said fourteen years ago, read it slowly and carefully. She made Francie and Neeley read it too. The undertaker stood first on one foot, then on the other. When all three Nolans were satisfied that the deed was in order, Katie handed over the money.

"Why should I want to cheat you, Mrs. Nolan?" he asked plaintively, as he put the money away carefully.

"Why should anyone want to cheat anybody?" she asked in return. "But they do."

The tin can stood in the middle of the table. It was fourteen years old and its strips were battered.

"Do you want me to nail it back down, Mama?" asked Francie.

"No," said mama slowly. "We won't need it any more. You see, we own a bit of land now." She placed the folded deed on top of the clumsy star bank.

Francie and Neeley remained out in the kitchen all the time the coffin was in the front room. They even slept in the kitchen. They didn't want to see their father in the coffin. Katie seemed to understand and did not insist that they go in and look at their father.

The house was full of flowers. The Waiters' Union, which had thrown Johnny out less than a week before, sent round an enormous pillow of white carnations with a purple ribbon running diagonally across it on which were the words in gold letters: *Our Brother*. The cops from the precinct, in memory of the capture of the murderer, sent a cross of red roses. Sergeant McShane sent a sheaf of lilies. Johnny's mother, the Rommelys and some of the neighbours sent flowers. There were flowers from dozens of Johnny's friends that Katie had never heard of. McGarrity, the saloon-keeper, sent a wreath of artificial laurel leaves.

"I'd throw it in the ash bin," said Evy indignantly when she read the card.

"No," said Katie gently, "I can't blame McGarrity. Johnny didn't *have* to go there."

(Johnny owed McGarrity over thirty-eight dollars at the time of his death. For some reason, the saloon-keeper said nothing to Katie about it. He cancelled the debt silently.)

The flat was sickly with the combined scents of roses, lilies and carnations. For ever after, Francie hated those flowers, but it pleased Katie to know how much people had thought of Johnny.

A few moments before they were to close the coffin lid on Johnny, Katie came out to the kitchen to the children. She put her hands on Francie's shoulders and spoke low.

"I heard some neighbours whispering. They said you won't look at your father because he wasn't a good father to you."

"He *was* a good father," said Francie fiercely.

"Yes, he was," agreed Katie. She waited, letting the children make their own decision.

"Come on, Neeley," said Francie. Hand in hand, the children went in to their father. Neeley looked quickly, then, afraid that he would start crying, he ran out of the room. Francie stood there with her eyes on the ground, afraid to look. Finally, she lifted her eyes. She couldn't believe that papa wasn't living! He wore his tuxedo suit, which had been cleaned and pressed. He had on a fresh dicky and collar and a carefully-tied bow tie. There was a carnation in his lapel and, above it, his Union button. His hair was shining and golden and as curling as ever. One of the locks was out of place and had fallen down on the side of his forehead a little. His eyes were closed as though he were sleeping lightly. He looked young and handsome and well-cared-for. She noticed for the first time how finely arched his eyebrows were. His small moustache was trimmed and looked as debonair as ever. All the pain and grief and worry had left his face. It was smooth and boyish-looking. Johnny was thirty-four years old when he died. But he looked younger now; like a boy just past twenty. Francie looked at his hands, crossed so casually over a silver crucifix. There was a circlet of whiter skin on his third finger, where he used to wear the signet ring that Katie had given him when they married. (Katie had taken it off to give to Neeley when he grew up.) It was queer to see papa's hands so quiet when she remembered them as always trembling. Francie noticed how narrow and sensitive-looking they were with the long and tapering fingers. She stared steadily at his hands and thought she saw them move. Panic churned up in her and she wanted to run away. But the room was full of people watching her. They would say she was running away because ... He *had* been a good father. He had! He had! She put her hand on his hair and put the lock back in place. Aunt Sissy came and put her arm around her and whispered: "It's time." Francie stepped back to stand with mama while they closed the lid.

At the Mass, Francie knelt on one side of mama and Neeley on the other. Francie kept her eyes on the floor, so that she wouldn't have to look at the flower-covered coffin standing on trestles before the altar. Once she stole a look at her mother. Katie was kneeling, staring straight ahead, her face white and quiet under the widow's veil.

When the priest stepped down and walked around the coffin, sprinkling holy water at the four corners of it, a woman sitting across the aisle sobbed wildly. Katie, jealous and fiercely possessive, even in death, turned sharply to look at the woman who dared weep for Johnny. She looked well at the woman, then turned her head away. Her thoughts were like torn bits of paper blowing around.

"Hildy O'Dair is old for her age," she thought. "It's like powder was sprinkled on her yellow hair. But she's not much older than me ... thirty-two or three. She was eighteen when I was seventeen. You go your way and I'll go my way. You mean you'll go her way, Hildy, Hildy ... he's my feller, Katie Rommely ... Hildy, Hildy ... but she's my best friend ... I'm not much good, Hildy ... I shouldn't have led you on ... you go your ... Hildy, Hildy. Let her cry, let her cry," thought Katie. "Someone who loved Johnny should cry for him and I can't cry. Let her ..."

Katie, Johnny's mother, and Francie and Neeley rode out to the cemetery in the first coach behind the hearse. The children sat with their backs to the driver. Francie was glad, because she couldn't see the hearse which led the procession. She saw the coach which followed. Aunt Evy and Aunt Sissy were in that one alone. Their husbands couldn't come because they were working and Granma Mary Rommely was staying at home to mind Sissy's new baby. Francie wished she were riding in the second coach. Ruthie Nolan wept and lamented during the whole of the ride. Katie sat in stony quiet. The

235

carriage was close and smelled of damp hay and stale horse manure. The smell, the closeness, the riding backwards and the tension gave Francie an unfamiliar feeling of sickness.

At the cemetery there was a plain wooden box standing beside a deep hole. They put the cloth-covered casket with its shiny handles into the plain box. Francie looked away when they lowered it into the grave.

It was a grey day and a chill wind was blowing. Little whirls of frozen dust eddied about Francie's feet. A short distance away, at a week-old grave, some men were stripping the withered flowers from the wire frames of the floral pieces heaped on the grave. They worked methodically, keeping the withered flowers in a neat heap and piling up the wire frames carefully. Theirs was a legitimate business. They bought this concession from the cemetery officials and sold the wire frames to the florists, who used them over and over again. No one complained because the men were very scrupulous about not tearing off the flowers until they were well withered.

Someone pushed a lump of cold damp earth into Francie's hand. She saw that mama and Neeley were standing at the edge of the grave and dropping their handfuls of earth in it. Francie walked slowly to the edge, closed her eyes and opened her hand slowly. She heard a soft thud after a second, and that feeling of sickness came back again.

After the burial the coaches went in different directions. Each mourner was to be taken to his own home. Ruthie Nolan went off with some mourners who lived near her. She didn't even say good-bye. All during the services she had refused to speak to Katie and the children. Aunt Sissy and Evy got into the carriage with Katie and Francie and Neeley. There wasn't room for five people, so Francie had to sit on Evy's lap. They were all very quiet on the way home. Aunt Evy tried to cheer them up by telling some new stories about Uncle Willie and his horse. But no one smiled because no one listened.

Mama made the coach stop at a barber's shop round the corner from their house.

"Go in there," she told Francie, "and get your father's cup."

Francie didn't know what she meant. "What cup?" she asked.

"Just ask for his cup."

Francie went in. There were two barbers there but no customers. One of the barbers sat on one of the chairs in a row against the wall. His left ankle rested on his right knee and he cradled a mandolin. He was playing "O, Sole Mio." Francie knew the song. Mr. Morton had taught it to them, saying the title was "Sunshine." The other barber was sitting on one of the barber chairs looking at himself in the long mirror. He got down from the chair as the girl came in.

"Yes?" he asked.

"I want my father's cup."

"The name?"

"John Nolan."

"Ah, yes. Too bad." He sighed as he took a mug from the row of them on a shelf. It was a thick white mug with "John Nolan" written on it in gold and in fancy block letters. There was a worn-down cake of white soap at the bottom of it and a tired looking brush. He prised out the soap and put it and the brush in a bigger unlettered cup. He washed Johnny's cup.

While Francie waited, she looked around. She had never been inside a barber shop. It smelled of soap and clean towels and bay rum. There was a gas-heater which hissed companionably. The barber had finished the song and started it over again. The thin tinkle of the mandolin made a sad sound in the warm shop. Francie sang Mr. Morton's words to the song in her mind.

> *Oh, what's so fine, dear,*
> *As a day of sunshine.*
> *The storm is past at last.*
> *The sky is blue and clear.*

Everyone has a secret life, she mused. Papa never spoke about the barber shop, yet he had come here three times a week to be shaved. Fastidious Johnny had bought his own cup, emulating men who were in better circumstances. He wouldn't be shaved with lather from the common cup. Not Johnny. He had come there three times a week—when he had the money—and sat in one of those chairs and looked in that mirror and talked with the barber about—maybe—whether the Brooklyns' had a good ball team that year or whether the Democrats would get in as usual. Perhaps he had sung when that other barber played the mandolin. Yes, she was sure that he had sung. Singing had come easier than breathing to him. She wondered if, when he had to wait, he read *The Police Gazette* lying on that bench?

The barber gave her the washed and dried cup. "Johnny

Nolan was a fine feller," he said. "Tell the mama that I, his barber, said this."

"Thank you," whispered Francie gratefully. She went out, closing the door on the sad sound of the mandolin.

Back in the coach, she held out the cup to Katie. "That's for you to have," said mama. "Neeley will have papa's signet ring."

Francie looked at her father's name in gold and whispered "Thank you" gratefully for the second time in five minutes.

Johnny had been on earth for thirty-four years. Less than a week ago he had walked on those streets. And now the cup, the ring and two unironed waiter's aprons at home were the only concrete objects left to connote that a man had once lived. There were no other physical reminders of Johnny, as he had been buried in all the clothes he owned with his studs and his fourteen-carat gold collar button.

When they got home they found that the neighbours had been in and straightened up the flat. The furniture had been put back in place in the front room and the withered leaves and fallen flower petals swept out. The windows had been opened and the rooms aired out. They had brought coal and made a great fire in the kitchen range and put a fresh white cloth on the table. The Tynmore girls had brought up a cake which they had baked themselves, and it stood on a plate and was already sliced. Floss Gaddis and her mother had bought a whole lot of sliced bologna. It took two plates to hold it. There was a basket of freshly sliced rye bread and the coffee-cups were set out on the table. There was a potful of freshly made coffee warming on the stove and someone had set a pitcher of real cream in the middle of the table. They had done all this while the Nolans were away. Then they had left, locked the door behind them and put the key under the mat.

Aunt Sissy, Evy, Mama, Francie, and Neeley sat at the table. Aunt Evy poured out the coffee. Katie sat for a long time looking at her cup. She remembered the last time Johnny had sat at that table. She did what Johnny had done; she pushed the cup away with her arm, put her head down on the table and cried in great ugly tearing sobs. Sissy put her arms around her and spoke in her gentle caressing voice.

"Katie, Katie, don't cry so. Don't cry so, else the child you'll soon be bringing into this world will be a sad child."

XXXVII

KATIE STAYED in bed the day after the funeral and Francie and Neeley wandered around the flat stunned and bewildered. Towards evening, Katie got up and made some supper for them. After they had eaten, she urged the children to go for a little walk, saying they needed the air.

Francie and Neeley walked up Graham Avenue towards Broadway. It was a bitterly cold and a still night, but there was no snow. The streets were empty. It was three days after Christmas and children were home playing with their new toys. The street lights were bleak and bright. A small icy wind coming in from the sea blew close to the ground. It whirled bits of dirty papers along the gutters.

They had grown out of childhood in the last few days. Christmas as Christmas had passed unnoticed since their father had died on Christmas Day. Neeley's thirteenth birthday had been lost somewhere in those last few days.

They came to the brilliantly-lighted façade of a big vaudeville house. Since they were reading children and read everything they came across, they stopped and automatically read the list of acts playing that week. Underneath the sixth act was a an announcement in large letters:

"Here next week! Chauncy Osborne, Sweet Singer of Sweet Songs. Don't miss him!"

Sweet Singer . . . Sweet Singer . . .

Francie had not shed a tear since her father's death. Neither had Neeley. Now Francie felt that all the tears she had were frozen together in her throat in a solid lump and the lump was growing . . . growing. She felt that if the lump didn't melt soon and change back into tears, she too would die. She looked at Neeley. Tears were falling out of his eyes. Then her tears came, too.

They turned into a dark side street and sat on the edge of the pavement with their feet in the gutter. Neeley, though weeping, remembered to spread his handkerchief on the kerb so that his new long trousers wouldn't get dirty. They sat close together because they were cold and lonesome. They wept long and quietly, sitting there in the cold street. At last, when they could cry no more, they talked.

"Neeley, why did papa have to die?"

"I guess God wanted him to die."

"Why?"

"Maybe to punish him."

"Punish him for what?"

"I don't know," said Neeley miserably.

"Do you believe that God put papa on this world?"

"Yes."

"Then He wanted him to live, didn't He?"

"I guess so."

"Then why did He make him die so quick?"

"Maybe to punish him," repeated Neeley, not knowing what else to answer.

"If that's true, what good is it? Papa's dead and he don't know that he's punished. God made papa the way he was and then said to Himself: I dare you to do anything about it. I just bet He said that."

"Maybe you shouldn't talk about God like that," said Neeley apprehensively.

"They say God's so great," said Francie scornfully, "and knows everything and can do everything. If He's so great, why didn't He help papa instead of punishing him like you said?"

"I just said *maybe*."

"If God has charge of all the world," said Francie, "and the sun and the moon and the stars and all the birds and trees and flowers and all the animals and people, you'd think He'd be too busy and too important—wouldn't you?—to spend so much time punishing one man—one man like papa."

"I don't think you should talk about God like that," said Neeley uneasily. "He might strike you down dead."

"Then let Him," cried Francie fiercely. "Let Him strike me down dead right here in the gutter where I sit!"

They waited fearfully. Nothing happened. When Francie spoke again, she was quieter.

"I believe in the Lord, Jesus Christ, and His Mother, Holy Mary. Jesus was a living baby once. He went barefooted like we do in the summer. I saw a picture where He was a boy and had no shoes on. And when He was a man He went fishing, like papa did once. And they could hurt Him too, like they couldn't hurt God. Jesus wouldn't go around punishing people. He *knew* about people. So I will always believe in Jesus Christ."

They made the sign of the cross as Catholics do when mentioning Jesus' name. Then she put her hand on Neeley's knee and spoke in a whisper.

"Neeley, I wouldn't tell anybody but you, but I don't

240

believe in God any more."

"I want to go home," said Neeley. He was shivering.

When Katie let him in she saw that their faces were tired, yet peaceful. "Well, they've cried it out," she thought.

Francie looked at her mother, then looked away quickly. "While we were gone," she thought, "she cried and cried until she couldn't cry any more." The weeping wasn't mentioned aloud by any one of them.

"I thought you'd come home cold," said mama, "so I made a warm surprise for you."

"What?" asked Neeley.

"You'll see."

The surprise was "hot chocolate" which was cocoa and condensed milk made into a paste and boiling water stirred into it. Katie poured the thick rich stuff into the cups. "And that's not all," she added. She took three marshmallows from a paper bag in her apron pocket and popped one into each cup.

"Mama!" said the children simultaneously and ecstatically. "Hot chocolate" was something extra special, usually reserved for birthdays.

"Mama is really somebody," thought Francie as she held her marshmallow down with her spoon and watched the melting white sworls vein the dark chocolate. "She knows we've been crying, but she's not asking questions about it. Mama never . . ." Suddenly the right word about mama came to Francie. "Mama never *fumbles*."

No, Katie never fumbled. When she used her beautifully-shaped but worn-looking hands, she used them with surety, whether it was to put a broken flower into a tumbler of water with one true gesture, or to wring out a scrub-cloth with one decisive motion—the right hand turning in, and the left out, simultaneously. When she spoke she spoke truly with the plain, right words. And her thoughts walked in a clear uncompromising line.

Mama was saying: "Neeley's getting too big to sleep in the same room with his sister. So I fixed the room your . . ." she barely hesitated over the next word, ". . . father and I used to have. That's Neeley's bedroom now."

Neeley's eyes jumped to his mother's. A room of his own! A dream come true; two dreams come true, long trousers and a room . . . His eyes saddened then as he thought of how these good things had come to him.

"And I'll share *your* room, Francie." Instinctive tact made Katie put it that way instead of saying: "You'll share *my* room."

"I wish I had my own room," thought Francie, with a flare of jealousy. "But it's right, I guess, that Neeley have it. There are only two bedrooms and he couldn't sleep with mama."

Knowing Francie's thought, Katie said: "And when it gets warm again, Francie can have the front room. We'll put her cot in there and put a nice cover on it in the day-time and it will be like a private sitting room. All right, Francie?"

"All right, Mama."

After a while, mama said: "We forgot the reading the last few nights, but now we'll start again."

"So things will go on just the same," thought Francie, a little surprised, as she took the Bible from the mantelpiece.

"Being," said mama, "that we lost Christmas this year, let's skip the part we're supposed to read and go to the birth of the Baby Jesus. We'll take turns reading. You start, Francie."

Francie read:

. . . and so it was, that, while they were there, the days were accomplished that she should be delivered. And she brought forth her first-born son, and wrapped him in swaddling clothes, and laid him in the manger; because there was no room for them in the inn.

Katie sighed sharply. Francie stopped reading and looked up inquiringly. "It's nothing," said mama. "Go on reading."

"No, it's nothing," Katie thought. "It's the time when I should feel life." Again the unborn child trembled faintly within her. "Was it because he knew of this coming child," she wondered silently, "that he stopped drinking at the last?" She had whispered to him that they were to have another child. Had he tried to be different when he knew? And knowing, did he die in the trying to be a better man? "Johnny . . . Johnny . . ." She sighed again.

And they read, each in turn, of the birth of Jesus and reading, they thought of Johnny dying. But each kept his thoughts.

When the children were ready to go to bed, Katie did something very unusual. It was unusual because she was not a demonstrative woman. She held the children close to her and kissed them good night.

"From now on," she said, "I am your mother and your father."

XXXVIII

JUST BEFORE Christmas vacation ended, Francie told mama that she wasn't going back to school.

"Don't you like school?" Mama asked.

"Yes, I do. But I'm fourteen now and I can get my working papers easy."

"Why do you want to go to work?"

"To help out."

"No, Francie. I want you to go back to school and graduate. It's only a few more months. June will be here before you know it. You can get your working papers for this summer. Maybe Neeley, too. But you're both going to high school in the autumn. So forget working papers and go back to school."

"But, Mama, how'll we get along till summer?"

"We'll manage."

Katie was not as confident as she sounded. She missed Johnny in more ways than one. Johnny had never worked steadily, but there had been the unexpected Saturday or Sunday night job with the three dollars it brought in. Then, too, when things got too terrible, Johnny had had a way of pulling himself together for a little while to get them over the bad places. But now, there was no Johnny.

Katie took stock. The rent was paid as long as she could keep those three tenements clean. There was a dollar and a half a week from Neeley's paper round. That would keep them in coal if they used a fire only at night. But wait! The twenty cents weekly insurance premium had to come out of that. (Katie was insured for a dime a week and each of the children for a nickel.) Well, a bit less coal and a little earlier to bed would take care of that. Clothes? Not to be thought of. Lucky Francie had those new shoes and Neeley the suit. The

243

big question, then, was food. Maybe Mrs. McGarrity would let her do the washing again. That would be a dollar a week. Then she'd get a few outside cleaning jobs. Yes, they'd get along somehow.

They got through to the end of March. By that time Katie was unwieldy. (The baby was due in May.) The ladies for whom she worked winced and looked away as they saw her, big with child, standing at the ironing-board in their kitchens; or saw her in an awkward sprawling position on her hands and knees scrubbing their floors. They had to help her out of pity. Soon they realized that they were paying a cleaning woman and doing most of the work themselves, anyhow. So, one after another, they told her they didn't need her any more.

A day came when Katie didn't have the twenty cents for the insurance collector. He was an old friend of the Rommelys and knew Katie's circumstances.

"I'd hate to see your policies lapse, Mrs. Nolan. Especially after you kept them up all these years."

"You wouldn't lapse me just because I got behind a little in my payments?"

"*I* wouldn't. But the company would. Look! Why don't you cash in the children's policies?"

"I didn't know you could do that."

"Few people know. They stop paying premiums and the company keeps mum. Time passes and the company just keeps the money already paid in. I'd lose my job if they knew I told you about this. But here's how I look at it: I insured your father and mother and all you Rommely girls and your husbands and children, and, I don't know, but I carried so many messages back and forth among you about birth and sickness and death that I feel like part of the family."

"We couldn't do without you," said Katie.

"Here's what you do, Mrs. Nolan. Cash in your children's policies but keep your own. If anything happens to one of the children—God forbid!—you could manage to get them buried. Whereas if something happened to you—also God forbid!—they couldn't get you buried without insurance money, now could they?"

"No, they couldn't. I must keep my own policy up. I wouldn't want to be buried as a pauper in Potter's Field. That's something they could never rise above; neither they, nor their children, nor their children's children. So I'll keep my policy and take your advice about the children's. Tell me what I have to do."

The twenty-five dollars that Katie got for the two policies got them through until the end of April. In five more weeks the child would be born. In eight more weeks Francie and Neeley would graduate from grade school. There was those eight weeks to be got through somehow.

The three Rommely sisters sat around Katie's kitchen table in conference.

"I'd help if I could," said Evy. "But you know Will's not been right since that horse kicked him. He's fresh to the boss and doesn't get along with the men, and it's got so that not a horse will go out with him. They put him on stable work, sweeping out manure and dumping broken bottles. They cut him to eighteen a week, and that doesn't go far with three children. I'm looking for odd cleaning jobs myself."

"If I could think of some way," began Sissy.

"No," said Katie firmly. "You're doing enough by taking Mother to live with you."

"That's right," said Evy. "Kate and I used to worry so about her living alone in one room and going out cleaning to make a few pennies."

"Mother's no expense and no trouble," said Sissy. "And my John don't mind having her around. Of course, he only earns twenty a week. And now there's the baby. I wanted to get my old job back, but Mother's too old to take care of the baby and the house. She's eighty-three now. I could work, but I'd have to hire somebody to look after Mother and the baby. If I had a job I could help you out, Katie."

"You just can't do it, Sissy. There's no way," said Katie.

"There's only one thing to do," said Evy. "Take Francie out of school and let her get working papers."

"But I want her to graduate. My children will be the first in the Nolan family to get diplomas."

"You can't eat a diploma," said Evy.

"Haven't you any men friends who could help you?" asked Sissy. "You're a very pretty woman, you know."

"Or will be, when she gets her shape back again," put in Evy.

Katie thought briefly of Sergeant McShane. "No," she said. "I have no men friends. There's always been Johnny and no

245

one else."

"I guess Evy's right then," decided Sissy. "I hate to say it, but you've got to put Francie to work."

"Once she leaves grammar school without graduating, she'll never be able to get into high school," protested Katie.

"Well," sighed Evy, "there's always the Catholic Charities."

"When the time comes," said Katie quietly, "that we have to take charity baskets, I'll plug up the doors and windows and wait until the children are sound asleep and then turn on every gas jet in the house."

"Don't talk like that," said Evy sharply. "You want to live, don't you?"

"Yes. But I want to live for *something*. I don't want to live to get charity food to give me enough strength to go back to get more charity food."

"Then it comes back to this again," said Evy. "Francie's got to get out and work. It's got to be Francie because Neeley is only thirteen and they won't give him his working papers."

Sissy put her hand on Katie's arm. "It won't be so terrible. Francie's smart and reads a lot, and that girl will get herself educated somehow."

Evy stood up. "Look! We've got to go." She put a fifty-cent piece on the table. Anticipating Katie's refusal, she spoke belligerently. "And don't think that's a present. I expect to be paid back some day."

Katie smiled. "You needn't holler so. I don't mind taking money from my sister."

Sissy took a short cut. As she leaned over to kiss Katie's cheek in good-bye, she slipped a dollar note in her apron pocket. "If you need me," she said, "send for me and I'll come, even if it's in the middle of the night. But send Neeley. It's not safe for a girl to walk through those dark streets past the coal-yards."

Katie sat alone at the kitchen table far into the night. "I need two months ... just two months," she thought. "Dear God, give me two months. It's such a little time. By that time my baby will be born and I'll be well again. By that time the children will be graduated from public school. When I'm boss of my own mind and my own body, I don't need to ask You for anything. But now my body is boss over me and I've got to ask You for help. Just two months . . . two months . . ." She waited for that warm glow that meant that she had established communication with her God. There was no glow. She tried again.

"Holy Mary, Mother of Jesus, you know how it is. You had children. Holy Mary . . ." She waited. There was nothing.

She placed Sissy's dollar and Evy's fifty-cent piece on the table. "That will get us through three more days," she thought. "After that . . .?" Not aware of what she did, she whispered: "Johnny, wherever you are, pull yourself together just one more time. One more time. . . ." She waited again, and this time the glow came.

And so it happened that Johnny helped them.

McGarrity, the saloon-keeper, couldn't get Johnny out of his mind. Not that McGarrity's conscience bothered him; no, nothing like that. He didn't force men to come into the saloon. Apart from keeping the door hinges so well oiled that the slightest touch made them swing open easily, he offered no more inducements than other saloon-keepers. His free lunch was no better than theirs and there was no beguiling entertainment other than that spontaneously contributed by his customers. No, it wasn't his conscience.

He missed Johnny. That was it. And it wasn't the money, either, because Johnny always owed him. He had liked having Johnny around because he gave class to the place. It was something, all right, to see that slender young fellow standing debonairly at the bar among the truck drivers and ditch-diggers. "Sure," admitted McGarrity, "Johnny Nolan drank more than was good for him. But if he didn't get it there he would have got it somewhere else. But he wasn't a rummy. He never got to cursing or brawling after he had a few drinks. Yes," decided McGarrity, "Johnny had been all right."

The thing that McGarrity missed was Johnny talking. "How that fellow could talk," he thought. "Why, he'd tell me about those cotton-fields down south or about the shores of Araby or sunny France just like he'd been there instead of getting the information out of those songs he knew. I sure liked to hear him talk about those far-off places," he mused. "But best of all, I liked to hear him talk about his family."

McGarrity used to have a dream about a family. This dream family lived far away from the saloon; so far that he had to hop a trolley to get home in the early morning after he locked up the saloon. The gentle wife of his dreams waited up for him and had hot coffee and something nice to eat ready. After eating, they'd talk ... talk about other things than the saloon. He had dream children—clean, pretty, smart children who were growing up sort of ashamed that their father ran a saloon. He was proud of their shame because it meant that he had the ability of begetting refined children.

Well, that had been his dream of marriage. Then he had married Mae. She had been a curvy, sensuous girl, with dark red hair and a wide mouth. But after a while of marriage, she turned into a stout, blowzy woman, known in Brooklyn as "the saloon type." Married life had been fine for a year or two, then McGarrity woke up one morning and found that it was no good. Mae wouldn't change into his dream wife. She liked the saloon. She insisted that they rent rooms above it. She didn't want a house in Flushing; she didn't want to do housework. She liked to sit in the saloon's back room day and night and laugh and drink with the customers. And the children that Mae gave him ran the streets like hoodlums and bragged about their father owning a saloon. To his grievous disappointment, they were proud of it.

He knew that Mae was unfaithful to him. He didn't care so long as it didn't get around to the extent that men laughed at him behind his back. Jealousy had left him years ago, when physical desire for Mae left him. He gradually grew indifferent about sleeping with her or with any other woman. Somehow, good talking had got tied up with good sex in his mind. He wanted a woman to talk to, one to whom he could tell all his thoughts; and he wanted her to talk to him, warmly, wisely and intimately. If he could find such a woman, he thought, his manhood would come back to him. In his dumb fumbling way he wanted union of mind and soul along with union of body. As the years passed, the need for talking intimately with a woman who was close to him became an obsession.

In his business he observed human nature and came to certain conclusions about it. The conclusions lacked wisdom and originality; in fact, they were tiresome. But they were important to McGarrity because he had figured them out for himself. In the first years of their marriage, he had tried to tell Mae about these conclusions, but all she said was: "I can imagine." Sometimes she varied by saying: "I can *just* imagine." Gradually then, because he could not share his inner self with her, he lost the power of being a husband to her and she was unfaithful to him.

McGarrity was a man with a great sin on his soul. He hated his children. His daughter, Irene, was Francie's age. Irene was a pink-eyed girl and her hair was of such a pale red that it, too, could be called pink. She was mean and stupid. She had been left back so many times that at fourteen she was still in the sixth grade. His son, Jim, ten years old, had no outstanding characteristic, excepting that his buttocks were always too fat for his breeches.

McGarrity had another dream; it was that Mae would come to him and confess that the children were not his. That dream made him happy. He felt that he could love those children if he knew they were another man's. Then he could see their meanness and their stupidity objectively; then he could pity them and help them. As long as he knew they were his, he hated them because he saw all of his own and Mae's worst traits in them.

In the eight years that Johnny had been patronizing McGarrity's saloon, he had spoken daily to McGarrity in praise of Katie and the children. McGarrity played a secret game during those eight years. He pretended that *he* was Johnny and that he, McGarrity, was talking so about Mae and his children.

"Want to show you something," Johnny said once, proudly, as he pulled a paper from his pocket. "My little girl wrote this composition in school and got 'A' on it, and she's only ten years old. Listen. I'll read it to you."

As Johnny read, McGarrity pretended that it was his little girl who had written the story. Another day, Johnny brought in a pair of crudely-made wooden book-ends and placed them on the bar with a flourish.

"Want to show you something," he said proudly. "My boy, Neeley, made these in school."

"My boy, Jimmy, made these in school," said McGarrity proudly to himself as he examined the book-ends.

Another time, to start him talking, McGarrity had asked: 'Think we'll get in the war, Johnny?"

"Funny thing," Johnny had answered. "Katie and I sat up till near morning talking about that very thing. I convinced her finally that Wilson will keep us out of it."

How would it be, McGarrity thought, if he and Mae sat up all night to talk about that, and how would it be if she said: 'You're right, Jim?" But he didn't know how it would be because he knew that could never happen.

So when Johnny died, McGarrity lost his dreams. He tried

to play the game by himself, but it didn't work out. He needed someone like Johnny to start him off.

About the time that the three sisters sat in Katie's kitchen talking, McGarrity got an idea. He had more money than he knew how to spend, and nothing else. Maybe through Johnny's children he could buy the way of dreaming again. He suspected that Katie was hard up. Maybe he could scare up a little easy work for Johnny's kids to do after school. He'd be helping them out ... God knows he could afford it, and maybe he'd get something in return. Maybe they would talk to him the way they must have talked to their father.

He told Mae he was going up to see Katie about some work for the children. Mae told him, cheerfully enough, that he'd be thrown out on his ear. McGarrity didn't think he'd be thrown out on his ear. As he shaved for the visit, he recalled the day that Katie had come in to thank him for the wreath.

After Johnny's funeral, Katie went around thanking each person who had sent flowers. She had walked straight through McGarrity's front door, disdaining the deviousness of the side door marked "Ladies' Entrance." Ignoring the staring men hanging on the bar, she had come straight to where McGarrity was. Seeing her, he had tucked up one bottom end of his apron into the belt, signifying that he was off duty for the moment and had come from behind the bar to meet her.

"I came to thank you for the wreath," she said.

"Oh, that," he said, relieved. He thought she had come to bawl him out.

"It was thoughtful of you."

"I liked Johnny."

"I know." She put her hand out. He looked at it dumbly for a moment before he got the idea that she wanted to shake him by the hand. As he wrung her hand, he asked: "No hard feelings?"

"Why?" she answered. "Johnny was free, white and over twenty-one." She had turned then and walked out of the saloon.

No, decided McGarrity, such a woman wouldn't throw him out on his ear if he came with well-meant intentions.

He sat ill at ease on one of the kitchen chairs talking t Katie. The children were supposed to be doing their home work. But Francie, head bent deceptively over her book, wa listening to Mr. McGarrity.

"I talked it over with my Missus," dreamed McGarrity, "and she agreed with me that we could use your girl. No hard work, you understand, just making the beds and washing a few dishes. I could use the boy downstairs, peeling eggs and cutting cheese into hunks, you know, for the free lunch at night. He wouldn't be anywhere near the bar. He'd work in the back kitchen. It would be for an hour or so after school and half a day on Saturday. I'd pay each two dollars a week."

Katie's heart jumped. "Four dollars a week," she figured to herself, "and the dollar and a half from the paper round. Both of them could stay in school. There'd be enough to eat. It would get us through."

"What do you say, Mrs. Nolan?" he asked.

"It's up to the children," she answered.

"Well?" He threw his voice in their direction. "What do you say?"

Francie pretended to tear herself away from her book. "What did you say?"

"Would you like to help Mrs McGarrity around the house?"

"Yes, sir," said Francie.

"And you?" He looked at Neeley.

"Yes, sir," echoed the boy.

"That's settled." He turned to Katie. "Of course it's only temporary until we can get a regular woman to take over the house and kitchen work."

"I'd rather it was temporary, anyhow," said Katie.

"You might be a little short." He worked his hand down into his pocket. "So I'll pay the first week's salary in advance."

"No, Mr. McGarrity. If they earn the money, they'll have the privilege of collecting it and bringing it home themselves at the end of the week."

"All right." But instead of taking his hand from his pocket, he closed it over the thick roll of notes. He thought: "I've got so much money that buys me nothing. And they haven't got anything." He had an idea.

"Mrs. Nolan, you know how Johnny and I done business. I gave him credit and he turned his tips over to me. Well, when he died, he was a little ahead." He took out the thick roll of notes. Francie's eyes popped when she saw all that money. McGarrity's idea was to say that Johnny was twelve dollars ahead and to give Katie that sum. He looked at Katie as he

251

took the rubber band off the money. Her eyes narrowed and he changed his mind about the twelve dollars. He knew she'd never believe it. "Of course, it isn't much," he said casually. "Just two dollars. But I figure it belongs to you." He detached two notes and held them out to her.

Katie shook her head. "I know there is no money owing us. If you told the truth, you'd say that Johnny owed you." Ashamed at being caught, McGarrity put the thick roll back in his pocket, where it felt uncomfortable against his thigh. "But, Mr. McGarrity, I do thank you for your kind intentions," Katie said.

Her last few words released McGarrity's tongue. He started to talk; he spoke of his boyhood in Ireland, of his mother and father and the many brothers and sisters. He spoke of his dream marriage. He told her everything that had been in his thoughts for years. He didn't run down his wife and children. He left them out of his story entirely. He told about Johnny; how Johnny had spoken daily of his wife and children.

"Take those curtains," McGarrity said, waving a thick hand at the half curtains made of yellow calico with a red rose design. "Johnny told me how you ripped up an old dress of yours and made kitchen curtains out of it. He said it made the kitchen look fine, like the inside of a Gypsy wagon."

Francie, who had abandoned the pretence of study, picked up McGarrity's last two words. "Gypsy wagon," she thought, looking at the curtains with new eyes. "So papa had said that. I didn't think he noticed the new curtains at the time. At least he didn't say anything. But he had noticed. He had said that nice thing about them to this man." Hearing Johnny spoken of so made Francie almost believe that he wasn't dead: "So papa had said things like that to this man." She stared at McGarrity with new interest. He was a short stocky man with thick hands, a short red neck and thinning hair. "Who'd ever guess," thought Francie, "looking at the outside of him, that he was so different inside?"

McGarrity talked for two hours without stopping. Katie listened intently to McGarrity *talking about Johnny*. When he stopped for a second, she gave him little transitional replies such as "Yes?" or *"Then* what?" or "And then . . .?" When he fumbled for a word, she offered him one, which he accepted gratefully.

And as he talked, a remarkable thing happened. He felt his lost manhood stirring within him. It wasn't the physical fact of

252

Katie in the room with him. Her body was swollen and distorted and he couldn't look at her without wincing inwardly. It wasn't the woman. It was the talking to her that was doing it.

It grew dark in the room. McGarrity stopped talking. He was hoarse and tired. But it was a new peaceful kind of tiredness. He thought, reluctantly, that he had to get back. The saloon would be filling up with men on their way home from work, stopping in for a pre-supper drink. He didn't like Mae behind the bar when a crowd of men were there. He got to his feet slowly.

"Mrs. Nolan," he said, fumbling with his brown derby, "could I come up here once in a while to talk?" She shook her head slowly. "Just to talk?" he repeated pleadingly.

"No, Mr. McGarrity," she said as gently as she could.

He sighed and went away.

Francie was glad to be so busy. It kept her from missing papa too much. She and Neeley got up at six in the morning and helped mama with the cleaning for two hours before they got ready for school. Mama couldn't work hard now. Francie polished the brass bell plates in the three vestibules and cleaned each banister spoke with an oiled cloth. Neeley swept out the cellars and swept down the carpeted stairs. Both of them got the filled ash-cans up on the kerb each day. It had been a problem because the two of them together couldn't so much as budge the heavy cans. Francie got the idea of tipping over the cans, dumping the ashes on the cellar floor, carrying the empty cans up to the kerb and then refilling them with coal buckets. It worked fine, even if it meant a lot of trips up and down the cellar. That left only the linoleum-laid halls for mama to scrub. Three of the tenants offered to scrub their own hallways until after Katie had had her baby, and that helped a whole lot.

After school, the children had to go to church for "instruction," since both were being confirmed that spring. After instruction, they worked for McGarrity. As he had promised, the work was easy. Francie made up four tumbled beds and washed a few breakfast dishes and swept the rooms. It took less than an hour.

Neeley had the same schedule as Francie, except that his paper round was added on. Sometimes he didn't get home for supper until eight o'clock. He worked in the kitchen back of

McGarrity's saloon. His job was to take the shells off four-dozen hard-boiled eggs, cut hard cheese into inch cubes and stick a toothpick in each cube and slice big pickles lengthwise.

McGarrity waited a few days until the children got used to working for him. Then he decided it was time to have them talk to him the way Johnny had. He went into the kitchen, sat down, and watched Neeley working. "He's the spitting image of his father," thought McGarrity. He waited a long time, letting the boy get used to him there, then he cleared his throat.

"Make any wooden book-ends lately?" he asked.

"No . . . no, sir," stammered Neeley, startled at the odd question.

McGarrity waited. Why didn't the boy start talking? Neeley shelled eggs faster. McGarrity tried again. "Think Wilson will keep us out of the war?"

"I don't know," said Neeley.

McGarrity waited a long time. Neeley thought he was checking up on the way he worked. Anxious to please, the boy worked so fast that he was finished ahead of time. He placed the last shelled egg in the glass bowl and looked up. "Ah! Now he's going to talk to me," thought McGarrity.

"Is that all you want done?" asked Neeley.

"That's all." Still McGarrity waited.

"I guess I'll go, then," ventured Neeley.

"All right, son," sighed McGarrity. He watched the boy walk out of the back door. "If he'd only turn round and say something . . . something . . . personal," thought McGarrity. But Neeley didn't turn round.

McGarrity tried Francie the next day. He came upstairs to the flat, sat down and said nothing. Francie got a little frightened and started sweeping towards the door. "If he comes at me," she thought, "I can run out." McGarrity sat quiet for a long time, thinking he was getting her used to him. He didn't know he was frightening her.

"Write any grade A, number one compositions lately?" he asked.

"No, sir."

He waited a while. "Do you think we'll get into this war?"

"I . . . I don't know." She edged closer to the door.

He thought: "I'm scaring her. She thinks I'm like that fellow in the hallway." Aloud he said: "Don't be afraid, I'm going. You can lock the door after me, if you want."

"Yes, sir," she said. After he had gone, Francie thought: "I uess he only wanted to talk. But I have nothing to say to im."

Mae McGarrity came up once. Francie was on her knees rying to poke out some dirt from behind the water-pipes nder the sink. Mae told her to get up and forget it.

"Lord love you, child," she said. "Don't be killing yourself vorking. This flat will be standing here long after you and I re dead and gone."

She took a mound of rosy jello out of the ice-box, cut it in alf and slid a portion on another plate. She garnished it berally with whipped cream, plunked two spoons on the able, sat down and indicated that Francie do the same.

"I'm not hungry," lied Francie.

"Eat, anyhow, to be sociable," Mae said.

It was the first time Francie had ever eaten jello and vhipped cream. It was so good, she had to remember her nanners and not gobble it down. As she ate, she thought: Why, Mrs. McGarrity's all right. Mr. McGarrity's all right, oo. Only I guess they aren't all right to each other."

Mae and Jim McGarrity sat alone at a little round table in ack of the saloon eating their usual hurried and silent supper. Jnexpectedly, she placed her hand on his arm. He trembled at he unexpected touch. His small light eyes looked into her arge mahogany-coloured ones and saw pity in them.

"It won't work out, Jim," she said gently. Excitement hurned up in him. "She knows!" he thought. "Why ... why ..*she understands*."

"There's an old saying," Mae continued. "Money won't buy verything."

"I know," he said. "I'll let them go, then."

"Wait until a couple of weeks after her kid is born. Give hem a show." She got up and walked out to the bar.

McGarrity sat there, torn apart by his feelings. "We held a onversation," he thought in wonder. "No names were menioned and nothing was said exactly in the words. But she new what I was thinking and I knew what she was thinking." Ie hurried after his wife. He wanted to hold on to that inderstanding. He saw Mae standing at the end of the bar. A usky teamster had his arm around her waist and was whisperng something in her ear. She had her hand over her mouth to old back her laughter. As McGarrity came in, the teamster emoved his arm sheepishly and moved down to stand with a group of men. As McGarrity went behind the bar, he looked into his wife's eyes. They were blank and had no understanding in them. McGarrity's face fell back into the old lines of grievous disappointment as he started his evening's work.

Mary Rommely was getting old. She was no longer able to go about Brooklyn alone. She had a longing to see Katie before her confinement, so she gave the insurance collector a message.

"When a woman gives birth," she told him, "death holds her hand for a little while. Sometimes he doesn't let go. Tell my youngest daughter that I would see her once more before her time comes."

The collector gave the message. The following Sunday, Katie went over to see her mother, taking Francie with her. Neeley begged off, saying he had promised to pitch for the Ten Eycks, who were trying to get up a ball game in the lots.

Sissy's kitchen was big and warm and sunny and spotlessly clean. Granma Mary Rommely was sitting by the stove in a low rocker. It was the only piece of furniture she had brought from Austria, and it had stood by the hearth in her family's hut for more than a hundred years.

Sissy's husband sat by the window, holding the baby while he gave it its bottle. After Mary and Sissy had been greeted, Francie and Katie greeted him.

"Hello, John," said Katie.

"Hello, Kate," he answered.

"Hello, Uncle John."

"Hello, Francie."

He never said another word during the entire visit. Francie stared at him, wondering about him. The family regarded him as temporary, as they had regarded Sissy's other husbands and lovers. Francie wondered whether he, himself, felt temporary. His real name was Steve, but Sissy always referred to him as "my John," and when the family spoke of him, they called him "The John" or "Sissy's John." Francie wondered whether the men in the publishing house where he worked called him John too. Did he ever protest? Did he ever say: "Look here, Sissy. My name is Steve and not John. And tell your sisters to call me Steve, too."

"Sissy, you're getting stouter," mama was saying.

"It's natural for a woman to put on a little weight after she's had a baby," said Sissy, with a straight face. She smiled at

Francie. "Would you like to hold the baby, Francie?"

"Oh, yes!"

"Without a word, Sissy's tall husband got up, gave over the baby and its bottle to Francie, and still without a word, walked out of the room. No one commented on his going.

Francie sat in his vacated chair. She had never held a baby in her arms before. She touched the baby's soft round cheek with her fingers as she had seen Joanna do. A thrill started at her finger-tips, went up her arm, and through her entire body. "When I get big," she decided, "I'll always have a new baby in the house."

While she held the baby, she listened to mama and granma talking and watched Sissy making up a month's supply of noodles. Sissy took a ball of stiff yellow dough, rolled it flat with the rolling-pin, then rolled the flat dough up like a jelly roll. With a sharp knife, she cut the roll into paper-thin strips, unwound the strips and hung them on a rack made of slender dowel sticks, which stood before the kitchen stove. This was to dry out the noodles.

Francie felt that there was something different about Sissy. She wasn't the old Aunt Sissy. It wasn't that she was a bit less slender than usual; the being different was something that did not have to do with the way she looked. Francie puzzled over it.

Mary Rommely wanted to hear every word of news, and Katie told her everything, starting from the end and working back. First she told of the children working for McGarritys, and how the money they brought in was keeping them. Then she went back to the day McGarrity had sat in her kitchen and talked about Johnny. She ended up with saying:

"I tell you, Mother, if McGarrity hadn't come along when he did, I don't know what would have happened. I was so low, that just a few nights before that, I had prayed to Johnny to help me. That was foolish, I know."

"Not foolish," said Mary. "He heard you and helped you."

"A ghost can't help anyone, Mother," said Sissy.

"Ghosts are not always those who pass through closed doors," said Mary Rommely. "Katie has told how her husband used to talk to this saloon man. In all those years of the talking Johnny gave away pieces of himself to this man. When Katie called on her man for help, the pieces of him came together in this man, and it was Johnny within the saloon man's soul that heard and came to her help."

Francie turned it over in her mind. "If that is so," she thought, "then Mr. McGarrity gave us back all those pieces of papa when he talked so long about him. There is nothing of papa in him now. Maybe that's why we can't talk to him the way he wants us to."

When it was time to leave, Sissy gave Katie a shoe-box full of noodles to take home. As Francie kissed her grandmother in goodbye, Mary Rommely held her close and whispered in her own language:

"In the month to come, give unto thy mother more than obedience and respect. She will have great need of love and understanding."

Francie didn't understand a word of what her grandmother had said, but she answered: "Yes, Granma."

Going home in the trolley, Francie held the shoe-box in *her* lap because mama had no lap now. Francie thought deep thoughts during the ride. "If what Granma Mary Rommely said is true, then it must be that no one ever dies, really. Papa is gone, but he's still here in many ways. He's here in Neeley, who looks just like him, and in mama, who knew him so long. He's here in his mother, who began him and who is still living. Maybe I will have a boy some day who looks like papa and has all of papa's good without the drinking. And that boy will have a boy. And that boy will have a boy. It might be there is no real death." Her thoughts went to McGarrity. "No one would ever believe there was any part of papa in *him*." She thought of Mrs. McGarrity and how she had made it easy for her to sit down and eat that jello. Something clicked in Francie's mind! She spoke to her mother.

"Aunt Sissy doesn't use that strong sweet perfume any more, does she, mama?"

"No. She doesn't have to, any more."

"Why?"

"She's got her baby now and a man to look after her and the baby."

Francie wanted to ask more questions, but mama had her eyes closed and was leaning her head back against the seat. She looked white and tired, and Francie decided not to bother her any more. She'd have to figure it out for herself.

"It must be," she thought, "that this using strong perfume is tied up somehow with a woman wanting a baby and wanting to find a man who can give her a baby and look after it and her too." She put that nugget of knowledge away with all the others that she was continually collecting.

Francie was beginning to get a headache. She didn't know whether it was caused by the excitement of holding the baby, the bouncing trolley-car, the idea of papa or the discovery about Sissy's perfume. Maybe it was because she was getting up so early in the mornings now, and being so busy all day. Maybe it was because it was the time in the month when she could look for a headache, anyhow.

"Well," Francie decided, "I guess the thing that is giving me this headache is life—and nothing else but."

"Don't be silly," said mama quietly, still leaning back with her eyes closed. "Aunt Sissy's kitchen was too hot. I have a headache myself."

Francie jumped. Was it getting so that mama could look right into her mind even with her eyes closed? Then she remembered that she had forgotten she was thinking, and had said that last thought about life out loud. She laughed for the first time since papa had died, and mama opened her eyes and smiled.

XXXIX

FRANCIE AND Neeley were confirmed in May. Francie was almost fourteen and a half years old and Neeley was just a year younger. Sissy, who was an expert seamstress, made Francie's simple white muslin dress. Katie managed to buy her white kid slippers and a pair of long white silk stockings. They were Francie's first silk stockings. Neeley wore the black suit he got for his father's funeral.

There was a legend in the neighbourhood that any three wishes made on that day would come true. One had to be an impossible wish, another a wish that you could make come true yourself, and the third had to be a wish for when you grew up. Francie's impossible wish was that her straight brown hair change into golden curly hair like Neeley's. Her second wish was that she'd have a nice speaking voice like mama and Evy and Sissy, and her third wish, for when she was grown up, was that she'd travel all over the world. Neeley wished, one: that he'd become very wealthy; two: that he'd get better marks on his report card; and three; that he wouldn't drink like papa when he grew up.

There was an iron-bound convention in Brooklyn that children must have their picture taken by a regular photographer when they were confirmed. Katie couldn't afford to have pictures made. She had to be content with letting Flossy Gaddis, who had a box camera, take a snapshot. Floss posed them on the edge of the pavement and snapped the picture, unaware that a trolley lumbered by at the instant of exposure. She had the snapshot enlarged and framed and presented it to Francie as a Confirmation Day present.

Sissy was there when the picture arrived. Katie held it and they all examined it over her shoulder. Francie had never been photographed before. For the first time she saw herself as others saw her. She was standing stiff and straight on the edge of the kerb, her back to the gutter and her dress blowing sidewise in the wind. Neeley stood close to her, was a head taller, and looked very wealthy and handsome in his freshly pressed black suit. The sun had slanted over the roofs in such a way that Neeley was in the sun and his face was clear and bright, while Francie looked dark and angry in the shadow. Behind both was the blurred trolley going by.

Sissy said: "I bet that's the only confirmation picture in the world with a trolley-car in it."

"It's a good picture," said Katie. "They look more natural standing on the street than in front of the picture-man's cardboard church window." She hung it up over the mantelpiece.

"What name did you take, Neeley?" Sissy asked.

"Papa's. Now I'm Cornelius John Nolan."

"That's a good name for a surgeon," commented Katie.

"I took mama's name," said Francie importantly. "Now my full name is Mary Frances Katherine Nolan." Francie waited. Mama did *not* say that was a good name for a writer.

"Katie, have you any pictures of Johnny?" Sissy asked.

"No. Just the one of both of us taken on our wedding day. Why?"

"Nothing. Only time passes so, doesn't it?"

"Yes," sighed Katie. "That's one of the few things we can be sure of."

Confirmation was over and Francie didn't have to go to instruction any more. She had an extra hour daily which she

260

was devoting to the novel she was writing to prove to Miss Garnder, the new English teacher, that she *did* know about beauty.

Since her father's death, Francie had stopped writing about birds and trees and My Impressions. Because she missed him so, she had taken to writing little stories about him. She tried to show that, in spite of his shortcomings, he had been a good father and a kindly man. She had written three such stories which were marked "C" instead of the usual "A." The fourth came back with a line telling her to remain after school.

All the children had gone home. Miss Garnder and Francie were alone in the room with the big dictionary in it. Francie's last four compositions lay on Miss Garnder's desk.

"What's happened to your writing, Frances?" asked Miss Garnder.

"I don't know."

"You were one of my best pupils. You wrote so prettily. I enjoyed your compositions. But these last ones . . ." She flicked at them contemptuously.

"I looked up the spelling and took pains with my penmanship and . . ."

"I'm referring to your subject matter."

"You said we could choose our own subjects."

"But poverty, starvation and drunkenness are ugly subjects to choose. We all admit these things exist. But one doesn't write about them."

"What does one write about?" Unconsciously, Francie picked up the teacher's phraseology.

"One delves into the imagination and finds beauty there. The writer, like the artist, must strive for beauty always."

"What is beauty?" asked the child.

"I can think of no better definition than Keats': 'Beauty is truth, truth beauty.' "

Francie took her courage into her two hands and said: "Those stories are the truth."

"Nonsense!" exploded Miss Garnder. Then, softening her tone, she continued: "By truth, we mean things like the stars always being there and the sun always rising and the true nobility of man and mother-love and love for one's country," she ended anti-climactically.

"I see," said Francie.

As Miss Garnder continued talking, Francie answered her bitterly in her mind.

"Drunkenness is neither truth nor beauty. It's a vice. Drunkards belong to jail, not in stories. And poverty. There is no excuse for that. There's work enough for all who want it. People are poor because they're too lazy to work. There's nothing beautiful about laziness."

(Imagine mama lazy!)

"Hunger is not beautiful. It is also unnecessary. We have well-organized charities. No one need go hungry."

Francie ground her teeth. Her mother hated the word "charity" above any word in the language, and she had brought up her children to hate it too.

"Now I'm not a snob," stated Miss Garnder. "I do not come from a wealthy family. My father was a minister with a very small salary."

(But it *was* a salary, Miss Garnder.)

"And the only help my mother had was a succession of untrained maids, mostly girls from the country."

(I see. You were poor, Miss Garnder, poor with a maid.)

"Many times we were without a maid and my mother had to do all the housework herself."

(And my mother, Miss Garnder, has to do all her own housework, and yes, ten times more cleaning than *that*.)

"I ,wanted to go to the state university but we couldn't afford it. My father had to send me to a small denominational college."

(But admit you had no trouble *going* to college.)

"And believe me, you're poor when you go to such a college. I know what hunger is, too. Time and time again my father's salary was held up and there was no money for food. Once we had to live on tea and toast for three days."

(So you know what it is to be hungry, too.)

"But I'd be a dull person if I wrote about nothing but being poor and hungry, wouldn't I?" Francie didn't answer. "*Wouldn't* I?" repeated Miss Garnder emphatically.

"Yes, ma'am."

"Now your play for graduation." She took a thin manuscript from her desk drawer. "Some parts are very good indeed; other parts, you've gone off. For instance," she turned a page, "here Fate says: 'And Youth what is thy ambition?' And the boy answers: 'I would be a healer. I would take the broken bodies of men and mend them.' Now *that's* a beautiful idea, Frances. But you spoil it here. 'Fate: That's what thou would'st be. But see! This is what thou shalt be.' Light shines on old man soldering bottom of ash-can. Old Man: 'Ah, once I thought to be a mender of men. Now I'm a mender of ...'"

Miss Garnder looked up suddenly. "You didn't by any chance mean that to be funny, did you, Frances?"

"Oh no, ma'am."

"After our little talk you can see why we can't use your play for graduation."

"I see." Francie's heart all but broke.

"Now Beatrice Williams has a cute idea. A fairy waves a wand and girls and boys in costume come out and there's one for each holiday in the year, and each one says a little poem about the holiday he represents. It's an excellent idea, but unfortunately Beatrice cannot make rhymes. Wouldn't you like to take that idea and write the verses? Beatrice wouldn't mind. We can put a note on the programme that the idea comes from her. That's fair enough, isn't it?"

"Yes, ma'am. But I don't want to use her ideas. I want to use my own."

"That's commendable, of course. Well, I won't insist." She stood up. "I've taken all this time with you because I honestly believe that you have promise. Now that we've talked things out, I'm sure you'll stop writing those sordid little stories."

Sordid. Francie turned the word over. It was not in her vocabulary. "What does that mean—sordid?"

"What-did-I-tell-you-when-you-don't-know-a-word?" sing-songed Miss Garnder drolly.

"Oh! I forgot." Francie went to the big dictionary and looked up the word. Sordid: *Filthy.* Filthy? She thought of her father wearing a fresh dicky and collar every day of his life and shining his worn shoes as often as twice a day. *Dirty.* Papa had his own mug at the barber shop. *Base.* Francie passed that up not knowing exactly what it meant. *Gross.* Never! Papa was a dancer. He was slender and quick. His body wasn't gross. *Also mean and low.* She remembered a hundred and one little tendernesses and acts of thoughtfulness on the part of her father. She remembered how everyone had loved him so. Her face got hot. She couldn't see the next words because the page turned red under her eyes. She turned on Miss Garnder, her face twisted with fury.

"Don't you *ever* dare use that word about us!"

"Us?" asked Miss Garnder blankly. "We were talking about your compositions. Why, Frances!" Her voice was shocked. "I'm surprised! A well-behaved girl like you. What would your mother say if she knew you had been impertinent to your teacher?"

Francie was frightened. Impertinence to a teacher was almost a reformatory offence in Brooklyn. "Please excuse me. Please excuse me," she repeated abjectly. "I didn't mean it."

"I understand," said Miss Garnder gently. She put her arm around Francie and led her to the door. "Our little talk has made an impression on you, I see. Sordid *is* an ugly word, and I'm glad you resented my using it. It shows that you understand. Probably you don't like me any more, but please believe that I spoke for your own good. Some day you'll remember what I said and you'll thank me for it."

Francie wished adults would stop telling her that. Already the load of thanks in the future was weighing her down. She figured she'd have to spend the best years of her womanhood hunting up people to tell them that they were right and to thank them.

Miss Garnder handed her the "sordid" compositions and the play, saying: "When you get home, burn these in the stove. Apply the match to them yourself. And as the flames rise, keep saying: 'I am burning ugliness. I am burning ugliness.'"

Walking home from school, Francie tried to figure the whole thing out. She knew Miss Garnder wasn't mean. She had spoken for Francie's good. Only it didn't seem good to Francie. She began to understand that her life might seem revolting to some educated people. She wondered, when she got educated whether she'd be ashamed of her background. Would she be ashamed of her people: ashamed of handsome papa, who had been so light-hearted, kind and understanding; ashamed of brave and truthful mama, who was so proud of her own mother, even though granma couldn't read or write; ashamed of Neeley, who was such a good honest boy? No! No! If being educated would make her ashamed of what she was, then she wanted none of it. "But I'll show that Miss Garnder," she vowed. "I'll show her I've got an imagination. I certainly will show her."

She started her novel that day. Its heroine was Sherry Nola, a girl conceived, born and brought up in sweltering luxury. The story was called THIS IS I, and it was the untrue story of Francie's life.

Francie had twenty pages written now. So far, it ran to

minute descriptions of the lush furnishings of Sherry's house, rhapsodies over Sherry's exquisite clothes, and course-by-course accounts of fabulous meals consumed by the heroine.

When it was finished, Francie planned to ask Sissy's John to take it over to his shop and get it published for her. Francie had a fine dream about how it would be when she presented her book to Miss Garnder. The scene was all worked out in her mind. She went over the dialogue.

FRANCIE (*as she gives book to Miss Garnder*): I believe you'll find nothing sordid in this. Please consider it as my term's work. I hope you won't mind its being published.

> (*Miss Garnder's jaw drops open. Francie takes no notice.*) It's a bit easier to read print, don't you think?

> (*As Miss Garnder reads, Francie stares out window, unconcernedly.*)

MISS GARNDER (*after reading*): Why, Frances! This is wonderful!

FRANCIE: What? (*With a start of remembrance.*) Oh, the novel. I dashed it off at odd moments. It doesn't take long to write things of which you know nothing. When you write of actual things, it takes longer, because you have to *live* them first.

Francie crossed that out. She wouldn't want Miss Garnder to suspect her feelings had been hurt. She rewrote it.

FRANCIE: What? (*Recalling.*) Oh! The novel. I'm glad you like it.

MISS GARNDER (*timidly*): Frances, could ... could I ask you to autograph it for me?

FRANCIE: But of course.

> (*Miss Garnder uncaps her fountain-pen and presents it, penpoint end towards herself, to Francie. Francie writes: "Compliments of M. Frances K. Nolan."*)

MISS GARNDER (*examining autograph*): What a distinctive signature!

FRANCIE: It's merely my legal name.

MISS GARNDER (*timidly*): Frances?

FRANCIE: Please feel as free to speak to me as in the old days.

MISS GARNDER: Could I ask you to write, "To my friend, Muriel Garnder" above your signature?

FRANCIE (*after a barely perceptible pause*): And why not? (*With a twisted smile*) I've always written what you asked me to write.

    (*Writes inscription*.)

MISS GARNDER (*low whisper*): Thank you.

FRANCIE: Miss Garnder ... not that it matters, now ... but
would you grade this work ... just for old times' sake?

    (*Miss Garnder takes red pencil. Writes large "A Plus" on
    book*.)

It was such a rosy dream that Francie started the next
chapter in a fever of excitement. She'd write and write and get
it done quickly, so the dream could come true. She wrote:

*"Parker," Sherry Nola asked her personal maid, "what's
cook giving us for dinner tonight?"*

*"Breast of pheasant under glass, I believe, with hot-house
asparagus and imported mushrooms and pineapple mousse,
Miss Sherry."*

"It sounds horribly dull," observed Sherry.

"Yes, Miss Sherry," agreed the maid respectfully.

"You know, Parker, I'd like to indulge a whim of mine."

"Your whims are the household's commands."

*"I'd like to see a lot of simple desserts and choose my dinner
from among them. Please bring me a dozen charlotte russe,
some strawberry shortcake and a quart of ice-cream—make it
chocolate—a dozen lady fingers and a box of French choco-
lates."*

"Very good, Miss Sherry."

A drop of water fell on the page. Francie looked up. No,
the roof wasn't leaking, it was merely her mouth watering. She
was very, very hungry. She went to the stove and looked into
the pot. It had a pale bone in it, surrounded by water. There
was some bread in the bread-box. It was a bit hard, but better
than nothing. She cut a slice and poured a cup of coffee and
dipped the bread into the coffee to soften it. As she ate, she
read what she had just written. She made an astonishing
discovery.

"Look here, Francie Nolan," she told herself, "in this story
you're writing exactly the same thing you wrote in those
stories Miss Garnder didn't like. Here, you're writing that
you're very hungry. Only you're writing it in a twisted roundabout silly way."

Furious with the novel, she ripped the copy-book apart and
stuffed it into the stove. When the flames began licking on it

her fury increased and she ran and got her box of manuscripts from under the bed. Carefully putting aside the four about her father, she crammed the rest of them into the stove. She was burning all her pretty "A" compositions. Sentences came out clearer for an instant before a sheet blackened and crumbled. *A giant poplar, tall and high, serene and cool against the sky.* Another: *Softly the blue skies arch overhead. 'Tis a perfect October day.* The end of another sentence ... *hollyhocks like distilled sunsets and larkspur like concentrate of heaven.*

"I never saw a poplar and I *read* somewhere about the sky arching and I never saw those flowers except in a seed catalogue. And I got A's because I was a good liar." She poked the papers to make them burn faster. As they changed into ashes, she chanted, "I'm burning ugliness. I am burning ugliness." As the last flames died away, she announced dramatically to the water-boiler, "There goes my writing career."

All of a sudden, she was frightened and lonely. She wanted her father, she wanted her father. He *couldn't* be dead, he just couldn't be. In a little while he'd come running up the stairs singing, "*Molly Malone.*" She'd open the door and he'd say "Hello, Prima Donna." And she'd say, "Papa, I had a terrible dream. I dreamed you were dead." Then she'd tell him what Miss Garnder had said and he'd find the words to convince her that everything was all right. She waited, listening. Maybe it *was* a dream. But no, no dream lasted that long. It was real. Papa was gone for ever.

She put her head down on the table and sobbed. "Mama doesn't love me the way she loves Neeley," she wept. "I tried and tried to make her love me. I sit close to her and go wherever she goes and do whatever she asks me to do. But I can't make her love me the way papa loved me."

Then she saw her mother's face in the trolley car when mama sat with her head back and her eyes closed. She remembered how white and tired mama had looked. Mama *did* love her. Of course she did. Only she couldn't show it in the ways that papa could. And mama *was* good. Here, she expected the baby any minute and she was still out working. Supposing mama died when she had the baby? Francie's blood turned icy at the thought. What would Neeley and she do without mama? Where could they go? Evy and Sissy were too poor to take them. They'd have no place to live. They had no one in all the world but mama.

"Dear God," Francie prayed, "don't let mama die. I know

that I told Neeley that I didn't believe in You. But I do! I do! I just *said* that. Don't punish mama. She didn't do anything bad. Don't take her away because I said I didn't believe in You. If You let her live, I'll give You my writing. I'll never write another story again if You'll only let her live. Holy Mary, ask your son, Jesus, to ask God not to let my mother die."

But she felt that her prayer was of no use. God remembered that she had said that she didn't believe in Him and He'd punish her by taking mama as He had taken papa. She became hysterical with terror and thought of her mother as already dead. She rushed out of the flat to look for her. Katie wasn't cleaning in their house. She went into the second house and ran up the three flights of stairs, calling "Mama!" She wasn't in that house. Francie went into the third and last house. Mama wasn't on the first floor. Mama wasn't on the second floor. There was one floor left. If mama wasn't there, then she was dead She screamed:

"Mama! Mama!"

"I'm up here," came Katie's quiet voice from the third floor. "Don't holler so."

Francie was so relieved that she all but collapsed. She didn't want her mother to know she had been crying. She searched for her handkerchief. Not having it, she dried her eyes on her petticoat and walked up the last flight slowly.

"Hello, Mama."

"Has something happened to Neeley?"

"No, Mama." (She always thinks of Neeley first.)

"Well, hello, then," said Katie smiling. Katie surmised that something had gone wrong in school to upset Francie. Well, if she wanted to tell her. . . .

"Do you like me, Mama?"

"I'd be a funny person, wouldn't I? if I didn't like my children."

"Do you think I'm as good-looking as Neeley?" She waited anxiously for mama's answer, because she knew that mama never lied. Mama's answer was a long time in coming.

"You have very pretty hands and nice long thick hair."

"But do you think I'm as good-looking as Neeley?" persisted Francie, *wanting* her mother to lie.

"Look, Francie, I know that you're getting at something in a roundabout way and I'm too tired to figure it out. Have a little patience until after the baby gets here. I like you and Neeley and I think you're both nice-enough-looking children. Now please try not to worry me."

Francie was instantly contrite. Pity twisted her heart as she saw her mother, so soon to bear a child, sprawled awkwardly on her hands and knees. She knelt beside her mother.

"Get up, Mama, and let me finish this hall. I have time." She plunged her hand into the pail of water.

"No!" exclaimed Katie sharply. She took Francie's hand out of the water and dried it on her apron. "Don't put your hands in that water. It has soda and lye in it. Look what it's done to my hands." She held out her shapely but work-scarred hands. "I don't want your hands to get like that. I want you to have nice hands always. Besides, I'm almost finished."

"If I can't help, can I sit on the stairs and watch?"

"If you've nothing better to do."

Francie sat watching her mother. It was so good to be there and know that Mama was alive and close by. Even the scrubbing made a safe, pleasant sound. Swish-a swish-a swish-a-swish-a went the brush. Slup-a slup-a slup-slup went the rag wiping up. Klunk, flump went the brush and rag as mama dropped them into the pail. Skrunk, skrunk went the pail as mama pushed it to the next area.

"Haven't you any girl friends to talk to, Francie?"

"No. I hate women."

"That's not natural. It would do you good to talk things over with girls your own age."

"Have you any women friends, Mama?"

"No, I hate women," said Katie.

"See? You're just like me."

"But I had a girl friend once and I got your father through her. So you see, a girl friend comes in handy sometimes." She spoke jokingly, but her scrub-brush seemed to swish out, you-go-your-way,-I'll-go-my-way. She fought back her tears. "Yes," she continued, "you need friends. You never talk to anybody but Neeley and me and read your books and write your stories."

"I've given up writing."

Katie knew then that whatever was on Francie's mind had to do with her compositions. "Did you get a bad mark on a composition today?"

"No," lied Francie, amazed as always by her mother's guess-work. She got up. "I guess it's time for me to go to McGarrity's now."

"Wait!" Katie put her brush and scrub rag in the pail. "I'm finished for the day." She held out her hands. "Help me to get up."

Francie grasped her mother's hands. Katie pulled heavily on them as she got to her feet clumsily. "Walk back home with me, Francie."

Francie carried the pail. Katie put one hand on the banister and put her other arm around Francie's shoulder. She leaned heavily on the girl as she walked downstairs slowly, Francie keeping time with her mother's uncertain steps.

"Francie, I expect the baby any day now and I'd feel better if you were never very far away from me. Stay close to me. And when I'm working, come looking for me from time to time to see that I'm all right. I can't tell you how much I'm counting on you. I can't count on Neeley because a boy's no use at a time like this. I need you badly now and I feel safer when I know you're nearby. So stay close to me for a while."

A great tenderness for her mother came into Francie's heart. "I won't ever go away from you, Mama," she said.

"That's my good girl." Katie pressed her shoulder.

"Maybe," thought Francie, "she doesn't love me as much as she loves Neeley. But she needs me more than she needs him, and I guess needed is almost as good as being loved. Maybe better."

XL

Two DAYS later, Francie came home for lunch and did not return to school in the afternoon. Mama was in bed. After Neeley was told to go back to school, Francie wanted to get Sissy or Evy, but mama said it wasn't time, yet.

Francie felt important being in sole charge. She cleaned the flat and looked over the food in the house and planned their supper. Every ten minutes she plumped up her mother's pillows and asked whether she wanted a drink of water.

Soon after three, Neeley rushed in out of breath, flung his books in a corner and asked whether it was time to run for anybody yet, Katie smiled at his eagerness and said it was no use taking Evy or Sissy away from their own affairs until it was necessary, Neeley went off to work with instructions to ask McGarrity if he could do Francie's work as well as his own, since Francie had to stay home with their mother. McGarrity not only agreed but helped the boy with the free lunch, so that Neeley was all finished at four-thirty. They had supper early. The sooner Neeley started with his papers, the quicker he'd be finished. Mama said she didn't want anything except a cup of hot tea.

Mama didn't want the tea after Francie brewed it. Francie worried because she wouldn't eat anything. After Neeley left on his paper route, Francie brought in a bowl of stew and tried to make her mother eat it. Katie lashed out at her; told her to leave her alone; that when she wanted something to eat, she'd ask for it. Francie poured it back into the pot, trying to hold back the hurt tears. She had only meant to help. Mama called her again and didn't seem mad any more.

"What time is it?" asked Katie.

"Five to six."

"Are you sure the clock isn't slow?"

"No, Mama."

"Maybe it's fast then." She seemed so worried that Francie looked out of the front window at Jeweller Woronov's large street clock.

"Our clock's right," reported Francie.

"Is it dark outdoors yet?" Katie had no way of knowing because even at bright noon only a dull grey light filtered through the air-shaft window.

"No, it's still light outdoors."

"It's dark in here," said Katie fretfully.

"I'll light the night candle."

Bracketed to the wall was a small shelf holding a plaster statue of the blue-robed Virgin Mary with her hands held out supplicatingly. At the foot of the image was a thick red glass filled with yellow wax and a wick. Next to it was a vase holding paper red roses. Francie put a lighted match to the wick. The candlelight glowed dully and ruby red through the thick glass.

"What time is it?" Katie asked after a little while.

"Ten after six."

"You're sure the clock is neither slow nor fast?"

"Just exactly right."

Katie seemed satisfied. But five minutes later she again demanded the time. It was if she had an important rendezvous to keep and was fearful of being late.

271

At half-past six Francie told her the time again and added that Neeley would be home in an hour. "The minute he comes in, send him for Aunt Evy. Tell him not to take the time to walk. Find a nickel car-fare for him and tell him, Evy, because she lives closer than Sissy."

"Mama, suppose the baby comes all of a sudden and I don't know what to do?"

"I couldn't be that lucky—to have a baby all of a sudden. What time is it?"

"Twenty-five to seven."

"Sure?"

"I'm sure. Mama, even if Neeley is a boy it would've been better if he stayed with you instead of me."

"Why?"

"Because he's always such a great comfort to you." She said it without malice or jealousy. It was a simple statement of fact. "While I . . . I . . . just don't know the right things to say to make you feel better."

"What time is it?"

"A minute after twenty-five to seven."

Katie was silent for a long time. When she spoke, she said the words quietly, as if speaking to herself. "No, men shouldn't be around at that time. Yet, women make them stand next to them. They want them to hear every moan and groan and see every drop of blood and hear every tear of the flesh. What is this twisted pleasure they get out of making the man suffer along with them? They seem to be taking revenge because God made them women. What time is it?" Without waiting for an answer, she continued: "Before they're married they'd *die* if a man saw them in curl crimpers or with their corsets off. But when they have a baby they want him to see them in the ugliest way a woman can be seen. I don't know why. I don't know why. A man thinks of the pain and agony that came to her out of their being together and then it isn't good any more to him. That's why many men start being unfaithful after the baby . . ." Katie hardly realized what she was saying. She was missing Johnny so terribly and thinking so, to rationalize his not being there. "Besides, there is this: If you love someone, you'd rather suffer the pain alone to spare them. So keep your man out of the house when your time comes."

"Yes. Mama. It's five after seven."

"See if Neeley's coming."

Francie looked and had to report that Neeley wasn't in sight yet. Katie's mind went back to what Francie had said about Neeley being a comfort.

"No, Francie, it's you who's the comfort to me now." She sighed. "If it's a boy, we'll call him Johnny."

"It will be nice, mama, when there are four of us again."

"Yes, it will." After that, Katie didn't say anything for a while. When next she asked the time, Francie told her it was a quarter past seven and that Neeley would be home soon. Katie instructed her to wrap Neeley's nightshirt, tooth-brush, a clean towel and a bit of soap in a newspaper, as Neeley was to remain at Evy's house for the night.

Francie made two more trips to the street with the bundle under her arm before she saw Neeley coming. He was running down the street. She ran to meet him; gave him the bundle, car-fare and instructions, and told him to hurry.

"How's mama?" he asked.

"Good."

"You sure?"

"Sure. I hear a trolley coming. You better run." Neeley ran.

When Francie got back she saw that her mother's face was bathed in sweat and that there was blood on her lower lip, as though she had bitten through it.

"Oh, Mama, Mama!" She took her mother's hand and held it to her own cheek.

"Wring a cloth out of cold water and wipe my face," mama whispered. After Francie had done so, Katie went back to what was incompleted in her mind. "Of course, you're a comfort to me." Her mind veered off to something that seemed irrelevant but wasn't. "I've always been meaning to read your A compositions, but I never had the time. I've a little time now. Would you like to read one to me?"

"I can't. I burned them all up."

"You thought about them, and wrote them, and handed them in, and got marks on them, and thought about them some more, and then you burned them up. And all through that, I never read one of them."

"That's all right, Mama. They weren't much good."

"It's on my conscience."

"They weren't much good, Mama, and I know you never had the time."

Katie thought: "But I always had time for anything the boy did. I *made* time for him." She continued her thought aloud. "But then, Neeley needs more encouragement. You can go on with what you have inside you, like I can. But he needs so much from outside."

"That's all right, Mama," Francie repeated.

"I couldn't do any different than I did," said Katie. "But it will always be on my conscience just the same. What time is it?"

"Nearly seven-thirty."

"The towel again, Francie." Katie's mind seemed to be trying to clutch at something. "And isn't there one left you can read?"

Francie thought of the four about her father, what Miss Garnder had said about them, and answered: "No."

"Then read something from the Shakespeare book." Francie got the book. "Read about ' 'twas on a night like this,' I'd like to have something pretty in my mind just before the baby comes."

The print was so small that Francie had to light the gas to read. As the light flared up, she had a good look at her mother's face. It was grey and contorted. Mama didn't look like mama. She looked like Granma Mary Rommely in pain. Katie winced away from the light and Francie shut it off quickly.

"Mama, we've read these plays so many times over that I almost know them by heart. I don't need a light or the book, Mama. Listen!" She recited:

The moon shines bright!—In such a night as this
When the sweet wind did gently kiss the trees
And they did make no noise; in such a night
Troilus ...

"What time is it?"
"Seven-forty."

> *... methinks mounted the Trojan walls,*
> *And sighed his soul toward the Grecian tents*
> *Where Cressida lay the night.*

"And did you ever find out who Troilus was, Francie? And Cressida?"

"Yes, Mama."

"Some day you must tell me. When I have time to listen."

"I will, Mama."

Katie moaned. Francie wiped the sweat away again. Katie held out her two hands as she had done that day in the hall.

274

Francie took the hands and braced her feet. Katie pulled and Francie thought her arms would come out of their sockets. Then mama relaxed and let go.

So the next hour passed. Francie recited passages she knew by heart—Portia's speech, Marc Antony's funeral oration: "Tomorrow and tomorrow"—the obvious things that are remembered from Shakespeare. Sometimes Katie asked a question. Sometimes she put her hands over her face and moaned. Without knowing she did so, and taking no note of the answer, she kept asking the time. Francie wiped off her face at intervals, and three or four times in that hour Katie held out her two hands to Francie.

When Evy arrived at half-past eight, Francie all but died of pure relief. "Aunt Sissy will be along in half an hour," announced Evy as she rushed into the bedroom. After a look at Katie, Evy pulled the sheet from Francie's cot, knotted one end to Katie's bedpost and put the other end in Katie's hand. "Try pulling on that for a change," she suggested.

"What time is it?" whispered Katie after she had taken a tremendous tug on the sheet; a tug that made the sweat stand out on her face again.

"What do you care?" answered Evy, cheerfully. "You're not going any place." Katie started a smile, but a pain spasm wiped it off her face. "We can do with a better light," decided Evy.

"But the gaslight hurts her eyes," objected Francie.

Evy took the glass globe from the parlour fixture, coated the outside with soap and attached it to the bedroom fixture. When she lit the gas, there was soft diffused light without glare. Although it was a warm May night, Evy built a fire in the range. She snapped out orders to Francie. Francie rushed around filling the kettle with water and placing it over the flames. She scoured the enamelled wash-basin and poured a bottle of sweet oil in it and set it on the back of the stove. The soiled clothes were dumped out of the wash-basket and it was lined with a ragged but clean blanket and set up on two chairs near the stove. Evy put all the dinner plates in the oven to heat and instructed Francie to put hot plates into the basket, remove them when they cooled and substitute other hot plates.

"Has your mother any baby clothes?" she asked.

"What kind of people do you think we are?" asked Francie scornfully, as she displayed a modest layette consisting of four hand-made flannel kimonos, four bands, a dozen hand-hemmed diapers and four threadbare shirts which she and Neeley had worn in turn as babies. "And I made everything myself, excepting the shirts," admitted Francie proudly.

"Hm. I see your mother's looking for a boy," commented Evy, examining the blue feather stitching on the kimonos. "Well, we shall see."

When Sissy arrived, the two sisters went into the bedroom, ordering Francie to wait outside. Francie listened to them talking.

"It's time to get the midwife," Sissy said. "Does Francie know where she lives?"

"I didn't make arrangements," Katie said. "There just isn't five dollars in the house for a midwife."

"Well, maybe Sissy and I can raise the money," began Evy, "if . . ."

"Look," Sissy said. "I bore ten—no—eleven children. You had three and Katie had two. Among us we had sixteen children. We ought to know enough to bring a baby."

"All right. *We'll* bring the baby," decided Evy.

Then they closed the bedroom door. Now Francie could hear the sound of their voices, but couldn't hear what they said. She resented her aunts shutting her out like that, especially when she had been in complete charge until they came. She took the cool plates from the basket, put them into the oven and took out two heated plates. She felt all alone in the world. She wished that Neeley was home, so that they could talk about olden times.

Francie opened her eyes with a start. She couldn't have been drowsing, she thought. She just *couldn't* have. She felt the plates in the basket. They were cold. Quickly she substituted hot plates. The basket had to be kept warm for the baby. She listened to the sounds from the bedroom. They had changed since she nodded. There was no more leisurely moving to and fro; no more quiet talking. Her aunts seemed to be running back and forth with quick short steps and their voices came in short sentences. She looked at the clock. Nine-thirty. Evy came out of the bedroom, shutting the door behind her.

"Here's fifty cents, Francie. Go out and get a quarter pound of sweet butter, a box of soda crackers and two navel oranges Tell the man you want navel. Say they're for a sick lady.'

"But all the stores are closed."

"Go down to Jewtown. They're always open."

"I'll go in the morning."

"Do as you're told," said Evy sharply.

Francie went unwillingly. Going down the last flight of stairs, she heard a hoarse guttural scream. She stopped, undecided whether to run back or to continue. She remembered Evy's sharp command and continued down the stairs. As she reached the door, there was another and more agonized scream. She was glad to get out on to the street.

In one of the flats, the ape-like teamster, ordering his unwilling wife to prepare for bed, heard Katie's first scream and ejaculated: "Jesus!" When the second scream came, he said, "I hope to Christ she don't keep me awake all night." His child-like bride wept as she unfastened her dress.

Flossie Gaddis and her mother were sitting in their kitchen. Floss was sewing on another costume, one of white satin intended for her delayed marriage to Frank. Mrs. Gaddis was knitting on a grey sock for Henny. Henny was dead, of course, but all of his life the mother had knitted socks for him and she couldn't let go of the habit. Mrs. Gaddis dropped a stitch when the first scream came.

Floss said: "The men have all the fun and women the pain." The mother said nothing. She trembled when next Katie cried out. "It seems funny," said Floss, "to be making a costume with *two* sleeves."

"Yes."

They worked a while in silence before Floss spoke again. "I wonder are they worth it? The children, I mean."

Mrs. Gaddis thought of her dead son and her daughter's withered arm. She said nothing. She bent her head over her knitting. She had come round to the place where she dropped a stitch. She concentrated on picking it up.

The spare Tynmore spinsters lay in their hard virginal bed. They groped for each other's hands. "Did you hear it, Sister?" asked Miss Maggie.

"Her time has come," answered Miss Lizzie.

"That's why I didn't marry Harvey—long ago when he asked me. I was afraid of *that*. So afraid."

"I don't know," Miss Lizzie said. "Sometimes I think it's better to suffer bitter unhappiness and to fight and to scream out, and even to suffer that terrible pain, than just to be . . .

277

safe." She waited until the next scream died away, "At least *she* knows she's *living*."

Miss Maggie had no answer.

The flat across the hall from the Nolans' was vacant. The remaining flat in the house was occupied by a Polish dock walloper, his wife and their four kids. He was filling a glass from a jug of beer on the table when he heard Katie.

"Women!" he grunted contemptuously.

"Shut up, you," snarled his wife.

And all the women in the house tensed each time Katie cried out, and they suffered with her. It was the only thing that women held in common—the sure knowledge of the pain of giving birth.

Francie had to walk a long way up Manhattan Avenue before she found a Jewish dairy open. She had to go to another store for the crackers and then find a fruit-stand that had navel oranges. As she came back, she glanced at the large clock in Knipe's Drug Store, and noted that it was nearly half-past ten. She didn't care what time it was except that it seemed so important to her mother.

When she walked into the kitchen she felt a difference. There was a new quiet feeling and an indefinable smell, new and faintly fragrant. Sissy was standing with her back to the basket.

"What do you think?" she said. "You have a baby sister."

"Mama?"

"Your mother's fine."

"So *that's* why I was sent to the store."

"We thought you knew too much already for fourteen," said Evy, coming out of the bedroom.

"I just want to know the one thing," said Francie fiercely. "Did mama send me out?"

"Yes, Francie, she did," said Sissy gently. "She said something about sparing those you love."

"All right then," said Francie, mollified.

"Don't you want to see the baby?"

Sissy stepped aside. Francie lifted the blanket from the baby's head. The baby was a beautiful little thing with white skin and downy black curls which grew down into a point on her forehead, like mama's. The baby's eyes opened briefly

Francie noticed that they were a milky blue. Sissy explained that all new babies had blue eyes and that probably they'd be dark as coffee-beans as she grew older.

"It looks like mama," Francie decided.

"That's what we thought," said Sissy.

"Is it all right?"

"Perfect," Evy told her.

"Not crooked or anything?"

"Certainly not. Where do you get such ideas?"

Francie didn't tell Evy how she was afraid the baby would be born crooked because mama had worked on her hands and knees up to the last minute.

"May I go in and see mama?" she asked humbly, feeling like a stranger in her own home.

"You can bring the plate in to her." Francie took the plate holding two buttered crackers in to her mother.

"Hello, Mama."

"Hello, Francie."

Mama looked like mama again, only very tired. She couldn't raise her head, so Francie held the crackers while she ate them. After they were gone, Francie stood holding the empty plate. Mama said nothing. It seemed to Francie that she and mama were strangers again. The closeness of the last few days was gone.

"And you had a boy's name picked out, mama."

"Yes. But I don't mind a girl, really."

"She's pretty."

"She'll have black curling hair. And Neeley has blond curling hair. Poor Francie got the straight brown hair."

"I *like* straight brown hair," Francie said defiantly. She was dying to know the baby's name, but mama seemed like such a stranger now that she didn't like to ask outright. "Shall I write the information out to send to the Board of Health?"

"No. The priest will send it in when she's christened."

"Oh!"

Katie recognized the disappointment in Francie's tone. "But bring in the ink and the book and I'll let you write down her name."

Francie took the Gideon Bible that Sissy had swiped nearly fifteen years ago, from the mantelpiece. She looked at the four entries on the flyleaf. The first three were in Johnny's fine careful hand.

> *January 1, 1901. Married. Katherine Rommely and John Nolan.*
> *December 15, 1901. Born. Frances Nolan.*
> *December 23, 1902. Born. Cornelius Nolan.*

The fourth entry was in Katie's firm back-hand slant.

> *December 25, 1915. Died. John Nolan. Age 34.*

Sissy and Evy followed Francie into the bedroom. They, too, were curious as to what Katie would name the baby. Sarah? Eva? Ruth? Elizabeth?

"Write this down." Katie dictated. "May 28, 1916. Born." Francie dipped her pen in the ink-bottle. "Annie Laurie Nolan."

"Annie! Such an ordinary name," groaned Sissy.

"Why, Katie? Why?" demanded Evy patiently.

"A song that Johnny sang once," explained Katie.

As Francie wrote the name, she heard the chords; she heard her father singing, *"And 'twas there that Annie Laurie."* ... Papa ... papa. . . .

". . . a song, he said, that belonged to a better world," Katie went on. "He would have liked the child named after one of his songs."

"Laurie is a pretty name," said Francie.

And Laurie became the baby's name.

XLI

LAURIE WAS a good baby. She slept contentedly most of the time. When she was awake she put in the time lying quietly and trying to focus her berry-brown eyes on her infinitesimal fist.

Katie nursed the baby, not only because it was the instinctive thing to do but because there was no money for fresh milk. Since the baby couldn't be left alone, Katie started her work at five in the morning, doing the other two houses first. She worked until nearly nine, when Francie and Neeley left for school. Then she cleaned her own house, leaving the door of her flat ajar in case Laurie cried. Katie went to bed immediately after supper each night and Francie saw so little of her mother that it seemed as if mama had gone away.

McGarrity didn't fire them after the baby's birth as he had planned. He really needed them now, because his business boomed suddenly in that spring of 1916. His saloon was crowded all the time. Great changes were taking place in the country, and his customers, like Americans everywhere, had to get together to talk things over. The corner saloon was their only gathering place, the poor man's club.

Francie, working in the flat above the saloon, heard their raised voices through the thin floor-boards. Often she paused in her work and listened. Yes, the world was changing rapidly and this time she knew it was the *world* and not herself. She heard the world changing as she listened to the voices.

It's a fact. They're gonna stop making liquor and in a few years the country will be dry.

A man that works hard has a right to his beer.

Tell that to the President and see how far you get.

This is a people's country. If we don't want it dry, it won't be dry.

Sure it's a people's country, but they're gonna push prohibition down your throat.

By Jesus, I'll make my own wine, then. My old man used to make it in the old country. You take a bushel of grapes . . .

G'wan! They'll never give wimmen the vote.

Don't lay any bets on it.

If that comes, my wife votes like I do, otherwise I'll break her neck.

My old woman wouldn't go to the polls and mix in with a bunch of bums and rummies.

. . . a woman President. That might be.

They'll never let a woman run the government.

There's one running it right now.

Like hell!

Wilson can't turn around and go to the bathroom 'less he asks Mrs. Wilson if it's okay by her.

Wilson's an old woman himself.

He's keeping us out of war.

That college professor!

What we need in the White House is a sound politician and not a school teacher.

*   *   *

281

...automobiles. Soon the horse will be a thing of the past. That feller out in Dee-troit's making cars so cheap that soon every working man can have one.

A labourer driving his own car! You should live so long!

Airplanes! Just a crazy fad. Won't last long.

The moving pitchers is here to stay. The thee-ayters is closing up one by one in Brooklyn. Take me: I'd rather see this here Charlie Chaplin any day than this here Corset Payton the wife goes for.

...wireless. Greatest thing ever invented. Words come through the air, mind you, without wires. You need a kind of a machine to ketch it and earphones to listen in....

They call it twilight sleep and a woman don't feel a thing when the kid comes. So when this friend tells my wife, she says that it's about time they invented something like that.

What're you talking about! Gaslight's out of date. They're putting 'lectricity even in the cheapest tenements.

Don't know what's got into the youngsters nowadays. They're all dance crazy. Dance ... dance ... dance....

So I changed my name from Schultz to Scott. The judge says what do you want to go and do that for? Schultz is a good name. He was German himself, see? Listen, Mac, I says ... that's just how I talked to him; judge or no judge. I'm through with the old country, I says. After what they done to them Belgian babies, I says, I want no part of Germany. I'm an American now, I says, and I want an American name.

And we're heading straight for war. Man, I can see it coming.

All we got to do is to elect Wilson again this autumn. He'll keep us out of war.

Don't bet on them campaign promises. When you got a Democrat president, you got a war president.

Lincoln was a Republican.

But the south had a Democrat president and they was the ones started the Civil War.

I ask you how long we gotta stand for it? The bastards sunk

282

*another one of our ships. How many do they gotta sink before
we get up enough nerve to go over there and lick hell out of
them?*

*We got to stay out. This country's getting along fine. Let
them fight their own wars without dragging us in.*

We don't want war.

War's declared. I'll enlist the next day.

You can talk. You're past fifty. They wouldn't take you.

I'd sooner go to jail than to war.

*A feller's got to fight for what he thinks is right. I'd be glad
to go.*

I got nothing to worry about. I got a double hernia.

*Let the war come. They'll need us working men then to
build their ships and their guns. They'll need the farmers to
grow their food. Then watch them come sucking around us.
Us labourers will have the God-damned capitalists by the
throat. They won't tell us. We'll tell them. By Jesus, we'll make
them sweat. War can't come quick enough to suit me.*

*Like I'm telling you. Everything is machines. I heard a joke
the other day. Feller and his wife going around getting food,
clothes, everything out of machines. So they come to this baby
machine and the feller puts money in and out come a baby. So
the feller turns around and says, give me the good old days.
The good old days! Yeah, I guess they're gone for ever.
Fill 'em up again, Jim.*

And Francie, pausing in her sweeping to listen, tried to put
everything together and tried to understand a world spinning
in confusion. And it seemed to her that the whole world
changed in between the time that Laurie was born and graduation day.

XLII

FRANCIE HARDLY had time to get used to Laurie when graduation night came round. Katie couldn't go to both graduations,
so it was decided that she go to Neeley's. And that was right.
Neeley shouldn't be deprived because Francie had felt like

changing schools. Francie understood but felt a bit hurt just the same. Papa would have gone to see her graduate if he were living. They arranged that Sissy go with Francie. Evy would stay with Laurie.

On the last night in June, 1916, Francie walked for the last time to the school she so loved. Sissy, quiet and changed since she got her baby, walked sedately beside her. Two firemen passed and Sissy never so much as noticed and there had been a time when Sissy couldn't resist a uniform. Francie wished Sissy hadn't changed. It made her feel lonesome. Her hand crept into Sissy's and Sissy squeezed it. Francie was comforted. Sissy was still Sissy underneath.

The graduates sat in the front part of the auditorium and the guests in the back. The principal made an earnest speech to the children about how they were going out into a troubled world and about how it would be up to them to build a new world after the war, which was sure to come to America. He urged them on to higher education, so that they would be better equipped for this world-building. Francie was impressed and vowed in her heart that she'd help carry the torch like he said.

Then came the graduation play. Francie's eyes burned with unshed tears. As the diluted dialogue droned on, she thought:

"My play would have done better. I would have taken the ash-bin out. I would have done whatever Teacher said if she had only let me write the play."

After the play, they marched up, got their diplomas and were graduates at last. The oath of allegiance to the flag and the singing of "The Star-Spangled Banner," clinched it.

And now came the time of Francie's Gethsemane.

It was the custom to present bouquets to the girl graduates. Since flowers were not allowed in the auditorium, they were delivered to the classrooms, where the teachers placed them on the recipient's desk.

Francie had to go back to her room to get her report card; also her pencil box and autograph book from her desk. She stood outside nerving herself for the ordeal, knowing her desk would be the only one without flowers. She was sure, because she hadn't told mama about the custom, knowing there was no money at home for such things.

Deciding to get it over with, she went in and walked straight to the teacher's desk, not daring to look at her own. The air was thick with flower scents. She heard the girls chattering and squealing with delight over their flowers. She heard the exchange of triumphant admiration.

She got her report card; four "A's" and one "C minus." The latter was her English mark. She used to be the best writer in school and here she ended up barely passing English. Suddenly, she hated the school and all the teachers, especially Miss Garnder. And she didn't care about not getting flowers. She didn't care. It was a silly custom, anyway. "I'll go to my desk and get my things," she decided. "And if anyone speaks to me, I'll tell them to shut up. And then I'll walk out of this school for ever and not say good-bye to anyone." She raised her eyes. "The desk without flowers on it will be mine." But there were no empty desks! There were flowers on every single one!

Francie went to her desk, reasoning that a girl had placed one of her bouquets there for a moment. Francie planned to pick it up and hand it to the owner, saying coolly: "Do you *mind*? I have to get something out of my desk."

She picked up the flowers—two dozen dark red roses on a sheaf of ferns. She cradled them in her arms, the way the other girls did, and pretended for a moment that they were hers. She looked for the owner's name on the card. But her own name was on the card! Her name! The card said: *For Francie on graduation day. Love from Papa.*

Papa!

The writing was in his fine careful hand, in the black ink from the bottle in the cupboard at home. Then it *was* all a dream, a long mixed-up dream. Laurie was a dream, and the working at McGarrity's, and the graduation play, and the bad mark in English. She was waking up now and everything would be all right. Papa would be waiting out in the hall.

But there was only Sissy in the hall.

"Then papa *is* dead," she said.

"Yes," said Sissy. "And it's six months now."

"But he *can't* be, Aunt Sissy. He sent me flowers."

"Francie, about a year ago he gave me that card all written out and two dollars. He said: 'When Francie graduates, send her some flowers for me—in case I forget.'"

Francie started to cry. It was only because she was sure, now, that nothing was a dream; it was because she was unstrung from working too hard and worrying about mama; because she didn't get to write the graduation play; because she got a bad mark in English; because she had been too well prepared not to receive flowers.

Sissy took her to the girls' wash-room and pushed her into a booth. "Cry loud and hard," she ordered, "and hurry up. Your mother will be wondering what's keeping us."

Francie stood in the booth, clutching her roses and sobbing. Each time the wash-room door opened and chattering announced incoming girls, she flushed the toilet so that the noise of the water would drown out her sobs. Soon she was over it. When she came out, Sissy had a handkerchief wet with cold water to hand her. As Francie mopped her eyes, Sissy asked whether she felt better. Francie nodded yes, and begged her to wait a moment while she said her good-byes.

She went into the principal's office and shook hands with him. "Don't forget the old school, Frances. Come back and see us some time," he said.

"I will," promised Francie. She went back to say good-bye to her classroom teacher.

"We'll miss you, Frances," said Teacher.

Francie got her pencil-box and autograph-book from her desk. She started to say good-bye to the girls. They crowded around her. One put her arm around her waist and two others kissed her cheek. They called out good-bye messages.

"Come to my house to see me, Frances."

"Write to me, Frances, and let me know how you're getting along."

"Frances, we have a telephone now. Ring me up some time. Ring me up tomorrow."

"Write something in my autograph-book, huh, Frances? So's I can sell it when you get famous."

"I'm going to summer camp. I'll put down my address."

"I'm going to Girls' High in September. You come to Girls' High, too, Frances."

"No. Come to Eastern District High with me."

"Girls' High!"

"Eastern District!"

"Erasmus Hall High's the best. You come there, Frances, with me and we'll be friends, all through high school. I'll never have any other friend but you, if you'll come."

"Frances, you never let me write in your autograph-book."

"Me neither."

"Gimme, gimme."

They wrote in Francie's all but empty book. "They're *nice*," Francie thought. "I could have been friends with them all the time. I thought they didn't want to be friends. It must have been me that was wrong."

They wrote in the book. Some wrote small and cramped; others, loose and sprawling. But all the writing was the handwriting of children. Francie read as they wrote:

> *I wish you luck, I wish you joy.*
> *I wish your first, a baby boy.*
> *And when his hair begins to curl,*
> *I wish you then, a baby girl.*
>   *Florence Fitzgerald.*

> *When you are married*
> *And your husband gets cross,*
> *Sock him with the poker,*
> *And get a divorce.*
>   *Jeannie Leigh.*

> *When night draws back the curtain.*
> *And pins it with a star,*
> *Remember I am still your friend,*
> *Though you may wander far.*
>   *Noreen O'Leary.*

Beatrice Williams turned to the last page in the book and wrote:

> *Way back here and out of sight.*
> *I sign my name, just for spite.*

She signed it: *Your Fellow-Writer, Beatrice Williams.* "She would say 'fellow-writer,'" thought Francie, still jealous about the play.

Francie got away at last. Out in the hall she said to Sissy: "Just one more good-bye."

"It's taking you the longest time to graduate," protested Sissy good-naturedly.

Miss Garnder sat at her desk in her brilliantly lighted room. She was alone. She wasn't popular, and so far no one had been to say good-bye. She looked up eagerly as Francie entered.

"So you've come to say good-bye to your old English teacher," she said, pleased.

"Yes, ma'am."

Miss Garnder couldn't let it go at that. She *had* to be a teacher. "About your mark: You haven't turned in work this

287

term. I should have failed you. But at the last moment I decided to pass you so that you could graduate with your class." She waited. Francie said nothing. "Well? Aren't you going to thank me?"

"Thank you, Miss Garnder."

"You remember our little chat?"

"Yes, ma'am."

"Why did you turn stubborn and stop handing in work, then?"

Francie had nothing to say. It was something she couldn't explain to Miss Garnder. She held out her hand. "Good-bye, Miss Garnder."

Miss Garnder was taken aback. "Well—good-bye, then," she said. They shook hands. "In time to come you'll see I was right, Frances." Francie said nothing. "Won't you?" Miss Garnder asked sharply.

"Yes, ma'am."

Francie went out of the room. She did not hate Miss Garnder any more. She didn't like her, but she felt sorry for her. Miss Garnder had nothing in all the world excepting a sureness about how right she was.

Mr. Jenson stood on the school steps. He took each child's hand in both of his and said: "Good-bye and God bless you." He added a personal message for Francie. "Be good, work hard, and reflect credit on our school." Francie promised that she would.

On the way home Sissy said: "Look! Let's not tell your mother, who sent the flowers. It will start her to remembering, and she's just about getting well after Laurie." They agreed to say that Sissy bought the flowers. Francie removed the card and put it in her pencil-box.

When they told mama the lie about the flowers she said: "Sissy, you shouldn't have spent your money." But Francie could tell that mama was pleased.

The two diplomas were admired and everyone agreed that Francie's was the prettier on account of Mr. Jenson's fine handwriting.

"The first diplomas in the Nolan family," said Katie.

"But not the last, I hope," said Sissy.

"I'm going to see to it that each of my children have three," said Evy: "grade school, high school and college."

"In twenty-five years," said Sissy, "our family will have a stack of diplomas this high." She stood on tiptoe and measured six feet from the ground.

Mama examined the report cards for the last time. Neeley had "B" in conduct, the same in physical education, and "C" in all his other subjects. Mama said: "That's good, son." She looked past Francie's "A's" and concentrated on the "C minus."

"Francie! I'm surprised. How did this happen?"

"Mama, I don't want to talk about it."

"And in English, too. Your best subject."

Francie's voice notched up higher as she repeated: "Mama, I don't want to talk about it."

"She always wrote the best compositions in school," explained Katie to her sisters.

"Mama!" It was almost a scream.

"Katie! Stop it!" ordered Sissy sharply.

"All right, then," surrendered Katie, suddenly aware that she was nagging and ashamed of herself.

Evy jumped in with a change of subject. "Do we have that party, or don't we?" she asked.

"I'm putting my hat on," Katie said.

Sissy stayed with Laurie while Evy, mama, and the two graduates went to Scheefly's Ice-Cream Saloon for the party. Scheefly's was crowded with graduation parties. The kids had their diplomas with them and the girls brought their bouquets. There was a mother or a father—sometimes both—at each table. The Nolan party found a free table at the back of the room.

The place was a medley of shouting kids, beaming parents and rushed waiters. Some kids were thirteen, a few fifteen, but most of them Francie's age—fourteen. Most of the boys were Neeley's classmates, and he had a great time hollering greetings across the room. Francie hardly knew the girls, nevertheless she waved and called out to them as gaily as though they had been close friends for years.

Francie was proud of mama. The other mothers had greying hair and most of them were so fat that their backsides slopped over the edges of the chair. Mama was slender and didn't look at all like going on thirty-three. Her skin was as smoothly clear and her hair as black and curling as it had ever been. "Put her in a white dress," thought Francie, "with a bunch of roses in her arms, and she'd look like any fourteen-year-old graduate—except for the line between her eyes that cut deeper since papa died."

They ordered. Francie had a mental list of all the soda flavours. She was going down the list so that she could say she had tasted all the kinds of sodas in the world. Pineapple was next and she ordered that. Neeley ordered the old stand-by, chocolate soda, and Katie and Evy chose plain vanilla ice-cream.

Evy made up little stories about the people in the place and kept Francie and Neeley laughing. Francie studied her mother from time to time. Mama wasn't smiling at Evy's jokes. She ate her ice-cream slowly and the line between her eyes deepened and Francie knew that she was figuring something out.

"My children," thought Katie, "have more education at thirteen and fourteen than I have at thirty-two. And still it isn't enough. When I think of how ignorant I was at their age. Yes, and even when I was married and had a baby. Imagine. I believed in witch's charms, then—what the midwife told me about the woman in the fish-market. They started in 'way ahead of me. They were never that ignorant.

"I got them graduated from grade school. I can't do more for them. All my plans . . . Neeley, a doctor, Francie in college . . . can't work them out now. The baby. . . . Have they enough in them to get somewhere alone? I don't know. The Shakespeare . . . the Bible . . . they know how to play piano, but they've stopped practising now. I taught them to be clean and truthful and not to take charity. Is that enough, though?

"They'll have a boss to please, soon, and new people to get along with. They'll get into other ways. Good? Bad? They won't sit home with me nights if they work all day. Neeley will be off with his friends. And Francie? Reading. . . . Away to the library . . . a show . . . a free lecture or band concert. Of course, I'll have the baby. The baby. She'll get a better start. When she graduates, the other two might see her through high school. I must do better for Laurie than I did for them. They never had enough to eat, never had right clothes. The best could do wasn't enough. And now they have to go out to work and they're still little children. Oh, if I could only get them into high school this autumn! *Please* God! I'll give twenty years off my life. I'll work night and day. But I can't of course. No one to stay with the baby."

Her thoughts were broken into by a wave of singing tha

rolled over the room. Someone started a popular anti-war song and the rest took it up.

I didn't raise my boy to be a soldier.
I brought him up to be my pride and joy ...

Katie resumed her thoughts. "There is no one to help us. No one." She thought briefly of Sergeant McShane. He had sent a big basket of fruit when Laurie was born. She knew he was retiring from the police force in September. He was going to run for Assembly-man from Queens, his home borough, next Election. Everyone said he'd be sure to get in. She had heard that his wife was very sick, might not live to see her husband elected.

"He'll marry again," thought Katie. "Of course. Some woman who knows all about social life ... help him ... the way a politician's wife must." She stared at her work-worn hands for a long time, then put them under the table as though she were ashamed of them.

Francie noticed. "She's thinking of Sergeant McShane," she guessed, remembering how mama had put on her cotton gloves that time long ago at the outing when McShane had looked at her. "He likes her," thought Francie. "I wonder does she know it? She must. She seems to know everything. I bet she could marry him if she wanted to. But he needn't think I'd ever call him father. My father is dead, and no matter who mama marries, he will only be Mr. So-and-So to me."

They were finishing the song.

There'd be no wars today,
If mothers all would say,
I didn't raise my boy to be a soldier.

"... Neeley," thought Katie. "Thirteen. If the war does come here, it will be over before he gets old enough to go, thank God."

Now Aunt Evy was singing softly to them, making up a parody on the song.

Who dares to place a moustache on his shoulder.

"Aunt Evy, you're *terrible*," said Francie as she and Neeley screamed with laughter. Katie jerked out of her thoughts and looked up and smiled. Then the waiter laid down the bill and they all grew silent, watching Katie.

"I hope she's not fool enough to tip him" thought Evy.

"Does mama know you're supposed to leave a nickel tip?" thought Neeley. "I hope so."

"Whatever mama does," thought Francie, "it will be the right thing."

It wasn't the custom to tip in the ice-cream saloons except on special parties, when you were supposed to leave a nickel. Katie saw that the bill was for thirty cents. She had one coin in her old purse, it was a fifty-cent piece, which she laid on the bill. The waiter took it away and brought back four nickels, which he laid in a row. He hovered near-by waiting for Katie to pick up three of them. She looked at the four nickels. "Four loaves of bread," she thought. Four pairs of eyes watched Katie's hand. Katie never hesitated once she put her hand on the money. With a sure gesture she pushed the four nickels towards the waiter.

"Keep the change," she said grandly.

Francie had all she could do not to stand up on her chair and cheer. "Mama is somebody," she kept saying to herself. The waiter scooped up the nickels happily and rushed away.

"Two sodas shot," groaned Neeley.

"Katie, Katie, how foolish," protested Evy. "I bet it's your last money, too."

"It is. But it may be our last graduation, too."

"McGarrity pays us four dollars tomorrow," said Francie, defending her mother.

"And he fires us tomorrow too," added Neeley.

"There'll be no money after that four dollars until they get jobs, then," concluded Evy.

"I don't care," said Katie. "For once I wanted us to feel like millionaires. And if twenty cents can make us feel rich, it's a cheap price to pay."

Evy recalled how Katie let Francie pour her coffee down the sink and said nothing more. There were many things she didn't understand about her sister.

The parties were breaking up. Albie Seedmore, the leggy son of a prosperous grocer, came over to their table.

"Go-to-the-movies-with-me-tomorrow-Francie?" he asked all on a breath. "I'll pay," he added hastily.

(A movie-house was letting the graduates attend the Saturday matinee two-for-a-nickel providing they brought their diplomas along as proof.)

Francie looked at her mother. Mama nodded her consent.

"Sure, Albie," accepted Francie.

"See you. Two. Tomorrow." He loped off.

"Your first date," said Evy. "Make a wish." She held out her little finger and crooked it. Francie hooked her little finger into Aunt Evy's.

"I wish I could always wear a white dress and carry red roses and that we could always throw money around like we did tonight," wished Francie.

BOOK FOUR

XLIII

"YOU GOT the idea now," said the forelady to Francie. "You'll make a good stemmer in time." She went away and Francie was on her own; the first hour of the first day of her first job.

Following the forelady's instructions, her left hand picked up a foot length of shiny wire. Simultaneously her right hand picked up a narrow strip of dark green tissue paper. She touched the end of the strip to a damp sponge then, using the thumb and first two fingers of each hand as a rolling machine, she wound the paper on the wire. She placed the covered wire aside. It was now a stem.

At intervals, Mark, the pimply-faced utility boy, distributed the stems to the "pet'lers," who wired paper rose petals to them. Another girl strung a calyx up under the rose and turned it over to the "leafer," who prised a unit, three dark glossy leaves on a short stem, from a block of leaves, wired the unit to the stem and turned the rose over to the "finisher," who wound a strip of heavier-textured green paper around the calyx and down the stem. The stem, calyx, rose and leaves were now one and seemed to have grown so.

Francie's back hurt and a shooting pain ran through her shoulder. She must have covered a thousand stems, she figured. Surely it was time for lunch. She turned round to look at the clock, and found that she had been working just one hour!

"Clock-watcher," commented a girl derisively. Francie looked up, startled, but said nothing.

She got a rhythm to her work and it seemed to come easier. *One.* She set aside the covered wire. *And a half.* She picked up a new wire and a strip of paper. *Two.* She moistened the paper. *Three-four-five-six-seven-eight-nine-ten.* The wire was covered. Soon the rhythm became instinctive, she didn't have to count and it wasn't necessary to concentrate. Her back relaxed and her shoulder stopped aching. Her mind was freed and she started to figure things out.

"This could be a whole life," she thought. "You work eight hours a day covering wires to earn money to buy food and to pay for a place to sleep so that you can keep living to come back to cover more wires. Some people are born and kept living just to come to this. Of course, some of these girls will marry; marry men who have the same kind of life. What will they gain? They'll gain someone to hold conversation with in the few hours at night between work and sleep." But she knew the gain wouldn't last. She had seen too many working couples who, after the children came and the bills piled up, rarely communicated with each other except in bitter snarls. "These people are caught," she thought. "And why? Because" (remembering her grandmother's repeated convictions) "they haven't got enough education." Fright grew in Francie. Maybe it would be so that she'd never get to high school; maybe she'd never have more education than she had at that moment. Maybe all her life she'd have to cover wires...cover wires...One...and a half...two...three-four-five-six-seven-eight-nine-ten. The same unreasoning terror came on her that had come where, as an eleven-year-old child, she had seen the old man with the obscene feet in Losher's Bakery. In her panic, she speeded up her rhythm so that she'd *have* to concentrate on her work and not have room to think

"New broom," observed a finisher cynically.

"Trying to make a hit with the boss," was the opinion of a pet'ler.

Soon even the speeding up became automatic and again Francie's mind was free. Covertly, she studied the girls at the long table. There were a dozen of them. Poles and Italians. The youngest looked sixteen and the oldest, thirty, and all were swarthy. For some unaccountable reason, all wore black dresses, evidently not realizing how unbecoming black was to dark skins. Francie was the only one wearing a gingham wash dress, and she felt like a silly baby. The sharp-eyed workers noticed her quick stares and retaliated with their own peculiar brand of hazing. The girl at the head of the table started it.

"Somebody at this table is got a dirty face," she announced. "Not me," answered the others one by one. When Francie's turn came they stopped work and waited. Not knowing what to answer, Francie remained silent. "New girl says nothing," summarized the ringleader. "So she's got the dirty face." Francie's face got hot, but she worked faster, hoping they'd drop the whole thing.

"Somebody is got a dirty neck." It started all over again. "Not me," answered the girls in order. When it came to Francie's turn she, too, said: "Not me." But instead of appeasing them, it gave them more material to work on.

"New girl says her neck ain't dirty."

"*She* says!"

"How does she know? Can she see her own neck?"

"Would she admit it if it was dirty?"

"They want me to do something," puzzled Francie. "But what? Do they want me to get mad and curse at them? Do they want me to give up this job? Or do they want to see me cry the way that little girl did long ago when I watched her clean the blackboard erasers? Whatever they want, I won't do it!" She bent her head over the wires and made her fingers fly faster.

The tiresome game went on all morning. The only respites were when Mark, the utility boy, came in. Then they let up on Francie a little in order to work on him.

"New girl, watch out for Mark," they warned her. "He was arrested twice for rape and once for white slavery."

The accusations were crudely ironical, considering the obvious effeminacy of Mark. Francie saw how the unfortunate boy flushed a brick-red at each taunt and she felt sorry for him.

The morning wore on. When it seemed that it would never end, a bell rang announcing lunch-time. The girls dropped their work, hauled out paper bags of lunch, ripped the bags open to form a table-cloth, spread out their onion-garnished sandwiches and started to eat. Francie's hands were hot and sticky. She wanted to wash them before she ate, so she asked her neighbour where the wash-room was.

"No spik Eeng-leash," answered the girl in exaggerated greenhorn dialect.

"Nix verstadt," said another, who had been taunting her in idiomatic English all morning.

"What's a wash-room?" asked a fat girl.

"Where they make washers," replied a wit.

Mark was collecting boxes. He stood in the doorway, his arms laden, made his Adam's apple go up and down twice, and Francie heard him speak for the first time.

"Jesus Christ died on the cross for people like you," he announced passionately, "and now you won't show a new girl where the terlet is."

Francie stared at him astonished. Then she couldn't help it—it had sounded so funny—she burst out laughing. Mark gulped, turned and disappeared down the hall. Everything changed then. A murmur ran round the table.

"She laughed!"

"Hey! The new girl laughed!"

"Laughed!"

A young Italian girl linked her arm in Francie's and said: "Come on, new girl, I'll show you the terlet."

In the wash-room, she turned on the water for Francie, punched down on the glass bowl of liquid soap and hovered over Francie solicitously while she washed her hands. When Francie would have dried her hands on the snowy, obviously-unused roller towel, her guide snatched her away.

"Don't use that towel, new girl."

"Why? It looks clean."

"It's dangerous. Some of the girls working here is clappy and you'll catch it if you use the towel."

"What'll I do?" Francie waved her wet hands.

"Use your petticoat like we do."

Francie dried her hands on her petticoat, eyeing the deadly towel with horror.

Back in the workroom, she found that they had flattened her paper bag and set out the two bologna sandwiches mama had fixed for her. She saw that someone had placed a nice red tomato on her paper. The girls welcomed her back with smiles. The one who had led the taunts all morning took a long swig out of a whisky bottle and then passed it to Francie.

"Take a drink, new girl," she ordered. "Them samwishes is dry going down alone." Francie shrank back and declined hastily. "Go ahead! It's only cold tea." Francie thought of the wash-room towel and shook her head "no" emphatically. "Ah" exclaimed the girl. "I know why you don't drink from my bottle. In the terlet, Anastasia scared you. Don't you believe her, new girl. The boss started that clappy talk hisself so's we wouldn't use the towels. That way he saves a couple dollars each week on laundry."

"Yeah?" said Anastasia. "I don't see none of youse using the towel."

"Hell, we only got half a hour for lunch. Who wants to vaste time washing hands? Drink up, new girl."

Francie took a long drink from the bottle. The cold tea was rong and refreshing. She thanked the girl and then tried to thank the donor of the tomato. Immediately each girl in turn denied giving it.

"What are you talking about?"

"What termater?"

"Don't see no termater."

"New girl brings a termater for lunch and don't even remember."

So they teased her. But now there was something warmly companionable about the teasing. Francie enjoyed the lunch period and was glad she had found out what they wanted from her. They had just wanted her to laugh—such a simple thing and so hard to find out.

The rest of the day passed pleasantly. The girls told her not to break her neck—that it was seasonable work and they'd all be laid off when the autumn orders had been made up. The quicker the orders were finished, the sooner they'd be fired. Francie, pleased at being taken into the confidence of these older, more experienced workers, obligingly slowed down. They told jokes all afternoon and Francie laughed at them all, whether they were funny or just plain dirty. And her conscience bothered her only a little bit when she joined the others in tormenting Mark, the martyr, who didn't know that if he would laugh but once, his troubles in the shop would be over.

It was a few minutes past noon on Saturday. Francie stood at the foot of the Flushing Avenue station of the Broadway El waiting for Neeley. She held an envelope containing five dollars—her first week's pay. Neeley was bringing home five dollars too. They had agreed to arrive home together and make a little ceremony out of giving the money to mama.

Neeley worked as errand-boy in a down-town New York brokerage house. Sissy's John had got him the job through a friend already working there. Francie envied Neeley. Each day he crossed the great Williamsburg Bridge and went into the strange big city while Francie walked to her work on the north side of Brooklyn. And Neeley ate in a restaurant. Like Francie, he had brought his lunch the first day, but the boys made fun of him, calling him the country boy from Brooklyn. After that, mama gave him fifteen cents a day for lunch. He told Francie how he ate in a place called the Automat, where you put a nickel in a slot and coffee and cream came out together—not too little, not too much, just a cupful. Franci wished she could ride across the bridge to work and eat in th

298

Automat instead of carrying sandwiches from home.

Neeley ran down the El steps. He carried a flat package under his arm. Francie noticed how he put his feet down at an angle so that the whole foot was on the step instead of just the heel part. This gave him sure footing. Papa had always come down stairs that way. Neeley wouldn't tell Francie what was in the package, saying that would spoil the surprise They stopped in a neighbourhood bank which was just about to close for the day and asked a teller to give them new one-dollar notes in exchange for their old money.

"What do you want new notes for?" asked the teller.

"It's our first pay and we'd like to bring it home in new money," explained Francie.

"First pay, eh?" said the teller. "That takes me back. It certainly takes me back. I remember when I took home my first pay. I was a boy at the time ... working on a farm in Manhasset, Long Island. Well, sir. ..." He went off into a biographical sketch while people in line shuffled impatiently. He ended: "... and when I turned my first pay over to my mother, the tears stood in her eyes. Yes, sir, the tears stood in her eyes."

He tore the wrapper from a bundle of new notes and exchanged their old money. Then he said: "And here's a present for you." He gave each a fresh-minted gold-looking penny which he took from the cash drawer. "New 1916 pennies," he explained. "The first in the neighbourhood. Don't spend them, now. Save them." He took two old coppers from his pocket and put them in the drawer to make up the deficiency. Francie thanked him. As they moved away, she heard the man next in line say as he leaned his elbow on the edge:

"I remember when I brought my first pay home to my old lady."

As they went out, Francie wondered whether everyone in line would tell about his first pay. "Everyone who works," said Francie, "has this one thing together: They remember about bringing home their first pay."

"Yeah," agreed Neeley.

As they turned a corner, Francie mused: "and the tears stood in her eyes." She had never heard that expression before, and it caught her fancy.

"How could that be?" Neeley wanted to know. "Tears have no legs. They can't 'stand.'"

"He didn't mean that. He meant it like when people say: 'I stood in bed all day.'"

"But 'stood' is no word that way."

"It is so," countered Francie. "Here in Brooklyn 'stood' is like the past tense of 'stay.'"

"I guess so," agreed Neeley. "Let's walk down Manhattan Avenue instead of Graham."

"Neeley, I have an idea. Let's make a tin-can bank without telling mama and nail it in your chest. We'll start it off with these new pennies, and if mama gives us any spending money, we'll each put ten cents in every week. We'll open it Christmas and buy presents for mama and Laurie."

"And for us, too," stipulated Neeley.

"Yeah. I'll buy one for you and you buy one for me. I'll tell you what I want when the time comes."

It was agreed.

They walked briskly, out-distancing loitering kids homeward bound from the junk-shops. They looked towards Carney's as they passed Scholes Street and noticed the crowd outside of Cheap Charlie's.

"Kids," said Neeley contemptuously, jingling some coins in his pockets.

"Remember, Neeley, when we used to go out selling junk?"

"That was a long time ago."

"Yeah," agreed Francie. It was, in fact, two weeks since they had dragged their last haul to Carney's.

Neeley presented the flat package to mama. "For you and Francie," he said. Mama unwrapped it. It was a pound box of Loft's peanut brittle. "And I didn't buy it out of my salary either," explained Neeley mysteriously. They made mama go into the bedroom for a minute. They arranged the ten new notes on the table, then called mama out.

"For you, Mama," said Francie, with a grand wave of her hand.

"Oh, my!" said Mama. "I can hardly believe it."

"And that's not all," said Neeley. He took eighty cents in change from his pocket and placed it on the table. "Tips for running errands fast," he explained. "I saved 'em all week. There was more, but I bought the candy."

Mama slid the change across the table to Neeley. "All the tips you make, you keep for spending money," she said.

(Just like papa, thought Francie.)

"Gee! Well, I'll give Francie a quarter out of it."

"No." Mama got a fifty-cent piece from the cracked cup and gave it to Francie. "That's Francie's spending money. Fifty cents a week." Francie was pleased. She hadn't expected that much of an allowance. The children overwhelmed their mother with thanks.

Katie looked at the candy, at the new notes and then at her children. She bit her lip, turned suddenly and went into the bedroom, closing the door after her.

"Is she mad about something?" whispered Neeley.

"No," said Francie. "She's not mad. She just didn't want us to see her start crying."

"How do you know she's going to cry?"

" 'Cause. When she looked at the money I saw that tears stood in her eyes."

XLIV

FRANCIE HAD been working two weeks when the lay-off came. The girls exchanged looks while the Boss explained that it was just for a few days.

"A few days, six months long," explained Anastasia for Francie's information.

The girls were going over to a Greenpoint factory which needed hands for winter orders, poinsettias and artificial holly wreaths. When the lay-off came *there*, they'd go on to another factory. And so on. They were Brooklyn migratory workers following seasonal work from one part of the borough to the other.

They urged Francie to go along with them, but she wanted to try new work. She figured that since she had to work, she'd get variety in it by changing her job each chance she got. Then, like the sodas, she could say she had tried every work there was.

Katie found an ad in *The World* that said a file clerk was wanted; beginner considered, age sixteen, state religion. Francie bought a sheet of writing-paper and an envelope for a penny and carefully wrote an application and addressed it to the ad's box number. Although she was only fourteen, she and her mother agreed that she could pass for sixteen easily. So she said she was sixteen in the letter.

Two days later, Francie received a reply on an exciting letterhead: a pair of shears lying on a folded newspaper with a pot of paste near-by. It was from the Model Press Clipping Bureau on Canal Street, New York, and it asked Miss Nolan to report for an interview.

Sissy went shopping with Francie and helped her buy a grown-up dress and her first pair of high-heeled pumps. When she tried on her new outfit, mama and Sissy swore that she looked like sixteen except for her hair. Her braids made her look very kiddish.

"Mama, please let me get it bobbed," begged Francie.

"It took you fourteen years to grow that hair," said mama, "and I'll not let you have it cut off."

"Gee, Mama, you're 'way behind the time."

"Why do you want short hair like a boy?"

"It would be easier to care for."

"Taking care of her hair should be a woman's pleasure."

"But, Katie," protested Sissy, "all the girls are bobbing their hair nowadays."

"They're fools, then. A woman's hair is her mystery. Daytimes, it's pinned up. But at night, alone with her man, the pins come out and it hangs loose like a shining cape. It makes her a special secret woman for the man."

"At night, *all* cats are grey," said Sissy wickedly.

"None of your remarks," said Katie sharply.

"I'd look just like Irene Castle if I had short hair," persisted Francie.

"They make Jew women cut off their hair when they marry so no other man will look at them. Nuns get their hair cut off to prove they're done with men. Why should any young girl do it when she doesn't have to?" Francie was about to reply when mama said: "We'll have no more arguments."

"All right," said Francie. "But when I'm eighteen I'll be my own boss. Then *you'll* see."

"When you're eighteen you can shave your scalp for all care. In the meantime..." She wound Francie's two heavy braids around her head and pinned them in place with bone hairpins which she took from her own hair "There!" She stepped back and surveyed her daughter. "It looks just like shining crown," she announced dramatically.

"It does make her look at least eighteen," conceded Sissy.

Francie looked in the mirror. She was pleased that sh

looked so old the way mama had fixed her hair. But she wouldn't give in and say so.

"All my life I'll have headaches carrying this load of hair around," she complained.

"Lucky you, if that's all gives you a life of headaches," said mama.

Next morning, Neeley escorted his sister to New York. As the train came on to the Williamsburg Bridge after leaving Marcy Avenue station, Francie noticed that many people seated in the car rose as if in accord and then sat down again.

"Why do they do that, Neeley?"

"Just as you get on the Bridge there's a bank with a big clock. People stand up to look at the time so's they know whether they're early or late for work. I betcha a million people look at that clock every day," figured Neeley.

Francie had anticipated a thrill when she rode over that Bridge for the first time. But the ride wasn't half as thrilling as wearing grown-up clothes for the first time.

The interview was short. She was hired on trial. Hours, nine to five-thirty, half an hour for lunch, salary seven dollars a week to start. First the Boss took her on a tour of inspection of the Press Clipping Bureau.

The ten readers sat at long sloping desks. The newspapers of all the states were divided among them. The papers poured into the Bureau every hour of every day from every city in every state of the Union. The girls marked and boxed the items sought and put down their total and their own identifying number on the top of the front page.

The marked papers were collected and brought to the printer, who had a hand press containing an adjustable date apparatus, and racks of slugs before her. She adjusted the paper's date on her press, inserted the slug containing the name, city, and state of the newspaper and printed as many slips as there were items marked.

Then, slips and newspaper went to the cutter, who stood before a large slanting desk and slashed out the marked items with a sharp curved knife. (In spite of the letter-head, there wasn't a pair of shears on the premises.) As the cutter slashed out the items, throwing the discarded paper to the floor, a sea of newspapers rose as high as her waist each fifteen minutes. A man collected this waste-paper and took it away for baling. The clipped items and slips were turned over to the paster, who affixed the clippings to the slips. Then they were filed, collected and placed in envelopes and posted.

Francie got on to the filing system very easily. In two weeks she had memorized the two thousand or so names of headings on the file-box. Then she was put into training as a reader. For two more weeks she did nothing but study the clients' cards, which were more detailed than the file-box headings. When an informal examination proved that she had memorized the orders, she was given the Oklahoma papers to read. The Boss went over her papers before they went to the cutter and pointed out her mistakes. When she got expert enough not to need checking, the Pennsylvania papers were added. Soon after she was given the New York State papers, and now had three states to read. By the end of August she was reading more papers and marking more items than any other reader in the Bureau. She was fresh to the work, anxious to please, had strong clear eyes (she was the only reader not wearing glasses), and had developed a photographic eye very quickly. She could take in an item at a glance and note immediately whether it was something to mark. She read between a hundred and eighty and two hundred newspapers a day. The next best reader averaged from a hundred to a hundred and ten papers.

Yes, Francie was the fastest reader in the Bureau—and the poorest paid. Although she had been raised to ten dollars a week when she went on reading, her runner-up received twenty-five dollars a week and the other readers received twenty. Since Francie never became friendly enough with the girls to be taken into their confidence, she had no way of knowing how grossly underpaid she was.

Although Francie liked reading newspapers and was proud to earn ten dollars a week, she was not happy. She had been excited about going to work in New York. Since such a tiny thing as a flower in a brown bowl at the library had thrilled her so, she expected that the great city of New York would thrill her a hundred times more. But it was not so.

The Bridge had been the first disappointment. Looking at it from the roof of her house, she had thought that crossing it would make her feel like a gossamer-winged fairy flying through the air. But the actual ride over the Bridge was no different than the ride above the Brooklyn streets. The Bridge was paved in pavements and traffic roads like the streets of

Broadway and the tracks were the same tracks. There was no different feeling about the train as it went over the Bridge. New York was disappointing. The buildings were higher and the crowds thicker; otherwise it was little different from Brooklyn. From now on, would all new things be disappointing, she wondered?

She had often studied the map of the United States and crossed its plains, mountains, deserts, and rivers in her imagination. And it had seemed a wonderful thing. Now she wondered whether she wouldn't be disappointed in that, too. Supposing, she thought, she was to walk across this great country. She'd start out at seven in the morning, say, and walk westward. She'd put one foot down in front of the other to cover distance, and, as she walked to the west, she'd be so busy with her feet and with realization that her footsteps were part of a chain that had started in Brooklyn, that she might think nothing at all of the mountains, rivers, plains, and deserts she came upon. All she'd notice was that some things were strange because they reminded her of Brooklyn and that other things were strange because they were so different from Brooklyn. "I guess there is nothing new, then, in the world," decided Francie unhappily. "If there is anything new or different, some part of it must be in Brooklyn and I must be used to it and wouldn't be able to notice it if I came across it." Like Alexander the Great, Francie grieved, being convinced that there were no new worlds to conquer.

She adapted herself to the split-second rhythm of the New Yorker going to and from work. Getting to the office was a nervous ordeal. If she arrived one minute before nine, she was a free person. If she arrived a minute after, she worried because that made her the logical scapegoat of the Boss if he happened to be in a bad mood that day. So she learned ways of conserving bits of seconds. Long before the train ground to a stop at her station, she pushed her way to the door to be one of the first expelled when it slid open. Out of the train, she ran like a deer, circling the crowd to be the first up the stairs leading to the street. Walking to the office, she kept close to the buildings so she could turn corners sharply. She crossed streets kitty-corner to save stepping off and on an extra pair of kerbs. At the building, she shoved her way into the lift, even though the operator yelled "Car's full!" And all this manoeuvring to arrive one minute before, instead of after, nine!

Once she left home ten minutes earlier to have more time. In spite of no need of hurry, she still pushed her way out of the train, flew up the steps, rushed through the streets economically and crowded into a full lift. She was fifteen minutes early. The big room was echoingly empty and she felt desolate and lost. When the other workers rushed in seconds before nine, Francie felt like a traitor. The next morning, she slept ten minutes longer and returned to her original timing.

She was the only Brooklyn girl in the Bureau. The others came from Manhattan, Hoboken, the Bronx, and one commuted from Bayonne, New Jersey. Two of the oldest readers there, sisters, had originally come from Ohio. The first day Francie worked at the Bureau one of the sisters said to her: "You have a Brooklyn accent." It had sounded like a shocked accusation and made Francie self-conscious of her speech. She took to pronouncing words carefully, lest she say things like "goil" for "girl," and "apperntment" instead of "appointment."

There were but two people in the Bureau to whom she could talk without embarrassment. One was the Boss-manager. He was a Harvard graduate, and in spite of a broad "a" which he used indiscriminately, his speech was plain and his vocabulary less affected than those of the readers, most of whom had graduated from high school and had picked up an extensive vocabulary from years of reading. The other person was Miss Armstrong, who was the only other college graduate.

Miss Armstrong was the special city reader. Her desk was isolated in the choicest corner of the room, where there was a north and an east window, the best light for reading. She read nothing but the Chicago, Boston, Philadelphia, and New York City newspapers. A special messenger brought her each edition of the New York City newspapers soon after it left the presses. When her papers were read up, she didn't have to pitch in, as the other readers did, and help the girls who were behind. She crocheted or manicured her nails while waiting for the next edition. She was the highest paid, receiving thirty dollars a week. Miss Armstrong was a kindly person and she took a helpful interest in Francie and tried to draw her out in conversation so that she wouldn't feel lonely.

Once in the wash-room, Francie overheard a remark about Miss Armstrong being the Boss's mistress. Francie had heard of but never seen one of those fabulous beings. Immediately she examined Miss Armstrong closely as a mistress. She saw that Miss Armstrong wasn't pretty; her face was almost simian with its wide mouth and flat, thick nostrils, and her figure was merely passable. Francie looked at her legs. They were long, slender and exquisitely moulded. She wore the sheerest of flawless silk stockings, and expensively-made high-heeled pumps shod her beautifully-arched feet. "Beautiful legs, then, is the secret of being a mistress," concluded Francie. She looked down at her own long thin legs. "I'll never make it, I guess." Sighing, she resigned herself to a sinless life.

There was a class system in the Bureau engendered by the cutter, printer, paster, paper-baler, and the delivery-boy. These workers, illiterate but sharp-witted, who for some reason called themselves The Club, assumed that the better-educated readers looked down on them. In retaliation, they stirred up as much trouble as possible among the readers.

Francie's loyalties were divided. By background and education, she belonged to The Club class, but by ability and intelligence she belonged to the readers' class. The Club was shrewd enough to feel this division in Francie and tried to use her as a go-between. They informed her of trouble-making office rumours, expecting that she would relay them to the readers and create dissension. But Francie wasn't friendly enough with the readers to exchange gossip with them and the rumours died with her.

So one day, when the cutter told her that Miss Armstrong was leaving in September, and that she, Francie, was to be promoted to the city reader job, Francie assumed this to be a rumour invented to arouse jealousy among the readers, all of whom expected the city reading job when and if Miss Armstrong resigned. She thought it was preposterous that she, a girl of fourteen, with nothing but a grade school education, would be considered eligible to take over the work of a thirty-year-old college graduate like Miss Armstrong.

It was nearing the end of August and Francie was worried because mama hadn't mentioned anything about her going to high school. She wanted desperately to go back to school. All the years of talk about higher education she had heard from her mother, grandmother, and aunts not only made her anxious to get more education but gave her an inferiority complex about her present lack of education.

She remembered with affection the girls who had written in

her autograph book. She wanted to be one of them again. They came out of the same life as she did; they were no further along. Her natural place was going to school with them, not working competitively with older women.

She didn't like working in New York. The crowds continually swarming about her made her tremble. She felt that she was being pushed into a way of life that she wasn't ready to handle. And the thing she dreaded worst about working in New York was the crowded El trains.

There had been that time in the train when, hanging from a strap and so tightly wedged in the crowd that she couldn't so much as lower her arm, she had felt a man's hand. No matter how she twisted and squirmed, she couldn't get away from that hand. When she swayed with the crowd as the cars swerved, the hand tightened. She was unable to twist her head to see whose hand it was. She stood in desperate futility, helplessly enduring the indignity. She could have called out and protested, but she was too ashamed to call public attention to her predicament. It seemed an eternity before the crowd thinned out enough for her to move to a different part of the car. After that, standing in a crowded train became a dreaded ordeal.

One Sunday, when she and mama brought Laurie over to see granma, Francie told Sissy about the man on the train, expecting that Sissy would comfort her. But her aunt treated it as a great joke.

"So a man pinched you on the El," she said. "I wouldn't let that bother me. It means you're getting a good shape and there are some men who can't resist a woman's shape. Say! I must be getting old! It's been years since anybody pinched me on the El. There was a time when I couldn't ride in a crowd without coming home black and blue," she said proudly.

"Is that anything to brag about?" asked Katie.

Sissy ignored that remark. "The day will come, Francie," she said, "when you're forty-five and have a shape like a bag of horses' oats tied in the middle. Then you'll look back and long for the old days when men *wanted* to pinch you."

"If she does look back," said Katie, "it will be because you put it in her mind, and not because it's anything wonderful to remember." She turned to Francie. "As for you, learn to stand in the train without holding on to a strap. Keep your hand down and keep a long, sharp pin in your pocket. If you feel a man's hand on you, stick it good with the pin."

308

Francie did as mama said. She learned to keep her feet without holding to a strap. She kept her hand closed on a long, vicious pin in her coat pocket. She hoped someone would pinch her again. She just hoped so, so that she could stab him with the pin. "It's all very well for Sissy to talk about shapes and men, but I don't like to be pinched in the back. And when I get to be forty-five, I certainly hope that I have something nicer to look back on and long for than being pinched by a stranger. Sissy ought to be ashamed. . . .

"What's the matter with me, anyhow? Here I stand criticizing Sissy—Sissy, who's been so darn good to me. I'm dissatisfied with my job when I should feel lucky having such interesting work. Imagine getting *paid* to read when I like to read so much, anyhow. And everyone thinks New York is the most wonderful city in the world and *I* can't even get to like New York. Seems like I'm the most dissatisfied person in the whole world. Oh, I wish I was young again when everything seemed so wonderful!"

Just before Labour Day, the Boss called Francie into his private office and informed her that Miss Armstrong was leaving to be married. He cleared his throat and added that Miss Armstrong was marrying him, in fact.

Francie's conception of a mistress broke and scattered. She had believed that men never married their mistresses—that they cast them aside like worn-out gloves. So Miss Armstrong was to become a wife instead of a worn-out glove. Well!

"So we'll need a new city reader," the Boss was saying. "Miss Armstrong herself suggested that we . . . ah . . . try *you* out, Miss Nolan."

Francie's heart jumped. She, city reader. The most coveted job in the Bureau! There had been truth, then, in The Club's rumours. Another preconceived idea gone. She had always assumed that all rumours were false.

The Boss planned to offer her fifteen a week, figuring he'd get as good a reader as his future wife was at half the salary. The girl should be tickled to death, too—a youngster like that . . . fifteen a week. She said she was past sixteen. She looked thirteen. Of course her age was none of his business as long as she was competent. The law couldn't touch him— hiring someone under age. All he'd have to say was that she deceived him as to her true age.

"There's a little rise along with the job," he said benignly.

Francie smiled happily and he worried. "Have I put my foot in it?" he thought. "Maybe she didn't expect a rise." He covered his blunder hastily. "...a small rise after we see how you work out."

"I don't know..." began Francie doubtfully.

"She's over sixteen," decided the Boss, "and she's going to hold me up for a big rise." To forestall her, he said: "We'll give you fifteen a week, starting...." He hesitated. No use being too good-natured. "...starting the first of October." He leaned back in his chair feeling as gracious as God Himself.

"I mean, I don't think I'll be here much longer."

"She's working me for more money," he thought. Aloud, he asked: "Why not?"

"I'm going back to school after Labour Day, I think. I meant to tell you as soon as my plans were settled."

"College?"

"High school."

"I'll have to put Pinsky on city," he thought. "She's getting twenty-five now, she'll expect thirty, and I'm right back where I started. This Nolan is better than Pinsky, too. Damn Irma! Where does she get the idea that a woman shouldn't work after marriage? She could keep right on ... keep the money in the family ... buy a home with it." He spoke to Francie.

"Oh! I'm sorry to hear that. Not that I don't approve of higher education. But I consider newspaper reading a darn fine education. It's a good live ever-growing contemporary education. While in school ... it's merely books. Dead books," he said contemptuously.

"I'll ... I'll have to talk it over with my mother."

"By all means. Tell her what your Boss said about education. And tell her I said," he closed his eyes and took the plunge, "that we'll pay you *twenty* dollars a week. Starting the first of November," he shaved off a month.

"That's an awful lot of money," she said in all honesty.

"We believe in paying our workers well so they stick with us. And...ah...Miss Nolan, please don't mention your future salary. It's more than anyone else is getting," he lied "and if they found out ..." he spread his hands in a gesture of futility. "You understand? No wash-room gossip."

Francie felt gracious as she set his mind at ease by assuring him that she'd never betray him in the wash-room. The Boss started to sign letters, indicating that the interview was over.

"That's all, Miss Nolan. And we must have your decision

the day after Labour Day."

"Yes, sir."

Twenty dollars a week! Francie was stunned. Two months ago she was glad to earn five dollars a week. Uncle Willie only earned eighteen a week and he was forty. Sissy's John was smart and earned but twenty-two-fifty a week. Few men in her neighbourhood earned as much as twenty a week, and they had families, too.

"With that money, our troubles would be over," thought Francie. "We could pay rent on a three-room flat somewhere, mama wouldn't have to go out to work and Laurie wouldn't be left alone so much. I guess I'd be mighty important if I could manage something like that.

But I want to go back to school!"

She recalled the constant harping on education in the family.

Granma: It will raise you up on the face of the earth.

Evy: Each of my three children will get three diplomas.

Sissy: And when mother goes—pray God not for a long time yet—and baby is big enough to start kindergarten, I'm going out to work again. And I'll bank my pay and when Little Sissy grows up I'll put her in the best college there is.

Mama: And I don't want my children to have the same hard-working life I have. Education will fix it so that their lives are easier.

"Still, it's such a good job," thought Francie. "That is, good right now. But my eyes will get worn out from the work. All the older readers have to wear glasses. Miss Armstrong said a reader's only good as long as her eyes hold out. Those other readers were fast too, when they first started. Like me. But now their eyes. . . . I must save my eyes . . . not read away from the job.

"If mama knew I could get twenty a week, maybe she wouldn't send me back to school, and I couldn't blame her. We've been poor so long. Mama is very fair in all things, but this money might make her see things in a different way, and it wouldn't be her fault. I won't tell her about the rise until after she decides about school."

Francie spoke to mama about school, and mama said, yes, they'd have to talk about it. They'd talk about it right after supper that night.

After finishing their supper coffee, Katie announced needlessly (since everybody knew it) that school was opening next week. "I want both of you to go to high school, but it's working out that only one of you can start this autumn. I'm saving every cent I can out of your pay so that next year both of you will be back in school." She waited. She waited a long time. Neither of the children answered. "Well? Don't you want to go to high school?"

Francie's lips were stiff as she spoke. So much depended on mama, and Francie wanted her words to make a good impression. "Yes, Mama. I want to go back to school more'n I'll ever want anything in my life."

"I don't want to go," said Neeley. "Don't make me go back to school, mama. I like to work and I'm going to get a two-dollar rise the first of the year."

"Don't you want to be a doctor?"

"No. I want to be a broker and make lots of money like my bosses. I'll get on to the stock market and make a million dollars some day."

"My son will be a great doctor."

"How do you know? I might turn out like Dr. Hueller on Maujer Street with an office in a basement flat and always wear a dirty shirt like him. Anyhow, I know enough. I don't need to go back to school."

"Neeley doesn't want to go back to school," said Katie. She spoke to Francie almost pleadingly. "You know what that means, Francie." Francie bit her lip. It wouldn't do to cry. She must keep calm. She must keep thinking clearly. "It means," said mama, "*that Neeley has to go back to school.*"

"I won't!" cried Neeley. "I won't go back, no matter what you say! I'm working and earning money and I want to keep on. I'm somebody now with the fellers. If I go back to school I'm just a punk kid again. Besides, you need my money, mama. We don't want to be poor again."

"You'll go back to school," announced Katie quietly. "Francie's money will be enough."

"Why do you make him go when he doesn't want to," cried Francie, "and keep me out of school when I want to go so much?"

"Yeah," agreed Neeley.

"Because if I don't make him, he'll never go back," said mama, "where you, Francie, will fight and manage to get back somehow."

"Why are you so sure all the time?" protested Francie. "I

a year I'll be too old to go back. Neeley's only thirteen. He'll still be young enough next year."

"Nonsense. You'll only be fifteen next autumn."

"Seventeen," corrected Francie, "going on eighteen; too old to start."

"What kind of silly talk is that?"

"Not silly. On the job, I'm sixteen. I have to look and act sixteen instead of fourteen. Next year I'll be fifteen in years but two years older in the way I'm living; too old to change back into a school-girl."

"Neeley will go back to school next week," said Katie stubbornly, "and Francie will go back next year."

"I hate both of you," shouted Neeley. "And if you make me go back I'll run away from home. Yes, I will!" He ran out slamming the door.

Katie's face set in lines of misery and Francie felt sorry for her. "Don't worry, Mama. He won't run away. He just said that." The instant relief that came into her mother's face angered Francie. "But I'm the one who'll go away and I won't make a speech about it. When the time comes that you don't need what I earn, I'll leave."

"What's got into my children who used to be so good?" asked Katie poignantly.

"Years have got into us." Katie looked puzzled. Francie explained, "We never did get working papers."

"But they were hard to get. The priest wanted a dollar for each baptismal certificate and I would have had to go to City Hall with you. I was nursing Laurie every two hours then, and couldn't go. We all figured it was easier for you both to claim to be sixteen and not have all the fuss."

"That part was all right. But saying we were sixteen, we had to *be* sixteen and you treat us like thirteen-year-old children."

"I wish your father were here. He understood things about you that I can't get to understand." Pain stabbed through Francie. After it passed, she told her mother that her salary was to be doubled on November first.

"Twenty dollars!" Katie's mouth fell open in surprise. "Oh my!" That was her usual expression when anything astonished her. "When did you know?"

"Saturday."

"And you didn't tell me till now."

"No."

"You thought if I knew that it would fix my mind about

you keeping on working."

"Yes."

"But I didn't know when I said it was right for Neeley to go back to school. You can see that I did what I thought was right and the money didn't come into it. Can't you see?" she asked pleadingly.

"No, I can't see. I can only see that you favour Neeley more than me. You fix everything for him and tell me that I can find a way myself. Some day I'll fool you, Mama. I'll do what I think is right for me and it might not be right in your way."

"I'm not worrying. Because I know that I can trust my daughter." Katie spoke with such simple dignity that Francie was ashamed of herself. "And I trust my son. He's mad now about doing what he doesn't want to do. But he'll get over it and do well in school. Neeley's a good boy."

"Yes, he's a good boy," conceded Francie, "but even if he was bad, you wouldn't notice it. But where I'm concerned . . ." her voice went ragged on a sob.

Katie sighed sharply but said nothing. She got up and started to clear the table. Her hand reached for a cup, and Francie, for the first time in her life, saw her mother's hand fumble. It trembled and couldn't connect with the cup. Francie put the cup in her mother's hand. She noticed a big crack in the cup.

"Our family used to be like a strong cup," thought Francie. "It was whole and sound and held things well. When papa died, the first crack came. And this fight tonight made another crack. Soon there will be so many cracks that the cup will break and we'll all be pieces instead of a whole thing together. I don't want this to happen, yet I'm deliberately making a deep crack." Her sharp sigh was just like Katie's.

The mother went to the wash-basket in which the baby was sleeping peacefully in spite of the bitter talking. Francie saw her mother's still fumbling hands take the sleeping child from the basket. Katie sat in her rocker near the window, held her baby tightly and rocked.

Francie almost went blind with pity. "I shouldn't be so mean to her," she thought. "What has she ever had but hard work and trouble? Now she has to turn to her baby for comfort. Maybe she's thinking that Laurie, whom she loves so and who is so dependent on her now, will grow up to turn against her like I'm doing now."

She put her hand awkwardly on her mother's cheek. "It's al

right, Mama. I didn't mean it. You're right and I'll do as you say. Neeley must go to school and you and I will see that he gets through."

Katie put her hand over Francie's. "That's my good girl," she said.

"Don't be mad at me mama, because I fought you. You yourself taught me to fight for what I thought was right, and I . . . I thought I was right."

"I know. And I'm pleased that you can and will fight for what you should have. And you'll always come out all right—no matter what. You're like me that way."

"And that's where the whole trouble is," thought Francie. "We're too much alike to understand each other because we don't even understand our own selves. Papa and I were two different persons and we understood each other. Mama understands Neeley because he's different from her. I wish I was different in the way that Neeley is."

"Then everything's all right now between us?" Katie asked, with a smile.

"Of course." Francie smiled back and kissed her mother's cheek.

But in their secret hearts each knew that it wasn't all right and would never be all right between them again.

XLV

CHRISTMAS AGAIN. But this year there was money for presents and lots of food in the ice-box and the flat was always warm now. When Francie came in off the cold street she thought that the warmth was like a lovers' arms around her drawing her into the room. She wondered, incidentally, exactly what a lover's arms felt like.

Francie took comfort out of not returning to school in the realization that the money she earned made life easier for them. Mama had been very fair. When Francie was raised to twenty dollars a week, mama gave her five dollars a week for herself to pay for her car-fare, lunches, and clothes. Also, Katie deposited five dollars each week in Francie's name in the Williamsburg Savings Bank—for college, she explained. Katie managed well on the remaining ten dollars and a dollar that

Neeley contributed. It wasn't a fortune, but things were cheap in 1916 and the Nolans got along fine.

Neeley had taken to school cheerfully when he found that many of his old gang were entering Eastern District High. He had his old after-school job back at McGarrity's and mama gave him one of the two dollars for pocket money. He was somebody in school. He had more spending money than most boys, and he knew *Julius Caesar* backwards, forwards, and upside down.

When they opened the tin-can bank, there was nearly four dollars in it. Neeley added another dollar, and Francie five, and they had ten dollars to spend for Christmas presents. The three of them went shopping the afternoon before Christmas, taking Laurie with them.

First they went to buy mama a new hat. In the hat store they stood behind mama's chair while she held the baby in her lap and tried on hats. Francie wanted her to have a jade-green velvet one, but there wasn't a hat of that colour to be found in Williamsburg. Mama thought she ought to get a black hat.

"We're buying the hat, not you," Francie told her, "and we say no more mourning hats."

"Try on this red one, mama," suggested Neeley.

"No. I'll try on that very dark green one in the window."

"It's a new shade," said the woman proprietor, getting it out of the window. "We call it moss green." She set it straight on Katie's brow. With an impatient flick of her hand, Katie tilted the hat over one eye.

"That's it!" declared Neeley.

"Mama, you look beautiful," was Francie's verdict.

"I like it," decided Mama. "How much?" she asked the woman. The woman drew a long breath and the Nolans girded themselves for bargaining.

"It's like this . . ." began the woman.

"How much?" repeated Katie inflexibly.

"In New York ten dollars would you pay for the same merchandise. But . . ."

"If I wanted to pay ten dollars I'd go to New York for a hat."

"Is that a way to talk? Exact copy, same hat in Wana-maker's is seven-fifty." Pregnant pause. "I'm going to give you identical hat for five dollars."

"I have exactly two dollars to spend on a hat."

"Get out of my store!" shouted the woman dramatically.

"All right." Katie gathered up the baby and got to her feet.

"You must be so hasty?" The woman pushed her back into the chair. She thrust the hat into a paper bag. "I'm letting you take it home for four-fifty. Believe me, my own mother-in-law shouldn't have it for that price!"

"I believe you," thought Katie, "especially if she's like my mother-in-law." Aloud she said: "The hat's nice, but I can only afford two dollars. There are lots of other hat stores and I ought to get one for that—not as good as this one, but good enough to keep the wind off my head."

"I want you should listen." The woman made her voice deep and sincere. "They say that by the Jews, money is everything. By me is different. When I got a pretty hat and it goes with a pretty customer, something happens in me here." She put her hand on her heart. "I get so . . . profits is nothing. I give free." She pushed the bag into Katie's hand. "Take the hat for four dollars. That's what is cost me wholesale." She sighed. "Believe me, a business woman I shouldn't be. Better I should be a picture painter."

And the bargaining went on. Katie knew when the price finally reached two-fifty that the woman wouldn't go lower. She tested her by pretending she was leaving. But this time the woman made no attempt to stop her. Francie nodded to Neeley. He gave the woman two dollars and fifty cents.

"You shouldn't tell nobody how cheap you got it," warned the woman.

"We won't," promised Francie. "Put the hat in a box."

"Ten cents extra is a box—what it costs me wholesale."

"A bag's good enough," protested Katie.

"This is your Christmas present," said Francie, "and it goes in a box."

Neeley got out another dime. The hat was wrapped in tissue and put in a box. "I give it to you so cheap, you should come back next time you buy a hat. But don't expect such bargains next time." Katie laughed. As they left, the woman said: "Wear it in good health."

"Thank you."

As the door closed on them, the woman whispered bitterly: '*Goyem!*' and spat after them.

On the street Neeley said: "No wonder mama waits five years to buy a new hat if it's all that trouble."

"Trouble?" said Francie. "Why, that's fun!"

Next they went to Seigler's to buy a sweater suit for Laurie's

Christmas. When Seigler saw Francie, he let loose a flood of abuse.

"So! At last you come in mine store! Is something maybe, other dry-goods stores ain't got and you come by me? Maybe by other store is dicky penny cheaper, but damaged stock, no?" He turned to Katie and explained: "So many years comes this girl to me to buy dickies and paper collars for the papa. Now for a whole year already, she don't come."

"Her father died a year ago," explained Katie.

Mr. Seigler gave his forehead a mighty blow with the flat of his hand. "Oi! By me is so big the mouth, so my foot always goes in," he apologized.

"That's all right," said Katie soothingly.

"It's this way by me: Nobody tells me nothing and I don't know till now."

"That's the way it always is," said Katie.

"And now," he asked briskly, getting down to business, "what can I show you?"

"A sweater suit for a seven-months-old baby."

"I got here exzactle size."

He took a blue woollen outfit from a box. But when they held it up to Laurie, the sweater reached only to her navel and the leggings went to just below her knees. They measured other sizes and found a two-year-old size that was just right. Mr. Seigler went into ecstasies.

"I'm in dry-goods business twenty years—fifteen on Grand Stritt and five on Graham Am-yer and never *ins Leben* do I see a seven months so big." And the Nolans glowed with pride.

There was no bargaining because Seigler's was a one-price store. Neeley counted out three dollars. They put the suit on the baby then and there. She looked cute with the zitful cap pulled down over her ears. The bright blue colour brought out the rosiness of her skin. You'd think she understood—the way she acted so pleased, flashing her two-toothed smile about indiscriminately.

"*Ach du Liebschen*," crooned Seigler, hands clasped prayerfully, "she should wear it in good health." This time the wish was not nullified by his spitting after them.

Mama went home with the baby and her new hat while Neeley and Francie continued their Christmas shopping. They bought small gifts for their Flittman cousins and something for Sissy's baby. Then it was time for their own gifts.

"I'll tell you what I want and you can buy it for me," said Neeley.

"All right. What?"

"Spats."

"Spats?" Francie's voice scaled up.

"Pearl-grey ones," he said firmly.

"If that's what you want . . ." she began, dubiously.

"Medium size."

"How do you know the size?"

"I went in and tried them on yesterday."

He gave Francie a dollar and a half and she bought the spats. She had the man wrap them in a gift box. On the street she presented the package to Neeley, while they frowned solemnly at each other.

"From me to you. Merry Christmas," said Francie.

"Thank you," he replied formally. "And now, what do you want?"

"A black lace dance-set in the window of that store near Union Avenue."

"Is that ladies' stuff?" asked Neeley uneasily.

"Uh-Huh. Twenty-four waist and 32 bust. Two dollars."

"You buy it. I don't like to ask for anything like that."

She bought the coveted dance-set—panties and brassiere made of scraps of black lace held together by narrow black satin ribbon. Neeley disapproved and muttered an ungracious: "You're welcome," to her thanks.

They passed the Christmas-tree kerb market. "Remember the time," said Neeley, "when we let the man chuck the biggest tree at us?"

"Do I? Every time I get a headache it's in the place where the tree hit me."

"And the way papa sang when he helped us get the tree up the stairs," recalled Neeley.

Several times that day the name or thought of papa had come up. And each time Francie had felt a flash of tenderness instead of the old stab of pain. "Am I forgetting him?" she thought. "In time to come, will it be hard to remember anything about him? I guess it's like Granma Mary Rommely says: 'With time, passes all.' The first year was hard because we could say, last 'lection he voted. Last Thanksgiving he ate with us. But next year it will be two years ago that he . . . and as time passes it will be harder and harder to remember and keep track."

"Look!" Neeley grabbed her arm and pointed to a two-foot fir-tree in a wooden tub.

"It's growing!" she cried out.

"What did you think? They all have to grow in the beginning."

"I know. Still and all you always see them cut off and get the idea that they grow chopped down. Let's buy it, Neeley."

"It's awful little."

"But it has roots."

When they brought it home, Katie examined the tree and the line between her eyes deepened as she figured something out. "Yes," she said, "after Christmas we'll put it on the fire escape and see that it gets sun and water and, once a month, horse manure."

"No, Mama," protested Francie. "You're not going to put that horse manure over on us."

As small children, gathering horse manure had been one of their most dreaded chores. Granma Mary Rommely kept a row of scarlet geraniums on her window-sill and they were strong and bright and clear-coloured because once a month either Francie or Neeley had to go out on the streets with a cigar box and fill it with two neat rows of manure balls. On delivery, granma made payment of two cents. Francie had been ashamed to gather horse manure. Once she had protested to Granma, who had answered:

"Ai, the blood runs thin in the third generation. Back in Austria, my good brothers loaded large wagons with the manure and they were strong and honourable men."

"They'd have to be," Francie had thought, "to work with stuff like that."

Katie was saying: "Now that we own a tree, we have to take care of it and make it grow. You can get manure in the dark of night if you're ashamed."

"There's so few horses now—mostly automobiles. It's hard to get," argued Neeley.

"Go on a cobble-stoned street where autos don't go, and if there isn't any manure, wait for a horse and follow him until there is."

"Gee whiz," protested Neeley, "I'm sorry we ever bought the old tree."

"What's the matter with us?" said Francie. "These aren't olden times. We've got money now. All we have to do is give some old kid on the block a nickel and he'll collect it for us."

"Yeah," agreed Neeley, relieved.

"I should think," said mama, "that you'd want to take care of your tree with your own hands."

"The difference between rich and poor," said Francie, "is that the poor do everything with their own hands and the rich hire hands to do things. We're not poor any more. We can pay to have some things done for us."

"I want to stay poor, then," said Katie, "because I like to use my hands."

Neeley, as always, became bored when his mother and sister began one of their figuring-out conversations. To change the subject, he said: "I bet Laurie's as big as that tree." They fished the baby out of her basket and measured her against the tree.

"Exzactle the same height," said Francie, imitating Mr. Seigler.

"I wonder which will grow the fastest?" said Neeley.

"Neeley, we've never had a puppy or a kitten. So let's make a pet out of the tree."

"Aw, a tree can't be a pet."

"Why can't it? It lives and breathes, doesn't it? We'll give it a name! Annie! The tree's Annie and the baby's Laurie and, together, they're the song."

"You know what?" asked Neeley.

"No. What?"

"You're crazy. That's what."

"I know it and isn't it wonderful? Today I don't feel like Miss Nolan, supposed to be seventeen and head reader of the Model Press Clipping Bureau. It's like olden times when I had to let you carry the junk money. I feel just like a kid."

"And you are," said Katie. "A kid just turned fifteen."

"Yeah? You won't think so when you see what Neeley bought me for Christmas."

"What you *made* me buy you," corrected Neeley.

"Show mama what you made me buy *you* for Christmas, smarty. Just go and show her," urged Francie.

When he showed mama, her voice scaled up like Francie's when she said: "Spats?"

"Just to keep my ankles warm," explained Neeley.

Francie showed her dance-set and mama let loose her "Oh, my!" of astonishment.

"Do you think that's what fast women wear?" asked Francie hopefully.

"If they do, I'm sure they all come down with pneumonia. Now let's see: What'll we have for supper?"

"Aren't you going to *object*?" Francie was disappointed because mama wasn't making a fuss.

"No. All women go through a black-lace-drawers time. You came to it earlier than most and you'll get over it sooner. I think we'll heat up the soup and have that and soup meat and potatoes. . . ."

"Mama thinks she knows everything," thought Francie resentfully.

They attended mass together Christmas morning. Katie was having a prayer said for the repose of Johnny's soul.

She looked very pretty in her new hat. The baby looked nice, too, in her new outfit. Neeley, wearing his new spats, manfully insisted on carrying the baby. As they passed Stagg Street, some boys hanging out in front of a candy store hooted at Neeley. His face got red. Francie knew they were making fun of his spats and to save his feelings, she pretended they hooted because he was carrying a baby and she offered to take Laurie. He refused the offer. He knew as well as she did that they were making fun of his spats and he was filled with bitterness at the narrow-mindedness of Williamsburg. He decided to put the spats away in the box when he got home and not wear them again until they moved to a more decent neighbourhood.

Francie was wearing her lace pants and freezing. Whenever an icy wind blew her coat apart and went through her thin dress, it was as if she had no underwear on at all. "I wish—oh how I wish I had my flannel bloomers on," she mourned. "Mama was right. A person could get pneumonia. But wouldn't give her the satisfaction of letting her know. I guess I'll have to put these lace things away until summer."

Inside the church, they pre-empted a whole front pew by laying Laurie full length on the seat. Several late-comers thinking there was an empty seat, genuflected at the pew entrance and prepared to enter. When they saw the baby stretched out over two places, they scowled fiercely at Katie who sat rigid and scowled back twice as fiercely.

Francie thought it was the most beautiful church in Brooklyn. It was made of old grey stone and had twin spires that rose cleanly into the sky, high above the tallest tenement

Inside, the high vaulted ceilings, narrow deep-set stained-glass windows and elaborately carved altars made it a miniature cathedral. Francie was proud of the centre altar, because the left side had been carved by Granpa Rommely more than half a century ago when, as a young fellow lately come from Austria, he had begrudgingly given his tithe of labour to his Church.

The thrifty man had gathered up the bits of gouged-out wood and taken them home. Stubbornly he had fitted and glued the scraps together and carved out three small crucifixes from the blessed wood. Mary gave one to each of her daughters, on their wedding day, with instructions that the crosses were to be passed on to the first daughter in each succeeding generation.

Katie's crucifix hung high on the wall over the mantelpiece at home. It would be Francie's when she married, and she was proud that it had come from the wood of that fine altar.

Today the altar was lovely with banked scarlet poinsettias and fir boughs, with the golden points of lighted slender white candles gleaming among the leaves. The thatched *crèche* was inside the altar rail. Francie knew that the tiny hand-carved figures of Mary, Joseph, the kings, and shepherds were grouped about the Child in the manger as they had first been grouped a hundred years ago, when they had been brought over from the old country.

The priest entered, followed by the altar boys. Over his other vestments he wore a white satin chasuble with a golden cross on the front and back. Francie knew that the chasuble was symbolic of the seamless garment, supposedly woven by Mary, that they had removed from Christ before they nailed Him to the cross. It was said that on Calvary, the soldiers, not wishing to divide the garment, had cast dice for it while Jesus was dying.

Absorbed in her thoughts, Francie missed the beginnings of the mass. She picked it up now, following the familiar Latin in translation.

To Thee, O God, my God, I will give praise upon the harp. Why art thou sad, my soul, and why dost thou disquiet me, chanted the priest in his deep rich voice.

Hope in God, for I will still give praise to Him, responded the altar boy.

Glory be to the Father and to the Son and to the Holy

Ghost.

As it was in the beginning, is now and ever shall be, world without end, Amen, came the response.

I will go unto the altar of God, chanted the priest.

To God, Who giveth joy to my youth, came the response.

Our help is in the name of the Lord.

Who made Heaven and earth.

The priest bowed and recited the *Confiteor.*

Francie believed with all her heart that the altar was Calvary and that again Jesus was offered up as a sacrifice. As she listened to the consecrations, one for His Body and one for His Blood, she believed that the words of the priest were a sword which mystically separated the Blood from the Body. And she knew, without knowing how to explain why, that Jesus was entirely present, Body, Blood, Soul, and Divinity in the wine in the golden chalice and in the bread on the golden plate.

"It's a beautiful religion," she mused, "and I wish I understood it more. No. I don't want to understand it all. It's beautiful because it's always a mystery, like God Himself is a mystery. Sometimes I say I don't believe in God. But I only say that when I'm mad at Him . . . Because I do! I do! I believe in God and Jesus and Mary. I'm a bad Catholic because I miss mass once in a while, and I grumble when, at confession, I get a heavy penance for something I couldn't help doing. But good or bad, I *am* a Catholic and I'll never be anything else.

"Of course, I didn't ask to be born a Catholic no more than I asked to be born an American. But I'm glad it turned out that I'm both these things."

The priest ascended the curved steps to the pulpit. "Your prayers are requested," intoned his magnificent voice, "for the repose of the soul of John Nolan."

"Nolan . . . Nolan . . ." sighed the echoes of the vaulted ceiling.

With a sound like an anguished whisper, nearly a thousand people knelt to pray briefly for the soul of a man only a dozen of them had known. Francie began the prayer for the souls in Purgatory.

Good Jesus, Whose loving heart was ever troubled by the sorrows of others, look with pity on the soul of our dear one

324

in Purgatory. Oh You, Who loved Your own, hear my cry for mercy....

XLVI

"IN TEN more minutes," announced Francie, "it will be 1917." Francie and her brother were sitting side by side with their stockinged feet inside the oven of the kitchen range. Mama, who had given strict orders to be called five minutes before midnight, was resting on her bed.

"I have a feeling," continued Francie, "that 1917 will be more important than any year we've ever had."

"You say that about every year," claimed Neeley. "First, 1915 was going to be the most important. Then 1916, and now, 1917."

"It *will* be important. For one thing, in 1917 I'll be sixteen for real instead of just in the office. And other important things have started already. The landlord's putting in wires. In a few weeks we'll have 'lectricity instead of gas."

"Suits me."

"Then he's going to rip out these stoves and put in steam heat."

"Gee, I'll miss this old stove. Remember how in olden times" (two years ago!) "I used to sit on the stove?"

"And I used to be afraid you'd catch on fire."

"I feel like sitting on the stove right now."

"Go ahead." He sat on the surface furthest away from the fire-box. It was pleasantly warm, but not hot. "Remember," Francie went on, "how we did our examples on this hearth-stone, and the time papa got us a real blackboard eraser and then the stone was like the blackboard in school, only lying down?"

"Yeah. That was a long time ago. But look! You can't claim 1917's going to be important because we'll have 'lectricity and steam heat. Other flats have had 'em for years. That's nothing important."

"The important thing about this year is that we'll get into the war."

"When?"

"Soon. Next week . . . next month."

"How do you know?"

"I read the papers every day, brother—two hundred of 'em."

"Oh, boy! I hope it lasts 'til I'm old enough to join the navy."

"Who's joining the navy?" They looked round, startled. Mama was standing in the bedroom doorway.

"We're just talking, Mama," explained Francie.

"You forgot to call me," said mama reproachfully, "and I thought I heard a whistle. It must be New Year's now."

Francie threw open the window. It was a frosty night without a wind. All was still. Across the yards, the backs of the houses were dark and brooding. As they stood at the window, they heard the joyous peal of a church bell. Then other bell sounds tumbled over the first pealing. Whistles came in. A siren shrieked. Darkened windows banged open. Tin horns were added to the cacophony. Someone fired off a blank cartridge. There were shouts and catcalls.

1917!

The sounds died away and the air was filled with waiting. Someone started to sing:

> Should auld acquaintance be forgot,
> And never brought to mind ...

The Nolans picked up the song. One by one, the neighbours joined in. And they all sang. But as they sang something disquieting came among them. A group of Germans were singing a round. The German words crowded into "Auld Lang Syne."

> Ya, das ist ein Gartenhaus,
> Gartenhaus,
> Gartenhaus,
> Ach, du schoene,
> Ach, du schoene,
> Ach, du schoene Gartenhaus.

Someone shouted: "Shut up, you lousy heinies!" In answer the German song swelled mightily and drowned out "Auld Lang Syne."

In retaliation, the Irish shouted a parody of the song across the dark back yards.

Yeah, das is a God-damned song,
God-damned song,
God-damned song,
Oh, du lousy,
Oh, du lousy,
Oh, du lousy heinie song.

Windows could be heard shutting as the Jews and Italians withdrew, leaving the fight to the Germans and Irish. The Germans sang lustier and more voices came in, until they killed the parody, even as they had killed "Auld Lang Syne." The Germans won. They finished their interminable rounds in shouting triumph.

Francie shivered. "I don't like Germans," she said. "They're so ... so persistent when they want something and they've always got to be ahead."

Once more the night was quiet. Francie grabbed her mother and Neeley. "All together now," she ordered. The three of them leaned out of the window and shouted:

"Happy New Year, everybody!"

An instant of silence, then out of the dark a thick Irish brogue shouted: "Happy New Year, youse Nolans!"

"Now who could that be?" puzzled Katie.

"Happy New Year, you dirty Irish mick!" Neeley screamed back.

Mama clapped her hand over his mouth and pulled him away, while Francie slammed the window down. All three of them were laughing hysterically.

"*Now* you did it!" gasped Francie, laughing so hard that she cried.

"He knows who we are and he'll come around here and fi ... fi ... fight," gurgled Katie, so weak from laughing that she had to hold on to the table. "Who ... who ... was it?"

"Old man O'Brien. Last week he cursed me out of this yard, the dirty Irish...."

"Hush!" said Mama. "You know that whatever you do when the new year starts, you'll do all year."

"And you don't want to go around saying, dirty-Irish-mick like a busted record, do you?" asked Francie. "Besides, you're a mick yourself."

"You, too," accused Neeley.

"We're all Irish, except mama."

327

"And I'm Irish by marriage," she said.

"Well, do us Irish drink a toast on New Year's Eve, or don't we?" demanded Francie.

"Of course," said mama. "I'll mix us a drink."

McGarrity had given the Nolans a bottle of fine old brandy for Christmas. Now Katie poured a small jiggerful of it into each of three tall glasses. She filled the rest of each glass with beaten egg and milk mixed with a little sugar. She grated nutmeg and sprinkled it on the top.

Her hands were steady as she worked, although she considered this drinking tonight as something crucial. She worried constantly that the children might have inherited the Nolan love of drink. She had tried to come to an attitude about liquor in the family. She felt that if she preached against it, the children, unpredictable individualists that they were, might consider drinking forbidden and fascinating. On the other hand, if she made light of it, they might consider drunkenness a natural thing. She decided neither to make nothing of it nor much of it; to proceed as though drinking was no more or less than something to be moderately indulged in at seasonal times. Well, New Year's was such a time. She handed each a glass. A lot depended on their reactions.

"What do we drink to?" asked Francie.

"To a hope," said Katie. "A hope that our family will always be together the way it is tonight."

"Wait!" said Francie. "Get Laurie, so she's together with us, too."

Katie got the patient sleeping baby out of her crib and carried her into the warm kitchen. Laurie opened her eyes, lifted her head and showed two teeth in a befuddled smile. Then her head went down on Katie's shoulder and she was asleep again.

"Now!" said Francie, holding up her glass. "To being together, always." They clicked glasses and drank.

Neeley tasted his drink, frowned, and said he'd rather have plain milk. He poured the drink down the sink and filled another glass with cold milk. Katie watched, worried, as Francie drained her glass.

"It's good," Francie said, "pretty good. But not half as good as a vanilla ice-cream soda."

"What am I worrying about?" sang Katie inwardly. "After all, they're as much Rommely as Nolan and we Rommelys are not drinking people."

"Neeley, let's go up on the roof," said Francie impulsively, "and see how the whole world looks at the beginning of a year."

"Okay," he agreed.

"Put your shoes on first," ordered mama, "and your coats."

They climbed the shaky wooden ladder. Neeley pushed the opening aside and they were on the roof.

The night was heady and frosty. There was no wind and the air was cold and still. The stars were brilliant and hung low in the sky. There were so many stars that their light made the sky a deep cobalt blue. There wasn't a moon, but the starlight served better than moonlight.

Francie stood on tiptoe and stretched her arms wide. "Oh, I want to hold it all!" she cried. "I want to hold the way the night is—cold without wind. And the way the stars are so near and shiny. I want to hold all of it tight until it hollers out: 'Let me go! Let me go!'"

"Don't stand so near the edge," said Neeley, uneasily. "You might fall off the roof."

"I need someone," thought Francie desperately. "I need someone. I need to hold somebody close. And I need more than this holding. I need someone to understand how I feel at a time like now. And the understanding must be part of the holding.

"I love mama and Neeley and Laurie. But I need someone to love in a different way from the way I love them.

"If I talked to mama about it, she'd say, 'Yes? Well, when you get that feeling don't linger in dark hallways with the boys.' She'd worry, too, thinking I was going to be the way Sissy used to be. But it isn't an Aunt Sissy thing, because here's this understanding that I want almost more than I want the holding. If I told Sissy or Evy, they'd talk the same as mama, although Sissy was married at fourteen and Evy at sixteen. Mama was only a girl when she married. But they've forgotten . . . and they'd tell me I was too young to be having such ideas. I'm young, maybe, in just being fifteen. But I'm older than those years in some things. But there is no one for me to hold and no one to understand. Maybe some day . . . some day. . . ."

"Neeley, if you *had* to die, wouldn't it be wonderful to die now—while you believed that everything was perfect, the way this night is perfect?"

"You know what?" asked Neeley.

"No. What?"

"You're drunk from that milk punch. That's what."

She clenched her hands and advanced on him. "Don't you say that! Don't you ever say that!"

He backed away, frightened at her fierceness. "Tha ... tha ... that's all right," he stammered. "I was drunk myself, once."

She lost her anger in curiosity. "Were you, Neeley? Honest?"

"Yeah. One of the fellers had some bottles of beer and we went down the cellar and drank it. I drank two bottles and got drunk."

"What did it feel like?"

"Well, first the whole world turned upside down. Then everything was like—you know those cardboard toots you buy for a penny, and you look in the small end and turn the big end, and pieces of coloured paper keep falling around and they never fall around the same way twice? Mostly, though, I was very dizzy. Afterwards I vomited."

"Then I've been drunk, too," admitted Francie.

"On beer?"

"No. Last spring, in McCarren's Park, I saw a tulip for the first time in my life."

"How'd you know it was a tulip if you'd never seen one?"

"I'd seen pictures. Well, when I looked at it, the way it was growing, and how the leaves were, and how purely red the petals were, with yellow inside, the world turned upside down and everything went around like the colours in a kaleidoscope—like you said. I was so dizzy I had to sit on a park bench."

"Did you throw up, too?"

"No," she answered. "And I've got that same feeling here on this roof tonight, and I know it's not the milk punch."

"Gee!"

She remembered something. "Mama tested us when she gave us that milk punch. I know it."

"Poor mama," said Neeley. "But she doesn't have to worry about me. I'll never get drunk again because I don't like to throw up."

"And she doesn't have to worry about me, either. I don

330

need to drink to get drunk. I can get drunk on things like the tulip—and this night."

"I guess it is a swell night," agreed Neeley.

"It's so still and bright . . . almost . . . holy."

She waited. If papa were here with her now. . . ,
Neeley sang.

> *Silent night. Holy night.*
> *All is calm, all is bright.*

"He's just like papa," she thought happily.

She looked out over Brooklyn. The starlight, half revealed, half concealed. She looked out over the flat roofs, uneven in height, broken once in a while by a slanting roof from a house left over from older times. The chimney pots on the roofs . . . and on some, the shadowing looming of pigeon cotes . . . sometimes, faintly heard, the sleepy cooing of pigeons . . . the twin spires of the Church, remotely brooding over the dark tenements. . . . And at the end of their street, the great Bridge that threw itself like a sigh across the East River and was lost . . . lost . . . on the other shore. The dark East River beneath the Bridge, and far away, the mist-grey skyline of New York, looking like a city cut from cardboard.

"There's no other place like it," Francie said.

"Like what?"

"Brooklyn. It's a magic city and it isn't real."

"It's just like any other place."

"It isn't! I go to New York every day and New York's not the same. I went to Bayonne once to see a girl from the office who was home sick. And Bayonne isn't the same. It's mysterious here in Brooklyn. It's like—yes—like a dream. The houses and streets don't seem real. Neither do the people."

"They're real enough—the way they fight and holler at each other and the way they're poor, and dirty, too."

"But it's like a dream of being poor and fighting. They don't really feel these things. It's like it's all happening in a dream."

"Brooklyn is no different than any other place," said Neeley calmly. "It's only your imagination makes it different. But that's all right," he added magnanimously, "as long as it makes you feel so happy."

Neeley! So much like mama, so much like papa; the best of each in Neeley. She loved her brother. She wanted to put her arms around him and kiss him. But he was like mama. He hated people to be demonstrative. If she tried to kiss him, he'd get mad and push her away. So, she held out her hand instead.

"Happy New Year, Neeley."

"The same to you."

They shook hands solemnly.

XLVII

FOR THE little while of the Christmas holidays, it had been almost like old times in the Nolan family. But after New Year's things reverted to the new routine which had grown on them since Johnny's death.

There were no more piano lessons, for one thing. Francie hadn't practised in months. Neeley did his piano playing evenings in the neighbourhood ice-cream saloons. He had been expert at ragtime and was becoming even more expert at jazz. He could make a piano talk—so people said—and he was very popular. He played for free sodas. Sometimes Scheefly gave him a dollar on a Saturday night for playing the whole evening. Francie didn't like it and spoke to her mother about it.

"I wouldn't let him, Mama," she said.

"But where's the harm in it?"

"You don't want him to get into the habit of playing for free refreshments like . . ." She hesitated. Katie picked up the sentence.

"Like your father? No, he'd never be like him. Your father never sang the songs he loved, like 'Annie Laurie' or 'The Last Rose of Summer.' He sang what the people wanted, 'Sweet Adeline' and 'Down by the Old Mill Stream.' Neeley's different. He'll always play what *he* likes and not care two cents whether anyone else likes it."

"You're saying, then, that papa was only an entertainer and that Neeley is an artist."

"Well . . . yes," admitted Katie defiantly.

"I think that's carrying mother love a little too far."

Katie frowned and Francie dropped the subject.

They had stopped reading the Bible and Shakespeare since Neeley started high school. He reported that they were study ng *Julius Caesar* and the principal read from the Bible each assembly period and that was enough for Neeley. Francie begged off reading at night because her eyes were tired from reading all day. Katie did not insist, feeling that they were now old enough to read or not—just as they wished.

Francie's evenings were lonely. The Nolans were together only at the supper hour, when even Laurie sat up to the table in her high chair. After supper Neeley went out, either to be with his gang or to play at some ice-cream saloon. Mama read the paper and then she and Laurie went to bed at eight o'clock. Katie was still getting up at five in order to have most of her cleaning done while Francie and Neeley were in the flat with the baby.)

Francie seldom went to the movies because they jumped around so and hurt her eyes. There were no shows to go to. Most of the stock companies had gone out of existence. Besides, she had seen Barrymore in Galsworthy's *Justice* on Broadway, and she was spoiled for stock companies after that. That past autumn she had seen a movie she liked: *War Brides* with Nazimova. She had hoped to see it again, but read in the papers that, because of the imminence of war, the film had been banned. She had a wonderful memory of journeying to a strange part of Booklyn to see the great Sarah Bernhardt in a one-act play in a Keith vaudeville house. The great actress was past seventy, but looked half that age from the stage. Francie couldn't understand the French, but she gathered that the play was written around the actress's amputated leg. Bernhardt played the part of a French soldier who had lost his leg in the war. Francie caught the word *Boche* from time to time. Francie would never forget the flaming red hair and the golden voice of Bernhardt. She treasured the programme in her scrap-book.

But those had been just three evenings out of months and months of evenings.

Spring came early that year and the sweet warm nights made her restless. She walked up and down the streets and through the park. And wherever she went, she saw a boy and a girl together; walking arm-in-arm, sitting on a park bench with their arms around each other, standing closely and in silence in a vestibule. Everyone in the world but Francie had a

333

sweetheart or a friend. She seemed to be the only lonely one in Brooklyn.

March, 1917. All the neighbourhood could think or talk about was the inevitability of war. A widow living in the flat had an only son. She was afraid he'd have to go and would be killed. She bought him a cornet and made him take lessons figuring he'd be put in an army band and play at parades and reviews only and be kept away from the front. People in the house were tormented almost to death by his incessant fumbling cornet practice. One harassed man, made crafty by desperation, told the mother that he had inside information that the military bands led the soldiers into action and invariably were the first ones killed. The terrified mother pawned the cornet immediately and destroyed the pawn-ticket. There was no more dreadful practising.

Each night at supper Katie asked Francie: "Has the war started yet?"

"Not yet. But any day now."

"Well, I wish it would hurry up and start."

"Do you want war?"

"No, I don't. But if it has to be, the sooner the better. The sooner it starts, the quicker it will end."

Then Sissy created such a sensation that the war was pushed into the background temporarily.

Sissy, who was done with her wild past, and who should have been settling down into the calm that precedes satisfied middle age, threw the family into a turmoil by falling madly in love with the John to whom she had been married for more than five years. Not only that, but she got herself widowed divorced, married, and pregnant—all in ten days' time!

The Standard Union, Williamburg's favourite newspaper was delivered as usual one afternoon to Francie's desk closing time. As usual, she took it home so that Katie could read it after supper. Francie would bring it back to the office the next morning and read and mark it. Since Francie never read newspapers outside of office hours, she had no way of knowing what was in that particular issue.

After supper, Katie sat by the window to look through the paper. An instant after turning the third page, she exploded her "Oh, my!" of utter astonishment. Francie and Neeley ran to look over her shoulder. Katie pointed to a heading:

HERO FIREMAN LOSES LIFE IN WALLABOUT
MARKET BLAZE

Underneath in small type was a sub-heading: "Had planned to retire on pension next month."

Reading the item, Francie discovered that the heroic fireman had been Sissy's first husband. There was a picture of Sissy taken twenty years ago—Sissy with a towering crimped pompadour and huge leg-o'-mutton sleeves—Sissy, sixteen years old. There was a caption under Sissy's picture. "Widow of heroic fire-fighter."

"Oh, my!" repeated Katie. "Then he never married again. He must have kept Sissy's picture all that time and when he died some men must have gone through his stuff and found—Sissy!

"I've got to go over there right away." Katie took off her apron and went to get her hat, explaining: "Sissy's John reads the papers. She told him she was divorced. Now that he knows the truth, he'll kill her. At least throw her out," she amended. "She'll have no place to go with the baby and mother."

"He seems like a nice man," said Francie, "I don't think he'd do that."

"We don't know what all he won't do. We don't know anything about him. He's a stranger in the family and always has been. Pray God I don't get there too late."

Francie insisted on going along and Neeley agreed to stay home with the baby on condition that he be told every single thing that happened.

When they got to Sissy's house, they found her rosy with excitement. Granma Mary Rommely had taken the baby and retired to the front room, where she sat in the dark and prayed for everything to come out all right.

Sissy's John gave them his version of the story.

"I'm away working in the shop, see? These here men come to the house and say to Sissy, 'Your husband's just been killed, see?' Sissy thinks they mean me." He turned on Sissy suddenly. "Did you cry?"

"You could hear me on the next block," she assured him. He seemed gratified.

"They ask Sissy what they should do with the body. Sissy asks is there any insurance, see? Well, it turns out there —for five hundred dollars, paid up ten years ago and still made out in Sissy's name. So what does Sissy go to work and do! She tells them to lay him out in Specht's Funeral Parlour, see? A five-hundred-dollar funeral she orders."

"I had to make the arrangements," apologized Sissy. "I'm his only living relation."

"And that's not all," he went on. "Now they're going to come around and give Sissy a pension. I won't stand for it!" he roared suddenly. "When I marry her," he went on more calmly, "she tells me she's a divorced woman. Now it turns out she's not."

"But there's no divorce in the Catholic Church," insisted Sissy.

"You wasn't married in the Catholic Church."

"I know. So I never considered I was married, and didn't think I had to get a divorce."

He threw his hands up in the air and moaned: "I give up!" It was the same cry of futile despair he had uttered when Sissy had insisted that she had given birth to the baby. "I marry her in good faith, see? And what does she do?" he asked rhetorically. "She turns right around and makes us live in adultery."

"Don't say that!" said Sissy sharply. "We're *not* living in adultery. We're living in bigamy."

"And it's got to stop right now, see? You're widowed from the first one and you're going to get a divorce from the second, and then you're going to marry me again, see?"

"Yes, John," she said meekly.

"And my name ain't John!" he roared. "It's Steve! Steve! Steve!" With each repetition of his name, he pounded on the table so hard that the blue glass sugar bowl with the spoon hanging around its rim clattered up and down. He pushed a finger into Francie's face.

"And you! From now on I'm Uncle *Steve*, see?"

Francie stared at the transformed man in dumb amazement.

"Well? What do you say?" he barked.

"Hel ... hel ... hello, Uncle Steve."

"That's more like it," he was mollified. He took his hat from a nail behind the door and jammed it on his head.

"Where are you going, John ... I mean, Steve?" asked Katie, worried.

"Listen! When I was a kid my old man always went out and got ice-cream when company came in his house. Well, this is *my* house, see? And *I* got company. So I'm going to get a quart of strawberry ice-cream, see?" He went.

"Isn't he wonderful?" sighed Sissy. "A woman could fall in

336

love with a person like that."

"Looks like the Rommelys have a man in the family at last," commented Katie dryly.

Francie went into the dark front room. By the light of the street lamp she saw her grandmother sitting at the window with Sissy's sleeping baby in her lap and amber rosary beads dangling from her trembling fingers.

"You can stop praying now, Granma," she said. "Everything's all right. He went out for ice-cream, see?"

"Glory be to the Father, and to the Son and to the Holy Ghost," praised Mary Rommely.

In Sissy's name, Steve wrote to her second husband at his last-known address and put "Please Forward" on the envelope. Sissy asked him to consent to a divorce so that she might remarry. A week later, a fat letter came from Wisconsin. Sissy's second husband informed her that he was well, had obtained a Wisconsin divorce seven years ago, had promptly remarried, settled down in Wisconsin, where he had a good job and was the father of three children. He was very happy, he wrote and in belligerently underlined words threatened that he intended to stay that way. He enclosed an old press clipping to prove that she had been legally informed of the divorce action by publication. He enclosed a photostatic copy of the decree (grounds: desertion), and a snapshot of three bouncing children.

Sissy was so happy at being divorced so quickly that she sent him a silver-plated pickle dish as a belated wedding present. She felt that she had to send a letter of congratulation also. Steve refused to write it for her, so she asked Francie to do it.

"Write that I hope he'll be very happy," dictated Sissy.

"But, Aunt Sissy, he's been married seven years and it's settled by now—whether he's happy or not."

"When you first hear that someone's married, it's polite to wish them happiness. Write it down."

"All right." She wrote it down. "What else?"

"Write something about his children ... how cute they are ... something like...." The words stuck in her throat. She knew he had sent the picture to prove that Sissy's stillborn children had not been his fault. That hurt Sissy. "Write that I'm the mother of a beautiful healthy baby girl and put a line under 'healthy'."

"But Steve's letter said you were only planning to get married. This man might think it funny that you got a baby so soon."

"Write it like I said," ordered Sissy, "and write that I expect another baby to be born next week."

"Sissy! You don't really!"

"Of course not. But write it down anyhow."

Francie wrote that down. "Anything else?"

"Say thanks for the divorce paper. Then say I got my own divorce a year before he got it. Only I forgot," she concluded lamely.

"But that's a lie."

"I *did* get the divorce before he did. I got it in my *mind*."

"All right. All right," surrendered Francie.

"Write that I'm very happy and intend to stay that way and put a line under those words like he did."

"Gosh, Sissy. *Must* you have the last word?"

"Yes. Just like your mother has to have it, and Evy and you too."

Francie made no more objections.

Steve got a licence and married Sissy all over again. This time a Methodist minister performed the ceremony. It was Sissy's first marriage by the Church, and at last she believed that she was truly married until death did the parting. Steve was very happy. He loved Sissy and had always been afraid of losing her. She had left her other husbands, casually and with no regrets. He had been afraid that she'd leave him, too, and take with her the baby whom he had grown to love dearly. He knew that Sissy believed in the Church ... any Church, Catholic or Protestant; that she'd never walk out on a church marriage. For the first time in their relationship, he felt happy, secure, and masterful. And Sissy discovered that she was madly in love with him.

Sissy came over one evening after Katie had gone to bed. She told her not to get up; that she'd sit in the bedroom and talk to her. Francie was sitting at the kitchen table pasting poems in old note-books. She kept a razor-blade at the office and cut out poems and stories she liked for her scrap-books. She had a series of them. One was labelled *The Nolan Book of Classical Poems*. Another, *The Nolan Volume of Contemporary Poetry*. A third was, *The Book of Annie Laurie*, in which

338

Francie was collecting nursery rhymes and animal stories to be read to Laurie when she was old enough to understand.

The voices coming from the dark bedroom made a soothing rhythm. Francie listened as she pasted. Sissy was saying:

". . . Steve, so fine and decent. And when I realized it, I hated myself on account of the others—outside of my husbands, I mean."

"You didn't tell him about the others?" asked Katie apprehensively.

"Do I look like a fool? But I wish with all my heart that he had been the first and only one."

"Woman talks that way," said Katie, "it means she's going to the change of life."

"How do you make that out?"

"If she never had any lovers, she kicks herself around when the change comes, thinking of all the fun she could have had, didn't have, and now can't have. If she had a lot of lovers, she argues herself into believing that she did wrong and she's sorry now. She carries on that way because she knows that soon all her womanness will be lost . . . lost. And if she makes believe being with a man was never any good in the first place, she can get comfort out of her change."

"I'm not going into any change of life," said Sissy indignantly. "In the first place I'm too young and in the second place I wouldn't stand for it."

"It has to come to all of us some day," sighed Katie.

There was terror in Sissy's voice. "Not to be able to have children any more . . . to be half a woman . . . get fat . . . have hair grow on your chin. I'll kill myself first!" she cried passionately. "Anyhow," she added complacently, "I'm nowhere near the change, because I'm that way again."

There was a rustle from the dark bedroom. Francie could visualize her mother raising herself on her elbow.

"No, Sissy! No! You can't go through that again. Ten times it's happened—ten children still-born. And it will be harder this time because you're going for thirty-seven."

"That's not too old to have a baby."

"No, but it's too old to get over another disappointment easily."

"You needn't worry, Katie. This child will live."

"You've said that each time."

"This time I'm sure because I feel that God is on my side," she said, with quiet assurance. After a while she said: "I told

339

Steve how I got Little Sissy."

"What did he say?"

"He knew all the while I hadn't given birth to her, but the way I claimed I had, got him mixed up. He said it didn' matter as long as I didn't have her by another man, and tha since we had her from birth almost he really feels that she's hi baby. It's funny how the baby looks like him. She has his dar eyes and the same round chin and the same small ears close t her head like him."

"She got those dark eyes from Lucia, and a million peop in the world have round chins and small ears. But if it mak Steve happy to think the baby looks like him, that's fine There was a long silence before Katie spoke again. "Sissy, d you ever get any idea from that Italian family as to who t father was?"

"No." Sissy, too, waited a long time before she continue "You know who told me about the girl being in trouble a where she lived and all?"

"Who?"

"Steve."

"Oh, my!"

Both were quiet for a long time. Then Katie said: "(course, that was accidental."

"Of course," agreed Sissy. "One of the fellows in his sh told him, he said: a fellow who lived on Lucia's block."

"Of course," Katie repeated. "You know funny things ha pen here in Brooklyn that have no meaning at all. L sometimes I'm walking on the street and I think of someon haven't seen maybe for five years and I turn a corner a there's that person walking towards me."

"I know," answered Sissy. "Sometimes I'm doing somethi that I never did before in my life and all of a sudden I ha the feeling that I did that same thing before—maybe another life. . . ." Her voice died away. After a while she sa "Steve always said he'd never take another man's child."

"All men say that. Life's funny," Katie went on. "A cou of accidental things come together and a person could mak lot out of them. It was just an accident that you got to kn about that girl. That same fellow must have told a dozen n in the shop. Steve just mentioned it to you accidentally. It w just by accident that you got in with that family and j accidental that the baby has a round instead of a square cl It's even less than accidental. It's . . ." Katie stopped to sea

340

tor a word.

Francie in the kitchen had become so interested that she forgot that she wasn't supposed to be listening. When she knew her mother was groping for a word, she supplied it unthinkingly.

"You mean *coincidental*, Mama?" she called out.

A shocked silence came from the bedroom. Then the conversation was resumed—but this time in whispers.

XLVIII

A NEWSPAPER LAY on Francie's desk. It was an "extra" and had come directly from the presses. The ink was still damp on its headlines. The paper had been there five minutes and as yet she had not picked up her pencil to mark it. She stared at the date.

April, 6, 1917.

The one-word headline was six inches high. The three letters were smudged at the edges and the word "WAR" seemed to waver.

Francie had a vision. Fifty years from now she'd be telling her grandchildren how she had come to the office, sat at her reader's desk and in the routine of work had read that war had been declared. She knew from listening to her grandmother that old age was made up of such remembrances of youth.

But she didn't want to recall things. She wanted to live things—or, as a compromise, relive rather than reminisce.

She decided to fix this time in her life exactly the way it was this instant. Perhaps that way she could hold on to it as a living thing and not have it become something called a memory.

She brought her eyes close to the surface of her desk and examined the patterned grain of the wood. She ran her fingers along the groove where her pencils rested, fixing the feel of the groove in her mind. Using a razor-blade, she nicked the next dot on one of her pencils and unravelled the paper. She held the ravelling in her palm, touched it with her forefinger, and noted its spiralling. She dropped it into the metal waste-basket, counting the seconds it took to fall. She listened intently so as not to miss its almost noiseless thud as it hit the bottom. She pressed her finger-tips to the damp headline, examined her inked finger-tips, then made finger-prints on a sheet of white paper.

Not caring about clients who might be mentioned on pages one and two, she detached the front sheet of the newspaper and folded the sheet into a careful oblong, watching the creases come under her thumb. She inserted it into one of the strong manilla envelopes that the Bureau used to post clippings in.

Francie heard, as if for the first time, the sound the desk drawer made when she opened it to get her purse. She noted the device of the purse's catch—the sound of its click. She felt the leather, memorized its smell and studied the whorlings of the black moire-silk lining. She read the dates on the coins in her change purse. There was a new 1917 penny which she put in the envelope. She uncapped her lipstick and made a line with it under her fingerprints. The clear red colour, the texture and the scent of it pleased her. She examined in turn the powder in her compact, the ridges on her nail-file, the way her comb was inflexible and the threads of her handkerchief. There was a worn clipping in the purse, a poem she had torn out of an Oklahoma newspaper. It had been written by a poet who had lived in Brooklyn, gone to the Brooklyn public schools and, as a young man, had edited *The Brooklyn Eagle*. She re-read it for the twentieth time, handling each word in her mind.

> *I am of old and young, of the foolish as much*
> *   as the wise;*
> *Regardless of others, ever regardful of others.*
> *Maternal as well as paternal, a child as well*
> *   as a man,*
> *Stuff'd with the stuff that is coarse, and*
> *   stuff'd with the stuff that is fine.*

The tattered poem went into the envelope. In the mirror of her compact she looked at the way her hair was braided—how the braids wound around her head. She noticed how her straight black eyelashes were uneven in length. Then her shoes were inspected. She ran her hand down her stockings, and for the first time noticed that the silk felt rough instead of smooth. The fabric of her dress was made of tiny cords. She turned back the hem and noticed that the narrow lace edge of her slip was diamond-shaped in design.

"If I can fix every detail of this time in my mind, I can keep this moment always," she thought.

Using the razor-blade, she clipped a lock of her hair, wrapped it in the square of paper on which were her finger-prints and lipstick mark, folded it, placed it in the envelope and sealed the envelope. On the outside she wrote:

"Frances Nolan, age 15 years and 4 months. April 6, 1917."

She thought: "If I open this envelope fifty years from now, I will be again as I am now and there will be no being old for me. There's a long, long time yet before fifty years . . . millions of hours of time. But one hour has gone already since I sat here . . . one hour less to live . . . one hour gone away from all the hours of my life.

"Dear God," she prayed, "let me be *something* every minute of every hour of my life. Let me be gay; let me be sad. Let me be cold; let me be warm. Let me be hungry . . . have too much to eat. Let me be ragged or well dressed. Let me be sincere—be deceitful. Let me be truthful; let me be a liar. Let me be honourable and let me sin. Only let me be *something* every blessed minute. And when I sleep, let me dream all the time so that not one little piece of living is ever lost."

The delivery-boy came by and slapped another city paper on her desk. This one had a two-word headline.

WAR DECLARED!

The floor seemed to swerve up, colours flashed before her eyes and she put her head down on the ink-damp paper and wept quietly. One of the older readers returning from the wash-room, paused at Francie's desk. She noticed the headline and the weeping girl. She thought she understood.

"Ah, the war!" She sighed. "You have a sweetheart or a brother, I presume?" she asked in her stilted readerish way.

"Yes, I have a brother," Francie answered truthfully enough.

"My sympathies, Miss Nolan." The reader went back to her desk.

"I'm drunk again," thought Francie, "and this time on a newspaper headline. And this is a bad one—I've got a crying jag."

The war touched the Model Press Clipping Bureau with its ailed finger and made it wither away. First, the client who was the backbone of the business—the man who paid out thousands of dollars a year for clippings on the Panama Canal

343

and such—came in the day after the declaration of war and said that since his address would be uncertain for a while, he'd call in person each day for his clippings.

A few days later, two slow-moving men with heavy feet came in to see the Boss. One of them pushed his palm under the Boss's nose, and what he saw in that palm made the Boss turn pale. He got a thick stack of clippings from the file-box of the most important client. The heavy-footed ones looked them over and returned them to the Boss, who put them in an envelope and put the envelope in his desk. The two men went into the Boss's lavatory, leaving the door ajar. They waited in there all day. At noon they sent the errand-boy out for a bag of sandwiches and a carton of coffee and they ate their lunch in the lavatory.

The Panama Canal client came in at four-thirty. In slow motion the Boss handed him the fat envelope. Just as the client put it in his inner coat pocket, the heavy ones strolled out of the lavatory. One of them touched the client on the shoulder. He sighed, took the envelope out of his pocket and surrendered it. The second heavy one touched him on the shoulder. The client clicked his heels together, bowed stiffly and walked out between the two men. The Boss went home with an acute attack of dyspepsia.

That evening, Francie told mama and Neeley how a German spy had been caught right in the office.

The next day, a brisk-looking man came in with a brief case. The Boss had to answer a lot of questions, and the brisk man wrote down the answers in spaces provided on a printed form. Then came the sad part. The Boss had to make out cheque for nearly four hundred dollars—the balance due on the involuntarily-cancelled account. After the brisk man left the Boss rushed out to borrow money to make the cheque good.

After that, everything went to pieces. The Boss was afraid to take in new accounts, no matter how innocent they seemed. The deluge of spring-published books which brought in hundreds of seasonal five-dollar author clients and dozens of hundred-dollar publisher clients, had not been a deluge but mere trickle. Houses were holding off important publication until things settled down a bit. Many research workers cancelled their accounts in expectation of being called up in the draft. Even if business had been normal the Bureau couldn't have handled it because the workers began to go.

The government, anticipating a man shortage, threw open Civil Service examinations for women workers in the big Thirty-fourth Street post office. Many of the readers took and passed the examination and were called to work immediately. The manual workers—The Club—left almost in a body to work in war project plants. They not only tripled their earnings but they received much praise for their unselfish patriotism. The Boss's wife came back to read and he fired all the remaining readers except Francie.

The huge loft echoed with emptiness as the three of them tried to carry on the business alone. Francie and the wife read, filed, and attended to the office work. The Boss slashed impotently at newspapers, printed blurry slips and pasted items askew.

In the middle of June, he gave up. He made arrangements for the sale of his office equipment, broke his lease, and settled the matter of refunds to clients very simply by saying: "Let 'em sue me."

Francie phoned the only other clipping bureau she knew of in New York and asked whether they needed a reader. She was told that they never hired new readers. "We treat our readers right," said an argumentative voice, "and never have to make replacements." Francie thought that was very nice, said so, and hung up.

She spent her last morning at the Bureau marking "Help Wanted" ads. She skipped the office jobs, knowing she'd have to start as a file clerk again. You didn't stand a chance in an office unless you were a stenographer and typist. Anyhow, she preferred factory work. She liked factory people better and she liked keeping her mind free while she worked with her hands. But of course mama wouldn't let her work in a factory again.

She found an ad that seemed a happy combination of factory and office; operating a machine in office surroundings. Communications Corporation offered to teach girls tele-type machine operating and to pay them twelve-fifty a week while they were learning. The hours were 5 p.m. to 1 a.m. At least it would give her something to do with her evenings—if she got the job.

When she went to say good-bye to the Boss, he told her that he'd have to owe her the last week's salary. He had her address, he said, and would send it. Francie said good-bye to the Boss, to his wife and to her final week's pay.

345

The Communications Corporation had a skyscraper office overlooking the East River in down-town New York. Along with a dozen other girls, Francie filled out an application after presenting a fervent letter of recommendation from her ex-Boss. She took an aptitude test, in which she answered questions which seemed silly—"which weighs the most, a pound of lead or a pound of feathers," was an example. Evidently she passed the test, for she was given a number, a locker key for which she had to pay a quarter deposit, and told to report the next day at five o'clock.

It wasn't quite four when Francie got home. Katie was cleaning in their house, and she looked upset when she saw Francie come up the stairs.

"Don't look so worried, Mama. I'm not sick or anything."

"Oh," said Katie, relieved. "For a moment I thought you had lost your job."

"I have."

"Oh, my!"

"And I won't get my last week's pay either. But I got another job . . . start tomorrow . . . twelve and a half a week I'll get a rise in time, I expect." Katie started to ask questions. "Mama, I'm tired. Mama, I don't want to talk. We'll talk about it tomorrow. And I don't want supper. I just want to go to bed." She went upstairs.

Katie sat on the steps and started to worry. Since war started, prices of food and everything else had sky-rocketed. In the past month, Katie had not been able to add to Francie's bank account. The ten dollars a week hadn't been enough. Laurie had to have a quart of fresh milk every day and the milk modifier was expensive. Then there had to be orange juice. Now with twelve-fifty a week . . . after Francie's expenses were taken out there'd be less money. Soon it would be vacation. Neeley could work during the summer. But what about the autumn? Neeley would return to high school. Francie had to get to high school that autumn. How? How? She sat there and worried.

Francie, after a brief glance at the sleeping baby, undressed and got into bed. She folded her hands under head and stared at the grey patch which was the air-shaft window.

"Here I am," she thought, "fifteen years old and a drifter. I've been working less than a year and I've had three jobs already. I used to think it would be fun to go from one job

346

the other. But now I'm scared. I've been fired from two jobs through no fault of my own. At each job I worked as best I could. I gave everything I could give. And here I'm starting all over again somewhere else. Only now I'm frightened. This time when the new boss says 'jump once,' I'll jump twice because I'll be afraid of losing the job. I'm scared because they're depending on me here for money. How did we ever get along before I worked? Well, there wasn't Laurie then. Neeley and I were smaller and could do with less, and of course papa helped some.

"Well . . . good-bye, college. Good-bye, everything, for that matter." She turned her face away from the grey light and closed her eyes.

Francie sat at a typewriter in a big room. There was a metal roof fastened over the top of Francie's machine so that she couldn't see the keyboard. An enormous chart of the keyboard diagram was tacked up in front of the room. Francie consulted the chart and felt for the letters under the shield. That was the first day. On the second day she was given a stack of old telegrams to copy. Her eyes went from the copy to the chart as her fingers groped for the letters. At the end of the second day she had memorized the position of the letters on the machine and didn't have to consult the chart. A week later they took the shield off. It made no difference now. Francie was a touch typist.

An instructor explained the workings of the tele-tape machine. For a day Francie practised sending and receiving dummy messages. Then she was put on the New York-Cleveland wire.

She thought it a wonderful miracle that she could sit at that machine and type and have the words come out hundreds of miles away on a piece of paper on the roller of a machine in *Cleveland, Ohio*! No less miraculous was that a girl typing away in Cleveland made the hammers of *Francie's* machine sound out the words.

It was easy work. Francie would send for an hour, then receive for an hour. There were two fifteen-minute rest periods in the work shift and half an hour for "lunch" at nine o'clock. Her pay had been increased to fifteen a week when she went on a wire. All in all, it wasn't a bad job.

The household adjusted itself to Francie's new schedule. She

347

left home soon after four in the afternoon and got home a little before two in the morning. She pressed the bell-button three times before she entered the hallway so that mama could be on the alert and make sure that Francie wouldn't be attacked by someone lurking in the hallways.

Francie slept mornings until eleven o'clock. Mama didn't have to get up so early because Francie was in the flat with Laurie. She started work in her own house first. By the time she was ready for the other two houses, Francie was up and looking after Laurie. Francie had to work on Sunday nights but she had Wednesday night off.

Francie liked the new arrangement. It took care of her lonely evenings, it helped mama out and gave Francie a few hours each day to sit in the park with Laurie. The warm sun did both of them a lot of good.

A plan took shape in Katie's mind and she spoke to Francie about it.

"Will they keep you on night work?" she asked.

"Will they! They're tickled to death. No girl wants to work nights. That's why they push it off on the new girls."

"I was thinking that maybe in the autumn you could keep on working nights and go to high school in the day-time. I know it'll be hard, but it could be done somehow."

"Mama, no matter what you say, I won't go to high school."

"But you fought to go last year."

"That was last year. That was the right time to go. Now it's too late."

"It's not too late and don't be stubborn."

"But what in the world could I learn in high school now? Oh, I'm not conceited or anything, but after all, I read eight hours a day for almost a year and I learned things. I've got my own ideas about history and government and geography and writing and poetry. I've read too much about people—what they do and how they live. I've read about crimes and about heroic things. Mama, I've read about *everything*. I couldn't sit still now in a classroom with a bunch of baby kids and listen to an old maid teacher drool away about this and that. I'd be jumping up and correcting her all the time. Or else I'd be good and swallow it all down and then I'd hate myself for . . . well . . . eating mush instead of bread. So I must not go to high school. But I *will* go to college some day."

"But you've got to go through high school before they'll le

348

you in college."

"Four years of high school . . . no, five. Because something would come up to delay me. Then four years of college. I'd be a dried-up old maid of twenty-five before I was finished."

"Whether you like it or not, you'll get to be twenty-five in time, no matter what you do. You might as well be getting educated while you're going towards it."

"Once and for all, Mama, I will not go to high school."

"We'll see," said Katie, as her jaw settled into a square line.

Francie said nothing more. But the set of her jaw was like her mother's.

However, the conversation gave Francie an idea. If mama thought she could work evenings and go to high school in the day, why couldn't she go to college that way? She studied a newspaper ad. Brooklyn's oldest and most reputable college was advertising summer courses available for college students wishing to take advanced work or to make up or work off conditions, and for high school students wishing to gain advance college credits. Francie thought she might come under the last heading. She wasn't exactly a high-school student, but she was eligible to be one. She sent for the catalogue.

From the catalogue she chose three courses with class meeting in the afternoon. She'd be able to sleep as usual until eleven, attend classes and go straight to work from the college. She chose Beginning French, Elementary Chemistry, and something called Restoration Drama. She figured up the tuition; a little over sixty dollars with laboratory fees. She had one hundred and five dollars in her savings account. She went to Katie.

"Mama, could I have sixty-five dollars of the money you've been saving for me towards college?"

"What for?"

"College, of course." She was deliberately casual for the drama of it. She was rewarded by the way mama's voice scaled up as she repeated after Francie:

"College?"

"Summer-school college."

"But-but-but," sputtered Katie.

"I know. No high school. But maybe I can get in if I tell 'em I don't want a diploma or any grades—that I just want the lessons." Katie got her green hat down from the closet shelf. "Where're you going, Mama?"

"To the bank for the money."

349

Francie laughed at her mother's eagerness. "It's after hours. The bank's closed. Besides, there's no hurry. Registration's a week off yet."

The college was located in Brooklyn Heights, another strange section of great Brooklyn for Francie to explore. As she filled out the registration form, her pen hovered over the question of previous education. There were three headings with blanks after them: Elementary Schools, High Schools, and Colleges, After a little thought, she crossed out the words and wrote in the space above them: "Privately educated."

"And when you come right down to it, that's no lie," she assured herself.

To her utter relief and astonishment, she was not challenged in any way. The cashier took her money and gave her a receipt for her tuition. She was given a registration number, a pass to the library, a schedule of her classes, and a list of the text-books she needed.

She followed a crowd to the college book-shop farther down the block. She consulted her list and ordered a "Beginning French" and an "Elementary Chemistry."

"New or second-hand?" asked the clerk.

"Why, I don't know. Which am I supposed to have?"

"New," said the clerk.

Someone touched her on the shoulder. She turned and saw handsome well-dressed boy. He said: "Get second-hand. Serves the same purpose as new and half the price."

"Thank you." She turned to the clerk. "Second-hand," she said firmly. She started to order the two books for the dram course. Again the touch on her shoulder.

"Uh, uh," said the boy negatively. "You can read them in the library before and after classes and when you get cuts."

"Thank you again," she said.

"Any time," he answered, and sauntered away.

Her eyes followed him out of the store. "Gosh, he's tall and good-looking," she thought. "College is certainly wonderful."

She sat in the El train on her way to the office, clutching the two text-books. As the train grated over the tracks its rhythm seemed to be, college-college-college. Francie started to feel sick. She felt so sick that she had to get off at the next station even though she knew she'd be late for work. She leaned against a penny weighing machine, wondering what was the matter with her. It couldn't have been anything she ate, because she had forgotten to eat her lunch. Then a thunderous thought came to her.

"My grandparents never knew how to read or write. Those who came before them couldn't read or write. My mother's sister can't read or write. My parents never even graduated from grade school. I never went to high school. But I, M. Frances K. Nolan, am now in college. Do you hear that, Francie? *You're in college!*

"Oh gosh, I feel sick."

XLIX

FRANCIE CAME away from her first chemistry lecture in a glow. In one hour she had found out that everything was made up of atoms which were in continual motion. She grasped the idea that nothing was ever lost or destroyed. Even if something was burned up or left to rot away, it did not disappear from the face of the earth; it changed into something else—gases, liquids, and powders. Everything, decided Francie after that first lecture, was vibrant with life and there was no death in chemistry. She was puzzled as to why learned people didn't adopt chemistry as a religion.

The drama of the Restoration, apart from the time-consuming reading required, was easy to manage after her home study of Shakespeare. She had no worries about that course nor the chemistry course. But when it came to Beginning French, she was lost. It wasn't really *beginning* French. The instructor, working on the knowledge that his students either had taken it before and flunked it, or had already had it in high school, sluffed over the preliminaries and got right down to translation. Francie, shaky enough regarding English grammar, spelling, and punctuation, didn't stand a chance with the French language. She'd never pass the course. All she could do was memorize vocabulary each day and try to hang

She studied going back and forth on the El. She studied in rest periods and ate her meals with a book propped up on the table before her. She typed out her assignments on one of the machines in the instruction-room of the Communications Corporation. She was never late or absent and she asked nothing more than to pass at least two of her courses.

The boy who had befriended her in the book-store became her guardian angel. His name was Ben Blake, and he was a most amazing fellow. He was a senior in a Maspeth high school. He was editor of the school magazine, president of his class, played half-back on the football team, and was an honour student. For the past three summers he had been taking college courses. He would finish high school with more than one year of college work out of the way.

In addition to his school work, he put in his afternoons working for a law firm. He drew up briefs, served summonses, examined deeds and records, and searched out precedents. He was familiar with the state's statutes and was completely capable of trying a case in court. Besides doing so well in school, he earned twenty-five dollars a week. His firm wanted him to come into the office full-time after his graduation from high school, read law with them, and eventually take the Bar exam. But Ben was contemptuous of non-college lawyers. He had a great mid-western college picked out. He planned to complete work for an A.B. degree and then enter law school.

At nineteen his life was planned out in a straight unswerving line. After passing the Bar exam he was all set to take over a country law practice. He believed that a young lawyer had more political opportunities in a small-town practice. He even had the practice picked out. He was to succeed a distant relative, an aged country lawyer who had a well-established practice. He was in constant touch with his future predecessor and received long weekly letters of guidance from him.

Ben planned to take over this practice and await his turn to be county prosecutor. (By agreement, the lawyers in this small county rotated the office among them.) That would be his start in politics. He'd work hard, get himself well known and trusted, and eventually be elected to the House of Representatives from his state. He'd serve faithfully and be re-elected. Then he'd come back and work himself up to the governorship of his state. That was his plan.

The amazing thing about the whole idea was that those who knew Ben Blake were sure that everything would come out the way he planned it.

In the meantime, in that summer of 1917, the object of his ambitions, a vast mid-western state, lay dreaming beneath a hot prairie sun—lay dreaming among its great wheat-fields and its unending orchards of wine-sap, Baldwin and northern spy apples—lay dreaming—unaware that the man who planned to occupy its White House as its youngest governor was, at the moment, a boy in Brooklyn.

That was Ben Blake; well-dressed, gay, handsome, brilliant, sure of himself, well liked by the boys, with all the girls crazy about him—and Francie Nolan tremulously in love with him.

She saw him every day. His fountain-pen flashed through her French assignments. He checked her chemistry work and cleared up obscurities in the Restoration plays. He helped her plan her next summer's courses and, obligingly enough, tried to plan out the rest of her life for her.

As the end of summer came near, two things saddened Francie. Soon she wouldn't be seeing Ben every day, and she wasn't going to pass the French course. She took Ben into her confidence about the latter sadness.

"Don't be silly," he told her briskly. "You paid for the course, you sat in class all summer, you're not a moron. You'll pass. Q.E.D."

"No," she laughed. "I'll flunk P.D.Q."

"We'll have to cram you for the final exam, then. We'll need a whole day. Now where can we go?"

"My house?" suggested Francie timidly.

"No. There'd be people around." He thought for a moment. "I know a good place. Meet me Sunday morning at nine, corner Gates and Broadway."

He was waiting for her when she stepped off the trolley. She wondered where in the world he'd take her in *that* neighbourhood. He took her to the stage door of a theatre given over to Broadway shows on the first lap of the road. He got through the magic door merely by saying " 'Morning, Pop" to the white-haired man sitting on a tilted chair in the sun beside the opened door. Francie then discovered that this amazing boy was a Saturday night usher in this theatre.

She had never been back-stage before, and she was so excited that she almost ran a temperature. The stage seemed vast and the roof of the theatre house seemed lost—so far away it was. As she walked across the stage, she changed her stride and walked slowly and stiff-leggedly as she remembered Harold Clarence walking. When Ben spoke she turned slowly, with dramatic intensity, and said in a throaty voice: "You" (pause: then with meaning) "spoke?"

"Want to see something?" he asked.

He pulled the curtain, and she saw the asbestos roll up like a

353

giant's shade. He turned on the foots and she walked out on the apron and looked over the thousand dark, empty, waiting raked seats. She tilted her head and threw her voice to the last row of the gallery.

"Hello, out there!" she called, and her voice seemed amplified a hundred times in the dark, waiting emptiness.

"Look," he asked good-naturedly, "are you more interested in the theatre or your French?"

"Why, the theatre, of course."

It was true. Then and there she renounced all other ambitions and went back to her first love, the stage.

Ben laughed as he cut off the foots. He brought down the curtain and placed two chairs facing each other. In some way he had got hold of the examination papers for five years back. From them he had made a master exam paper, using the questions asked most frequently and those seldom asked. Most of the day he drilled Francie in these questions and answers. Then he had her memorize a page from Molière's *Le Tartufe* and its English translation. He explained:

"There'll be one question in the exam tomorrow that will be absolute Greek to you. Don't attempt to answer it. Do this: State frankly that you can't answer the question, but that you are offering in its stead an excerpt from Molière with translation. Then write down what you've memorized and you'll get away with it."

"But suppose they ask for that exact passage in a regular question?"

"They won't. I picked out a very obscure passage."

Evidently she got away with it, for she passed the examination in French. True, she passed with the lowest mark, but she consoled herself with the idea that passing was passing. She did very well on the chemistry and drama examinations.

Acting on Ben's instructions, she came back for the transcript of her grades a week later and met him by arrangement. He took her to Huyler's for a chocolate soda.

"How old are you, Francie?" he asked over the sodas.

She calculated rapidly. She was fifteen at home, seventeen at work. Ben was nineteen. He'd never speak to her again if he knew she was only fifteen. He saw her hesitation and said:

"Anything you say may be used against you."

She took her courage into her two hands and quavered boldly: "I'm ... fifteen." She hung her head in shame.

"Hm. I like you, Francie."

"And I love you," she thought.

"I like you as much as any girl I've ever known. But of course, I have no time for girls."

"Not even for an hour, say, on Sunday?" she ventured.

"My few free hours belong to my mother. I'm all that she has."

Francie had never heard of Mrs. Blake until that moment. But she hated her because she pre-empted those free hours, a few of which would have made Francie happy.

"But I'll be thinking of you," he continued. "I'll write if I have a moment." (He lived half an hour from her.) "But if you ever need me—not for any trivial reason, of course—drop me a line and I'll manage to see you." He gave her one of the firm's cards with his full name, Benjamin Franklin Blake, written in the corner.

They parted outside of Huyler's, shaking hands warmly. "See you next summer," he called back as he walked away. Francie stood looking after him until he turned the corner. Next summer! It was only September, and next summer seemed a million years away.

She had enjoyed the summer school so much that she wanted to matriculate in the same college that autumn, but she had no way of raising the more than three hundred dollars required for tuition. In a morning spent in studying catalogues in the Forty-second Street, New York, Library, she discovered a college for women in which tuition was free to residents of New York.

Armed with her transcripts, she went over to register. She was told that she couldn't matriculate, lacking a high-school education. She explained how she had been permitted to go to summer school. Ah! That was different. There courses were given for credit only. No degree was offered in summer courses. She asked couldn't she take courses now without expecting a degree. No. If she were past twenty-five, she might be permitted to enter as a special student and take courses without being a candidate for a degree. Francie regretfully acknowledged that she was not yet past twenty-five. There was an alternative, however. If she were able to pass the entrance regents' examinations, she would be permitted to enrol, regardless of high-school credits.

Francie took the examinations and flunked everything but

chemistry.

"Oh, well! I should have known," she told her mother. "I[f] people could get into college that easy, no one would eve[r] bother with high school. But don't worry, Mama, I know wha[t] the entrance examinations are now, and I'll get the books an[d] study and take those examinations next year. And I'll pas[s] next year. It can be done and I'll do it. You'll see."

Even if she had been able to enter college, it wouldn't hav[e] worked out, because she was put on the day shift after all. Sh[e] was now a fast and expert operator, and they needed her i[n] the day when the traffic was heaviest. They assured her tha[t] she could go back on night work in the summer if she wishe[d]. She got her next rise. She was now earning seventeen-fifty [a] week.

Again the lonely evenings. Francie roamed the Brookly[n] streets in the lovely nights of autumn and thought of Ben.

("If you ever need me, write, and I'll manage to see you.[)]

Yes, she needed him, but she was sure he'd never come [if] she wrote: "I'm lonely. Please come and walk with me a[nd] talk to me." In his firm schedule of life there was no headi[ng] labelled "Loneliness."

The neighbourhood seemed the same, yet it was differe[nt]. Gold stars had appeared in some of the tenement windo[ws]. The boys still got together on the corner or in front of a pe[nny] candy store of an evening. But now, often as not, one of t[he] boys would be in khaki.

The boys stood around harmonizing. They sang "A Sha[ck] in Old Shantytown" and "When You Wore a Tulip," "D[ear] Old Girl," "I'm Sorry I Made You Cry," and other son[gs]. Sometimes the soldier boy led them in war songs: "O[ver] There," "K-K-K-Katie" and "The Rose of No Man's Lan[d]."

But no matter what they sang, always they finished off w[ith] one of Brooklyn's own folk songs: "Mother Machre[e]," "When Irish Eyes Are Smiling," "Let Me Call You Sw[eet]heart," or "The Band Played On."

And Francie walked past them in the evenings and w[on]dered why all the songs sounded so sad.

L

Sissy expected her baby late in November. Katie and Evy went to a lot of trouble to avoid discussing it with Sissy. They were certain it would be another still-birth, and they reasoned that the less said about it, the less Sissy would have to remember afterwards. But Sissy did such a revolutionary thing that they *had* to talk about it. She announced that she was going to have a *doctor* when the baby came, and that she was going to a *hospital*.

Her mother and sisters were stunned. No Rommely woman had had a doctor at childbirth, ever. It didn't seem right. You called in a midwife, a neighbour woman, or your mother, and you got through the business secretively and behind closed doors and kept the men out. Babies were women's business. As for hospitals, everyone knew you went there only to die.

Sissy told them they were way behind the times; that midwives were things of the past. Besides, she informed them proudly, she had no say in the matter. Her Steve insisted on the doctor and the hospital. And that wasn't all.

Sissy was going to have a Jewish doctor!

"Why, Sissy? Why?" asked her shocked sisters.

"Because Jewish doctors are more sympathetic than Christian ones at a time like that."

"I've nothing against the Jews," began Katie, "but ..."

"Look! Just because Dr. Aaronstein's people look at a star when they pray and our people look at a cross has nothing to do with whether he's a good doctor or not."

"But I'd think you'd want a doctor of your own faith round at a time of ..." (Katie was going to say "death," but checked herself in time) ... "birth."

"Oh sugar!" said Sissy contemptuously.

"Like should stick to like. You don't see Jews calling on Christian doctors," said Evy, thinking she had made a telling point.

"Why should they," countered Sissy, "when they and everybody else know that the Jewish doctors are smarter?"

The birth was the same as all the others. Sissy had her usual easy time made easier by the skill of the doctor. When the baby was delivered, she closed her eyes tightly. She was afraid to look at it. She had been so sure that this one would live. But now that the time had come, she felt in her heart that it wouldn't be so. She opened her eyes finally. The baby was lying on a near-by table. It was still and blue. She turned her head away.

"Again," she thought. "Again and again and again. Eleven times. Oh God, why couldn't You let me have one? Just one out of the eleven? In a few years my time of child-bearing will be over. For a woman to die at last . . . knowing that she has never given life. Oh, God, why have You put Your curse on me?"

Then she heard a word. She heard a word that she had never known. She heard the word "oxygen."

"Quick! Oxygen!" she heard the doctor say.

She watched him work over her baby. She saw a miracle that transcended the miracles of the saints her mother had told her about. She saw the dead blue change to living white. She saw an apparently lifeless child draw a breath. For the first time she heard the cry of a child she had borne.

"Is . . . is . . . it alive?" she asked, afraid to believe.

"What else?" The doctor shrugged his shoulders eloquently "You've got as fine a boy as I've ever seen."

"You're *sure* he'll live?"

"Why not?" Again the shrug. "Unless you let him fall out of a three-storey window."

Sissy took his hands and covered them with kisses. And Dr Aaron Aaronstein was not embarrassed about her emotional ism the way a Gentile doctor would have been.

She named the baby Stephen Aaron.

"I've never seen it to fail," said Katie. "Let a childless woman adopt a baby and bang! A year or two later she's sure to have one of her own. It's as if God recognized her good intentions at last. It's nice that Sissy has two to bring up because it's no good to bring up one child alone."

"Little Sissy and Stevie are just two years apart," said Francie. "Almost like Neeley and me."

"Yes. They'll be company for each other."

Sissy's living son was a great wonder of the family until Uncle Willie Flittman gave them something else to talk about Willie tried to enlist in the army and was turned down whereupon he threw up his job with the milk company, came home, announced that he was a failure, and went to bed. He wouldn't get up next morning or the morning after. He said was going to stay in bed and never get up as long as he lived

358

All his life he had lived as a failure, and now he was going to die as a failure, and the sooner the better, he stated.

Evy sent for her sisters.

Evy, Sissy, Katie, and Francie stood around the big brass bed in which the failure had ensconsed himself. Willie took one look at the circle of strong-willed Rommely women and wailed: "I'm a failure." He pulled the blanket up over his head.

Evy turned her husband over to Sissy and Francie watched Sissy go to work on him. She put her arms around him and held the futile little fellow to her breast. Sissy convinced him that not all the brave men were in trenches—that many a hero was risking his life daily for his country in a munitions factory. She talked and talked until Willie got so excited about helping to win the war that he jumped out of bed and made Aunt Evy scurry around getting him his trousers and shoes.

Steve was foreman now, at a munitions factory on Morgan Avenue. He got Willie a good-paying job there with time and a half for overtime.

It was a tradition in the Rommely family that the men keep for themselves any tips or overtime money that they earned. With his first cheque for overtime work, Willie bought himself a bass drum and a pair of cymbals. He spent all of his evenings (when he didn't have to work overtime) practising on the drum and cymbals in the front room. Francie gave him a dollar harmonica for Christmas. He fastened it to a stick and attached the stick to his belt so he could play the harmonica while riding a bicycle no hands. He tried to manipulate the guitar, harmonica, drum, and cymbals all at once. He was practising to be a one man band.

And so he sat in the front room evenings. He blew into the harmonica, strummed the guitar, thumped the great drum, and clashed the brass cymbals. And he grieved because he was a failure.

LI

WHEN IT got too cold to go walking, Francie enrolled in two evening classes at the Settlement House—sewing and dancing.

She learned to decode paper patterns and to run a sewing machine. In time she hoped to be able to make her own clothes.

She learned "ballroom" dancing, although neither she nor her partners ever expected to set foot in something called a ballroom. Sometimes her partner was one of the brilliantine-haired neighbourhood sheiks, who was a snappy dancer and made her watch her steps. Sometimes he was a little old boy of fourteen in knee-breeches and she made him watch his steps. She loved dancing and took to it instinctively.

And that year began to draw to a close.

"What's that book you're studying, Francie?"

"That's Neeley's geometry book."

"What's geometry?"

"Something you have to pass to get into college, Mama."

"Well, don't sit up too late."

"What news do you bring me of my mother and sisters?" Katie asked the insurance collector.

"Well, for one thing I just insured your sister's babies, Sara and Stephen."

"But she's had them insured since birth—a nickel a week policy."

"This is a different policy. Endowment."

"What does that mean?"

"They don't have to die to collect. They get a thousand dollars each when they're eighteen. It's insurance to get them through college."

"Oh, my! First a doctor and hospital to give birth, then college insurance. What next?"

"Any mail, Mama?" asked Francie as usual when she came home from work.

"No. Just a card from Evy."

"What does she say?"

"Nothing. Except they've got to move again on account of Willie's drumming."

"Where're they moving now?"

"Evy found a one-family house in Cypress Hills. I wonder whether that's in Brooklyn?"

"It's out East New York way—where Brooklyn changes to Queens. It's around Crescent Street, the last stop on

roadway El. I mean it used to be the last stop until they
xtended the El to Jamaica."

Mary Rommely lay in her narrow white bed. A crucifix
ood out on the bare wall above her head. Her three daugh-
rs and Francie, her eldest grand-daughter, stood by her bed.
"Ai. I am eighty-five now and I feel that this is my last time
sickness. I wait for death with courage I gained from living.
will not speak falsely and say to you: 'Do not grieve for me
en I go.' I have loved my children and tried to be a good
other, and it is right that my children grieve for me. But let
ur grief be gentle and brief. And let resignation creep into
Know that I shall be happy. I shall see face to face the
at saints I have loved all my life."

Francie showed the snapshots to a group of girls in the
reation-room.
"This is Annie Laurie, my baby sister. She's only eighteen
nths old, but she runs all over the place. And you ought
hear her talk!"
'She's cute."
'This is my brother, Cornelius. He's going to be a doctor."
He's cute."
This is my mother."
She's cute. And so young-looking."
And this is me on the roof."
The roof's cute."
I'm cute," said Francie, with mock belligerence.
We're all cute." The girls laughed. "Our supervisor's cute—
old wagon. I hope she chokes."
hey laughed and laughed.
What are we all laughing at?" asked Francie.
Nothing." They laughed harder.

Send Francie. The last time I asked for sauerkraut he
ed me out of the store," complained Neeley.
You've got to ask for Liberty Cabbage now, you dope,"
Francie.
Don't call each other names," chided Katie absent-
ledly.
Did you know they changed Hamburg Avenue to Wilson
ue?" asked Francie.
War makes people do funny things," sighed Katie.

"You going to tell mama?" asked Neeley apprehensively.

"No. But you're too young to go out with that kind of girl. They say she's wild," said Francie.

"Who wants a tame girl?"

"I wouldn't care, only you don't know anything at a about—well—sex."

"I know more than you, anyhow." He put his hand on h hip and squealed in a lisping falsetto: "Oh, Mama! Will have a baby if a man just kisses me? Will I, Mama? Will I?"

"Neeley! You listened that day!"

"Sure! I was right outside the hall and heard every word

"Of all the low things...."

"You listen, too. Many's the time I caught you when mar and Sissy or Aunt Evy were talking and you were supposed be asleep in bed."

"That's different. I have to find out things."

"Check!"

"Francie! Francie! It's seven o'clock. Get up!"

"What for?"

"You've got to be at work at eight-thirty."

"Tell me something new, Mama."

"You're sixteen years old today."

"Tell me something new. I've been sixteen for two ye now."

"You'll have to be sixteen for another year, then."

"I'll probably be sixteen all my life."

"I wouldn't be surprised."

"I *wasn't* snooping," said Katie indignantly. "I needed a ther nickel for the gas-man and I thought you wouldn't c You look in *my* pocket-book for change many a time."

"That's different," said Francie.

Katie held a small violet box in her hand. There scented gold-tipped cigarettes in it. One was missing from full box.

"Well, now you know the worst," said Francie, "I smok *Milo* cigarette."

"They smell nice anyway," said Katie.

"Go ahead, mama. Give me the lecture and get it with."

"With so many soldiers dying in France and all, the wo

not going to fall apart if you smoke a cigarette once in a while."

"Gee, mama, you take all the fun out of things—like not objecting to my black lace trousers last year. Well, throw the cigarettes away."

"I'll do no such thing! I'll scatter them in my bureau drawer. They'll make my night-gowns smell nice."

"I was thinking," said Katie, "that instead of buying each other Christmas presents this year, that we put all the money together and buy a roasting chicken and a big cake from the bakery and a pound of good coffee and . . ."

"We have enough money for food," protested Francie. "We don't have to use our Christmas money."

"I mean to give to the Tynmore girls for Christmas. No one takes lessons from them now—people say they're behind the times. They don't have enough to eat, and Miss Lizzie's been so good to us."

"Well, all right," consented Francie, not very enthusiastically.

"Gee!" Neeley kicked the table leg viciously.

"Don't worry, Neeley," laughed Francie. "You'll get a present. "I'll buy you *fawn*-coloured spats this year."

"Aw, shut up!"

"Don't say 'shut up' to each other," chided Katie absentmindedly.

"I want to ask your advice, Mama. There was this boy I met summer school. He said he might write, but he never has. I want to know would it look forward if I sent him a Christmas card?"

"Forward? Nonsense! Send the card if you feel like it. I hate all those flirty-birty games that women make up. Life's too short. If you ever find a man you love, don't waste time hanging your head and simpering. Go right up to him and say: 'I love you. How about getting married?' That is," she added hastily, with an apprehensive look at her daughter, "when you're old enough to know your own mind."

"I'll send the card," decided Francie.

"Mama, we decided, Neeley and I, that we'd like coffee instead of milk punch."

"All right." Katie put the brandy bottle back in the cupboard.

"And make the coffee very strong and hot and fill the cups with half coffee and half hot milk and we'll toast 1918 in *cafe au lait*."

"*Si'l vous plait*," put in Neeley.

"Wee-wee-wee," said mama. "*I* know some French words too."

Katie held the coffee-pot in one hand and the saucepan of hot milk in the other and poured both into the cups simultaneously. "I remember," she said, "when there was no milk in the house. Your father would put a lump of butter in his coffee—if we had butter. He said that butter was cream in the first place and just as good in coffee."

Papa ... !

LII

ONE SUNNY day in the spring when Francie was sixteen, she walked out of the office at five o'clock and saw Anita, a girl who operated a machine in her row, standing in the doorway of the Communications Building with two soldiers. One, short, stubby, and beaming, held Anita's arm possessively. The other, tall and gangling, stood there awkwardly. Anita detached herself from the soldiers and drew Francie aside.

"Francie, you've *got* to help me out. Joey's on his last leave before his unit goes overseas and we're engaged."

"If you're engaged already you're doing all right and don't need anybody's help," said Francie jokingly.

"I mean help with that other fellow. Joey just *had* to bring him along, darn it. Seems like they're buddies and where one goes the other goes. This other fellow comes from some high town in Pennsylvania and doesn't know a soul in New York and I *know* he'll stick around and I'll never get to be alone with Joey. You've *got* to help me out, Francie. Three girls turned me down already."

Francie took a speculative look at the Pennsylvania fellow standing ten feet away. He didn't look like much. No wonder the other three girls refused to help out Anita. Then his eyes met hers and he smiled a slow, shy smile and somehow, when he wasn't good-looking, he was nicer than good-looking. The shy smile decided Francie.

"Look," she said to Anita, "if I can catch my brother where he works I'll give him a message for my mother. If he's left I'll have to go home because my mother will worry if I don't turn up for supper."

"Hurry up, then. Phone him," urged Anita. "Here!" She fished in her pocket-book. "I'll give you the nickel for the call."

Francie phoned from the corner cigar store. It just happened that Neeley was still at McGarrity's. She gave him the message. When she got back, she found that Anita and her Joey had gone. The soldier with the shy smile was all alone.

"Where's 'Nita?" she asked.

"I reckon she's run out on you. She went off with Joe."

Francie was dismayed. She had expected it to be a double date. What in the world was she to do with this tall stranger now?

"I don't blame them," he was saying, "wanting to be alone. I'm an engaged man myself. I know how it is. The last leave—the only girl."

"Engaged, then?" thought Francie. "At least he wouldn't try any romancing."

"But that's no reason why *you* should be stuck with me," he went on. "If you'll show me where to get the subway to Thirty-fourth Street—I'm a stranger in this city—I'll go back to the hotel room. A person can always write letters, I guess, when there's nothing else to do." He smiled his lonely, shy smile.

"I've already phoned my folks that I won't be home. So if you'd like...."

"*Like?* Gosh! This is my lucky day. Well, gee, thanks, Miss ..."

"Nolan. Frances Nolan."

"My name's Lee Rhynor. It's really Leo, but everybody says 'Lee.' I'm sure pleased to meet you, Miss Nolan." He held out his hand.

"And I'm pleased to meet you, Corporal Rhynor." They shook hands.

"Oh, you noticed the stripes." He smiled happily. "I suppose you're hungry after working all day. Any special place you'd like to go for supper ... I mean dinner?"

"*Supper's* okay. No. No special place. You?"

"I'd like to try some of this here chop suey I heard about."

"There's a nice place up around Forty-second Street. With

365

music."

"Let's go!"

On the way to the subway he said: "Miss Nolan, do you care if I call you Frances?"

"I don't care. Everyone calls me Francie, though."

"Francie!" He repeated the name. "Francie, another thing: Would you mind if I sort of made believe that you were my best girl—just for this evening?"

"Hm," thought Francie, "fast worker."

He took the thought out of her mind. "I guess you think I'm a fast worker, but it's this way: I haven't been out with a girl in nearly a year, and a few days from now I'll be on a boat heading for France, and after that I don't know what may be. So for these few hours—if you don't mind—I'd consider it a great favour."

"I don't mind."

"Thanks." He indicated his arm. "Hang on, best girl." As they were about to enter the subway, he paused. "Say 'Lee,' " he ordered.

"Lee," she said.

"Say: 'Hello, Lee. It's good to see you again, dear.' "

"Hello, Lee. It's so good to see you again..." she said shyly. He tightened his arm.

The waiter at Ruby's put two bowls of chop suey and a fat pot of tea between them.

"You pour out my tea so it's more home-like," said Lee.

"How much sugar?"

"I don't take sugar."

"Me either."

"Say! We have exactly the same tastes, don't we?" he said.

Both were very hungry and they stopped talking in order to concentrate on the slippery wet food. Every time Francie looked up at him he smiled. Every time he looked down at her she grinned happily. After the chop suey, rice, and tea were all gone, he leaned back and took out a packet of cigarettes.

"Smoke?"

She shook her head. "I tried it once and didn't seem to like it."

"Good. I don't like a girl who smokes."

Then he started to talk. He told her all that he could remember about himself. He told her of his boyhood in a small Pennsylvania town. (She remembered the town from

366

reading its weekly newspaper in the press clipping bureau.) He told her about his parents and his brother and sisters. He spoke of his school days—parties he had gone to—jobs he had worked at—he told her he was twenty-two—how he had come to enlist at twenty-one. He told her about his life at the army camp—how he got to be corporal. He told her every single thing about himself. Excepting the girl he was engaged to back home.

And Francie told him of her life. She told only of the happy things—how handsome papa had been—how wise mama was—what a swell brother Neeley was, and how cute her baby sister was. She told him about the brown bowl on the library desk—about the New Year's night she and Neeley had talked on the roof. She didn't mention Ben Blake because he never entered her thoughts. After she had finished, he said:

"All my life I've been so lonely. I've been lonely at crowded parties. I've been lonely in the middle of kissing a girl and I've been lonely at camp with hundreds of fellows around. But now I'm not lonely any more." He smiled his special slow, shy smile.

"That's the way it was with me too," confessed Francie, "except I've never kissed any boy. And now for the first time I'm not lonely either."

The waiter again replenished their almost filled waterglasses. Francie knew it was a hint that they had sat there too long. People were waiting for tables. She asked Lee the time. Almost ten o'clock! They had been talking for nearly four hours!

"I have to start for home," she said regretfully.

"I'll take you home. Do you live near the Brooklyn Bridge?"

"No. The Williamsburg."

"I hoped it was the Brooklyn Bridge. I thought that if I ever got to New York, I'd like to walk across the Brooklyn Bridge."

"Why not?" suggested Francie. "I can get a Graham Avenue trolley from the Brooklyn end that will take me right to my corner."

They took the I.R.T. Subway to Brooklyn Bridge, got out and started to walk across. Half way over they paused to look down on the East River. They stood close together and he held her hand. He looked up at the skyline on the Manhattan shore.

"New York! I've always wanted to see it, and now I've seen it. It's true what they say—it's the most wonderful city in the world."

"Brooklyn's better."

"It hasn't got skyscrapers like New York, has it?"

"No. But there's a *feeling* about it—Oh, I can't explain it. You've got to live in Brooklyn to know."

"We'll live in Brooklyn some day," he said quietly. And her heart skipped a beat.

She saw one of the cops who patrolled the Bridge coming towards them.

"We'd better move," she said uneasily. "The Brooklyn Navy Yard's right over there and that camouflaged boat anchored there is a transport. The cops are always watching out for spies."

As the cop came up to them Lee said: "We're not going to blow up anything. We're just looking at the East River."

"Sure, sure," said the cop. "Don't I know how it is on a fine May night? Wasn't I young meself once and not so long ago, as you might think?"

He smiled at them. Lee smiled back and Francie grinned at both of them. The cop glanced at Lee's sleeve.

"Well, so long, General," said the cop. "Give 'em hell when you get over there."

"I'll do that," promised Lee.

The cop went on his way.

"Nice guy," commented Lee.

"Everybody's nice," said Francie happily.

When they got to the Brooklyn side, she said that he was not to take her the rest of the way home. She had often gone home alone late at night when working on the night shift. she explained. He'd get lost if he tried to find his way back to New York from her neighbourhood. Brooklyn was tricky that way. You had to live there in order to find your way about, she said.

In truth, she didn't want him to see where she lived. She loved her neighbourhood and wasn't ashamed of it. But she felt that to a stranger who didn't know about it the way she did, it might seem a mean and shabby place,

First she showed him where to get the El that would return him to New York. Then they walked over to where she had to get the trolley. They passed a one-window tattoo shop. Inside sat a young sailor with his sleeve rolled up. The tattoo artist sat before him on a stool with his pan of inks near-by. He was pricking out an arrow-pierced heart on the sailor boy's arm. Francie and Lee stopped to stare in the window. The sailor waved at them with his free arm. They waved back. The artist looked up and made signs that they were welcome to enter. Francie frowned and shook her head: "No."

Walking away from the store, Lee said with wonder in his voice: "That fellow was actually getting tattooed! Gosh!"

"Don't you ever ever *ever* let me catch you getting tattooed," she said, with playful severity.

"No. Mother," he answered meekly, and they laughed.

They stood on the corner waiting for the trolley. An awkward silence came between them. They stood apart and he kept lighting cigarettes and discarding them before they were half smoked. Finally a trolley came in sight.

"Here comes my car," said Francie. She held out her right hand. "Good night, Lee."

He threw away the cigarette he had just lighted.

"Francie?" He held out his arms.

She went to him and he kissed her.

The next morning Francie dressed in her new navy blue faille suit with the white georgette crêpe blouse and her Sunday patent leather pumps. She and Lee had no date—had made no arrangements to meet again. But she knew he'd be waiting for her at five o'clock. Neeley got up from bed as she was about to leave. She asked him to tell mama she wouldn't be home for supper.

"Francie's got a feller at last! Francie's got a feller at last!" chanted Neeley.

He went to Laurie, who was sitting by the window in her high chair. There was a bowl of oatmeal on the chair's tray. The baby was busily engaged in spooning out the oatmeal and dumping it on the floor. Neeley chucked her under the chin. "Hey! Dopey! At last Francie's got a feller."

A faint line appeared on the inner edge of the child's right eyebrow (the Rommely line, Katie called it) as the two-year-old tried to understand.

"Fran-nee?" she said in a puzzled way.

"Listen, Neeley, I got her out of bed and gave her her oatmeal. It's your job to feed her now. And don't call her Dopey."

As she came out of the hallway on to the street, she heard

her name called. She looked up. Neeley was hanging out of the window in his pyjamas. He sang at the top of his voice:

> *There she goes*
> *On her toes,*
> *All dressed up*
> *In her Sunday clothes . . .*

"Neeley, you're terrible! Just terrible!" she called up to the window. He pretended not to understand.

"Did you say he was terrible? Did you say he had a big moustache and a baldy head?"

"You better go feed the baby," she hollered back.

"Did you say you were going to have a baby, Francie? Did you say you were going to have a baby?"

A man passing on the street winked at Francie. Two girls coming by arm-in-arm had a terrific fit of giggling.

"You damned kid!" screamed Francie in impotent fury.

"You cursed! I'm gonna tell mama, I'm gonna tell mama, I'm gonna tell mama you cursed," chanted Neeley.

She heard the trolley coming and had to run for it.

He was waiting for her when she got out to walk. He met her with that smile.

"Hello, my best girl." He tucked her arm within his.

"Hello, Lee. It's good to see you again."

". . . dear," he prompted.

"Dear," she added.

They ate at the Automat—another place she had wanted to see. Since smoking wasn't permitted there and Lee couldn't sit still for long without smoking, they didn't linger to talk after coffee and dessert. They decided to go dancing. They found a dime-a-dance place just on Broadway where service men were given half rates. He bought a strip of twenty tickets for a dollar and they started to dance.

They had gone but half-way round the floor when Francie discovered that his gangling awkwardness was extremely deceptive. He was a smooth and skilful dancer. They danced, holding each other closely. There was no need for conversation.

The orchestra was playing one of Francie's favourite songs "Some Sunday Morning."

> *Some Sunday morning,*
> *When the weather's fine.*

She hummed the chorus as the vocalist sang it.

> *Dressed up in gingham,*
> *What a bride I'll be.*

She felt Lee's arm tighten around her.

> *I know my girl friends,*
> *They're gonna envy me.*

Francie was so happy. Once more around the floor, then the vocalist sang the chorus once again, this time varying it slightly in honour of the soldiers present.

> *Dressed up in khaki,*
> *What a groom you'll be.*

Her arm tightened around his shoulders and she rested her cheek on his tunic. She had the same thought Katie had had seventeen years ago dancing with Johnny—that she'd willingly accept any sacrifice or hardship if she could only have this man near her for always. And like Katie, Francie gave no thought to the children who might have to help her work out the hardship and sacrifice.

A group of soldiers were leaving the hall. As was the custom, the orchestra cut off the song they were playing and went into "Till We Meet Again." Everyone stopped dancing and sang a farewell to the soldiers. Francie and Lee held hands and sang, even though neither was quite certain of the words.

> *...When the clouds roll by*
> *Then I'll come back to you.*
> *Then the skies will seem more blue ...*

There were cries of "Good-bye, soldier!" "Good luck, soldier!" "Till we meet again, soldier." Then the departing soldiers stood in a group and sang the song. Lee pulled Francie towards the door.

"We'll leave now," he said. "So that this moment will remain a perfect memory."

They walked down the stairs slowly, the song following them. As they reached the street, they waited until the song died away.

. . . pray each night for me,
Till we meet again.

"Let it be our song," he whispered, "and think of me every time you hear it."

As they walked, it started to rain and they had to run and find shelter in the doorway of a vacant store. They stood in the protected and dark doorway, held each other's hand and watched the rain falling.

"People always think that happiness is a far-away thing," thought Francie, "something complicated and hard to get. Yet, what little things can make it up; a place of shelter when it rains—a cup of strong hot coffee when you're blue; for a man, a cigarette for contentment; a book to read when you're alone—just to be with someone you love. Those things make happiness."

"I'm leaving early in the morning."

"Not for France?" Suddenly she was jolted out of her happiness.

"No, for home. My mother wants me for a day or two before . . ."

"Oh!"

"I love you, Francie."

"But you're engaged. That's the first thing you ever told me."

"Engaged," he said bitterly. "Everybody's engaged. Everybody in a small town is engaged or married or in trouble. There's nothing else to do in a small town.

"You go to school. You start walking home with a girl— maybe for no other reason than that she lives out your way. You grow up. She invites you to parties at her home. You go to other parties—people ask you to bring her along; you're expected to take her home. Soon no one else takes her out. Everybody thinks she's your girl and then . . . well, if you don't take her around, you feel like a heel. And then, because there's nothing else to do, you marry, and it works out all right if she's a decent girl (and most of the time she is) and you're a half-way decent fellow. No great passion, but a kind of affectionate contentment. And then children come along and you give them the great love you kind of miss in each other. And the children gain in the long run.

"Yes, I'm engaged all right. But it isn't the same between her and me as it is between you and me."

"But you're going to marry her?"

He waited a long time before he answered.

"No."

She was happy again.

"Say it, Francie," he whispered. "Say it."

She said: "I love you, Lee."

"Francie..." there was urgency in his voice, "I may not come back from over there and I'm afraid...afraid. I might die...die, never having had anything...never...Francie, *can't* we be together for a little while?"

"We are together," said Francie innocently.

"I mean in a room...alone...Just till morning when I leave?"

"I...couldn't."

"Don't you *want* to?"

"Yes," she answered honestly.

"Then why..."

"I'm only sixteen," she confessed bravely. "I've never been with...anybody. I wouldn't know how."

"That makes no difference."

"And I've never been away from home overnight. My mother would worry."

"You could tell her you spent the night with a girl friend."

"She knows I have no girl friend."

"You could think of some excuse...tomorrow."

"I wouldn't need to think of an excuse. I'd tell her the truth."

"You *would*?" he asked in astonishment.

"I love you. I wouldn't be ashamed...afterwards if I stayed with you. I'd be proud and happy and I wouldn't want to lie about it."

"I had no way of knowing, no way of knowing," he whispered, as if to himself.

"*You* wouldn't want it to be something...sneaky, would you?"

"Francie, forgive me. I shouldn't have asked. I had no way of knowing."

"Knowing?" asked Francie, puzzled.

He put his arms around her and held her tightly. She saw that he was crying.

"Francie, I'm afraid...so afraid. I'm afraid that if I go away I'll lose you...never see you again. Tell me not to go home and I'll stay. We'll have tomorrow and the next day.

We'll eat together and walk around or sit in a park or ride on top of a bus and just talk and be with each other. Tell me not to go."

"I guess you have to go. I guess that it's right that you see your mother once more before.... I don't know. But I guess it's right."

"Francie, will you marry me when the war's over—*if* I come back?"

"*When* you come back, I'll marry you."

"Will you, Francie? ... please, will you?"

"Yes."

"Say it again."

"I'll marry you when you come back, Lee."

"And, Francie, we'll live in Brooklyn."

"We'll live wherever you want to live."

"We'll live in Brooklyn, then."

"Only if *you* want to, Lee."

"And will you write to me every day? *Every* day?"

"Every day," she promised.

"And will you write to me tonight when you get home and tell me how much you love me, so that the letter will be waiting for me when I get home?" She promised. "Will you promise never to let anyone kiss you? Never to go out with anyone? To wait for me ... no matter how long? And if I don't come back, never to *want* to marry anyone else?"

She promised.

And he asked for her whole life as simply as he'd ask for a date. And she promised away her whole life as simply as she'd offer a hand in greeting or farewell.

It stopped raining after a while and the stars came out.

LIII

SHE WROTE that night as she had promised—a long letter in which she poured out all her love and repeated the promises she had given.

She left a little earlier for work to have time to post the letter from the Thirty-fourth Street post office. The clerk at the window assured her that it would reach its destination tha' afternoon. That was Wednesday.

She looked for but tried not to expect a letter Thursday night. There hadn't been time—unless he, too, wrote immediately after they had parted. But, of course, he had to pack maybe—get up early to make his train. (It had never occurred to her that *she* had managed to find time.) There was no letter Thursday night.

Friday, she had to work straight through—a sixteen-hour shift—because the company was short-handed on account of an influenza epidemic. When she got home a little before two in the morning, there was a letter propped against the sugar bowl on the kitchen table. She ripped it open eagerly.

"Dear Miss Nolan:"

Her happiness died. It couldn't be from Lee because he'd write, "Dear Francie." She turned the page and looked at the signature. "Elizabeth Rhynor (Mrs.)." Oh! His mother. Or a sister-in-law. Maybe he was sick and couldn't write. Maybe there was an army rule that men about to go overseas couldn't write letters. He had asked someone to write for him. Of course. That was it. She started to read the letter.

"Lee told me all about you. I want to thank you for being so nice and friendly to him while he was in New York. He arrived home Wednesday afternoon, but had to leave for camp the next night. He was home only a day and a half. We had a very quiet wedding, just the families and a few friends . . ."

Francie put the letter down. "I've been working sixteen hours in a row," she thought, "and I'm tired. I've read thousands of messages today and no words make sense right now. Anyhow, I got into bad reading habits at the Bureau—reading a column at a glance and seeing only one word in it. First I'll wash the sleep out of my eyes, have some coffee, and read the letter again. This time I'll read it right."

While the coffee heated, she splashed cold water on her face, thinking that when she came to the part of the letter that said 'wedding" she'd go on reading and the next words would be: 'Lee was best man. I married his brother you know."

Katie, lying awake in her bed, heard Francie moving about in the kitchen. She lay tense . . . waiting. And she wondered what it was she waited for.

Francie read the letter again.

". . . wedding, just the families and a few friends. Lee asked me to write and explain why he hadn't answered your letter. Again thank you for entertaining him so nicely while he was in your city. Yours truly, Elizabeth Rhynor (Mrs.)."

There was a postscript.

"I read the letter you sent Lee. It was mean of him to pretend to be in love with you and I told him so. He said to tell you he's dreadfully sorry. E.R."

Francie was trembling violently. Her teeth made little biting sounds.

"Mama," she moaned. "*Mama!*"

Katie heard the story. "It's come at last," she thought, "the time when you can no longer stand between your children and heartache. When there wasn't enough food in the house you pretended that you weren't hungry so they could have more. In the cold of a winter's night you got up and put your blanket on their bed so they wouldn't be cold. You'd kill anyone who tried to harm them—I tried my best to kill that man in the hallway. Then one sunny day they walk out in all innocence and they walk right into the grief that you'd give your life to spare them."

Francie gave her the letter. She read it slowly and as she read, she thought she knew how it was. Here was a man of twenty-two who evidently (to use one of Sissy's phrases) had been around. Here was a girl sixteen years old; six years younger than he. A girl in spite of bright-red lipstick and grown-up clothes and a lot of knowledge picked up here and there—who was yet tremulously innocent; a girl who had come face to face with some of the evil of the world and most of its hardships, and yet had remained curiously untouched by the world. Yes, she could understand her appeal for him.

Well, what could she say? That he was no good or, at best, just a weak-man who was easily susceptible to whoever he was with? No, she couldn't be so cruel as to say that. Besides, the girl wouldn't believe her anyhow.

"Say something," demanded Francie. "Why don't you say something?"

"What can I say?"

"Say that I'm young—that I'll get over it. Go ahead and say it. Go ahead and lie."

"I know that's what people say—you'll get over it. I'd say it

376

too. But I know it's not true. Oh, you'll be happy again, never fear. But you won't forget. Every time you fall in love it will be because something in the man reminds you of *him*."

"Mother. . . ."

Mother! Katie remembered. She had called her own mother "mama" until the day she had told her that she was going to marry Johnny. She had said: "Mother, I'm going to marry . . ." She had never said "mama" after that. She had finished growing up when she stopped calling her mother "mama." Now Francie . . .

"Mother, he asked me to be with him for the night. Should I have gone?"

Katie's mind darted around looking for words.

"Don't make up a lie, Mother. Tell me the truth."

Katie couldn't find the right words.

"I promise you that I'll never go with a man without being married first—if I ever marry. And if I feel that I must—without being married, I'll tell you first. That's a solemn promise. So you can tell me the truth without worrying that I'll go wrong if I know it."

"There are two truths," said Katie finally.

"As a mother, I say it would have been a terrible thing for a girl to sleep with a stranger—a man she had known less than forty-eight hours. Horrible things might have happened to you. Your whole life might have been ruined. As your mother, I tell you the truth.

"But as a woman . . ." she hesitated. "I will tell you the truth as a woman. It would have been a very beautiful thing. Because there is only once that you love that way."

Francie thought: "I should have gone with him then. I'll never love anyone as much again. I wanted to go and I didn't and now I don't want him that way any more because *she* owns him now. But I wanted to and I didn't and now it's too late." She put her head down on the table and wept.

After a while Katie said: "I got a letter, too."

Her letter had come several days ago, but she had been waiting for the right time to mention it. She decided that this was a good time.

"I got a letter," she repeated.

"Who . . . who wrote?" sobbed Francie.

"Mr. McShane."

Francie sobbed louder.

"Aren't you interested?"

Francie tried to stop crying. "All right. What does he say?" she asked listlessly.

"Nothing. Except he's coming to see us next week." She waited. Francie showed no further sign of interest. "How would you like Mr. McShane for a father?"

Francie's head jerked up. "Mother! A man writes that he's coming to the house. Right away you think things. What makes you think you know everything all the time?"

"I don't *know*. I don't know anything, really. I just *feel*. And when the *feeling* is strong enough, then I just *say* I know. But I don't. Well, how would you like him as a father?"

"After the botch I've made of my own life," said Francie bitterly (and Katie didn't smile), "I'm the last person to hand out advice."

"I'm not asking for your advice. Only I'd know better what to do if I knew how my children felt about him."

Francie suspected that her mother's talking about McShane was a trick to divert her thoughts, and she was angry because the trick had almost worked.

"I don't know, Mother. I don't know anything. And I don't want to talk about anything any more. Please go away. Please go away and let me alone."

Katie went back to bed.

Well, a person can cry only so long. Then he has to do something else with his time. It was five o'clock. Francie decided it was no use going to bed; she'd have to get up again at seven. She discovered that she was very hungry. She had nothing to eat since noon the day before, except a sandwich between the day and night shift. She made a pot of fresh coffee, some toast, and scrambled a couple of eggs. She was astonished at how good everything tasted. But while she was eating, her eyes went to the letter and the tears came again. She put the letter in the sink and set a match to it. Then she turned on the tap and watched the black ashes go down the drain. She resumed her breakfast.

Afterwards she got her box of writing paper from the cupboard and sat down to write a letter. She wrote:

Dear Ben: You said I was to write if ever I needed you. So I'm writing....

She tore the sheet in half.

"No! I don't want to need anybody. I want someone to
ed me . . . *I want someone to need me*."
She wept again, but not so hard this time.

LIV

was the first time Francie had seen McShane without his
iform. She decided that he looked very impressive in his
ensively-tailored double-breasted grey suit. Of course, he
sn't as good-looking as papa had been; he was taller and
re massive. But he was handsome in his own way, decided
ncie, even though his hair was grey. But gosh he was awful
for mother. True, mother wasn't so young either. She was
ng on thirty-five. Still, that was much younger than fifty.
yhow, no woman need be ashamed to have McShane for a
band. While he looked exactly what he was, a shrewd poli-
an, his voice was gentle when he spoke.

hey were having coffee and cake. With a pang, Francie
iced that McShane was sitting in her father's place at the
le. Katie had just finished telling him all that had hap-
ed since Johnny died. McShane seemed amazed at the
gress they had made. He looked at Francie.

So this slip of a girl got herself to college last summer!"

And she's going again this summer," announced Katie
dly.

There's wonderful for you."

And she works, in the bargain, and earns twenty dollars
ek now."

All that and good health, too?" he asked in honest amaze-
t.

The boy is half-way through high school."

No!"

And he works at this and that afternoons and evenings.
etimes he earns as much as five dollars a week outside of
ol."

A fine lad. One of the finest of lads. And look at the health
im—would you now."

ancie wondered why he commented so much on the
h, which they themselves always took for granted. Then
emembered about his own children; how most of them

had been born but to sicken and die before they grew up. N
wonder he thought healthiness such a remarkable thing.

"And the baby?" he inquired.

"Go get her, Francie," said Katie.

The baby was in her crib in the front room. It was suppos
to be Francie's room, but all had agreed that the baby need
to sleep where there was air. Francie picked up the sleepi
child. She opened her eyes and instantly was ready for an
thing.

"Bye-bye, Fran-nee? Park? Park?" she said.

"No, sweet. Just an introduction to a man."

"Man?" said Laurie doubtfully.

"Yes. A great big man."

"Big man!" repeated the child happily.

Francie brought her out to the kitchen. The baby was tr
a beautiful thing to see. She had a fresh dewy look in her p
flannel nightgown. Her hair was a mass of soft black cu
Her widely-set-apart dark eyes were luminous and there wa
dusky rose colour in her cheeks.

"Ah, the baby, the baby," crooned McShane. " 'Tis a r
she is. A wild rose."

"If papa were here," thought Francie, "he'd start to s
'My Wild Irish Rose.' " She heard her mother sigh and w
dered whether she, too, was thinking. . . .

McShane took the baby. The child sat on his knees, stiffe
her back away from him and stared at him doubtfully. K
hoped she wouldn't cry.

"Laurie!" she said. "Mr. McShane. Say Mr. McShan

The child lowered her head, looked up through her las
smiled knowingly and shook her head, "no."

"No may-mane," she stated. "Man?" she shouted tri
phantly. "Big man!" She smiled at McShane and said wh
lingly. "Take Laurie bye-bye? Park? Park?" Then she re
her cheek against his coat and closed her eyes.

"*Aroon, aroon*," McShane crooned.

The child slept in his arms.

"Mrs. Nolan, you're wonderin' why I came tonight.
your wonderin' be over. I came to ask a personal questi
Francie and Neeley got up to leave. "No. Don't be le
chilthern. The question would be concernin' you as we
your mother." They sat down again. He cleared his th
"Mrs. Nolan, time has passed since your husband—Go

is soul. . . ."

"Yes. Two and a half years. God rest his soul."

"God rest his soul," echoed Francie and Neeley.

"And my wife—'tis a year since she's been gone. God rest er soul."

"God rest her soul," echoed the Nolans.

"I have been waitin' many years and now the time has come hen 'tis no longer disrespect to the dead to speak out.

"Katherine Nolan, I'm askin' to keep company with you. bject, a weddin' in the autumn."

Katie looked quickly at Francie and frowned. What was the atter with mother anyhow? Francie wasn't even *thinking* of ughing.

"I am in a position to take care of you and the three ilthern. With my pension and salary and income from real ate in Woodhaven and Richmond Hill, I have over ten ousand dollars a year. I have insurance, too. I offer to put e boy and girl through college and I promise to be a faithful sband in the future as I was in the past."

"Have you thought this over, Mr. McShane?"

"I don't need to be thinkin'. Sure didn't I make up me mind e years ago when I saw you first at the Mahony Outin'? vas then I asked the girl if it was her mother you were."

"I am a scrub-woman without education." She stated it as a t, not an apology.

"Education! And sure, who was it taught *me* to read and te? Nobody but meself."

"But a man like you—in public life—needs a wife who ws social business—who can entertain his influential ness friends. I'm not that kind of a woman."

"My office is where I do my business entertainin'. My home here I live. Now I'm not meanin' you wouldn't be a credit ne—you'd be a credit to a better man: But I'm needin' no nan to help me out in my business. I can handle that elf, thank you. Need I be sayin' I love you . . ." he tated before calling her by her first name, ". . . Katherine? it is time you want to think it over?"

"No. I don't need time to think it over. I will marry you, McShane.

"Not for your income. Although I'm not overlooking that. thousand a year's a lot of money. But so is one thousand eople like us. We've had little money and are well trained bing without it. It's not for sending the children to college.

Your help will make it so easy. But without help at all, I kno'
we'd manage some way. It's not for your grand public pos
tion, although it'll be fine to have a husband to be proud o

"I will marry you because you are a good man and I'd li
to have you for my husband."

It was true. Katie had made up her mind to marry him—
he asked her—simply because life was incomplete without
man to love her. It had nothing to do with her love f
Johnny. She'd always love him. Her feeling for McShane w
quieter. She admired and respected him and she knew she'd
a good wife to him.

"Thank you, Katherine. Sure it's little enough I'm givin'
exchange for a pretty young wife and three healthy chilthern
he said in sincere humility.

He turned to Francie. "As the eldest, do you be approvin'

Francie looked at her mother, who seemed to be waiting
her to speak. She looked at her brother. He nodded.

"I think my brother and I would like to have you for a .
Tears came into her eyes as she thought of her father and
couldn't say the next word.

"Now, now," said McShane soothingly, "I'll not have y
worryin'." He turned to Katie.

"I'm not askin' that the two oldest call me 'father.' T
had a father and he as fine a lad as God ever made—the w
he was always singin'."

Francie felt her throat tightening.

"And I won't be askin' that they take my name—No
bein' the fine name it is.

"But this little one I'm holdin'—the one who never loo'
on a father's face: Would you be lettin' her call me fat
and lettin' me legally adopt her and give her the name t
you and I will be carryin' together?"

Katie looked at Francie and Neeley. How would they t
it—their sister called McShane instead of Nolan? Fra
nodded approval. Neeley nodded approval.

"We will give you the child," said Katie.

"We can't call you 'father,'" said Neeley suddenly. "
we'll call you 'dad,' maybe."

"I'm thankin' you," said McShane simply. He relaxed
smiled at them. "Now I'm wonderin' if I could smoke
pipe?"

"Why, you could have smoked any time without aski'
said Katie in surprise.

"I didn't want to be takin' privileges before I was entitled to hem," he explained.

Francie took the sleeping baby from him in order to let him moke.

"Help me put her to bed, Neeley."

"Why?" Neeley was thoroughly enjoying himself and didn't vant to leave.

"To fix the blankets in the crib. Somebody's got to do it hile I hold her." Didn't Neeley know *anything*? Didn't he now that maybe McShane and mother wanted to be alone r a minute, at least?

In the darkness of the front room, Francie whispered to her rother. "What do you think of it?"

"It's sure a good break for mama. Of course, he isn't pa...."

"No. No one will ever be ... papa. But apart from that, he's nice man, though."

"Laurie's going to have a mighty easy life all right."

"Annie Laurie McShane She'll never have the hard time had, will she?"

"No. And she'll never have the fun we had, either."

"Gosh! We *did* have fun, didn't we, Neeley?"

"Yeah!"

"Poor Laurie," said Francie pityingly.

BOOK FIVE

LV

FRANCIE JUMPED as someone tapped her on the shoulder. The
she relaxed and smiled. Of course! It was one o'clock in th
morning, she was through, and her "relief" had come to tak
over the machine.

"Let me send just one more," begged Francie.

"The way some people like their jobs!" smiled the "relief
Francie typed her last message slowly and lovingly. She w
glad it was a birth announcement rather than a notification
a death. The message was her farewell. She hadn't told anyo
she was leaving. She was afraid she'd break down and cry
she went around saying good-bye. Like her mother, she w
afraid of being openly sentimental.

Instead of going directly to her locker, she stopped off in t
big recreation room, where some girls were making the m
of their fifteen-minute rest period. They were grouped arou
a girl at the piano and were singing, "Hello, Central, Give
No Man's Land."

As Francie walked in, the pianist drifted into another so
inspired by Francie's new grey autumn suit and her grey sue
pumps. The girls sang: "There's a Quaker Down in Qua
Town." A girl put her arm around Francie and drew her i
the circle. Francie sang with them.

> *Down in her heart I know, she's not so slow . . .*

"Francie, where'd you ever get the idea for an all-g
outfit?"

"Oh, I don't know—some actress I saw when I was a
Don't remember her name, but the show was *The Minist*
Sweetheart.

"It's *cute!*"

> *She has that "meet me later" look . . .*
> *My little Quaker down in Quaker town.*

Do-o-o-own To-o-o-o-own, harmonized the girls in a gr
finale.

Next they sang: "You'll Find Old Dixieland in France."
Francie went over to stand at the great window from which
she could see the East River twenty storeys below. It was the
last time she'd see the river from that window. The last time of
anything has the poignancy of death itself. This that I see now,
she thought, to see no more this way. Oh, the last time how
early you see everything; as though a magnifying light had
been turned on it. And you grieve because you hadn't held it
dearer when you had it every day.

What had Granma Mary Rommely said? "To look at
everything always as though you were seeing it either for the
first or last time: Thus is your time on earth filled with glory."
Granma Mary Rommely!

She had lingered on for months in her last illness. But a time
had come when Steve came just before dawn to tell them.
"I'll miss her," he said. "She was a great lady."

"You mean a great woman," said Katie.

Why, puzzled Francie, had Uncle Willie chosen that time
to leave his family? She watched a boat glide under the Bridge
before she resumed her thoughts. Was it that one less Rommely woman to be accountable to made him feel more free?
Had her death given him the idea that there was such a thing
as escape? Or was it (as Evy claimed) that he was able, in his
drunkenness, to take advantage of the confusion created by
Granma's funeral to run away from his family? Whatever it
was, Willie was gone.

Willie Flittman!

He had practised desperately, until he got so that he could
play all the instruments at once. Then as a one-man band he
competed with others at a movie house on amateur night. He
won the first prize of ten dollars.

He never came home with the prize money and his instruments, and no one in the family had seen him since.

They heard about him now and then. It seemed that he was
playing the streets of Brooklyn as a one-man band and living
on the pennies he collected. Evy said he'd be home again when
the snow started to fly, but Francie, for one, doubted it.

Evy got a job in the factory where he had worked. She
earned thirty dollars a week and got along fine, except at
night, when, like all Rommely women, she found it hard to get
along without a man.

*   *   *

Francie, standing at the window overlooking the rive recalled how always there had been something dream-lik about Uncle Willie. But then, so many things seemed lik dreams to her. That man in the hallway that day: Surely th had been a dream! The way McShane had been waiting f mother all those years—a dream. Papa dead. For a long tim that had been a dream, but now papa was like someone wh had never been. The way Laurie seemed to come out of dream—born the living child of a father five months dea Brooklyn was a dream. All the things that happened there ju *couldn't happen*. It was all dream stuff. Or was it all real a true and was it that she, Francie, was the dreamer?

Well, she'd find out when she got out to Michigan. If th were that same dream feeling about Michigan, then Fran would know that she was the one dreaming.

Ann Arbor!

The university of Michigan was there. And in two m days she would be on a train heading for Ann Arbor. Sumr school was over. She had passed the four subjects she h elected. Crammed by Ben, she had passed the regents' coll entrance examinations, too. That meant that she, sixteen an half years old, could now enter college with half a ye freshman credits behind her.

She had wanted to go to Columbia in New York or Ade in Brooklyn, but Ben said that part of education was adap oneself to a new environment. Her mother and McShane agreed. Even Neeley said it would be a good thing for he go far off to college—she might get rid of her Brooklyn ac that way. But Francie didn't want to get rid of it any n than she wanted to get rid of her name. It meant that *belonged* some place. She was a Brooklyn girl with a Broo' name and a Brooklyn accent. She didn't want to change in bit of this and a bit of that.

Ben had chosen Michigan for her. He said it was a lit state college, had a good English department and low tui Francie wondered, if it was so good, why he hadn't mat lated there instead of at the university of another mid-we state. He explained that eventually he would practice in state, enter into its politics and he might as well be classn with its prominent citizens of the future.

Ben was twenty now. He was in the Reserve Officers' T ing Corps of his college and he looked very handsome i uniform.

Ben!

She looked at the ring on the third finger of her left hand. en's high school ring. "M.H.S. 1918." Inside was engraved: B.B. to F.N." He had told her that while he knew *his* mind, e was too young to know *hers*. He gave her the ring to bind hat he called their understanding. Of course, it would be five ore years before he'd be in a position to marry, he said. By at time she'd be old enough to know her own mind. Then, if ere were still the understanding, he'd ask her to accept other kind of ring. Since Francie had five years in which to ake up her mind, the responsibility of deciding whether or t to marry Ben did not weigh too heavily upon her.

Amazing Ben!

He had graduated from high school in January, 1918, had tered college immediately, taken a staggering number of urses and had come back to summer school in Brooklyn to e more work, and—as he confessed at the end of the sion—to be with Francie again. Now, in September, 1918, was returning to college to start his junior year!

Good old Ben!

Decent, honourable, and brilliant. *He* knew his own mind. 'd never ask one girl to marry him and the next day go off l marry another girl. *He'd* never ask her to write out her e and then let someone else read the letter. Not Ben . . . not . Yes, Ben was wonderful. She was proud to have him for riend. But she thought of Lee.

ee!

Where was Lee now?

He had sailed away to France on a transport just like the she now saw slipping out of the harbour—a long boat its swirls of camouflage and the silent white faces of its usand soldier passengers, looking from where she stood, so many white-headed pins in a long awkward pin ion.

Francie, I'm afraid . . . so afraid. I'm afraid that if I go y I'll lose you . . . never see you again. Tell me not to ..")

I guess that it's right that you see your mother once more re . . . I don't know. . . .")

e was with the Rainbow Division—the Division even now ing into the Argonne Woods. Was he even now lying dead ance under a plain white cross? Who would tell her if he ? Not the woman in Pennsylvania.

"(Elizabeth Rhynor [Mrs.]")

Anita had left months ago to work somewhere else and ha
left no address. No one to ask . . . not one to tell her.

Fiercely she wished he were dead, so that the woman .
Pennsylvania could never have him. In the next breath sl
prayed: "Oh God, don't let him be killed and I won't cor
plain no matter who has him. Please . . . Please!"

Oh time . . . time, pass so that I forget!

("You'll be happy again, never fear. But you won't forget.

Mother was wrong. She *had* to be wrong. Francie wanted
forget. It was four months since she had known him, but s
couldn't forget. ("Happy again . . . but you'll never forget
How could she be happy again if she couldn't forget?

Oh Time, Great Healer, pass over me and let me forg

("Every time you fall in love it will be because something
the man reminds you of *him*.")

Ben had the same slow smile. But she had thought she was
love with Ben last year—long before she had seen Lee. So th
didn't work out.

Lee, Lee!

The recreation period was over and a new bunch of g
came in. It was their recreation period now. They floc
around the piano and started on a sequence of "Smile" son
Francie knew what would come.

Run, run, you fool, before the waves of hurt start breaki
But she couldn't move.

They did Ted Lewis' song: "For When My Baby Smiles
Me." From that it was inevitable that they go into, "There /
Smiles That Make You Happy."

And then it came.

> *Smile the while*
> *You kiss me sad adieu . . .*

(". . . think of me every time you hear it. Think of me. .

She ran out of the room. She snatched her grey hat and
new grey purse and gloves from her locker. She ran for
elevator.

She looked up and down the canyon-like street. It was c
and deserted. A tall man in uniform stood in the shado
doorway of the next building. He walked out of the dark
came towards her with a shy lonely smile.

She closed her eyes. Granma had said that the Romn

388

women had the power of seeing the ghosts of their beloved
dead. Francie had never believed it, because she had never
seen papa. But now...now...

"Hello, Francie."

She opened her eyes. No, he wasn't a ghost.

"I had an idea that you'd feel blue—your last night on the
job—so I came to take you home. Surprised?"

"No. I thought you'd come," she said.

"Hungry?"

"Starved!"

"Where do you want to go? Want to get some coffee at the
Automat or would you like chop suey?"

"No! *No!*"

"Child's?"

"Yes. Let's go to Child's and have butter-cakes and coffee."

He took her hand and drew her arm through his.

"Francie, you seem so strange tonight. You're not mad at
me, are you?"

"No."

"Glad I came?"

"Yes," she said quietly. "It's good to see you, Ben."

LVI

SATURDAY! THE last Saturday in their old home. The next day
was Katie's wedding day and they were going straight to their
new home from the church. The movers were coming Monday
morning for their stuff. They were leaving most of their
furniture for the new janitress. They were taking only their
personal belongings and the front-room furniture. Francie
wanted the green carpet with the big pink roses, the cream-
coloured lace curtains and the lovely little piano. These things
were to be installed in the room set aside for Francie in their
new home.

Katie insisted on working as usual that last Saturday morning. They laughed when mother set out with her broom and
pail. McShane had given her a banking account with a thousand dollars in it as a wedding present. According to Nolan
standards, Katie was rich now and didn't have to do another
lick of work. Yet, she insisted on working that last day.

389

Francie suspected that she had a sentimental feeling about the houses and wanted to give them a last good cleaning before she left.

Shamelessly, Francie searched for the cheque book in her mother's purse and examined the only stub in the fabulous folder.

No: *1*
Date: *9-20-18*
To: *Eva Flittman*
For: *Because she's my sister*
Total: *1000.00*
Amt this cque: *200.00*
Bal fwd: *800.00*

Francie wondered why that amount? Why not fifty dollars or five hundred? Why two hundred? Then she understood. Two hundred was the amount Uncle Willie was insured for; what Evy would have collected had he died. No doubt Katie considered Willie as good as dead.

No cheque had been made out for Katie's wedding dress. She explained that she didn't want to use any of that money for herself until after she had married the giver. In order to buy the dress, she had borrowed the money she had saved for Francie, promising to give her a cheque for it as soon as the ceremony was over.

On that last Saturday morning Francie strapped Laurie into her two-wheeled sulky and took her down on the street. She stood on the corner for a long time watching the kids lug their junk up Manhattan Avenue to Carney's junk shop. Then she walked up that way and went into Cheap Charlie's during a lull in business. She put a fifty-cent piece down on the counter and announced that she wanted to take all the picks.

"Aw, now, Francie! *Gee*, Francie," he said.

"I don't have to bother picking. Just give me all the stuff on the board."

"Aw, *lissen*"

"Then there aren't any prize numbers in that box, are there Charlie?"

"Christ, Francie, a feller is got to make a living and it come slow in this business—a penny at a time."

"I always thought those prizes were fake. You ought to be ashamed—fooling little kids that way."

"Don't say that, I give them a penny's worth of candy for each cent they spend there. The pick is just so's it's more interesting."

"And it makes them keep coming back—hoping."

"If they don't go here, they go across to Gimpy's, see? And it's better they come here, because I'm a married man," he said virtuously, "and I don't take girls in my back room, see?"

"Oh, well. I guess there's something in what you say. Look! Have you got a fifty-cent doll?"

He dredged up an ugly-faced doll from under the counter. "I only got a sixty-nine-cent doll, but I'll let you have it for fifty cents."

"I'll pay for it if you'll hang it up as a prize and let some kid win it."

"But look, Francie: A kid wins it. *All* the kids expect to win then see? It's a bad example."

"Oh, for sweet Christ's sake," she said, not profanely but prayerfully, "let somebody win something just *once*!"

"All right All right! Don't get excited now."

"I just want one little kid to get something for nothing."

"I'll put it up and I won't take the number out of the box, either, after you go. Satisfied?"

"Thanks, Charlie."

"And I'll tell the winner the doll's name's Francie, see?"

"Oh no, you don't! Not with the face that doll's got."

"You know what, Francie?"

"What?"

"You're getting to be quite a girl. How old are you now?"

"I'll be seventeen in a couple of months."

"I remember you used to be a skinny long-legged kid. Well, I think you'll make a nice-looking woman some day—not pretty, but something."

"Thanks for nothing." She laughed.

"Your kid sister?" he nodded at Laurie.

"Uh-huh."

"First thing you know she'll be lugging junk and coming in here with her pennies. One day they're babies in buggies and the next day they're in here taking picks. Kids grow up quick in this neighbourhood."

"*She'll* never lug junk. And she'll never come in here, either."

"That's right. I hear you're moving away."

"Yes, we're moving away."

"Well, the best of luck, Francie."

She took Laurie to the park, lifted her out of the sulky and let her run around on the grass. A boy came by selling pretzels and Francie bought one for a penny. She crumbled it into bits and scattered it on the grass. A flock of sooty sparrows appeared from nowhere and squabbled over the bits. Laurie stumbled about trying to catch them. The bored birds let her get within inches of them before they lifted their wings and took off. The child screamed with delighted laughter each time a bird flew away.

Pulling Laurie along in the sulky, Francie went over for a last look at her old school. It was but a couple of blocks from the park which she visited every day, but for some reason or other, Francie had never gone back to see it since the night she graduated.

She was surprised at how tiny it seemed now. She supposed the school was just as big as it had ever been, only her eye had grown used to looking at bigger things.

"There's the school that Francie went to," she told Laurie.

"Fran-nee went to school," agreed Laurie.

"Your papa came with me one day and sang a song."

"Papa?" asked Laurie, puzzled.

"I forgot. You never saw your papa."

"Laurie saw papa. Man. *Big* man." She thought Francie meant McShane.

"*That's* right," agreed Francie.

In the two years since she had last looked on the school, Francie had changed from a child to a woman.

She went home past the house whose address she had claimed. It looked little and shabby to her now, but she still loved it.

She passed McGarrity's saloon. Only McGarrity didn't own it any more. He had moved away early in the summer. He had confided in Neeley that he, McGarrity, was a man who had his ear to the ground and was therefore in a position to hear prohibition coming. He was getting all set for it, too. He bought a large place on the Hempstead Turnpike out on Long Island and was systematically stocking its cellars with liquor against the day. As soon as prohibition came, he was going to open up what he called a Club. He had the name picked out: The Club Mae-Marie. His wife was going to wear an evening dress and be a hostess, which was right up her alley, McGarrity explained. Francie was sure that Mrs. McGarrity would be very happy as a hostess. She hoped that Mr. McGarrity would be happy some day, too.

After lunch she went around to the library to turn in her books for the last time. The librarian stamped her card and shoved it back to her without, as was usual, looking up.

"Could you recommend a good book for a girl?" asked Francie.

"How old?"

"She is eleven."

The librarian brought up a book from under the desk. Francie saw the title: *If I Were King*.

"I don't really want to take it out," said Francie, "and I'm not eleven years old."

The librarian looked up at Francie for the first time.

"I've been coming here since I was a little girl," said Francie, "and you never looked at me till now."

"There are so many children," said the librarian fretfully. "I can't be looking at each one of them. Anything else?"

"I just want to say about the brown bowl ... what it has meant to me ... the flower always in it."

The librarian looked at the brown bowl. There was a spray of pink wild aster in it. Francie had an idea that the librarian was seeing the brown bowl for the first time also.

"Oh, that! The janitor puts the flowers in. Or somebody. Anything else?" she asked impatiently.

"I'm turning in my card." Francie pushed the wrinkled dog-eared card covered with stamped dates across the desk. The librarian picked it up and was about to tear it in two when Francie took it back from her.

"I guess I'll keep it after all," she said.

She went out and took a last long look at the shabby little library. She knew she would never see it again. Eyes changed after they look at new things. If in the years to be she were to come back, her new eyes might make everything seem different from the way she saw it now. The way it was now was the way she wanted to remember it.

No, she'd never come back to the old neighbourhood.

Besides, in years to come there would be no old neighbourhood to come back to. After the war the city was going to tear down the tenements and the ugly school where a woman

393

principal used to whip little boys, and build a model housing project on the site; a place of living where sunlight and air were to be trapped, measured and weighed, and dolled out so much per resident.

Katie banged her broom and pail in the corner with that final bang that meant she was through. Then she picked up the broom and pail again and replaced them gently.

As she dressed to go out—she was going for a last-minute fitting of the jade-green velvet dress she had chosen to be married in—she fretted because the weather was so mild for the end of September. She thought it might be too warm to wear a velvet dress. She was angry that the autumn was so late in coming that year. She argued with Francie when Francie insisted that autumn *was* here.

Francie knew that autumn had come. *Let* the wind blow warm, *let* the days be heat hazy; nevertheless autumn had come to Brooklyn. Francie knew that this was so because now, as soon as night came and the street lights went on, the hot chestnut-man set up his little stand on the corner. On the rack above the charcoal fire chestnuts roasted in a covered pan. The man held unroasted ones in his hand and made little crosses on them with a blunt knife before he put them in the pan.

Yes, autumn had surely come when the hot chestnut-man appeared—no matter what the weather said to the contrary.

After Laurie had been tucked into her crib for her afternoon nap, Francie packed a few last things in a wooden Fels-Naphtha soap-box. From over the mantelpiece she took down the crucifix and the picture of her and Neeley on Confirmation Day. She wrapped these things in her First Communion veil and placed them in the box. She folded her father's two waiters' aprons and put them in. She wrapped the shaving-cup with the name "John Nolan" on it in gilt block letters in a white georgette crêpe blouse which Katie had put in the "give-away" basket because its lace jabot had torn badly in the wash. It was the blouse Francie had worn that rainy night when she stood in the doorway with Lee. The doll named Mary and the pretty little box which had once held ten gilded pennies were stowed away next. Her sparse library went into the box: the Gideon Bible, *The Complete Works of Wm*

Shakespeare, a tattered volume of *Leaves of Grass*, the three scrap-books—*The Nolan Volume of Contemporary Poetry*, *The Nolan Book of Classical Poems*, and *The Book of Annie Laurie*.

She went into the bedroom, turned back her mattress and took from under it a notebook in which she had kept a desultory diary during her thirteenth year, and a square manilla envelope. Kneeling before the box, she opened the diary and read a random entry dated September 24th, three years ago.

> *Tonight when I took a bath, I discovered I was changing into a woman.*
> *It's about time!*

She grinned as she packed the diary in the box. She looked at the writing on the envelope.

Contents:
1 sealed envelope to be opened in 1967.
1 diploma.
4 stories.

Four stories, which Miss Garnder had told her to burn. Ah, well. Francie remembered how she had promised God she'd give up writing if He wouldn't let mother die. She had kept her promise. But she knew God a little better now. She was sure that He wouldn't care at all if she started to write again. Well, maybe she'd try again some day. She added her library card to the contents of the envelope, made an entry for it on the envelope and put that in the box. Her packing was finished. All her possessions, except her clothes, were in that box.

Neeley came running up the stairs whistling: "At the Dark-town Strutters' Ball." He burst into the kitchen peeling off his coat.

"I'm in a hurry, Francie. Have I got a clean shirt?"

"There's one washed but not ironed. I'll iron it for you." She put the iron to heat while she sprinkled the shirt and set the ironing-board on two chairs. Neeley got the shoe-shine set from the closet and proceeded to put a higher shine on his already flawlessly polished shoes.

"Go somewhere?" she asked.

"Yup. Just got time to catch the show. They've got Van and Schenck and boy, can Schenck sing! He sits at the piano like this." Neeley sat at the kitchen table and demonstrated. "He sits sideways and crosses his legs, looking out at the audience. Then he leans his left elbow on the music-rack and picks out the tune with his right hand while he sings." Neeley went into a fair imitation of his idol singing: "When You're a Long, Long Way From Home."

"Yup, he's swell. Sings the way papa used to . . . a little." Papa!

Francie looked for the union label in Neeley's shirt and pressed that first.

("That label is like an ornament . . . like a rose that you wear.")

The Nolans sought for the union label on everything they bought. It was their memorial to Johnny.

Neeley looked at himself in the glass hanging over the sink. "Do you think I need a shave?" he asked.

"Not for five years yet."

"Aw, shut up!"

"Don't-say-shut-up-to-each-other," said Francie, imitating her mother.

Neeley smiled and proceeded to scrub his face, neck, arms, and hands. He sang as he washed.

> *There's Egypt in your dreamy eyes,*
> *A bit of Cairo in your style. . . .*

Francie ironed away contentedly.

Neeley was dressed at last. He stood before her in his dark blue double-breasted suit, fresh white shirt with the soft turned-down collar and a polka dot bow tie. He smelled fresh and clean from washing and his curly blond hair gleamed.

"How do I look, Prima Donna?"

He buttoned up his coat jauntily, and Francie saw that he wore their father's signet ring.

It was true then—what granma had said: that the Rommely women had the gift of seeing the ghosts of their beloved dead. Francie saw her father.

"Neeley, do you remember 'Molly Malone'?"

He put a hand in his pocket, turned away from her and sang.

In Dublin's fair city,
The girls are so pretty . . .

Papa . . . .papa!

Neeley had the same clear true voice. And how unbelievably handsome he was! So handsome that, even though he wasn't sixteen years old yet, women turned to look after him with a sigh when he walked down the street. He was so handsome that Francie felt like a dark drab alongside of him.

"Neeley, do you think I'm good-looking?"

"Look! Why don't you make a novena to St. Theresa about it? I think a miracle might fix you up."

"No. I mean it."

"Why don't you get your hair cut off and wear it in curls like the other girls instead of those chunks wound around your head?"

"I have to wait until I'm eighteen on account of mother. But do you think I'm good-looking?"

"Ask me again when you fill out a little more."

"Please tell me."

He examined her carefully, then said: "You'll pass." She had to be satisfied with that.

He had said he was in a hurry, but now he seemed reluctant to go.

"Francie! McShane . . . I mean dad, will be here for supper tonight. I'm working afterwards. Tomorrow will be the wedding and a party in the new house tomorrow night. Monday I have to go to school. And while I'm there you'll be getting on that Wolverine train for Michigan. There'll be no chance to say goodbye to you alone. So I'll say good-bye now."

"I'll be home for Christmas, Neeley."

"But it won't be the same."

"I know."

He waited. Francie extended her right hand. He pushed her hand aside, put his arms around and kissed her on the cheek. Francie clung to him and started to cry. He pushed her away.

"Gee, girls make me sick," he said. "Always so mushy." But his voice was ragged as though he, too, was going to cry.

He turned and ran out of the flat. Francie went out into the hallway and watched him run down the steps. He paused in the well of darkness at the foot of the stairs and turned to look back up at her. Although it was dark, there was brightness where he stood.

So like papa . . . so like papa, she thought. But he had more strength in his face than papa had had. He waved to her. Then he was gone

Four o'clock.
Francie decided to get dressed first, and then fix supper so that she'd be all ready when Ben came to call for her. He had tickets and they were going to see Henry Hull in *The Man Who Came Back*. It was their last date until Christmas because Ben was leaving for college tomorrow. She liked Ben. She liked him an awful lot. She wished that she could love him. If only he wasn't so sure of himself all the time. If only he'd stumble—just once. If once he needed her. Ah, well. She had five years to think it over. She stood before the mirror in her white slip. As she curved her hair over her head in washing, she remembered how she had sat on the fire-escape when a little girl and watched the big girls in the flats across the yards getting ready for their dates. Was someone watching her as she had once watched?

She looked towards the window. Yes, across two yards she saw a little girl sitting on a fire-escape with a book in her lap and a bag of candy at hand. The girl was peering through the bars at Francie. Francie knew the girl, too. She was a slender little thing of ten, and her name was Florry Wendy.

Francie brushed out her long hair, braided it and wound the braids around her head. She put on fresh stockings and white high-heeled pumps. Before she slipped a fresh pink linen dress over her head, she sprinkled violet sachet powder on a square of cotton and tucked it inside her brassiere.

She thought she heard Fraber's wagon come in. She leaned out of the window and looked. Yes, the wagon had come in Only it wasn't a wagon any more. It was a small motor-truck with the name in gilt letters on the sides and the man making preparations to wash it wasn't Frank, the nice young man with rosy cheeks. He was a little bandy-legged, draft-exempt fellow

She looked across the yards and saw that Florry was still staring at her through the bars of the fire-escape. Francie waved and called:

"Hello, Francie."

"My name *ain't* Francie," the little girl yelled back. "It' *Florry*, and you know it, too."

"I know," said Francie.

She looked down into the yard. The tree whose lea

398

umbrellas had curled around, under and over her fire-escape, had been cut down because the housewives complained that washing on the lines got entangled in its branches. The landlord had sent two men and they had chopped it down.

But the tree hadn't died ... it hadn't died.

A new tree had grown from the stump and its trunk had grown along the ground until it reached a place where there were no wash-lines above it. Then it had started to grow towards the sky again.

Annie, the fir-tree that the Nolans had cherished with waterings and manurings, had long since sickened and died. But this tree in the yard—this tree that men chopped down ... this tree that they built a bonfire around, trying to burn up its stump—this tree lived!

It lived! And nothing could destroy it.

Once more she looked at Florry Wendy reading on the fire-escape.

"Good-bye, Francie," she whispered.

She closed the window.

Fiction

☐	**Castle Raven**	Laura Black	£1.75p
☐	**Options**	Freda Bright	£1.50p
☐	**Bad Company**	Liza Cody	£1.50p
☐	**Chances**	Jackie Collins	£2.50p
☐	**Brain**	Robin Cook	£1.75p
☐	**The Entity**	Frank De Felitta	£1.95p
☐	**The Dead of Jericho**	Colin Dexter	£1.50p
☐	**Whip Hand**	Dick Francis	£1.75p
☐	**Saigon**	Anthony Grey	£2.50p
☐	**The White Paper Fan**	Unity Hall	£1.75
☐	**Solo**	Jack Higgins	£1.75
☐	**The Rich are Different**	Susan Howatch	£2.95
☐	**Smash**	Garson Kanin	£1.75
☐	**Smiley's People**	John le Carré	£1.95
☐	**The Conduct of Major Maxim**	Gavin Lyall	£1.75
☐	**The Master Mariner Book 1: Running Proud**	Nicholas Monsarrat	£1.50
☐	**Fools Die**	Mario Puzo	£1.95
☐	**The Throwback**	Tom Sharpe	£1.75
☐	**Wild Justice**	Wilbur Smith	£2.50
☐	**Cannery Row**	John Steinbeck	£1.50
☐	**That Old Gang of Mine**	Leslie Thomas	£1.75
☐	**Caldo Largo**	Earl Thompson	£1.7
☐	**Ben Retallick**	E. V. Thompson	£1.9

All these books are available at your local bookshop or newsagent, or can be ordered direct from the publisher. Indicate the number of copies required and fill in the form below
....

Name..
(Block letters please)

Address..

....

Send to CS Department, Pan Books Ltd, PO Box 40, Basingstoke, Hants
Please enclose remittance to the value of the cover price plus:
35p for the first book plus 15p per copy for each additional book ordered
to a maximum charge of £1.25 to cover postage and packing
Applicable only in the UK

While every effort is made to keep prices low, it is sometimes
necessary to increase prices at short notice. Pan Books reserve
the right to show on covers and charge new retail prices which
may differ from those advertised in the text or elsewhere